Had the Queen Lived

Had the Queen Lived:

An Alternative History of Anne Boleyn

Raven A. Nuckols

authorHOUSE®

AuthorHouse™
1663 Liberty Drive
Bloomington, IN 47403
www.authorhouse.com
Phone: 1-800-839-8640

First published by AuthorHouse 10/07/2011

ISBN: 978-1-4634-4580-5 (sc)
ISBN: 978-1-4634-4581-2 (hc)
ISBN: 978-1-4634-4582-9 (ebk)

Library of Congress Control Number: 2011914152

Printed in the United States of America

Contents

Table of Illustrations

Author's Note

This book is dedicated to the many historians who have spent countless hours tirelessly researching the history of the Tudor period, and to their contribution to the understanding of so controversial and influential an epoch in English history; an era whose effects still reverberate to this day. Their works have inspired this alternative history, which takes a new perspective on the story of Anne Boleyn by exploring the ramifications if certain events had not occurred, and postulating the effects of other events that could have occurred, but did not.

As a personal note of thanks I would like especially to recognize the work of Professor Eric Ives, historians Allison Weir, David Starkey, and Derek Wilson, and many others who inspired this story. I also would like to thank my family and friends for all their encouragement in making this book a reality. I dedicate this book to Jose, for without his love and support this might not have been possible.

Epigraph

"Good Christian people, I am come hither to die, for according to the law, and by the law I am judged to die, and therefore I will speak nothing against it. I am come hither to accuse no man, nor to speak anything of that, whereof I am accused and condemned to die, but I pray God save the king and send him long to reign over you, for a gentler nor a more merciful Prince was there never: and to me he was ever a good, a gentle and sovereign lord. And if any person will meddle of my cause, I require them to judge the best. And thus I take my leave of the world and of you all, and I heartily desire you all to pray for me. O Lord have mercy on me, to God I commend my soul."

—Anne Boleyn, May 19th, 1536

Introduction

The tragic love story of King Henry VIII and Anne Boleyn continues to captivate audiences around the world nearly five hundred years after its end. The years they spent together and what they accomplished revolutionized not only England, but the rest of the world. As a result of their legacy, the Anglican Church is still headed by the British monarch, currently Queen Elizabeth II of England, and the groundwork was laid for the foundations of a British Empire and Commonwealth that would last for centuries, and whose impact continues to reverberate.

On her own, Anne Boleyn remains one of the most controversial figures in British history, revered by some, reviled by others. Henry's second wife, she defied the standards of her time and was truly a powerful force in her own right. Her life has been well chronicled over the years since her tragic end—executed for treason on the grounds of the Tower of London—however, this book is an imagining of an alternative history that might have come to pass. This book examines what might have happened had Anne given birth to the longed-for son she miscarried in the winter of January 1536; both the rewards for her, and the consequences for the whole of England.

Chapter 1

Prologue: 1525-1536

England in the 1520's was undergoing a significant religious reformation towards Protestantism. Up until the 16th century, the country had been faithful to Catholicism, and the faithful answered to the patriarch of the church, the Pope. The Pope was God's messenger on Earth, a lifetime appointee to the throne of St. Peter, elected by the Catholic Church conclave, a group of high ranking Cardinals representing each region of the world. At that time, with Catholicism the dominant form of Christianity and the masses of Europe so heavily influenced, even directed, by their Catholic clergy, the Pope held enormous sway over the Kings and Emperors of Christian Europe.

It was widely believed in the Middle Ages and the Renaissance that Kings received their mandate to rule directly from God, and that gave the Pope—as God's emissary on Earth—tremendous influence over the secular rulers of Europe. Popes had the power to call for war, as in the Crusades, and vast European armies were often at Rome's beck and call. Within countries they commanded vast bureaucracies through networks of churches, monasteries, abbeys and so on, providing services to the people, collecting revenues from both the clergy and the laity, and often these systems were far more organized than the civil authorities. These bureaucracies were jealously protected by Rome, with ecclesiastical courts demanding authority over clergy charged with crimes, and freedom from interference (including taxation) from the state. Kings often resented this rival power's interference in their kingdom's affairs, but none had attempted to break free from Rome's control so directly as would Henry VIII of England.

King Henry VIII had come to power in 1509 and swiftly sought to make an impact. To serve any other faith but Catholicism was socially and politically dangerous. Nevertheless, for centuries discontent with the Roman Church had been quietly brewing and a new generation of reformers lay just beneath the surface of outward obedience to the existing order. To disclose publicly one's true feelings—if they differed from the dogma of the Church—was to risk denouncement as a heretic, imprisonment, and even death. The government was prone to using torture and execution to dispose of its enemies, whether a threat were real or merely perceived. As the reformist movement went from a simmer to a boil, religious exchanges among countrymen became ever more fervent.

Under the feudal system that had persisted until the early Renaissance, the still strengthening civil states allowed the authority of the church to remain almost unrivaled. Popes knew well how to manage such egomaniacal personalities as Kings and, when it suited them, the Church also manipulated Kings into doing its bidding, thus maintaining Rome's stronghold.

Under the pre-Reformation system, the Pope and his convocation of Bishops were responsible for determining holy doctrine, advising countries on how to spread Christ's true word and for serving as the intermediaries through which the Kings of Europe could seek God's favor. Kings paid for these services heavily, not only in fees, but also in diplomatic favors like supporting the Holy Wars declared by Rome. For instance, if a country was starting to stray from the faith, the Pope would ask another country to cut off the offending country's their economic supply chain to force it back into the fold. If that failed to work, he would call for military action against the offending country. By so easily manipulating all of Europe, it could be argued that the Vatican was the preeminent European power in the Middle Ages, with influence over both life and death on a mass scale. The Pope would also at times call for Holy Wars, in Christ's name, to ensure the successful spread of Catholicism and add territory, resources, and widen the base for financial support to the Vatican.

Religion offered up answers to life's difficult questions, explaining the higher power of God, rules for behavior such as the duties owed by the common people to the state, and how by following such edicts the poor could hope to win salvation for their immortal souls in the afterlife. The church controlled the people by making them fear the eternal consequences of disobedience. In the Middle Ages, sermons that interpreted the meaning of Biblical text were often preached in Latin to teach that disobeying God's true word (as passed through the clergy, of course) would lead to a soul's eternal damnation. This was a brilliant public relations campaign, using the dual tactics of stoking both fear and hope, threats of damnation or the promise of salvation, to beholden the Church's followers to the existing order.

The church also relied on its ability to describe what it called the immense power of Christ to reward the faithful; both by promising an eternity in heaven in the afterlife, and even in saying the most faithful (i.e. obedient and repentant) might see their Earthly burdens lessened by a forgiving God. When circumstances in one's world went out of control, one could turn to prayer, confession, fasting, and supporting the church. Priests and clergy reassured laymen that God would answer all prayers and that, while it may take just a little time, God would come through to support his children, so long as they believed in Him and His Church. They provided an outlet of hope, support, and a listening ear when desperate commoners needed it most. Those who could afford it—such as the monarchy and most of the nobility—maintained a private chaplain on retainer at all times, for just such spiritual emergencies.

Rome's ability to channel both the positive message of Christ and exploit the fear of Satan allowed it to maintain control of a massive bureaucracy that European kings both resented and envied, making the Reformation such a pivotal turning point in history. Never before had Rome been so boldly and blatantly challenged. For centuries, people had genuinely believed from birth that both their lives and eternal fates were in God's hands alone, and that they owed God, through His Holy Church, their devotion and their money, to secure favor and ensure eventual salvation. The church's massive operating organization included maintaining lavish buildings, retaining a large staff of clergy and servants, and of course requiring significant financial support for daily upkeep. Rome had several means of raising these funds, including the selling of indulgences, imposing high vestment and ordinance fees, and requiring high tithes each year from parishioners. For centuries this was the status quo. No one had dared challenge the Catholic Church. It was this opulence—even more than the meddling in affairs of secular government—that would spark the coming revolution from within.

Martin Luther was a devout monk who for years piously practiced his ministry in contentment, until he was extended a formal invitation to visit the Vatican to further his theological education. During this visit, he came to disagree with key papal applications of scripture, but far worse, he witnessed such abuses by his beloved Church that he would start the process of reevaluating whether the institution he had sworn to uphold was deserving of his loyalty.

Upon his return to Germany he penned the document known to us today as the Ninety-five Theses. The formal name for this work was *The Disputation of Martin Luther on the Power and Efficacy of Indulgences.* These theses outlined the corruptions of the Church and detailed exactly how it was building excessive wealth with fees it charged to Christendom, such as charging both commoners and the nobility alike for blessings. Enraging Luther the most was the selling of indulgences, which held the promise of minimizing or forsaking time in purgatory—or even guaranteeing a soul's passage directly into heaven—by paying the church. Purgatory was the place souls went after their human lives had passed to reflect upon and be punished for their worldly misdeeds until they emerged purged and purified from sin and deserving of entry into heaven; depending upon the grievousness of those sins, a person's soul could remain in this torment for quite some time (never quite clear, but implicitly a very long while). The Catholic Church commonly used threats of purgatory to keep followers in line.

The selling of indulgences basically meant that the rich could afford to buy their way out of purgatory and go straight from the afterlife to heaven with no atonement for their sins, all so that the Vatican could continue to buy opulent tapestries, artwork, sculptures, and adorn its buildings' walls with magnificent frescoes. Luther was disgusted, for he truly believed in all that the faith had taught him of equality before God and the corruptions of wealth; to hear that the rich could simply buy their way out of doing penance for their sins was more than he could take.

The thesis he wrote also challenged commonly accepted practices such as baptisms, the very doctrine of purgatory, interpretation of various rites based on passages in both the Old and New Testaments, and the Church's take on how to guarantee the salvation of souls. Luther's anger over these practices led him to post his theses on the door of the All Saints Church in Wittenberg, a common practice known at the time for inviting formal academic debate.

When the theses were distributed, they rocked Europe to its core. After centuries of buildup of frustration over clerical abuse, here was a pious monk who was brave enough to stand up alone against the powerful institution of the Catholic Church. Luther, although at first calling chiefly for reforms to existing practices, had sparked the start of the Protestant movement that would permanently divide Christianity. To understand how truly significant this call for reform was in the context of the figures in this book, each of the factors applying to how it took shape in England must be reviewed. In so examining these factors, it is possible to see how the politics, theology, sociology, and history of the country under the period of Tudor rule created the perfect climate for reform.

The Tudor dynasty began with the end of the Wars of the Roses, during which the noble houses of Lancaster and York fought out their claims to the throne of England for thirty years between 1455 through 1485. Both lines claimed entitlement to the throne based on complicated lines of marriage and descent tracing back through to the Conquest in 1066 that had won England for the Norman and Plantagenet monarchs for centuries. These houses ended their long rivalry at the Battle of Bosworth in August 1485, when Henry Tudor (descending from the House of Lancaster) seized power on the battlefield from Richard III (the last monarch of the House of York). Tudor became King Henry VII and officially founded the House that would bear his name. The new King would have several children, and groomed his eldest, Prince Arthur, as the heir apparent. He had arranged for his son to marry Princess Katherine of Aragon from Spain, the daughter of Isabella I of Castile and Ferdinand II of Aragon, the monarchs who would drive the Muslim Caliphate from Spain, unify their country, fund the discovery of the New World and build a Spanish Empire.

Arthur and Katherine married in November 1501, when he was only fifteen years old. The marital alliance with ascendant Spain re-established England as a serious diplomatic player in European affairs. Unfortunately, the Prince suffered from a poor immune system and was known for bouts of repeated and lengthy illness. The Prince died only a few months after marriage, in April 1502, leaving Katherine a foreign widow claiming they had never consummated the marriage. She in fact swore this in confession. As a result of her declaration, and the English King not wanting to lose her rather large dowry; Henry VII amended the marriage contract to have Princess Katherine of Spain wed the next son in line, Henry.

Henry was only 12 when his father pre-contracted him to his former sister-in-law, who was five years his elder. To accomplish this, a special dispensation from the Pope had to be obtained, due to a passage in the Old Testament in the Book of Leviticus stating it the sin of incest to have relations with your brother's wife if she had been known carnally to him, and that the couple would be childless. The entire dispensation rested on the sole testimony of Katherine, who continued to adamantly claim her virginity and deny that she and Arthur had consummated their union due to the Prince's failing health. This claim would prove critical in the years to come. Due mainly to Katherine's adamant claims of virginity, Pope Julius II easily granted the dispensation and the marriage ceremony to Prince Henry was conducted in June 1509 at Westminster Abbey.

Henry VII reigned for twenty-three mostly peaceful years and was a fiscally conservative king who left his family (mostly his heir) a large fortune. The king died April 21st, 1509. Prince Henry was decreed King Henry VIII later the same day. Henry and Katherine were married two months later and the young couple seemed genuinely happy. The people were hopeful at the prospect of a youthful and vibrant King and the change he could bring. Henry was handsome, tall, kind, and passionately loved learning. He was fluent in several languages including Latin, composed poetry and several music ballads. He also was athletic, known for his love of hunting and sport. The people lovingly nicknamed him, *"The Renaissance King."*

Over the preceding decade of the 1500s Cardinal Thomas Wolsey had served in Henry VIIs administration as the King's royal chaplain; based on his diligent service and discretion, Wolsey was rewarded with appointments as both Lord Chancellor and as the Archbishop of York. His wealth rivaled only that of the King. He was the real source of power behind the crown, acting as a royal agent for a young King Henry VIII who wanted to spend his days hunting and his nights in lustful pursuits. Wolsey placated Henry's every desire and catered to his ego. This careful calculation of how to play to Henry VIII's moods brought him closer to the King and he even formed a genuine friendship with the monarch, who had the greatest respect for Wolsey.

Wolsey was also an aggressive minister of state who managed to engage England with the mainland powers of Europe, playing one side off of the other. His tactics in diplomacy in some ways were revolutionary and his strategies and manipulations worked well in his favor. His goal in these games was to interject England into European affairs as a major force to be reckoned with, leaving behind England's prior status as a merely secondary player to be called upon as backup when major established kingdoms such as France or Spain needed assistance. Wolsey very nearly succeeded in his efforts and along the way he managed to create many enemies, who were envious of his hold over the King. Among these in particular were the Duke of Norfolk, the Duke of Suffolk, and an up-and-coming courtier named Thomas Boleyn.

1.1 The Lady Anne

Anne Boleyn was the daughter of Thomas Boleyn and Elizabeth Howard, the daughter of one of England's most distinguished noble families. As a result of her father's post as an Ambassador, in 1520, the family accompanied Henry VIII to meet with his French rival King Francis I, at the *"Field of Cloth of Gold"* summit in Calais. It was at this pivotal and glorious meeting, where Mary and Anne Boleyn were serving as ladies-in-waiting to Queen Mary of France, that Thomas Boleyn was able to introduce both of his daughters to the English king.

By this time, Mary Boleyn had been the mistress of King Francis I, a fact that was well known at the French court and that Francis had no issue with sharing with Henry, most likely in an attempt to make his English rival jealous. At this summit, Henry called for Mary Boleyn also to become his own mistress. The affair would last well beyond the summit and carry on nearly five years. At that time, Thomas Boleyn was encouraging Mary to keep Henry's interests in the bedroom as best she could, so as to secure further advancement for their family. By whatever means necessary Mary was ordered by her father to keep Henry's interest in her and not to be simply a fleeting pleasure in the royal bedchamber.

In his post as Ambassador, Thomas had sent his other daughter, Anne, to serve in both the courts of the Netherlands under Archduchess Margaret of Austria, and then again to the French court as a lady-in-waiting to Henry's sister Queen Mary. During these various duties Anne had cultivated her education and refined her social graces. In France she learned fashion, theology, courtly games, dancing, knitting, cards, and gained a wide depth of experience from witnessing the licentiousness of the French court and its damaging consequences. This opportunity allowed her to perfect her fluency in French, and to learn the arts of courtly love.

Thomas had also arranged for Mary to serve alongside her sister Anne as a lady-in-waiting to Queen Mary, but Anne's sister had gained quite the reputation for unladylike behavior, making no secret of her often frequent and illicit affairs. No evidence exists that suggests Anne's character was anything short of impeccable while in either court, and she only surrounded herself with reputable women known for their virtue and honor. She did not want to make the same mistakes that Mary had made. Yet upon her return to England she had grown from a precocious youth to a well rounded and sophisticated young lady. When she returned home, Thomas Boleyn's relationship with the King of England had only grown and he was able to secure Henry's favor and place his daughters as a ladies-in-waiting to Queen Katherine.

To shield the King from any impropriety, Mary was immediately married off in 1520 to a Sir William Carey of Aldenham, while she continued her five year affair with the King. It is speculated that at least one of Mary's children was fathered by the King, although this cannot be confirmed as Henry never claimed any children by her, as he had with another of his mistresses. She finally left court in March 1526 with the birth of her second child. As Mary returned with her husband to the country, Anne was left alone at court, where she thrived. Anne watched the natural progression of her sister's promising rise and abrupt fall from grace. Instead of focusing on the wealth and position her family gained from the liaison, she only saw the disastrous consequences to Mary's reputation that resulted and how Mary's lack of will and intellect to use the situation to her favor had eventually led to her downfall. Anne would learn from her sister's lack of ambition and would not make the same mistakes.

Mary and Anne were opposites in nearly every way. While Mary had blonde hair, fair skin and blue eyes, which met the typical 16th century standards of beauty, Anne's features were described as not particularly handsome, with a thin frame and olive skin, dark hair, and dark eyes. Mary was quiet, demure and subservient, whereas Anne was passionate, intelligent, and exciting. Anne certainly stood out among her contemporaries and fully engaged them with her charm and wit to enhance her social standing. At court she truly was a force to be reckoned with.

Although Henry and Anne had already met at the Anglo/French summit in 1520, it was not until March 1522 that they became better acquainted. That month, a magnificent pageant was held at court to celebrate the joint alliance of England and Spain against France, along with the accompanying betrothal of Henry and Katherine's daughter, the young Princess Mary, to the Spanish King. This match was extremely promising for England as, by this time, the Spanish King was head of Europe's growing Superpower, benefiting from the unification of Spain under his parents, the growing Spanish dominions in the Americas, and his status—based on the web of interrelationships among European nobles—as Holy Roman Emperor, ruling the many principalities and states of Central Europe (modern Germany and most of the non-Slavic lands between France in the west, northern Italy, and North and Baltic Seas). Princess Mary was only six years old when her pre-contract treaty of marriage with King Charles V of Spain (also known as the Holy Roman Emperor) was executed, but this was of little consequence. These types of treaties were negotiated often to secure land rights, alliances, wealth, and maintain or enhance diplomatic standing in international affairs. It was a purely political move orchestrated most likely by Cardinal Wolsey.

Wolsey had been instrumental in arranging such alliances, and treated them as long-term projects to secure England's standing. In fact, the engagement that would cement the Anglo-Spanish alliance would not come to fruition for nearly a decade, the Princess Mary and the Emperor would have to wait eight years to marry. Time would show that the Emperor was not that patient. Regardless of the practical considerations of this treaty, the alliance provided an opportunity for Henry's court to compete on the same level of grandiosity with the rest of European courts. When the Spanish delegation arrived, they were welcomed to every accommodation the English King could afford.

As part of the lavish entertainments surrounding the celebration of the great treaty and engagement, the English court held a play at which the ladies and the gentlemen of the court represented prized and scorned social values. Anne (foreshadowing the trait that would be her greatest strength) played the part of perseverance. Henry also starred in the pageant. Historians believe that it was in this play that Henry began his infatuation with Anne. It brought the two of them together in close proximity and allowed Anne to showcase her dancing, acting and rare form of beauty to the King. Henry was captivated by her instantly. Certainly the two interacted during the play, but there is no evidence to suggest this marked the start of their affair, for which documentation of Henry's feelings would only come four years later. Nevertheless, it was during these days that Henry, with Anne as a lady-in-waiting to his Queen, would start to learn of the wit, charm and drive of Anne Boleyn. His infatuation with this incredible lady would change the face of England forever.

When Henry did begin to pursue Anne he was initially captivated by her strikingly different appearance. That initial interest led to his discovery of her remarkable personality. Not only in looks did Anne stand out, but in her speech, fashion, mannerisms, and overall acumen. Contemporary accounts noted that she dressed, spoke, and behaved more like a French woman than an English woman. She was known for introducing French fashions into the court and was noted to have made a variety of changes to her accessories and dress every single day. An expensive habit to be sure, but on her father's salary one they could afford and ultimately one that got the rest of the court talking, which was after all the point. Unlike the typical standards of subservient and docile women at court, Anne was no wall flower. Her vibrant personality radiated at dances, and she injected herself into discussions above her station concerning theology, diplomacy, the sciences, and other serious European affairs. She could intelligently hold her own against some of the most highly educated scholars of the day, including the King. She also enjoyed playing cards and going on hunts, two main passions of Henry's.

Henry hated writing in general, but when it came to his feelings for Anne he would come to put pen to paper and write a series of beautiful letters that have managed to survive and are stored in the Vatican today. The letters show the deep affection Henry felt for Anne and suggest that she was showing reluctance to accept his interest. The majority of Anne's letters have been, unfortunately, lost to us. In the meantime, between 1522, when the play was performed, and 1525, when Henry admitted in writing to his feelings for Anne, he also was still sleeping with her sister Mary; only towards the end of 1525 did that affair end.

The first letter we have to Anne is from 1526, where the King admits to his infatuation for her, extending over a year, dating the start of their flirtation to around 1525. Henry wrote the most charming letters to Anne asking, and in some places even begging, for her to acknowledge his feelings and return them. Anne played her course cautiously. It must have been flattering in every sense to have the most powerful man in the realm pursuing her; but it also could have come with grave consequences. The facts were that he was married; he had a Queen, a wife and a mother for a potential heir. Anne was also incredibly pious and, above everything else, she valued society's convention that "her maidenhead" should be reserved for her husband. Seeing no possible reason that Katherine might be set aside in favor of herself, Anne kept Henry at a distance, giving him just enough hope to continue to pursue her while allowing the King's affections to grow.

Henrys purpose, at least at first, was likely to merely bed Anne, as he had done with so many others so many times before. Anne would have none of it and resisted his every attempt, citing her honor and recalling how her sister had so recently fallen. Her refusal to sleep with him was all it took to enhance his desire to possess her even further. As King it was indeed a rare instance when he did not receive his every whim and desire from any of his subjects. Anne's refusal intrigued him and, perhaps for the first time, put him in the same league as any other suitor seeking a lady's hand. She was incredibly resilient against his attempts, and he made many. He sent gifts of fine jewels, fabrics, even sent her meat for her table that he had hunted himself. He wrote poetry for her, engaged her in deep intellectual conversations and sought every opportunity to be in her presence. She returned the jewels he sent her deeming that she was not worthy to receive them, only enticing him further.

Concurrent with the rise in Henry's affections for Anne had been growing discord within his marriage, largely related to Henry's desire to secure his dynasty and avoid another civil war for the throne. Professor Eric Ives, Anne's biographer, dates trouble in the royal marriage to approximately 1524. Through multiple miscarriages, still births, and deaths in infancy, Queen Katherine had only managed to produce a single living heir, the Princess Mary. Katherine was now approaching 40 and according to her physicians, she no longer menstruated and was unable to bear another child.

Up until this point England had only had one female ruler and it was widely accepted in their culture at this time, that a woman was unfit to rule. Henry was focusing on the legacy that he would leave behind and was acutely aware that, of the Tudor dynasty, he was only the second monarch, and only the first to peacefully inherit the crown. Without a strong male heir to inherit the throne, Henry feared that the Tudor line would be finished. He was determined to have the heir he desired and, with his wife's failure to produce one, began to take steps indicating that he might seek an heir elsewhere.

Before Henry began pursuing Anne, he had been carrying on an affair with another one of Katherine's ladies-in-waiting, Elizabeth Blount. Bessie, as she was called, became pregnant in 1518 and since her husband was away at his estates the child was more than likely the King's. Fortunately for Henry, the child turned out to be the longed for son and he was named Henry Fitzroy and created Duke of Richmond and Somerset in a vain attempt to legitimize a bastard as heir apparent, even over his legitimate daughter, Princess Mary. With Katherine unable to give him a son and with only a bastard who legally could not inherit the throne—no matter how badly Henry wanted Fitzroy to be in line to do so—the King had to find other means of consolation. Seeing no reason to visit Katherine's bed any longer, these visits practically stopped altogether, except on rare occasions in 1524. As it happened, Henry would find a more direct way to pursue an heir.

1.2 Putting Away a Queen

The King tasked Wolsey to begin searching for a way to divorce Katherine and find a new European bride, preferably a young lady who would be capable of giving him a male heir. Henry ordered his minister to obtain the divorce by any means necessary. The issue was so controversial that it was termed the "King's Great Matter" which lasted several years and became the scandal of the decade across all of Europe. The issue of dissolving his marriage and his growing feelings for Anne were two separate for quite some time. The Lady Anne was a commoner and thus would not be fit to marry and become Queen, so as Wolsey commenced the search for a replacement Anne was not even in his thoughts. Mainly this was because Henry had not informed his minister that he had fallen deeply in love with Anne. Perhaps the King reasoned that, as much as he wanted Anne, his duty to the state and the House of Tudor forced him to choose a European Princess, or lady of equally noble standing, to preserve centuries of dynastic marital alliances between countries.

It was not long before Anne Boleyn became a household name mainly for being called a home wrecker, a whore, and Henry's mistress, breaking up a marriage with the widely admired Queen Katherine. None of this in fact was true; Henry had carried on multiple carnal affairs before he fell in love with Anne and despite her (perhaps manipulatively) resisting Henry's affections, Anne was labeled a whore anyway and blamed for the breakdown of his marriage. The reality is that it was Henry who wanted the separation from Katherine, who was unable to provide him with the male heir he so desperately desired. In the beginning of their courtship, Anne was not being seriously considered as an answer to Henry's troubles, only as a companion to meet his emotional and physical desires. This would soon change.

The turning point came when Henry (whether of his own accord or by other persuasions) became convinced that Anne could solve both of his issues. By divorcing Katherine and replacing her with Anne, the hope for a legitimate succession could at long last be realized. The challenge to Henry was that his strongest argument for annulling his marriage with Katherine had already been overcome prior to their marriage by special Papal dispensation. Nevertheless, Henry's lawyers had been arguing that, for the sake of peace in England as well as the preservation of his majesty's soul, the marriage needed to be annulled on the grounds of incest, and that it was indeed unlawful for him to have lain with his brother's wife. The other obstacle to overcome was Anne's lowly status, which could very easily be remedied by her own elevation to the nobility, granting her a title and making her worthy of meeting foreign dignitaries and even Kings of Europe.

The King's lawyers, Stephen Gardiner and Edward Fox, were dispatched to meet with the Pope, who was being held in captivity at Orvieto in Italy on orders of the Spanish Emperor (based on their own disputes over various Italian states). In addition to their legal arguments and diplomatic maneuvering, Fox and Gardiner had also been specifically instructed by his majesty to make it clear to the Pope that, if he failed to satisfy the King's demands, England's allegiance to the papacy would be severed. When the lawyers arrived at Orvieto, the Spanish let them through to present their argument, realizing they were not there to remove the Pope from his captivity, but only to appeal to him on the King of England's behalf.

As far as the Catholic Church was concerned, Henry's marriage was legal, binding, and valid, as were any heirs produced from that marriage, making Princess Mary the rightful and legitimate heir to the English throne. If the Pope agreed to the annulment it would be a complete loss of face from a 20-year old decision made by his predecessor in good faith. On the other hand, Popes typically sought to keep Kings happy (to secure their own bargaining positions and retain Church properties) and therefore would often grant such motions without much hindrance or objection. Henry's petition would prove to be the exception to the rule. As a stalling technique, the Pope advised the lawyers that he would read their arguments very carefully and only then would pronounce a verdict; this was not exactly the answer they had come for. Only after such time that the Pope came to a judgment would he send dispatches back to England of his decision; this would prove to be after a very long period of time. By the time the English lawyers had arrived, the Pope had already been briefed on Henry's infatuation with Anne and believed that he wanted a divorce on the sole grounds of intending to replace the Queen with his mistress instead of Henry's claims of genuinely stricken conscience for marrying his brother's widow and violating God's law.

Dissatisfied, the lawyers did as their King commanded them and before departing threatened to break all ties with Rome if Henry did not achieve satisfaction, a threat the Pope did not take at all seriously. After all, no King had ever broken ranks with the Church and he did not expect that to happen now. The lawyers would not see satisfaction as they prepared to head back to England. Little did they realize that Henry's rage against the Church was only growing.

When the Pope finally did take action, he sent Cardinal Campeggio as the papal legate in his stead to review the case and decide the matter. The Cardinal, however, was on strict papal orders not to come to any final judgment and to use any means necessary to disrupt the King's plans to terminate his marriage. These tactics worked for seven long years. Henry's strong faith had made him reticent to rush toward a break from Rome. Henry saw himself as being tested, just as he had read, had so often happened to great men and kings in the Bible. Meanwhile, Anne was growing ever more impatient that she was now in her late twenties and still was not married; she even threatened to leave the King if he could not give her satisfaction. The pair quarreled over this issue intensely, with most of these arguments leaving the King begging Anne not to leave him and swearing that it would just be a matter of time before they would marry.

At this stage, Wolsey still knew little of Anne's status as more than a possible mistress, and indeed, as Henry's true love; he was only concerned with how to bring the divorce proceedings about, with Rome stalling.

Wolsey was deeply conflicted by the King's demand. Either decision he could make would cost him dearly. Although he was the senior-most official of state, he was also a Cardinal and served as the Papal representative in England. A great portion of his personal wealth, which had allowed him to afford to build lavish palaces, came from this office. Wolsey knew that by supporting the divorce he would be planting enemies about him who sought to replace him. Also, since the Catholic Church did not believe in divorce, he would be viewed as a hypocrite to his own followers.

Wolsey was in an impossible situation. If he chose not to support the divorce and fight against it, he risked angering the King and losing his titles, offices, wealth, power, or worse. If he were to support and achieve the divorce he would alienate the very source of his power, his seniority in the Church, and neutralize the reason for his elevation to the Chancellorship in the first place. During his time serving Henry, he had made many enemies in the Privy Council who would love nothing more than to seek his downfall. Should he support and arrange this divorce, Wolsey feared they would do exactly that. He also doubted the King's protection against his enemies' attempts if the divorce did not come around as quickly as Henry desired.

Queen Katherine had always regarded Wolsey as her bitter enemy. The Queen saw in Wolsey a corrupt man of the cloth with a mistress, two bastard children, and wealth rivaling, perhaps even surpassing, that of the King. She held him liable for the many unfortunate deaths of otherwise innocent political rivals, and for the ruin of anyone who threatened his position. While Wolsey certainly carried out matters concerning the Queen much more severely than even Henry had originally intended, he was nevertheless carrying out the King's orders. Katherine further blamed him for his complicity in the elevation of Henry's bastard child by her former lady-in-waiting, and thus for threatening Princess Mary's rightful claim to the throne. He also was responsible for sending the Princess away from her mother to be raised by Governesses and servants, and for reading her private correspondence with her family in Spain; because of Wolsey's tactics the Queen would only be able to visit her daughter once a year to assess her progress.

The final act came when Wolsey had arranged the Blackfriars Trial in 1529 to investigate the Queen's claim of virginity with her former husband, Prince Arthur. The trial was Wolsey's plan to remove Katherine from the throne by force, which the King vigorously embraced. Henry had tried in private, by gentler and kinder means, to convince Katherine to renounce her throne and go into a nunnery; such attempts were to no avail. He even promised to take care of her financially in any palace of her choosing the rest of her life; again, Katherine denied him. When the trial idea came up Wolsey convinced Henry it could work and he jumped at the chance to be rid of her once and for all. The King expected the outcome to be a foregone conclusion, but he would be sadly mistaken. The trial consisted of a legatine court authorized by the Pope and conducted in the Dominican Friary of the Parliament Chamber in London. Cardinal Campeggio represented His Holiness the Pope, who was not in attendance.

If it could be proven that Katherine had lied about her virginity and had, indeed, consummated her marriage with then-Prince Arthur, the marriage would be annulled, the Lady Mary would be declared a bastard, and the King would be left free to remarry. Confident in his case, the King opened the proceedings, presenting a passionate opening argument for his cause. He spoke highly of Katherine and their time together, and how much he detested why things had come to a trial, but concluded by advising the court to make no mistake this marriage was never legal and should not have been judged thus. It is said he found the very inability of Katherine to produce a living male heir as proof that God Himself condemned the marriage. His argument was said to be so moving that few in the court believed Katherine could be innocent.

The Queen was represented by Bishop John Fisher as her counsel. One of the main legal arguments that Katherine's defense had made at Blackfriars had been to appeal to Rome to pronounce a final verdict on the matter. This outraged Henry; by appealing to Rome this argument made the King also subject to the Vatican. With Anne's encouragement, Henry began designs towards winning a separation. At the conclusion of the first few days of the trial, Anne persuaded him to deny the application to appeal to Rome and played on his own fears of vulnerability, that he would be made a subject to Rome if he allowed Katherine's request to go through.

All appeared to be going well for the King until Katherine made a dramatic move. In a final, desperate act to win back her husband and retain her crown, Katherine dropped to her knees at Henry's feet, before the entire court, and begged him to be merciful and consider that she was still a maid when she married him; she beseeched him to consider the truth of the matter before God, and let her keep her honor. The dramatic gesture stunned the court, and was followed by the Queen's immediate departure, never to return.

While he would succeed in shedding himself of his wife and Queen, Henry was humiliated; her uncharacteristic act of defiance had taken place not in private, which was to be expected, but in open court. Further, the crowd had rallied to the Queen's side, much to Henry's chagrin and highlighting to him even further the conflicted position of a King who seeks to rule in his lands, but is yet subservient to the judgments of churchmen.

Despite Katherine's dramatic testimony, Wolsey would not be placated, he continued on, even after Katherine's departure. He miraculously found servants who attended Prince Arthur the night of his wedding and testified to the consummation of the marriage. These witnesses claimed that the Queen was inaccurate in her statements to the court and that Arthur had himself bragged to having taken her. To this day, the truth of the matter rests with Prince Arthur and Queen Katherine; however, the show trial was enough for Henry to feel validated in his cause.

Unfortunately, the trial did not produce the outcome the King so desired and that Wolsey so desperately needed. The court, based solely on Cardinal Campeggio's orders, decided to delay proceedings yet again, until the Pope himself could answer the arguments made in the record. Wolsey and Campeggio were the principal deciders on the panel and when Campeggio failed to yield the appropriate verdict, Wolsey knew he was finished. Perhaps this was the final strain on the once strong bond of trust and loyalty between Henry and his minister. It was also exactly the ammunition the Boleyns needed if they were to successfully bring down the Cardinal. Wolsey had been untouchable until now. With this single act of a broken promise, his enemies, including Boleyn, could take him down with little trouble. As for Katherine, she never changed her story.

In 1531 Queen Katherine was ordered to leave court and head to a rundown palace called the More, because Henry was planning finally to wed Anne. Two years later, Katherine was moved to Kimbolton Castle. The castle had been known for its draftiness and was in a severe state of disrepair, but, most importantly, it was secluded. It was vital to Henry and Anne that Katherine be kept as far away from court as possible; to diminish any hope her supporters might have for her re-instatement. Another harsh condition set upon Katherine was that she was not allowed to see or write to her daughter, the Lady Mary. Her position was also downgraded to the Dowager Princess instead of allowing to call herself Queen and was officially forbidden by Henry to do so; a move she intentionally denied. While she was allowed at rare times to have visitors, she chose to keep to her rigid schedule of church masses instead. She had been deathly ill for quite some time from cancer of the heart, another ailment that was not medically understood at the time. Anne had taken her place in all but name and was moved into the palace, staying in the Queen's former chambers; causing great scandal at court. Yet still, Anne did not relent, and refused to give Henry her maidenhead.

1.3 Schism

During the preparation for the trial, Anne and her faction privately built a substantial case against Wolsey, claiming corruption, fraud, and theft against his majesty. The faction consisted of her father Thomas, her brother George, her Uncle Thomas Howard, the Duke of Norfolk, and their sometime adversary Charles Brandon Duke of Suffolk, who was Henry's closest friend. Privately, Brandon disliked the Boleyns, but he absolutely hated Wolsey for his hold over the King, and joined forces with the Boleyns to bring him down. Brandon also needed to regain Henry's favor after having illegally married the King's sister, Mary Tudor, in May 1515, without first seeking the King's permission. In return for Brandon's participation in the scheme, Norfolk promised to bring Brandon back to court and into Henry's good graces.

If this group was to be successful in its venture it needed nothing short of absolute and irrefutable proof that Wolsey was falsely serving two Masters and thus failing the King. They played on Henry's ego and Anne provided him books from allegedly heretical authors such as William Fish, who examined matters of church and state and argued that Kings should be the ultimate authority in their kingdom, answerable only to God and not to Rome. Anne also let the King know that Wolsey intentionally banned these books to keep them from him, fearful that the King would take his rightful power, thereby inflaming Henry further.

The King absorbed these words like a sponge. They fueled his desire, beyond his initial wishes merely for a divorce, to instead want to be fully his own master and take absolute power. After all, was he not the King of England? Why need he beg from Rome permission to conduct the affairs of state within his kingdom? As these questions began racing in his head,

Henry prepared for the most radical move thus far in his reign. The people too were calling for Reformation against the corruption and abuses of the clergy. Monasteries throughout the whole of the realm were wealthy and the splendor of some rivaled even the estates of the highest ranks of the nobility.

The strict control over interpretation of liturgy was held in tight control by the Church. To be able to attend mass and hear the service only in Latin, the people had to trust in the accuracy of what their Priests were interpreting for them. This only fed into a system wherein the clergy must pay to obtain training on how to read and understand Latin to relay it to lay people, and then pay the church in order to give the lessons. Payments to the church were endless and everywhere. Luther's theses presented a direct and uncompromising challenge to the Church about the extent of the Church's power. Ironically enough, while Luther's manifesto did not specifically engage the issue of translating the Bible into the vernacular, once the Reformation was underway, this became a central tenet of change. Other theological scholars in England, principally William Tyndale, Hugh Latimer, Thomas Cranmer and John Fish, adapted Luther's call for reform with the utmost passion, although such reformers were still called heretics and prosecuted by Cardinal Wolsey.

Among the most prominent of the reformers was William Tyndale, a highly educated theological scholar, born in the early 1490s, who received a Bachelor and Master Degrees from Cambridge and Oxford, respectively. He was ordained by the Catholic Church as a priest in the early 1520s and devoted his career to continuous academic study. To support himself, he tutored several pupils on a variety of subjects. His greatest passion, however, was his translation work. It was this work that inspired his lifetime commitment towards spreading education.

Tyndale yearned for the broadest collective understanding of the New Testament by everyone. It came as no surprise to either the state or the people that the Church strongly resisted this translation. Tyndale's excitement to bring the people God's true word in terms they could understand led him to join a movement that would rock the church to its foundations. He devoted himself to translating the Bible from Latin into English in the mid-1520s, but he was also an accomplished author of books focusing on the abuses of the Church and enforcing its interpretation of God's truth according to what he deemed anti-Christian practices. Upon hearing news of his works, Cardinal Wolsey sought Tyndale's arrest.

Disappointed but undeterred, Tyndale fled to Germany upon his release, seeking refuge to practice his writing and develop his ideas in a safe environment. In 1525, his first published work, a partial English translation of the New Testament, was printed in Cologne; unfortunately, it was pulled from the press before the complete version could be finished. Despite Prussia's Fredrick I warmly embracing reformist ideas, there were still a large number of Catholic followers throughout German lands and when the church was notified of the printing of Tyndale's book the work was immediately pulled. Those who carried, transported or possessed Tyndale's translation, much less read it, were placing themselves at grave risk of arrest for heresy.

Meanwhile, back in England, the timing of events and placement of allies could not have been arranged more perfectly to aid the anti-Wolsey faction in their maneuverings. The official works against Wolsey were gathered into a volume and given to Henry in July 1529, just before he was to retire for a summer progress with Anne, where she could no doubt seek to influence him further against Wolsey. Anne's father was elevated to a title and a new position, as Lord Rochford and Comptroller of the King's Household. This great honor would leave him in a unique position to uncover financial corruption and lay the blame directly at Wolsey's feet. Evidence was presented to accuse Wolsey of having robbed his master blind for years, with the money being diverted to causes the Cardinal supported, including the building of Universities and his lavish palaces.

The evidence of these alleged crimes was presented to the King; it was shortly thereafter that the King stripped him of all of his appointments, with the exception of the Archbishopric of York, which continued to bring him lucrative annual payments. Wolsey was formally charged with treason by right of *praemunire,* an offense in which an official of the government usurps the power of the state by consulting with and acting upon advice from a foreign agent. Wolsey was near sixty years old when he was arrested in 1529 and taken to the Tower of London to await trial. En route to the prison in November 1530 he collapsed and died of unknown causes. His famous last words were *"If I had served my God as diligently as I served the King, He would not have given me over in my grey hairs."*

With Wolsey removed and his former clerk Thomas Cromwell now acting as the King's new minister except in name, that went to Thomas More; Anne grew ever more impatient with the divorce proceedings. Henry acted swiftly and decisively to consolidate his own authority. He delivered on his previous threat to the Pope and in 1529 ordered his council and advisers to draft up documents breaking away from the bonds of servitude to the Catholic Church in Rome. By February 1531, the final documents, edited several times, were finally ready for Henry's signature. That same month he presented his doctrine to the clergy. Although not a single member voted in favor of making the King Head of a new Church of England, the silence of the clerics, ironically under the canon law precept of *qui tacet consentire videtur* ("he who is silent, is assumed to consent"), was used to validate the law. The King had claimed leadership of the church in England, the clergy said nothing, and so he had broken the Catholic establishment by default. Archbishop Thomas Cranmer, who had been the first to suggest that the King's Great Matter was a theological one and not a legal one, was chosen by the King and confirmed by the Vatican in a vain attempt to appease the King. With the Church broken and Henry's first marriage annulled, English history had forever changed.

1.4 A Coronation

On September 1st, 1532, Henry made Anne the first female Marquess of Pembroke, in her own right, with the title passing down to her heirs. Promoting Anne to this new rank of nobility made her worthy of presenting to European Kings as his new wife, which he did several months later. Anne had accompanied him as Queen in all but name. As a result of spending the majority of her life being raised in the service of the Queen of France, it was only fitting when Henry in the winter of 1532 took Anne back to Calais, the site of their first meeting at the summit with the French in 1520. With her new nobility, despite descending from the merchant class, and with his divorce complete and free to marry, Henry formally introduced Anne Boleyn to King Francis I as his fiancé and the future Queen of England. It was during this trip in the winter of 1532, a visit that was years in the making, that Anne finally yielded her virginity to her king.

June 1st, 1533 was an historic day. The actual wedding ceremony had already secretly taken place six months previously on January 25th, 1533, with Charles Brandon, the Duke of Suffolk, and George Boleyn standing as witnesses. Anne had a bridesmaid attendant as a witness for her as well, the Lady Berkeley. The ceremony took place in Dover after the couple returned from a successful diplomatic venture at Calais with Francis I of

France. The desire for an expedient marriage was due to Anne's delicate condition, as she was now with child and needed for her potential son to be made legitimate. The King was thrilled at last to have a potential heir by Anne; however, the court erupted in scandal since Queen Katherine was still officially recognized by European powers and the Vatican. Paying no mind to these foes of his new union, he dispatched his Lord Privy Seal and newly created Secretary of State, Thomas Cromwell, to making arrangements for the official ceremony and coronation proceedings. Cromwell had succeeded More when he resigned over the elevation of Anne to replace the Queen.

The official announcement of Anne's new position came with the Easter Service on April 12th, 1533. The coronation was to be held June 1st. Preparations for the ceremony had been underway for only a short time. Two weeks in May 1533 was all the time the King's subjects had to make ready the route. The Mayor of London was in charge of the proceedings and it was his responsibility to ensure security so that all would go well. This was a large responsibility given that there was both a waterway procession and one within the city. The Tower of London had housed monarchs before their coronation proceedings for the last several centuries. Rooms were specially prepared for the new Queen at a large expense to the crown. Renovations were under the direction of Thomas Cromwell. Within the Tower several rooms had to be completely rebuilt for the festivities, as they had not been used in many years and had fallen into a state of complete disrepair. According to Professor Eric Ives, the Queen's rooms were held within the inner ward and contained a dining room, great chamber, and a great gallery.

On May 29th, 1533, at 1 P.M., the official proceedings got underway. For three magnificent days the court followed from her residence at Greenwich Palace to the Tower of London. Anne was taken by a large fleet of over 300 ships marked with Anne's badge that carried the entire court from Greenwich. As the ships made their way down river, the coast line was littered with gun bearers saluting Anne with both gun and cannon fire. Henry thanked the people for their magnificent reception of his new bride, and the couple made their way to spend the next two days enjoying festivities at the Tower. The finest tapestries, liveries, jewelry, horses, wine, and meats were all prepared for her arrival.

On June 1st Anne awoke early for the festivities. According to a contemporary account, her long dark hair was fixed to flow loosely down her back. The royal treasurer brought the Queen's jewels from the Tower to adorn her on her journey. Anne must have been about five months pregnant. On the day of the ceremony participants were ready by 7 A.M. as Anne was still preparing. It took her close to two hours before the ceremony got underway. The court's fleet was late to leave the Tower to head down river to Westminster Abbey, where the actual coronation rites would be performed. The Abbey had been a pivotal place of worship and official functions since the original building was dedicated in 1065 A.D. Its rich history has seen many coronations, funerals, baptisms, and other royal events.

The waterway procession was astonishing. Many barges released gunfire saluting Anne and her retinue as she traveled to the city. The crowds lining the river banks were large, though their shouts were limited. The main streets in London that Anne would go down would be Gracechurch Street and Cornhill, which were lined with the finest fabrics of the day and, where possible, with the Queen's badge as well. Gracechurch Street still exists today and, although it is now lined with businesses, tourists can take the route Anne walked during the ceremony and proves to be a popular tourist attraction. Among the attendants were the Mayor of London, servants in the Chapel Royal, the Abbot of Westminster along with other monks and clergy, and of course the Archbishop of Canterbury, Thomas Cranmer, who would perform the rites of coronation.

Anne had chosen the French Ambassador to England, Jean de Dinteville, along with twelve servants dressed in blue, yellow, and white to accompany her through the streets of London. Her selection of the Ambassador itself evoked reaction. The English people of the time were not fond of the French for a variety of reasons; mainly the excellent propaganda campaign the English monarchs had used for centuries to claim the right to the French throne. They viewed the French as haughty usurpers who were too focused on pleasures of the flesh. By the time the Queen's barge had reached the city, the fanfare of the waterway procession would radically change. Unlike at previous coronation processions through the cities, where the crowds lining the streets were plenty and cheering loudly, for Anne's procession, the number of people in the city was relatively small and without much applause. It could be viewed that those who attended did so more out of curiosity at the new Queen than to pledge their allegiance to her.

Upon entering Westminster Abbey, it is most likely that Anne made her way through the main entrance, the North Transept, proceeding with her retinue to the nave of the chapel where the ceremony would be performed. It is not known how many people were waiting inside the church to greet or glimpse the new Queen, but most likely only the nobility and those persons authorized by Henry or Anne were in attendance. According to Professor Eric Ives, Anne walked down the aisle wearing a robe of purple velvet, signifying royalty, trimmed with ermine. Her ladies proceeded thereafter, according to their rank in the nobility, with the Dowager Duchess of Norfolk, Anne of York, carrying Boleyn's beautiful train.

The right of coronation itself was short but solemn. When she arrived at the high altar Anne was greeted by Archbishop Cranmer and other senior members of the clergy. Henry was not in official attendance, in accordance with custom of the time; but he did watch his bride from the gallery above. After mass she was seated and the rite of coronation was spoken in Latin, during which she was crowned and then given the scepter and orb of the monarchy. Anne was to be the first Queen to wear St. Edward's crown at her coronation, a rite previously only allowed for male monarchs. This was the highest honor anyone in England could win, especially so for a female in that time. She was also the last monarch to be crowned apart from their spouse. It was now official, she was the Queen, divinely ordained.

Once the procession was over, a great feast was arranged where Anne presided over the highest ranks of the English elite, sitting at a marble table. She was attended during the meal by two prominent ladies, the Countess of Worcester and the Dowager Countess of Oxford. A few hundred people participated in the meal, which was a grand affair. The court was known for consuming huge quantities of food, so much so that a single meal's provisions could have fed entire villages for days. Musicians would announce the arrival of each course, an astonishing twenty eight for the Queen alone. Following that was another twenty four courses at a second meal, followed by a third feast with twenty three dishes. Excessive overindulgence was definitively at work for this feast, and the cooks and kitchen servants worked around the clock for weeks to prepare.

The following day a great jousting tournament was held to honor the new Queen. Allies of Katherine remarked that the entire affair was without luster and left much to be desired. Cromwell, at Henry's direction, was already preparing a declaration for Parliament honoring

Anne—and only Anne—as Queen. Anyone found to be paying homage to the former Queen Katherine would suffer stiff penalties. There was no reason initially to suspect that beyond this Act there would be any further dramatic changes to daily life for the people, but all that they knew was about to come undone. Henry and Anne continued to enjoy their newfound marriage and entered into a period of relative bliss as preparations approached for the birth of their child.

1.5 The First Heir

At the end of August 1533, the couple was in residence at Greenwich Palace to prepare her "lying in" for the birth. Labor pains had been ongoing only a short while. Princess Elizabeth was born shortly after three in the afternoon and was named after both Henry and Anne's mothers on September 7th, 1533. Henry met the news of the Princess' birth with mixed reaction. He was very pleased to see that Anne was capable of producing a healthy, living heir, but he had so desperately longed for a son and was privately devastated. A girl was viewed as useless in dynastic succession. Regardless, he loved Elizabeth and held an extravagant christening for her three days after her birth at the Church of the Observant Friars.

There were a total of twenty-one attendants in the church, many of whom were from the conservative faction at court and had favored Queen Katherine. It is interesting to note that the Duke of Suffolk carried the Princess to the altar. According to Professor Ives, Anne's other enemies, including Gertrude Courtenay Marchioness of Exeter, and Catherine Willoughby Duchess of Suffolk, were both made partial Godmothers. Both presented lavish gifts, while angered and shamed at having to recognize Anne and the new bastard Princess. Both women were loyal to Queen Katherine and resented their posts at the christening. Upon further review of the contemporary documents, it appears these appointments were intentional slights, perhaps at Anne's direction, although this cannot be proven.

Archbishop Cranmer of Canterbury was made Godfather to the child. The traditional royal *te deum* was sung throughout churches in London, along with the ringing of the church bells. At the closing of the ceremony, Elizabeth was brought back to her mother's chambers, accompanied by a retinue of over 500 torchbearers. The magnificent display was meant to reinforce the new regime, although it did little to sway public opinion, especially those maintaining their allegiance to the Pope.

The printers were notified of the change from Prince to Princess that day and announcements reached London before spreading throughout the realm and then Europe. Spain and the Vatican viewed the birth of Elizabeth as a proof positive that Henry was wrong in the eyes of God and they were relishing in it; for overthrowing Katherine for a harlot, his efforts would bear no son. This news was a welcome relief to the Catholic faithful, who hoped that soon Henry would recognize Anne for what she was and return to Katherine. The former Queen's following still believed her capable of providing a son, although the reality was that she was well into menopause.

Over the next years, the new Princess Elizabeth was given title to the palace at Hatfield, servants, and the Lady Bryan was appointed as her Governess; however, despite the many favors bestowed upon her daughter, Anne's insecurity about the Lady Mary worried her constantly. She recognized that Henry had great love for his first daughter, although he often would deny it, inspiring Anne's sometimes erratic behavior. She greatly feared that the King would change his mind and make Mary once again heir apparent instead of Elizabeth.

To help alleviate his Queen's fears, Henry next assigned Mary to serve the new Princess in a position he hoped would force her to accept her new place; however, Katherine's and Mary's supporters laid sole blame for this purposeful and vindictive slight at the feet of Anne. The Princess Mary's entire way of life had been reduced to one of a lowly servant, far removed from her previous station. She not only had to bear witness to an infant Princess outranking her and replacing her in the line of succession, she had to serve the infant. This serious slight made her supporters at court furious, but most kept their views to themselves. They were well aware that Anne was incredibly powerful and moving against her would only be to their own detriment.

Elizabeth was never meant to rule, at least not in her father's eyes. Women at that point, especially royal women, were only prizes to be traded in the European marriage market to cement alliances between powers. The expected male heir that would eventually, hopefully come was to be the official ruler; the Princess' place would be in learning and devotion. Elizabeth would be expected to follow in the same traditions of demonstrating obedience and subservience that were expected of women of her time. In fact, royal women had those duties amplified since their every action was conducted in the spotlight of the royal court. Royalty would be a heavy burden to bear.

1.6 Acts of Succession

The first submission of the clergy recognizing King Henry VIII as Supreme Head of the Church of England came about in 1531. It would be only two more years before the next phase of reforms under which Henry sought to truly free England from Rome. On February 6th, 1533, Parliament passed the Act of Restraint of Appeals. It stated that all legal appeals on matters touching English rights were forbidden to be heard in any other territory but England. This Act was made in reaction to the former Queen Katherine's pleas to Rome to interfere in her marital disputes. Henry wanted none of it. Written entirely by Cromwell at the King's behest, the Act also made it illegal to appeal to any other nation.

Clever and deliberate, Cromwell tied the language of the Act to the *praemunire* policy, making violations of the Act treasonous. Reaction to the Act sent out shock waves to the religious and legal communities. When Rome was notified of the law, Pope Clement VII drafted a Bull of Excommunication to damn Henry and expel him from the community of Christian believers. Nevertheless, the Bull was not officially issued and was used more to maintain pressure on the King and try to extort him by threatening his base of support with still largely Catholic England. Under the Bull, the Pope would give Henry until September 1533 to return to Queen Katherine or see the Bull carried out. Defiant in the face of papal authority, Henry continued on his course.

Archbishop Cranmer was a cleric who came to Henry's attentions at Cromwell's behest and was responsible for resolving the King's Great Matter as a theological problem. As a result of this he earned Henry and Anne's trust and, at the death of Archbishop Warham Henry, in March 1533 the King appointed him to the prestigious office of Archbishop of Canterbury. Interestingly enough, while Henry was trying to free his kingdom from the shackles of Rome, he insisted that Cranmer's appointment be confirmed by the Pope. In a desperate attempt to placate the King and keep him from withdrawing England from the Catholic Church, the Pope authorized the appointment, not realizing how much harm he had just done.

Once officially appointed to the post, Cranmer set right to work. After weeks of agonizing research on Henry's divorce case, on May 23rd, 1533, Archbishop Cranmer pronounced judgment that the marriage between Henry VIII and Katherine of Aragon was officially null and void. Only five days after issuing the divorce decree to Katherine, Cranmer proclaimed Henry's marriage to Anne as valid and binding in the eyes of the law and God. Until she died, Katherine never accepted Cranmer's verdict and the Lady Mary never forgave him; both of these issues would be of little consequence. In alliance with the King, despite his office, Cranmer spoke out boldly and publicly against the practices and abuses of the Catholic Church. He had written pamphlets and preached sermons on the divine justice of Henry's actions and how he had freed the English people from a corrupt and abominable Pope.

When word reached the Pope of Cranmer's verdict, after years of stalling, Rome on March 23rd, 1534, issued the papal edict pronouncing Henry and Katherine's marriage valid. Katherine and her supporters clung on to hope, believing that the Pope's declaration would cause Henry to change course; it did just the opposite. His advisors continued preparing the country for the new reforms taking place. Even though Henry's personal feelings for his state minister were not warm, he was wise to reward Cromwell in April of 1534 for the part he had played by granting him the office of Chancellor of the Exchequer and Secretary of State.

The First Act of Succession of January 1534 declared the Lady Mary Tudor a bastard and removed her from the succession entirely; it called the Princess Elizabeth Tudor the heir presumptive. It also required that all subjects were to swear their allegiance to the new Queen and Princess, vowing that they recognize their divine right to rule. Further, Parliament also passed the Ecclesiastical Appointments Act of 1534, stating that nominations for bishopric offices would come directly from the King, and then be voted upon by the clergy. At no point in English history had a monarch ever enjoyed such absolute authority over the church. The clerical appointments were a sure sign that the King could now control the church in his realm, and thus wield absolute influence over his people. To deny his majesty these rights was treason, meaning instant torture and death. Political prisoners were subjected to cruel and horrifying fates for denying a duty due the crown. While Anne had every reason to celebrate, she was deeply insecure about the overwhelming upset of the people. She convinced Henry that, following the Act of Succession, all who were so asked should need to swear the oath of allegiance, recognizing her and Princess Elizabeth's legitimacy. Cromwell set about drawing up the oath and began distributing it to the people by Easter of that year.

A year later Parliament passed the Treasons Act of 1535, making it a treasonous offense against the crown for any subject to deny taking any oath his majesty required. The Treasons Act was used as catch-all to capture anyone speaking out against the King's new marriage or his new place as head of the church. It was written in such a way that traditional processes, such as Bills of Attainder authorizing arrests, would not have to be sought before a person could be tried. A Bill of Attainder was a legal device used to arrest accused criminals without the crown first proving the deeds alleged. The most important provision of the bill was that it denied the accused a right to trial, to legal representation, or to speak in one's own defense at a trial. It was by far the most expeditious means for the crown to secure political enemies in prison. The Act also made it treason for any person to speak or act out against their majesties in any way that would deprive them of the crown or bring them harm. These Acts had been a direct result of his breaking with the Church of Rome.

By mid-summer, July of 1534, an estimated 7,300 people had sworn the oath, agreeing that the King was the Supreme Head of the English Church, and to the Act of Supremacy and the Act of Succession. Out of all of the subjects of whom the oath was demanded, only two high ranking persons blatantly refused to swear to the Act of Supremacy. They were Sir Thomas More and Bishop Fisher.

1.7 Martyrs: Sir Thomas More and Bishop Fisher

Sir Thomas More was a statesman, lawyer, philosopher, author, and prominent political figure at the English court. After the death of Cardinal Wolsey in 1530, More had replaced him briefly as Lord Chancellor. Bishop Fisher served as Queen Katherine's legal counsel at the Blackfriars Trial. Both men served in positions of honor and distinction and had earned the respect of most of the court, and the people both at home and abroad. They were also loyal to their faith and put fidelity to their beliefs above secular matters.

On April 13th, 1534, Bishop Fisher refused to swear the newly legislated oath, while More refused only the Act of Supremacy, claiming to have no issue with the Act of Succession. Mores' conscience would not let him swear that the King was head of the church; he felt it would damn his soul for all eternity. While he held no fault to other men who had done so and even understood why they did, he could not and would not change his position on the matter. There was nothing in the King's behavior while More had served him that would make More fear that the King might put him to death. Rather, Henry had told More that he should look to God first, then to his King; however, when the time came for More to make that choice, Henry could not handle being second to Rome in matters of faith. More was sent to the Tower on April 17th. He was a model prisoner and even allowed to have his family visit him. Winning the renowned dissidents' compliance with the oath would have been a most dramatic way of quelling further opposition and demonstrating to the public that all should simply accept the new order. Alternatively, if they would not break to the King's will, their severe punishment would also inspire compliance.

Bishop Fisher was released in order to be given the opportunity to once more swear to the Oath of Supremacy and the Oath of Succession; he swore to neither. Therefore, on April 26th, 1534, Fisher was sent to the Tower on charges of treason for refusing the oath. Additional evidence was needed for this charge, and so a hired hand of Cromwell, Sir Richard Rich, was sent to interrogate and trap both More and Fisher. Rich was a highly respected, yet manipulative Solicitor General and also the head prosecutor for the crown. Disguising his intent by playing at innocent conversation he coaxed Fisher to say that the King was not, and could never be, Supreme Head of the Church. Before his trial, Fisher was removed from his diocese and declared a commoner.

The results of Fisher's subsequent trial were a foregone conclusion. When the Pope heard of Fisher's imprisonment in May 1535, he elevated the loyal Bishop to Cardinal, in hopes of inspiring leniency, but Henry reportedly refused to allow delivery to the Tower of Fisher's red cardinal's hat, and said that he would send Fisher's head to Rome instead. Fisher was found guilty of the charges against him June 17th, 1535, at Westminster Hall. Although his conviction for treason merited a brutal sentence including disembowelment, hanging, drawing and quartering, the King reduced it to a quicker, more merciful beheading on June 23rd; it was the only leniency Henry would grant.

The people of London were angry at the King for sentencing Fisher to die. The upcoming holiday celebrating St. John the Baptist had the public considering how much Fisher was being treated like the beheaded saint. Making Fisher a martyr was the last thing Henry wanted to accomplish, but neither would he accept second place to the Pope within his own Kingdom.

Having resigned himself to his death and made his peace with God, Cardinal Fisher was beheaded at Tower Hill on June 22nd, 1535. His body lay on the executioner's block for nearly ten hours before a groundskeeper took it away for soldiers to bury in a makeshift grave. Fisher's head was placed on a post overlooking London Bridge. Centuries later, on May 19th, 1935, Pope Pius XI would canonize Fisher as a saint for his sacrifice for the Church; he would share that honor, on that same day, with his ally Sir Thomas More.

Cromwell had visited More twice during his imprisonment in the Tower, once in April, and again on June 3rd, to persuade him to either accept the oath or confess, both efforts were to no avail. More's answer in April, as described by witnesses, remains dramatized and known today: "*I did none harm, I say none harm, and I think none harm. If this be not enough to keep a man alive then I long not to live.*" He told the minister that he debated neither the King's nor Pope's titles and was the King's true subject. During the second visit, Cromwell brought Archbishop Cranmer, but Mores' conscience would not permit him to swear that the King of England was the head of the English Church.

When that tactic did not work, Cromwell again sought out the services of Sir Richard Rich to collect evidence from More. Rich arrived at the Tower on June 12th to obtain a confession by means of the same ruse he had used on Bishop Fisher, but More was far too clever to make an outright confession. Instead, Rich probably contrived the evidence against More. Rich falsely reported to his masters that More had confessed and even alleged statements which More denied having made. Rich's purportedly false testimony was all that was needed to find More guilty.

The trial was held at Westminster Hall on July 1st, 1535. Everyone knew the King wanted More's blood, and More responded to the show trial by announcing that he hoped God would send the King good counsel, a direct and public slight at Cromwell. He was found guilty and sentenced to die, and again the King commuted the harsh sentence for treason to a more mercifully quick beheading on July 6th, 1535 at Tower Hill. More's head replaced Fisher's on a post overlooking London, for all to see as a visible reminder of the penalty for disobedience. More's body was buried in St. Peter ad Vincula Church within the Tower of London.

In time, Henry would come to repent More's death. He had been a cherished friend and perhaps one of the only true councilors the King ever had. More's family assets and home were stripped from them and they were downgraded in society, reduced to living as peasants just a short while after his death. Henry, on the other hand, despite his sorrow and sense of loss at More's death, would not allow himself to accept responsibility for the execution. The King would continue to blame More for his stubbornness in not recognizing Henry's rightful authority, as a subject should. Nevertheless, More's death haunted Henry the rest of his life.

Chapter 2

A New World Begins

Winter of 1536 proved very harsh. Most of the land to the north was covered in snow. Servants of the crown struggled to keep a continuous amount of wood for the fireplaces of the enormous lodgings of the court. The rivers froze over and trade routes were often quite difficult to get supplies through. Despite the hardships, the court kept busy playing indoor games such as tennis and cards, gossiping, dancing and having lavish feasts to pass the time.

In December of 1535 Katherine made her will, realizing her end was approaching and that she would meet her maker soon. Her attendants helped her sign her name and write a final letter to Henry.

"*My most dear lord, King and husband, The hour of my death now drawing on, the tender love I ouge [owe] thou forceth me, my case being such, to commend myselv to thou, and to put thou in remembrance with a few words of the healthe and safeguard of thine allm [soul] which thou ougte to preferce before all worldley matters, and before the care and pampering of thy body, for the which thoust have cast me into many calamities and thineselv into many troubles. For my part, I pardon thou everything, and I desire to devoutly pray God that He will pardon thou also. For the rest, I commend unto thou our doughtere Mary, beseeching thou to be a good father unto her, as I have heretofore desired. I entreat thou also, on behalve of my maides, to give them marriage portions, which is not much, they being but three. For all mine other servants I solicit the wages due them, and a year more, lest they be unprovided for. Lastly, I makest this vouge [vow], that mine eyes desire thou aboufe all things.—Katharine the Quene."*

Katherine died January 7th, 1536, around two in the afternoon at Kimbolton Castle. Autopsies were not typically performed on a Queen out of religious observances; however, in Katherine's case, an exception was made. Her heart had blackened in her illness. Anne was immediately blamed for causing her death through poisoning, a common explanation at the time for all causes not well understood. This alleged poisoning on Anne's part could not have happened; Anne had ladies-in-waiting surrounding her constantly and had not even seen Katherine since she served under her nearly five years before.

Regardless, because of Anne's reputation, she was blamed anyway. Katherine's final attendants reported that she confined herself to one room within the spacious castle, perhaps for her better comfort. She had complained often of stomach pain and had difficulty keeping any food down. It most likely would have been difficult for her to eat anyway; from her symptoms it appears Queen Katherine died of heart disease, which restricts the muscles pumping blood into the heart and makes basic functions like breathing far more painful and difficult. These symptoms could have been caused by blood leaking from her heart into her gastrointestinal track. Since medicine was still very much in its infancy, it is difficult with absolute certainty to say how long the Queen had been suffering from her ailments. Katherine, whom the King had rejected, betrayed, and ultimately discarded, had died a frail, lonely, sick woman, in a ruined castle.

Upon hearing the news of Katherine's death, Anne and her supporters rejoiced. Henry on the other hand was initially genuinely stricken over his former Queen's death, at least for a brief while. A groom of the Privy Chamber delivered Katherine's will to him around 11 P.M. the evening of her death. Before getting ready for bed, he read it with a stoic expression, and as he read, slowly, a single tear had formed and fallen down his cheek. Never one to fret too long over a bad situation, he crumpled up the letter and threw it across the room.

The following day he changed his attitude as he realized that, with Katherine's removal, the constant looming threat of war with Spain had been eliminated. Although Katherine had been estranged from her husband and died as technically only a Dowager Princess, she was allowed to be buried at Peterborough Cathedral bearing her crest with the full rights and honors befitting her station. No other public ceremony was performed marking her death and her allies mourned in private, out of fear of reprisals should they do so openly.

The next several days were devoted to preparing for a celebration festival. Anne was at last the only and rightful Queen of England. She had made her place at court and she and Henry believed that it could no longer be disputed, debated, or threatened by her enemies; at least for a while. That would not stop the rest of Europe from proclaiming her Henry's "official mistress" instead of Queen, and declaring the Princess Elizabeth a bastard. The Lord and Viscount Rochford (her father and brother, respectively) visited the Queen in her chambers at Greenwich, toasting to their security. For a time at least, Anne had nearly every reason to feel secure for herself and her heir.

Henry could also rejoice. With Katherine's death there remained a possibility that could potentially re-open diplomatic relations and trading with the Holy Roman Emperor (Charles V, King of Spain), at least after sufficient mourning time had passed. This was essential to trade and keeping peace in Europe. Henry ordered Cromwell to orchestrate a joust, followed by a magnificent banquet and a dancing reception, inviting the nobility and all of the heads of Europe, minus Spain, naturally. The invitation to the Vatican was in especially ill taste and was Anne's idea entirely.

The event took place on January 24th, 1536, at Greenwich. At the time it was said that the Spanish color of mourning was yellow, and during these engagements the Queen wore it proudly, supposedly out of respect for Katherine; however, no conclusive research can confirm this. Yellow during this period did mean God's light, but it also was worn by both common and political prisoners in Spain about to be executed. Black was the traditional color of mourning, but Anne wanted to prove a point that a new dynasty had finally begun with Katherine officially out of the picture and that point was made loud and clear. When Spanish Queens and the nobility mourned it was in the traditional color black, not yellow. This choice of color, regardless of the purported reason, was distasteful, even for Anne, but certainly understandable under the circumstances. Anne was finally the only true Queen and was reveling in it.

Nevertheless, Henry and Anne had no reason to be downcast. Their celebration made it plain to all in attendance that Anne's station could no longer be questioned. The festival was a marvelous affair. At one point during the ceremony, Henry gathered everyone's attention and announced that the Queen was with child, receiving thunderous applause. The couple embraced and kissed, and Henry asked for everyone who had a drink to cheer to his future (presumptive) son. Contemporary witnesses remarked it was more like a wedding reception than a funeral acknowledgement. The nobility was brought out in splendor. Invitations from the King and Queen were not merely requests one could choose to shake off; despite many of the nobility's personal feelings towards the Queen.

Anne attended the initial festival but retired back to her chambers before the jousting tournament began later that day. At the time she was around four months pregnant and it was believed in her time that too much activity could potentially upset the unborn child. Many courtiers in attendance were still loyal followers of Katherine's, genuinely grieving at the Queen's passing. They begrudgingly appeared at this festival to show allegiance and good faith to Henry, and possibly not to risk their own heads by their refusal to attend. The three-year old Princess Elizabeth was brought from Hatfield by her Governess, Lady Salisbury, to be shown off to the court and spoiled in loving affection from her parents. The jousting tournament was held at three in the afternoon with the top nobles of the day scheduled to perform. Before the performance Anne retired back to the palace so she and her ladies-in-waiting could retire to her chambers and read by the fire to pass the time.

The King himself was prepared to ride this day and had his stablemen, tailors and armory prepare the necessary materials for the occasion. Among the competitors, he was to joust his long time friend, close companion and former brother-in-law, Charles Brandon. Brandon had married the King's sister Mary behind his back in March 1515. Unfortunately Mary Tudor died in 1533 and later that same year Charles married Catherine Willoughby, his ward. Despite this betrayal, the friendship was repaired after the Boleyn faction had ousted Cardinal Wolsey, and Brandon had regained the King's good graces for his part in the affair. While the day may have been cold and jousting in January seems an odd affair, due to the cold weather, the crowds and court withstood the cool temperatures to see the magnificent display the King had prepared. The royal badge of an intertwined *H* and *A* appeared on fine gold cloth hanging all around the stands. Court servants passed out free snacks of turkey legs and nuts to the crowd, along with free ale as they watched the proceedings get underway. Jousting was just as much about entertainment as it was public relations, and it was vital to reinforce the monarchy and for Henry to boost his own ego by showing his realm that he was excelling in all his glory.

2.1 The *Duke* Has Fallen!

Henry and Brandon got into position with their lances drawn towards one another, awaiting the call from the referee to charge. Lances drawn, armor on, and cheering fans waiting, the two set off towards one another, barely able to see through the small slits left in their helmets for their eyes. The cold winds that blew that day had been heavy, and the participants had been warned that a strong enough gust could play a factor.

As the call was shouted, a huge burst of wind spooked Charles' horse, causing it to buck wildly and throw Brandon nearly fifty feet into the waiting stands. A shocked crowd watched on as the King immediately halted his horse, yelling for help for his friend. Witnesses reported the crowd letting out a loud gasp followed by silence with very few whispers. Catherine Brandon was present and immediately began crying hysterically and yelling her husband's name, although it was custom for women to let the men handle these situations. Physicians and groomsmen rushed to the Duke's side to check his condition before Henry could dismount and fully realize what had happened.

A scared Henry ordered his personal physicians to move Charles carefully into one of the preparing tents to treat him. The physicians were not optimistic. Charles had lost a significant amount of blood and his right shoulder was severely wounded with pieces of wood stuck in his flesh. These pieces, presumably broken off from the makeshift stand, had gotten in the wound. Had they not been removed as carefully, quickly and delicately as possible, they would have likely allowed infection to set in, leading perhaps to sepsis, a deadly form of prolonged infection that often leads to death.

The King's own personal physician, Dr. William Butts, was on hand that day to oversee the tournament. He carefully extracted each piece of wood from Brandon's shoulder. Brandon felt none of it; when he hit his head it immediately sent him into a temporary coma lasting several hours. From how he landed he suffered massive head trauma leaving him with a large gash on the right side of his head that bled for hours, according to physicians' aides. The aides were able to stop the bleeding, but it would be no telling how long Brandon may be unconscious for. Four hours into the coma, the King told his groom to have Cromwell prepare papers for passing his estate and jointure to his wife Catherine should he not survive.

Meanwhile, as the doctors, friends, and the King himself desperately tried to revive Brandon, Henry prayed to God to save his friend and not to let him die. He kept repeating his prayers until finally Charles opened his eyes and asked what had happened. The King was the first to hug him and shout happily "he's alive! Thank God man, he's alive!" through tears of joy.

Brandon had no recollection of what had happened to him and later told his physicians that the last thing he remembered was that wind had blown dust into his eye and he could not see his lance once the call to run had been made. After that, everything went black. The King asked for how long Brandon had been unconscious and how severely he had been hurt. Dr. Butts answered that Brandon would be fine, but that large amounts of wooden splinters had broken off and speared themselves into his shoulder, perhaps causing permanent damage. It was very well possible that he might never joust again, but only time would tell. He put Brandon on a strict regimen of a marigold and wheat extract that he would take twice daily while the physician would continue to visit him to work on his shoulder. One of Brandon's groomsmen ran over to notify his hysterical wife Catherine and to have her head back to the preparing tent to see her husband and that he was finally awake.

Queen Anne's father, Lord Rochford, was the greatest source of comfort for the King that day, and assisted in all of the doctors' and King's requests to help Brandon, putting aside his personal feelings. His behavior was a politically shrewd move ensuring his relationship to the King. Dr. Butts ordered Brandon back to his chambers in the palace where he could be watched around the clock and ordered he not be moved for any reason. He then advised Henry that nothing more could be done but to monitor Brandon's vitals and ease his pain, and that the King should rejoin the Queen in the palace and await news of the Duke's return to health. He vowed to keep Henry apprised of Brandon's progress on a daily basis, and if the Duke's condition should change, but he was optimistic that in a few months he would make a full recovery with only slight—albeit permanent—damage to his right shoulder.

Henry returned to the palace immediately notifying Anne, who outwardly comforted her husband as he wept for his friend. Inwardly, the Queen could not have been more overjoyed. Although Charles Brandon had been co-conspirators with her family during the opposition to their mutual enemy Cardinal Wolsey, the Boleyns and Brandon had never been true allies. Regardless, Henry was genuinely shaken by what he had witnessed his friend go through; Anne played the caring and loving wife. She held him and listened to him talk about how devastating it was watching Charles nearly die and advised him to visit Charles every day. Despite her jealousy over others with the King's ear, she loved her husband and wanted to see him happy. Henry stayed with Anne as they both awaited news.

Shortly thereafter, a groom of Dr. Butts notified Henry and Anne that Brandon was asking for him. Anne encouraged him to be with his friend. He kissed her, told her how much he loved her, and that he would return soon. Anne and her ladies prayed for Brandon's safe return to health and the Queen read parts of the English Bible to her ladies for the remainder of the afternoon. She remained in excellent spirits. Although Brandon had been seriously injured, it was an excellent sign that Henry ran first to her, instead of to his mistress, one of Anne's own ladies-in-waiting, Jane Seymour. He kept his promise and later that evening Henry and Anne fell asleep holding one another.

2.2 Jane

Jane Seymour came to court as a lady-in-waiting to Queen Katherine of Aragon sometime between 1527 and 1532. She was described as pale, with blonde hair, blue eyes, and of little mirth. While her general features were favored by the beauty standards of the day, as hers were manifest she was considered to be of no great mention. Her initial appearance at court was probably due largely to her brother Edward having received distinguishing service marks at military affairs, earning him a knighthood in 1528. Serving Henry's first Queen brought continued honor to the Seymour family and solidified them in the King's good graces.

As a lady-in-waiting she spent tireless hours on needlepoint, which Katherine had insisted her ladies do for distribution to the poor. Jane was an expert needlewoman and some of her works were passed down generations later and retained with the Seymour family until the late 18th century. Her meek demeanor served well with Katherine's natural disposition. As she came to know Queen Katherine, Jane grew to admire the Queen's grace, dignity, and poise. To Jane, Katherine was everything a Queen should be. Her own ambitions certainly could not dream to reach so high, and it can be reasoned that Katherine's virtues greatly influenced Jane's development at court. Jane had always envisioned herself marrying a fellow courtier and living a comfortable but modest life, one befitting her current station. That was as far as Jane's ambitions went. It is unclear if Jane and Anne would have served under Katherine at the same time, but they certainly were aware of one another.

Jane is estimated to have been born in 1508 at the family residence at Wolf Hall in Wiltshire. Born to Sir John Seymour and Margery Wentworth, she was the first girl and the fifth of ten children. Her father, Sir John, had long been an ally of the King, and a noted courtier. They had served together in military campaigns in the early part of Henry's reign. Through her mother's grandmother, Anne Say, Jane was the second cousin to Anne Boleyn and related to Thomas Howard, the Duke of Norfolk. Their family estate was also a working farm that the family used to gain additional income by selling their crops, and employed plenty of tenants to work the fields. The family managed the property of close to 130 acres. It was a steady job for hundreds of local commoners. While the family was certainly glad to have a daughter in their line of sons, daughters also required a dowry before they could be married off to a family of means that could adequately care for her in the lifestyle she was accustomed to. That would require quite a lot of money.

Her education was lacking and left room to be desired if she were to be placed at court as a lady of distinction, in hopes of making a match with a suitable husband. She was educated only in the minimal standards of domestic duties. The curriculum consisted of a lady's duties in running a household, managing servants, and basic medical cures for common ailments. She was raised as a Catholic and held very strong beliefs towards the papacy that did not falter with the Reformation.

In May 1528, a heavy case of "the sweating sickness" broke out in London and spread throughout the realm. This was the fourth bout of the sweat that had hit the city since the late 1400's. The sweat spread quickly and was highly acute in nature. It began with a sense of anxiety and fear, followed by cold chills and pain in the upper body, especially the neck. Its symptoms resembled the flu. After the cold chills had passed, a severe case of sweating started, with the body attempting to rid itself of the virus by burning it with fever, but climbing to a dangerous temperature range. Ultimately, as a result of probably heat exhaustion, the victims would have a strong desire to sleep, and often times did not wake up.

Anne had caught the sweat in 1528 while courting with the King, but she managed to survive, to Henry's great relief. She fully recovered at her family estate at Hever and was reunited with Henry upon her remarkable recovery. She is one of the few documented cases on record of a person becoming sick with the sweat and making a full recovery; as a result she had the antibodies to fight off the next bout should it come around and not mutate to a different strain. The cause was most certainly the filthy and vile living conditions of the day, as there were few sanitary measures taken in large cities, or indeed, anywhere. It was common for "piss pots" containing feces and urine to be thrown into the same street as merchants selling food. This direct cross-contamination of deadly pathogens was responsible for the illness; which scientists now believe was a deadly form of the Hantavirus; a biohazard level four virus isolated and identified during the Korean War in the 1950's when soldiers began coming down with similar symptoms as the sweating sickness. Hanta is spread by the feces of animals and it is believed that this could be a possible vector for the virus, mixed in with that of humans in areas of poor sanitation. In the pre-modern age, the disease proved disastrous.

While it killed far fewer than the Black Plague in the Middle Ages, it still took with it hundreds of thousands of lives. Most citizens viewed these plagues as punishment from God for sins, instead of the reality of the unsanitary conditions around them. As a result of the many deaths it caused, the court was dispersed when the sickness arose, with the King taking refuge in seclusion with only a few servants, in a desperate attempt to flee from its grasp. When the sweat came it took several of Jane's siblings. Perhaps the hardest death for her parents was that of her eldest brother, John, in whom the family had been placing their highest ambitions. Instead, it would be the younger brother, Edward, who would achieve the station toward which the Seymour's had aimed for John. As tragic as this sweating sickness was, it removed thousands of people, bringing with it openings and opportunities for those still alive and ambitious enough to exploit them.

Thanks to Edward placing her at court, Jane was able to watch Henry and Anne's affair grow. Jane was rather plain and dull, with such a reserved manner that it was unlikely that she would stand out at court. Due to her demure nature, she was able to observe many illicit activities, including forbidden love. Jane hated Anne for everything she represented, mainly due to the direct pain she had caused her mistress, Queen Katherine. She witnessed the devastating effects that the breakdown of the royal marriage had caused but she also learned how to land a King with games of emotional and physical torment. She watched how Queen Katherine had, for the most part, handled Henry's affair her own ladies-in-waiting, while still holding her head high with remarkable dignity and poise.

Life at court under Katherine had been one of comfort, but Jane did watch as her fellow ladies-in-waiting were matched off for marriages, or even minor dalliances with lovers at court, while she had no serious prospects. With none coming her way, on her brother's advice, she returned home to Wolf Hall at some point between 1532 and 1533 to contemplate her future and resign herself to a quaint life in the country. Jane was graciously granted leave from her post to attend to her affairs and by the time she retired back home she would have been around 25, typically an older age for receiving marriage proposals. It was now becoming critical to marry her off as quickly as possible or she might risk becoming a spinster and burden to her aging parents; worst of all, she may have become too old to bear children. Jane's future at this point in her life was incredibly grim.

The late 1520's and early 1530's saw few accomplishments for Jane in courtship, social climbing, or any other aspect of life for a woman at court. Because she was shy she failed to use the time at court to seek a potential mate. It is believed she stayed in residence at Wolf Hall, practicing her needlepoint and other activities to pass the time. Certainly she must have pondered her own fate. Even back at home she watched as those around her were married off, only this time, instead of fellow courtiers, those being wed were her own siblings. Her brother Edward was married to Anne Stanhope and the two ladies became fast friends. Edward and his family were rarely at Wolf Hall for visits but when they did appear they brought with them news of the court. Thomas Seymour, Edward's younger brother, also had ambition and used Edward's connections to place himself at court, albeit in a low ranking position.

The only marriage prospect Jane had was a match with William Dormer. The Dormers were a successful family from Buckinghamshire.

The head of the house was Sir Robert, a Member of Parliament. The family had built their wealth through generations of wool trading and careful social climbing. The match came to the Seymour family through the dealings of Sir Francis Bryan, a good friend of the family and cousin to the King. While Sir Francis' motives for working so diligently on finding Jane a suitable husband are unclear, his efforts were nearly successful and negotiations on a pre-marriage contract were underway. Unfortunately for Jane, the Dormers could not see their son married to her. They felt the Seymour's were too low socially.

Instead, the Lady Dormer visited the residence of the Sidney's, neighboring, higher-ranking courtiers, to ask for their daughter Mary's hand in marriage to William. This contract with the Sidney family ensured that Jane was removed completely from any future negotiations with the family. William and Mary were promptly married on January 11th, 1535. Mary Sidney brought with her the social comfort and handsome dowry that the Dormers expected.

Jane was embarrassed at the loss of her only prospect. Edward, Thomas, her father, and Sir Francis Bryan did their best to support and reassure her that another match would be coming. It did little to assuage her concerns. It is believed that Sir Francis once again attempted to help Jane by recommending her for placement in Anne's household. It took some serious convincing on his part, being that Jane was not fond of Anne at all. She wanted nothing to do with "the King's whore" and was not certain she saw a point in returning back to the same court where she saw no prospects. She was also concerned at all the rumors her brother had been telling her about how loosely Anne ran the court. Sir Francis overcame her fears by telling her this may be the only way she would find a suitable match. He warned her that if she stayed home it would be near impossible to find one. Through some very carefully crafted persuasion, Jane finally agreed. When Sir Francis returned to the court he appealed directly to the King on this matter and it was a matter of weeks before Jane was placed in Anne's service as her new lady-in-waiting. Despite her personal feelings to the contrary, in January 1535 she had returned to court and was attending Queen Anne.

This court was very different from when she served under Katherine. For one thing, Anne had all her ladies dress in French fashions, which were far more revealing than previous English fashions had been. These gowns were outfitted with the finest textiles, pearls and jewels. Anne felt that her ladies were a direct representation of her and as such wanted to ensure that they dressed in the latest fashions, always looking their best, so when foreign dignitaries came to pay their respects they would regale their own courts with tales of how well her ladies were kept.

Jane was uncomfortable with being so lavishly dressed, even under direct order; she was much more at ease in a plain servant's outfit as she had worn under Katherine. Also, the attitudes of this court, instead of being somber and filled with continuous prayer and deep piety, featured nights spent dancing and reveling in good cheer. Perhaps the hardest thing for Jane to come to terms with was the enforced reading of the English Bible on a daily basis with its Protestant leanings, which Anne kept in her chambers and would often recite to her ladies. The Queen did attend mass and was very pious, but she also knew how to appreciate life to the fullest, a value which Katherine saw little use for.

Jane was caught off guard by these radical changes, but like everyone else she was forced to adapt. The ladies played cards, learned new dances, prayed regularly from the new English Bible, and flirted as never before. Anne often taught her ladies new dances that she had learned in France, taught them how to speak French, played cards with them, listened to stories about their own lives, and treated them as both servants and dear friends. She was known to be overly generous to her ladies, which is one of the many reasons each year saw hundreds of applications for new positions in her household. The new maids and groomsmen of the Queen's Privy Chamber swore their oath of office, which declared that they were to be gracious, virtuous, modest, humble, and above all obedient in the execution of their duties. Jane would represent these pledges honorably, at least mostly.

It was common for Kings to take mistresses when their Queens were with child, and Henry was no exception. Two alleged mistresses were documented between 1533 and 1535, with neither causing serious risk to Queen Anne. The conservative factions to which Edward Seymour belonged were attentive to the ever shifting perceptions of Henry's desires and eagerly awaited an opportunity to supplant Anne. Upon her return to court, Jane had already been aware of and in contact with one alleged mistress nicknamed the *Imperial Lady* for her great support of the Lady Mary.

Although documentation on the extent of Jane's relationship with the mistress was not known, Eustace Chapuys, the long serving Spanish

Ambassador to the English court, had written in his dispatches that Jane was in the favor of the new lady. The King had known of Jane a long time, but she had not made a serious impression beyond being a servant to the crown. Certainly she was given gifts on New Years, as were the other ladies-in-waiting, but she was shown no more favor than that. It was most likely at a visit to Wolf Hall by the King and Queen in September 1535, that Jane managed to capture the King's interest. It is difficult to imagine that during this visit anything illicit in nature happened, with Anne present.

During Christmastime 1535, Anne announced her pregnancy to Henry as his gift. Her conception date is estimated to have been sometime around October, perhaps occurring shortly after the couple's visit to Wolf Hall. By this time the Queen was close to three months pregnant and just barely starting to show. Her slender frame allowed her to lose baby weight quickly and she went back to her original shape after the birth of Elizabeth two years earlier. The couple was seen as joyous with one another, laughing and affectionate. They even exchanged beautifully extravagant gifts with one another and enjoyed several dances together. For all their public joy, with Anne's pregnancy, it was once again time for Henry to set about to find a temporary mistress.

To Henry, Jane represented everything opposite of his wife. She was demure, where Anne was passionate; she was pale and blonde, where Anne was olive and dark; she was humble and modest, where Anne was boastful and ambitious; she was ill educated, where Anne was refined and sophisticated. The contrast between these two women could not have been greater, and it was in Jane's different virtues that he found solace. For all the love he bore the Queen, something about Jane intrigued him. He found it appealing to engage with a woman so gentle natured and amenable to his every whim. While no contemporary evidence survives suggesting the exact date when the King began his pursuit of Jane, the first indication of his interest is a letter dated February 10th, 1536, in which Chapuys wrote that Henry had a new amour.

The Seymour's saw this coupling as their opportunity to unite with the conservative faction, restore the rightful Princess Mary to the succession, and reverse the Acts that the Reformation had caused. Jane was their tool to achieve all of this, using the same tactics she had seen employed years before by Anne. It was a dangerous game she was about to play, but if it bore fruit she could be the next Queen of England. For a woman with no marriage prospects at all, this fantasy must have seemed both terrifying and irresistible.

Henry's new infatuation would play hard to get, with much coaching from Edward. At some point prior to January 1536, Henry had given Jane a locket with only his picture inside of it, a gift of favor. It was not long thereafter that Anne found out what was transpiring and went into a blind rage, ripping the necklace from around Jane's neck and hurting her own hand in the process. She was furious that this lowly servant in her own household had managed to capture her husband's affections; surely he could have picked a lady not serving her everyday to be his whore. The anger was certainly understandable; she knew well that Jane was copying her own moves. Anne continued to abuse her maid emotionally, verbally and physically at every available opportunity. The entire court was well aware of the new lady in Henry's eye and some set about wooing her. Jane's price tag would be the same as her predecessors had been—marriage or nothing.

Mary's supporters were certainly aware of Jane's presence and her sympathy towards their cause. Chapuys kept her informed daily of even the smallest, most seemingly insignificant detail. A new Catholic wife would bring none of the consequences in Europe or domestic unhappiness that Anne's marriage had resulted in. Jane could solve long-standing resentments with Spain, reunite England with Rome, and return Protestants to status as heretics. Anne had every reason to be genuinely worried about this mistress. The plan was simple, increase Jane's standing in the King's affections until he thought only of his desire for her; fill his majesty's mind with increasingly negative thoughts toward the Boleyns, and recruit new allies to their cause. Anne had to go, no matter the cost. They had seen how easily swayed the King was once before when a woman refused him, perhaps it could work again.

The King however, was not looking to leave his wife; he had been down this road before, and while his affections for Jane grew stronger daily, he did not want to be coerced again to marriage. This entire game was no easy feat and for it to be even remotely successful, Jane would need intimate details of the King's true nature, his fears, his desires and most of all, how to play upon his passions. Those vital details she would get from Edward and her father. The little pawn was moving across the board, heading straight for the Queen.

2.3 Out with the New, In with the Old

Charles Brandon awoke groggy and with a severe headache. Notes from eyewitnesses at the time recall him asking his attendants where he was and how he'd gotten there. His wife Catherine stayed by his side day and night and assured him all was well. The doctors were treating his shoulder, head and other injuries as best they could, but he had lost a great deal of blood and he would need to remain in the doctor's care for several more weeks. He was laid in his chambers and news of his condition was taken to both of their majesties. Henry ordered that he be kept updated of Brandon's condition daily and that Brandon be given the very best medical care. The King continued to visit daily with Charles and Catherine and deepened his bond with both of them. His recovery was slow, taking nearly three months. The King refused nearly all embassies and foreign delegations while his friend recuperated. He focused on domestic matters and his family.

Chapuys continued writing to Lady Mary, optimistic about her chances of being reinstated, especially with Jane in the picture. Chapuys was setting the Lady Mary up for false hope. Still, it brought poor Mary good spirits, at least for a time. She suffered from multiple ailments including migraines and other disorders most likely brought on by psychosomatic trauma. Relations were still strained between England and Spain but, under the circumstances, with Henry refusing all visitors while attending to his injured friend, his refusing a meeting with Spain was thankfully not interpreted as a sign of disfavor. Unfortunately for the Spanish Ambassador, during this time of stress Henry was not turning to Jane, he was finding comfort in the Queen.

The King, when not keeping vigil over Brandon, would spend hours talking with Anne late into the night about things past, memories of his friend, and what he hoped for the future for all his friends, family and his kingdom. Henry wanted to spend time with those whom he loved and who could provide comfort and reminisce with him. These were things Jane Seymour could not do, as she barely knew Brandon and certainly could not stroll down memory lane with Henry as Anne could. Further, Brandon's fall reminded Henry of his own mortality.

Henry realized that it could just as easily have been he who was thrown from the horse that day. He thought of the consequences had he suffered Brandon's injuries. It could have been him, wracked with pain and of barely sound mind; it could have been Anne thrown into hysterics at sight of the tragedy, and in the delicate early stages of her pregnancy, with her prior miscarriage, who but God could say what such a shock might have done to both her, and to his potential heir? With these thoughts in mind, Henry put aside his boisterous ego and spent more time with Anne and Elizabeth, needing to feel close to his own family and cherishing those moments with them. He had an epiphany that his family and his future was what had to come first. He had done well to play his lustful passions in his youth, but seeing Brandon lying there unconscious caused him nightmares. That could very easily have been him. Now he would focus on his family and his unborn child, who hopefully would turn out to be the son he so longed for.

Henry was well aware of the friction between his wife and his injured best friend, but Anne put aside her personal inclinations and supported her husband. It does not seem likely that during such an emotionally trying time for Henry that she would be brazen in her comments and actions, as her husband's friend lay near death. Further, she had no reason to risk such provocation. As jealous as she may have been over Henry's affair with Jane while she was pregnant, she well understood it was custom for a King to seek temporary solace to lay with another woman while his wife was with child.

Anne may not have cared for Brandon, but certainly would not have wanted to see any genuine harm come to him, in this manner at least. His injury after all brought Henry to her bedside every night, pregnant or not, and was slowly but surely pushing away any affection he had towards Jane. She had every reason to be grateful. She had just celebrated her predecessor's death and, with her primary threat removed, she had every opportunity to bring her husband closer to her instead of pushing him away. Being affectionate towards Brandon and his wife during such a delicate time would be the most effective means of retaining Henry's interests. If anything, doing the opposite of this could prove to be at least injudicious, even self-harming; two traits Anne did not possess. She instead redirected any anger about the King's taking a mistress solely towards Jane.

Although the relationship between Brandon and Anne had never been friendly, they both shared a common love for the King. It would have been unwise for the Queen or any of her faction to outwardly exploit in open court Brandon's injuries as a means of enhancing their agenda; privately, however, such manipulation was another matter. The reforms were progressing smoothly, the Boleyn family held the most power at court, and the Queen's pregnancy was progressing well.

There are two powerful arguments to be made in favor of the Queen's actions during this time. Her rage towards Jane was well documented and understandable; however, with the counsel of her father and brother, Anne was able to channel that rage away from her husband, at least for the most part. They certainly argued about his affairs; she would not have been the type to let it go. Nevertheless, during Brandon's recovery, Henry was genuinely stressed and attempting to balance his infrequent indiscretions with Jane with his increasing sense of domestic security with the Queen's developing pregnancy. Because Henry had taken so much care to spend nearly every night with Anne, she had let up on her typical harping about his affairs and attempted to make the most of their time together to bring him closer to her.

Rumors at court, started by Chapuys and Spanish sympathizers, had the Boleyn faction using spells and witchcraft to bring about Brandon's injuries, just as they had supposedly caused Katherine's poisoning, but neither the court nor the King were inclined to believe such wild accusations. He continued to visit Anne's chamber and supped with her each night for weeks. In private they reminisced about times at court with Brandon. Anne played her own part brilliantly. She had a real chance to bring Henry closer to her, out of love instead of manipulation. She even went to visit Brandon and his wife with the King, bringing them gifts and showing them favor. At Anne's own insistence, she vowed to hold a welcome-back banquet in Brandon's honor upon his full recovery, much to the King's great joy and surprise.

Brandon and Catherine saw right through Anne's Act. While Anne utterly detested Brandon, she saw it as an opening for her to make new alliances. Always the consummate politician, she strategically played her next few emotional moves to bolster her position and make the King more loyal to her than ever. It worked well. Her tenderness in Henry's time of need, and towards someone against whom she had had a history of grievance, brought her husband closer to her than ever before. For Henry, it validated the reason he fell in love with her in the first place. Henry spent every night in Anne's chambers for the next four months.

Anne's brother George proved to be an outlet for her frustration over Jane's attempted plotting to sneak messages to Henry through her brother Edward, lying about where she had been at odd hours when she should have been waiting on her Queen and hiding possessions such as jewelry or letters that Henry had sent Jane, which the Queen went looking for in her chambers. It was difficult for George to withstand his sister's tantrums, but he did so for the security of their family and, being her closest advisor, she placed absolute trust in his judgments. Anne had a short fuse and scary temper. Her fits of rage were legendary and no one was spared a severe tongue lashing by her.

The best piece of advice that George provided was not to pay Jane any attention, as that would only elevate her in importance and make her an official rival. In private with George, when her ladies were not present, Anne would reveal her real feelings of intense rage. This was perhaps one of the most difficult things for her to do as, prior to Brandon's fall, the King had been sending Jane gifts and was preparing to have her brother Edward elevated to the Privy Chamber. His feelings for Jane had been beyond obvious. She would pace back and forth, her mind constantly filled with irrational thoughts, wondering if Henry meant to put her aside in place of Jane. George would calm her from these manias, after all she was pregnant once more, and would urge her to stop her agitations for the sake of her child, lest she miscarry and then leave them truly vulnerable.

The Queen made several bedside visits to Charles Brandon, bringing him herbs and other remedies and vowing to keep him in her great affections. She even visited with his wife, bringing her gifts and showing great humility and piety towards the grieving wife. The ploy did not work at all to the afflicted, but it still pleased the King greatly. When Henry was informed of Anne's goodwill missions, he remarked to Cromwell that he had never loved Anne more than he did in her generosity over Brandon's recovery. Chapuys' dispatches of the time admitted of the change in the Queen's behavior, but noted with typical cynicism that it was nothing more than a lion attempting to bait its prey before pouncing. Anne even reached out to former ladies who might have been slighted, including some of the Lady Mary's own servants, bestowing gifts on them and elevating the now-bastard daughter's household's wages. Brandon and Catherine hated every move Anne made, but they too would not risk angering the King by betraying their real feelings about the Queen. They would wait, confident that their time would come.

Brandon recovered—partially at least—around the middle of April, although he would always have trouble with his shoulder and would never be able to hold lance to joust again. The physicians of the day had no remedy for such wounds other than to keep him stable, prescribe certain herbal concoctions to take daily, and recommend rest and prayer. Brandon requested of Henry that he be allowed to retire to his estates in the country with his wife; he had missed seeing his children and he felt the country air might do him some good.

Henry gave Brandon his blessing and told him not to stay away too long. Dr. Butts released him from care, but was cautious to tell Brandon not to put too much stress on the injured arm or he could risk tearing his shoulder, which would be incurable. In time, Brandon recovered from some of his wounds, but he would never be the same.

Brandon suffered from what was likely a severe concussion and his speech was often slow. His associates recognized a noticeable change in his behavior at Privy Council meetings. He suffered from insomnia and became paranoid and anxious at things that previously would not have bothered him. He was also incredibly irritable and known for swift and sudden mood changes, quickly forgetting altogether why he was angry in the first place. In one infamous incident he threw a heavy goblet at his wife Catherine—claiming she brought him the wrong ale—and hit her in the head, causing a gash in her forehead.

She went to her sister's house for the better part of two weeks to recuperate; worse yet, he claimed to have no memory of having so assaulted his wife. When Catherine finally came back, she removed anything sharp in the house that he might find and use to harm himself, her, or their children. He had never been violent before this head trauma. Brandon apologized to her and attempted to make it up to her by buying her three new dresses with matching head pieces and fine jewels from Italy.

He would have recurring nightmares and seeing liveries or jousting equipment would put him in a very volatile mood and bring memories of that day flooding back. Today, a person with these symptoms might be thought to be suffering from Traumatic Brain Injury, or even a form of Post Traumatic Stress Disorder. At the time, all that was known was that Brandon was much more volatile since his injury.

It leaves one to speculate how different Henry's reign might have been had it been he, rather than his friend, who had suffered those injuries during that fateful joust . . . .

While Catherine attempted to soothe Brandon's new emotional state, it became almost unbearable over the next few years and the two would eventually become estranged. He would spend the rest of his life trying to win her love back, sometimes successfully, but often times not. The King was told of his hardships and for his part bestowed upon Brandon a recently converted monastery in Yorkshire for his health and increased his revenues on other land holdings by 3,000 pounds a year. Now that Brandon was healing, the King continued conducting the affairs of state while continuing to visit Anne daily.

Henry had visited Jane and brought her gifts frequently up until Brandon's fall. After that, the visits became less frequent and soon stopped altogether. The last gift she received from the King was on January 28th. It was clear to everyone that Brandon's accident had ceased his desire for Jane, although the conservatives would not give up hope. Jane simply could not relate to Henry on the fundamental emotional level that he needed. She only knew of Brandon, but had spent no time with him and had no memories to share and knew nothing of his personality.

Henry desired a companion who could relate to how he was feeling out of genuine shared experience, not a mistress demanding marriage of all things. Jane's family urged her to be patient and continue her course, but Henry saw right through it. As a result of both Jane's actions and his need for bonding, the King no longer brought Jane gifts or had her share his table. When they did speak, it was brief, with no sign of the true affection or admiration that had once been progressing on a natural romantic course.

The Seymour family was furious. Edward was nervous that should anyone of privilege uncover their plot there could be lethal consequences. The conservatives had tried, and failed miserably, to execute a marital coup d'état. The Boleyn's still reigned supreme and with this turning of affection all were on cautious ground, but Jane's fate had been sealed during her final visit with Henry in early February 1536. She kept on neutral topics and asked about Brandon, trying to bring back his interest by playing it safe. She suggested a game of cards and it was obvious when she let him win. There was no longer any spark or connection to her. Instead, the King was bored and ended their meeting early. This was the last visit they would have.

Edward Seymour retained his seat at Privy Council meetings, but his input was not widely sought. He was asked less frequently to comment on matters of genuine importance and instead given supervisory tasks such as "Keeper of the Stables," a post he did not relish. Furthermore, when he was at the Privy Council he tended to intentionally argue, merely for the sake of arguing, with any suggestions made by either Lord or Viscount Rochford. Had he been wise enough to truly evaluate and understand what a valuable post he held, he could have cultivated the endless opportunities it held. Being the Keeper of the Stables brought him into almost daily contact with the King, allowing an unseen advantage over most of the other courtiers.

Unfortunately for Seymour, he despised the position. He felt it was beneath him and showed his displeasure with every ounce of indignation he could. With the writing on the wall, Sir John ordered Jane back to Wolf Hall, a tactic that Anne herself had used many times at Hever to rekindle the King's interests when they would appear to wane; however, in the case of Jane, out of sight would indeed prove out of mind. In her absence, the Queen banished the maid from ever returning to her service due to "abandonment." Sir John received the order as his daughter was on her way home for good.

While her supporters found it merely unnerving to lose this battle, Jane was most likely humiliated. There is still no evidence as to Jane's mindset during these events, but one can speculate that she was offended at the loss of so great a man, and possibly lapsed into a brief but deep depression over all that had occurred. She was most likely thankful that this was her last time at court, as it was a very volatile, stressful and overall unhappy time for her. She was approaching her late twenties, a time when she should have been married with several children. Instead she was heading back home, again with no prospects. Ultimately, she decided not to fight for Henry and wanted to find a husband and make a good marriage away from court. The King only sent Sir John a message of good will that Easter and had no further contact with Jane. The Seymour's had finally lost.

Jane would wait another two years until any significant marriage prospects arose. Her father had found one in George Esmond, a mere blacksmith's apprentice, but the eldest son of a close friend with whom he had served in the time of Henry VII. Sir John weighed the pre-contract carefully, to ensure the best possible match for his daughter, but after Jane's fall from the King's good graces, possible matches with noblemen would be few. Her age was not only a consideration for aesthetics; it was a factor in childbirth. With these elements in mind the decision was made to execute the marriage agreement.

On July 27th, 1538, Jane married George Esmond after only a few weeks of courting, and moved with her new husband to a small farm house just two and a half miles from Wolf Hall. Later that year she conceived their first child, a son whom she named after her husband, George Jr. She followed with seven more children over the years. One set of twins, Emily and Mary, three more sons, Joseph, John, David and a final girl named Margaret, in tribute to her mother. Jane kept an excellent home and relished being a wife and mother. She had no regrets about leaving court and had no intentions to ever go back. The family would struggle on George's meager earnings but they were happy. John would save up his earnings to open up his own blacksmithing shop, which turned out to be a one of a kind in its area due to the vastness of the village, and proved to be successful. So successful in fact, it afforded him sending his eldest child, George Jr. to study law when he came of age.

Chapuys on occasion kept in touch with Jane and his last dispatch from 1543 regarding her would report that the family was lacking in all but love. She had outwardly conformed to the Reformation but, in private, still attended Catholic mass illegally in the family basement with only the family and, when she could afford it, would call upon a chaplain to pray for their souls. Her involvement in politics was over and she settled down comfortably to motherhood and domestic life. She explained to Chapuys that she had secretly yearned for this all her life and would die a proud woman after all. She passed in 1554 and was buried in a family cemetery.

2.4 A Country Reforms

In March 1536 the Queen had been told by her ladies, as confirmed by Lord Rochford, that Cromwell was diverting revenues from dissolved monasteries to the King's exchequer instead of to educational or humanitarian causes. The Queen was outraged at Cromwell's insolence, and confronted him about the uses of these new revenues. This intransigence was unacceptable; it put the Reformation in jeopardy and could possibly invalidate these changes altogether by not keeping the promise of reform to the people. Cromwell replied that his plan was to make Henry the wealthiest monarch in all of Europe, a motive he thought she would surely support. The temper she had worked so hard to control was instead unleashed. She raged at Cromwell, calling him names not fit for a man of his elevated status, and warned him that if he did not distribute those revenues to other useful purposes for the good of the realm, she would have him dealt with, reminding him of More's fate and storming out of the room.

Realizing this was no idle threat, and without many friends, Cromwell carefully reviewed his options. He had made serious enemies. His inexperience in such a high position definitely showed. Cromwell would attempt to execute his wishes at a whim instead of negotiating to clarify simple misunderstandings, leading to the impoverishment or deaths of hundreds of innocent persons at perceived evidence of treason. He was blood thirsty; there was no doubt about it. While it is difficult to tell what exactly was going on in his mind when the King was taking Cromwell's word of traitors and was openly sentencing others to death, we can ascertain perhaps he thought by killing off these alleged traitors that it would clear his realm of these criminals and endear him to his people. If that was the King's plan it backfired.

The nobility loathed Cromwell because he was not of high birth and yet had achieved such a coveted position. The commons hated him because he was destroying the very life of their communities by destroying their monasteries. The gentry hated him because he sided with the landowners on the illegal practice of enclosures and rarely supported solving their grievances. Cromwell was finding it more difficult to locate true friends at court, and those he did, he had mainly kept through bribes. Most of the court was out for his blood. He had no security with the King and now also with the Queen, his one time ally, and had to begin looking elsewhere for friends in high places that did not already hold a grudge against him. This would prove to be no easy task. Anne and Cromwell's relationship would never be repaired, and Cromwell would continue trying to aid Anne's enemies, wherever possible, even as his circle of allies shrank.

In one instance, during the week of Easter, this conspiring went so far as to involve . . . a kiss. The King had invited Chapuys to kiss the Queen's cheek, a rare privilege held only for those in royal favor. The Ambassador was less than pleased with the invite; however, to decline the great honor would be a sign that his master was not welcoming of English friendship. It could include revoking vital revenues and English support in the Spanish conflict with the French, who were threatening Spanish territory in Italy. Chapuys had to find a clever way out of this potential debacle. Speaking with Cromwell about the invite and Spain's desire to unite Spain and England against the French, Cromwell revealed a perfect solution to the Ambassador's problems.

When greeted before entering the chapel for service, as expected, the King invited Chapuys to kiss the Queen's cheek; the Ambassador politely declined, protesting that he could not accept the honor until such time as he had proved himself worthy. Although it was a sign of disrespect to Anne, it was executed artfully; however, Anne showed she would not be outmaneuvered. During the same service, Anne hid behind the doors of the chapel until Chapuys entered. Upon seeing Anne, the Ambassador was obligated to show her respect to avoid an international incident, infuriating him at being tricked by the Queen he considered a whore.

1536 brought with it changes not only to religious doctrine, but in politics as well. Throughout the early part of the year, appointments were made to reformist sympathizers or Boleyn allies on a far larger scale, impacting all areas of court life. On February 4th, George served as a proxy vote to the recognition of a new peerage for Lord Delaware. On April 14th Lord Rochford was given revenues previously belonging to the Bishopric of Norwich. Lands at Colley Weston formerly belonging to the Duke of Richmond, the King's bastard son, were given to Anne instead.

Parliament had been in session debating vigorously to combine the legal system of Wales with that of England. In April, the resolution was passed and known as *An Acte for Laws and Justice to be ministered in Wales in like forum as it is in this Realm.* This Act allowed England to reconcile administrative differences in legal application that had long been a headache. Not only out of administrative concerns, Henry ordered Cromwell in 1535 to devise changes to Wales, fearful that the gentry in that area would be a serious threat to his power base. It was difficult prior to the passing of this Act for the King's councilors to collect revenues, distribute clear titles and land grants, nominate sheriffs and hear civil cases in court. Wales had not seen a change in its legal statutes since the creation of *Laws in Wales Acts* in the late 1280s.

Under that old system, the nobles retained unequal privilege that commoners could little contest and the application of laws varied greatly from parish to parish within Wales. For obvious reasons, nobles contested the passing of this Act because it now made them equal to the commons in matters of state. Further, it commanded that the official language to be used in Wales was henceforth to be English and not their native tongue. No other language would be acceptable in the state's eyes, including in the training of barristers and appointment of law enforcement or tax collectors on behalf of the crown. The people of Wales would now be required to formally adjust to the language spoken in the rest of the kingdom. The language provision may appear at first glance to have been added for the ease of the King's administrators, but in application it transformed the Welsh people to adopt an Anglican system over time. The Act remained in effect until it was formally repealed in 1993.

Perhaps one of the most significant changes Henry made was to order the English universities to discontinue teaching canon law. This was to include its history, application in law, basis in authority and its effects on divinity. Canon law was what the entire English legal system had been based on, a holdover from the allegiance to Rome. Canon law was the principle of applying Catholic ecclesiastical practices to administer justice in a kingdom.

The next legal system adopted was Civil Law, a system of law based on Roman secular law passed by either a monarch or a legislative body. Students would go on to graduate with degrees such as the Doctorate in Civil Law. Under this civil law system, judges held the power during trial to conduct questioning of a prisoner. While Parliament would continue to legislate, judges would remain the sole administers of justice and rarely used juries. With this significant change in the courts, Henry completed the cycle of Reformation, extending the changes in authority over religion to consolidate his authority over the state as well. Subjects were to obey the King and Parliament for secular reasons, not only providing validation for the Acts of Supremacy but enforcing their key provisions in law.

Along with government reforms, advances in other fields such as astronomy, mathematics, and the arts were also emerging. The Reformation not only removed the shackles of religious ideology, it allowed the open exchange of free ideas. During the time of the Tudors, astronomy was a relatively new field with emerging breakthroughs. In the fourteenth century, the principle of Occom's Razor had been developed by William of Occum, a pioneer in the field of logic, which states that the solution featuring the fewest variables to a hypothetical problem is most likely to be correct. This principle of scientific evaluations still applies today. Such scientific advances sparked the beginning of the remarkable advances that would later spread through Europe and make possible the discoveries of the Age of Enlightenment to come.

Prior to Henry's secularization of England, the intellectual efforts of scholars at work in the universities often contrasted with the common beliefs in the community. The reason for this was because most of the commons were illiterate and lacked the money to afford to attend universities to receive education. Had those resources been available on a massive scale technological, scientific and intellectual breakthroughs would have occurred faster in England as a result of a highly literate population. Without education, the commons turned to answers such as God or the Devil (aka witchcraft) for things they could not explain when often times there was a perfectly rational explanation for most events. Answers for explaining the universe in which the illiterate people lived were based on religious principles. Secular alternatives for explaining the universe were often seen as either heretical or outright witchcraft. Scientists had to be careful to conduct their experiments so as to minimize the potential for persecution by the ecclesiastical authorities.

The Queen was a huge proponent of education and thus helped to eliminate or remove as best she could, persecution from scientific trials to help explain basic parts of the world in which the Tudors lived and the universe itself. Liberated from these fears, England's scientists developed and helped to accelerate the Renaissance and usher in a new age in not only astronomy, but cosmology, physics and advanced mathematics.

As the world around them changed, for those living under Tudor rule, these impressive advances in science would pass with little notice. The political and religious reforms under which the subjects were now to abide would encompass every aspect of their lives—for better or for worse. For Anne, her world was filled with an abundance of hope. Hope of the birth of a future Prince, and hope for a reformed England that she had made possible.

Chapter 3

The Birth of a Prince

The Queen now set about making preparations for the birth. She also set about detailing her plan for education trust divestitures and religious house reformations. The new policy still awaiting Parliamentary approval was not to destroy monasteries but to re-indoctrinate them with the Anglican movement and introduce the use of William Tyndale's English Bible in the pulpit. Anne understood that for their reforms to be successful the people would need to be educated in their own tongue. These were causes Anne was passionate about and she charged ahead, although there were some at court who felt the Queen was overreaching herself, both in political affairs and, at the risk of her child.

The final month approaching her pregnancy came easily and was moderately peaceful, despite the revelry of the equally expectant court. Hans Holbein was invited to paint the royal family. The sitting took several hours but produced one of the finest family portraits of the age; unfortunately this work was lost to us in the Great Fire of London in 1666. Henry kept busy ruling his kingdom and set about enforcing courtesies at court, such as banning public urination on the court grounds and replacing antiquated plumbing and kitchen systems in the palaces. The kitchen chambers at both Hampton Court and York Palace were remodeled with a relatively new technology that would allow for hot and cold running water, facilitating healthier preparation of food for the enormous court. Henry took a keen interest in these palaces and enjoyed seeing them renovated into places regal and majestic. Cromwell's extensive record keeping helped document the King's enormous spending on such projects, and in providing the giant cadre of servants that such estates required to maintain them.

Meanwhile, Lord Rochford controlled the affairs of the Queen's household by monitoring servants' performance. To instill loyalty to the Boleyns, Lord Rochford provided generous gifts and other benefits, not only to the servants themselves, but to their families. Most of the servants were so grateful to receive such benefits that they remained loyal, and harsher tactics were rarely needed to enforce obedience. Lord Rochford was definitely the mastermind when it came to using illicit tactics to get his way. George and Anne could be if the appropriate situation called for it, but it was not in their nature the same way it was with their father. Lord Rochford was not shy about using blackmail or extortion when generosity failed to work.

3.1 The "lying in"

Although the pre-summer months were already becoming scorching hot, Anne had her ladies-in-waiting shut the windows and put dark cloth over them, letting little if any light in to help keep the heat down. She also ordered no fireplaces be lit either in her chamber or the chambers on either side of her. She slept with only one sheet and the lightest gown she could find to wear while in her chamber. As May approached, she rarely went outside except when duty called or to greet a foreign Ambassador, but the rest of the court was so hot that she preferred the sanctity of her own cooler chamber.

To help pass the time she ordered new books from France be sent to her, so she had some material to read newer than the old supply she had read at least a dozen times. She continued her prayer and needlepoint but found it so exhausting that she opted to read more instead. As few candles as possible were lit to help keep down the heat and, to give her ladies a break from the temperature, she permitted them to wear appropriate but loose garments, rather than the typical elaborate gowns while in her chamber.

This was proving to be one of the hottest summers on record and in Anne's delicate state she needed to be kept cool at all times. She called it a voluntary "lying in" due to her pregnancy, even though it was just an attempt to avoid the weather. The baby was kicking more and she occasionally had bouts of heartburn. Henry chose to visit almost daily unless he got caught up with that day's business or was out hunting. Once he discovered how much cooler Anne's own chambers were, he ordered his groomsmen to match their treatment of his own chambers.

The birth of the royal heir was widely anticipated by all. Anne and Henry had consulted with several astrologers who, along with her physicians, claimed with certainty that the child was to be a boy. With confidence in that judgment, announcements were printed and wine barrels and tailors stood anxiously by, awaiting the order for new liveries in honor of the Prince-to-be. A son would bring the political, diplomatic and dynastic security that the Tudors so desperately needed. If a male heir was not born, England would need to align with one of the top European powers, potentially giving up control of their kingdom.

Childbearing in the sixteenth century was a brutal and grueling process, one that was potentially lethal to both mother and child. Many children did not survive past infancy. The infant mortality rate was incredibly high due to medical standards being very low, and the overall birthing process being not well understood by most. Safe delivery of the child depended on the skill of a midwife, the healthy constitution of the mother, and divine providence. Religion played a significant role to all involved. It provided one of the only real comforts available for the mother.

The birthing chamber had to be prepared for delivery weeks in advance. For the expectant mother, the "lying in" process was a significant and formalized ritual. She would be inducted into the birth chamber, signifying the end of marital relations, for several weeks until the birth, and usually upwards of 40 days after. For a Queen, above all, the "lying in" was celebrated as an important rite. The Queen's retinue of ladies, senior nobles, and their families were in attendance when the Archbishop performed the "lying in" ceremony.

Because a Queen's childbirth would result in an heir to the kingdom, the sex, health, constitution, and all other personal factors of the mother and child would be called divinely inspired. Her majesty took to her "lying in" period officially in late May with only her ladies attending her. Normally a Queen would take to her chamber several weeks prior to birth; however, Anne would take to her unofficial "lying in" chamber only 10 days before. The expectant mother would typically be placed near a fire for warmth, since cold was believed harmful to the body by bringing sickness and being near fire was thought to provide a physical barrier to evil spirits, but with the brutal heat of that summer, Anne insisted on changes to the ritual.

Some of the attendants in the room thought she was mad for going against tradition and demanding the room be kept cool but she could have cared less. This was her pregnancy, her child and her comfort; she wanted it cool and so it was. Once the "lying in" had begun, men were not allowed near her and any male attendants were replaced by capable women, mostly midwives and their assistants, to care for the expectant mother. When Anne heard that preparations were being made for her "lying in" chamber, she demanded that it match the level of cool air that her own chamber had, or she was going to give birth right there in her bed. It took another day and a half of preparation, but the midwives attendants did as the Queen commanded and by the time Anne made her way down the hall to the "lying in" room it was just as she ordered. With that, according to legend, she said *"good, now I can give birth to my son."*

The process of childbirth during this time was a delicate ritual understood by few men, which contained part mystical and part religious rights to be observed for the birth of a new child. Unbeknownst to the women of the time, several of the special requirements of the "lying in" chamber had real, practical benefits to mother and child. The white linen that was favored for the room, chosen for its symbolic purity, would also ensure cleanliness, although these hygienic implications were unknown at the time. Additionally, the white material was dye-free and thus was both hypoallergenic and would further reduce the likelihood of infection.

Unfortunately, few comforts were provided for pregnant women in those days, and royalty was no exception. A cross was placed within the sanctity of the birth chamber so that the mother could pray to God for the safe, speedy and healthy delivery of the child. Prior to the Reformation, English women also prayed to the Saints for a healthy child and safe delivery.

There was little else to ease suffering during the pains of birth, as there were neither antibiotics nor pain medications of any real use in England at that time, although primitive apothecaries provided "medicinal remedies" in the form of herbs which provided no real relief. Apothecaries dispensed these so-called medicines, as an early equivalent to a modern day pharmacy, and served as a general place for medical counsel. For the poor, an apothecary was far cheaper than calling for a physician that many could not afford.

Physicians in those days advised herbal remedies based on traditional folklore passed down for generations. These plants and herbs, including roses, aquilegia, meadow plant, and others were used to moderate pain, encourage the smooth delivery of the child, and even inspire more breast milk production by the mother. Reference guides for physicians were still very primitive, probably for fear of printing any material that could be perceived to be of an obscene nature, even when greater precision was necessary, even essential, for health reasons. Gynecological books of that period often reflect a romantic and unrealistic view of the process.

A midwife and her attendants were trained in the delicate art of childbirth, and those fortunate enough to be selected for royal service were ladies of the utmost standing in their family line. Training was passed down to select apprentices, making their service prestigious and invaluable. Technically, they were required to be licensed, participate in the church, and embody a deeply religious background. The licensing requirements were imposed during Henry's time and could well have been established to show compliance with the policies of the Reformation. One of the midwife's vital duties was emergency baptism. The rite was performed in case the infant should die prematurely, without a proper christening, to ensure that a child's soul would be saved should a Priest not be readily available. This infant baptism was solely a reformist principle. It later became a tenant of the Ten Articles officially establishing evangelical doctrine in England. It was vital to the aristocracy to employ some semblance of control over those who were assisting in birth; it also showed how well-connected royal persons were to have reputable ladies as experienced midwives about them.

As a senior advisor to the King, Cromwell too continued to have a prominent role in the preparations. Cromwell had in his possession the *Bible of Midwifery*, which had been used by royal families for generations to pass down advice, superstitions, and strict rules of governance regarding childbirth. One main contributor was none other than Henry's own grandmother, the Lady Margaret Beaufort. She believed in strict rules of observance and that any deviation from those set birthing policies fail, it would displease God. While she was alive she enforced these rules to the smallest degree. Katherine's attendants had also added to the book during her deliveries. It was typically kept in the safe keeping of the state minister, hence how Cromwell became its guardian, and was only to be used for preparation of the "lying in" and delivery.

3.2 Cometh an Heir

On May 21st, 1536, Anne began experiencing heavy cramps. Concerned that this could potentially be a bad sign, she called for her midwife immediately. At her request, Anne immediately set in motion plans for her ladies to begin the "lying in" process, without the pomp and ceremony that had accompanied Elizabeth's arrival. Should Anne or the child be in danger, there was no time for such novelties. During the last three months of a Queen's pregnancy, the midwife was living at court in case of such emergencies. The "lying in" took place that afternoon after the Queen was moved from her chambers to the birth room. The midwife, her assistants, and supplies took less than an hour to prepare. The cramping continued through the late evening.

After examining the Queen, the midwife found no damage to the child. Anne was just experiencing some early contractions; the midwife recommended Anne change her breathing style and her ladies keep her as comfortable as possible. They called for herbal remedies to help Anne sleep and ease her discomfort. The following morning she awoke rested and rejuvenated, the cramps had subsided, and she insisted on continuing her plans of renovating the religious houses. The midwife resisted Anne's attempts to exert herself and carefully thwarted those who could obtain access to her, for example, blocking the interference of Lord and Viscount Rochford, who could otherwise bring Anne diversions from the outside, which could not only contaminate the birthing chamber but excite the Queen into premature labor. The King was made aware of Anne's condition and celebrated with his men, toasting to the health of mother and child. He took his nobles out hunting that day in celebration. For her sake and her child, Anne's physicians advised her to stay in her chambers until the contractions started.

On the outside, Viscount Rochford had initiated a public relations campaign to mitigate negative reactions towards the Queen. With Cromwell's coordination, the King's subjects were given free wine, quilts, bread and meats, all generously delivered whilst plays were put on for the people, showcasing the religious reforms and poking fun at the Pope. Plans for a museum at the Tower of London housing the royal jewels were also drawn up at Anne's insistence, as a means of retrieving revenues lost from Cromwell's recent monastery diversions. These funds were then used towards educational/poor trusts of her choosing. An added benefit was to bring the people more in touch with their heads of state. During her confinement Anne and her attendants had made beautiful quilts for the poor. Henry embraced these examples of his wife's activism and received letters about Anne's activities while she was confined so that he might publicly insist that it was his idea to show the people such Christian charity.

On June 17th, while already "lying in", Anne reported more intense contractions. Due to her delicate condition, and the possibility of causing premature labor, her ladies kept her occupied by sewing, reading, dancing, praying, card playing and conversing on the Queen's vision of reformation. She debated scripture with her attendants and sought theological opinions from them, rare behaviors for a Queen. She listened intently to their ideas, some appealed to her, others did not. Intently focusing on the child she was to bear, she let any slights go for the time being, but would catalog them for future use, should the need arise.

Twelve days later, around 1 P.M. of June 29th, 1536, Anne went into labor. The contractions were sudden, intense, and quick with the labor lasting only 34 minutes. This delivery went much easier than her first. The midwife rejoiced and cried out *"Your Majesty has given birth to a son!"* as the ladies in the room burst into tears, followed by laughter and applause. Queen Anne had, at last, birthed the precious Tudor son that would secure the dynasty. She burst into tears, joining her ladies in praising God, and called for King Henry. The Prince was immediately christened by the midwife, as a precautionary measure; but this time, there was no need. The child was healthy and able, of moderate length and weight, about seven pounds. He had received Henry's bright blue eyes, and showed signs of Anne's dark hair.

The King was immediately notified by her chief lady-in-waiting, Madge Shelton, as she ran past the Yeoman shouting the news, interrupting a session of the Privy Council to tell the King in exasperation that he had a son. Typically, news of the birth would reside with the King's Chief Groom, but Madge disregarded ceremony for value of the news she would deliver.

The King immediately slammed his fists on the table and a laughed heartily with joy. He ran over and hugged Madge, thanked God, and shouted at his men *"I have a son! I have a son! God has not abandoned me! Bless His mercy I have a son!"* As the men cheered and exchanged hugs at the securing of the dynasty, the King ran to the Queen's birth chamber to welcome his son. He grabbed Anne and with a strong hug and kiss thanked her for her blessing and her duty, then laughed and roared *"Bring him to me, I want to see my SON!"* The midwife appeared at once, bringing the baby boy into his father's arms as he began to weep, holding his heir. This account was witnessed and chronicled by the midwife attendant, Shellie Flatley.

The Queen told the King that the child had not yet been named, and she had left that honor to him. *"I shall name him Henry, that he too may someday be King Henry of England. Go and tell the printers to announce the birth, I want the whole of the kingdom to share in the joy of this day."*

Embracing his son, Henry and Anne shared a kiss. One final exam of the Queen and child gave them both clean bills of health. The midwife assured the couple of the Prince's good posture and lack of any visible signs of health problems. The King inquired into the Prince's christening, had he been fed yet, had he cried much after his birth, how blue his eyes were, and all the details that fascinate the parent of a new child. The heir Prince reinvigorated Henry, who had not felt so sprightly and in control of his destiny in years. The gamble had been worth it; Anne had done her duty and was now untouchable. She had her midwife bring her father and brother to meet their new family member and celebrate with her and Henry. The two were now the proud parents of the next Tudor king.

3.3 Promises of Joy . . .

The evening of the Prince's birth the royal family held a magnificent festival in the Great Chamber with all the nobles, courtiers and retainers invited to dance, rejoice, and toast the new Prince. There were hundreds of people who ate at the King's pleasure and expense daily, putting an enormous burden on the kitchen staff, but these celebratory feasts went so far as to be endurance tests for all involved. Kitchen staff worked constantly to provide main course after main course, and so many were served in a single setting that it was not uncommon for those attending to periodically induce vomiting to make room for later courses. This feast is documented to have included venison, mutton, chicken, fowl, crawfish, eel, capons, partridge, oxen, pork, beef, herons and even peacock.

The Queen was not in attendance, as she was still in "churching," mode, one of the rituals accompanying childbirth in the 16th century. Churching was performed to ensure that there were no complications with the mother or the child and usually lasted around 40 days, long enough to ensure that she had been thoroughly cleansed and purified to be released back into society and ultimately back into marital relations again. For royal women and especially Queens, churching was an elaborate ceremony dictated by strict rules governing how a Queen was to be removed from her "lying in" process and re-introduced back into her duties as Queen of state.

Once a woman—especially a Queen—delivered a child, a ceremony was performed notifying all and sundry that she was ready to be reintroduced back into marital relations. This was mainly done to protect the health of the mother and protect the integrity of the lineage. The utmost security was also ensured, with all Yeomen, and even additional hired guards standing watch. Only four hundred persons of the court were allowed to be in attendance when the Prince was near. As the print shops went about quickly making the birth announcements, clergy set about ringing church bells, and councilors notified diplomats, dignitaries and foreign leaders of the news. In addition to the announcements, the King at once commissioned from Master Holbein a painting of his son—only three days old—to be made available en mass for his people.

Elizabeth was brought by Lady Salisbury from Hatfield to meet her new brother. The three-year-old Princess took quickly and kindly to her new brother, wanting to hold him and touch him, attempting to understand who he was to her and how delicate he was. Anne's brother George informed the Queen how the affair went. During her churching, Anne instead celebrated with her maids in the "lying in" chamber, toasting to all with good cheer.

Henry showed how important this birth was to him by diving into detailed preparations for even the most intimate details of the Prince's christening ceremony at Westminster Abbey. He reviewed safety concerns, gifts, foods, entertainment, and other areas. He personally wrote letters following the announcements to King Francis of France and Spain's king, the Holy Roman Emperor, Charles V, gushing about the birth. He then chose the Lord Rochford, the Duke of Suffolk, and Cromwell to serve equally as godfathers. No one served as Godmother this time around. Anne had wanted Lady Madge Shelton, a lady-in-waiting and her cousin, to be made Godmother, but she was not of noble blood and so her request was denied. Anne did have some say in the ceremony, personally visiting the Prince often to monitor his feeding and sleeping schedule, and with her personal tailor she selected his christening gown. Henry chose the Duchess of Suffolk to walk the Prince down the aisle towards the baptismal altar followed by the Queen's ladies-in-waiting and several high ranking members of the clergy and Privy Chamber. A few days later the new Prince, the first who would be born into leadership of the Church of England, was prepared for his official christening.

The ceremony took place in the Nave of Westminster on July 2nd at six in the evening, with Archbishop Cranmer officiating. All of the court of London was invited, including foreign Ambassadors, dignitaries, nobles, and courtiers, to bear witness to the prize of the Tudor crown. Unlike at Anne's coronation, the streets were lined with thousands of people, all hoping to catch a glimpse of the future King. Shouts of joy and cheer were heard for miles leading up to the procession en route to the church. Nevertheless, it was one thing to finally celebrate the birth of the royal heir; however, embracing the Queen was another matter entirely and it would take time for the people to feel warmth for Anne, as well, if at all.

Interestingly, considering the importance of the occasion to the witnesses present, official custom forbade their majesties from attending the christening. As such, the King stood next to the bed at the palace where Anne continued her "lying in", awaiting the moment when they would receive the Prince afterward. Both the King and Queen were wearing their official robes of state since this was a formal occasion. Elizabeth was also at the ceremony with her Governess.

Very strict guidelines dictated how guests were to be arranged in the halls, chamber, and church. Their every movement was choreographed, as if an elaborate dance, with each guest fully understanding well ahead of time where they were to be during the ceremony. Guests were arranged by their title, dressed accordingly, with their retainers and servants wearing their masters liveries, occupying standing room only. The Godfathers and European Ambassadors walked last to the church, following the officiating members of the clergy, with the Grooms of the King's Privy Chamber guiding them to their proper places. Lord Rochford was given the honor of carrying Prince Henry into the church prior to turning him over at the church doors to the Duchess of Suffolk who would carry him to the altar.

The procession just to get to the altar took two hours, it was eight in the evening by the time Cranmer began his blessings.

There are conflicting reports from Chapuys and a Privy Chamber groom as to how magnificent the ceremony truly was. The Imperial Ambassador could always be counted upon to discount any recognition of the Queen and described the event to his master in Spain as uncomfortable, against God, and lacking in true regal presence. By contrast, a member of court detailed the elaborate liveries of the servants, along with the beautiful dresses of the ladies. For a group that may not have wanted to attend, this collection of nobles had certainly brought out their absolute best attire for the occasion. Chapuys did concede that the number of attendees was far larger than for the christening of the Princess Elizabeth. This would be the single highest compliment, as it was all that the Ambassador could muster.

If the festivities truly were smaller than might have been expected, it is just as likely that this was a deliberate decision by the King, who quickly grew to be highly protective of his heir. While the people lined the streets and additional security was deployed, inside the church was even more tightly controlled. After the sweating sickness outbreak, Henry had developed an unhealthy paranoia of all things resembling illness or filth, and demanded that a strict ceiling be put on the number of people permitted in the Prince's presence, to reduce the likelihood of illness to the Prince's person.

Although there was only an elementary understanding of the connection between cleanliness and illness, Henry would take no chances and ordered that the Prince's undergarments be disposed of after a single use, preferring that anything resembling filth be kept away from the precious youth. The servants had never seen anything like it before, but after all, Henry was a new father and he wanted to take every precaution possible to ensure that the heir to the Tudor line had the very best care he could find.

To ensure the health of his son, every possible consideration was given to the Prince's care. He ordered that only those persons whom he had selected could attend the boy, and that his chambers be scrubbed three times a day. Those who cared for the Prince directly had to be of outstanding moral character. His majesty would take no chances on any immoral persons influencing his son's character. He also decreed that no person below the rank of knight could wait on the young Prince at any time. It was nothing strange for infants not to survive past a few weeks and, having had painful personal experience with this, Henry left nothing to chance.

Ironically, emphasis on apparent cleanliness while not understanding the germ theory of disease, led to some increased risk factors for the Prince. All servants and dinnerware that the Prince would touch would also be of the highest standards of cleanliness, but it is documented that servants ministering to the child were so often forced to scrub their hands, and so hard, that their skin would be raw, sore, and often covered with blisters, making them potentially more susceptible to infections that might be passed on before manifesting direct symptoms. Should the King be notified that servants waiting upon the Prince had this condition they were immediately replaced.

Outer garments could not be so easily disposed of, or so vigorously boiled and washed before re-use, because they often incorporated hand sewn pearls, diamonds and incredibly delicate lace that could be easily destroyed. Nevertheless, Anne would often order that a garment be sealed away after a single wearing, justifying the extravagance as making an excellent display for the people to see, and a source of income as well, as the King's subjects would pay handsomely to see these garments.

In a sense, Anne displayed great ingenuity in charging to see the Prince's attire. This was the first such example of profiting from one's celebrity. She had managed to create a public museum requiring an admission cost of two ducats. The money went into the royal coffers but, surprisingly, thousands lined up to see the Prince's fine garments. People came from all over the kingdom to see his attire. Anne had not witnessed anything like it and it gave her a far broader idea.

Henry on the other hand, had apparently been validated by God with the Prince's birth. Suddenly, all the turmoil and all the labor that taking Anne as his wife had required seemed worth the sacrifices; the victory boosted his own sense of self and gave him greater serenity and confidence in the correctness of his decisions. Another element of Henry's personality that had changed with this birth was that he found himself growing closer to God.

The King would spend long hours talking to the Prince, holding him, reading to him and telling him of the great King he would someday become. Servants would often catch him retelling the story of Henry V's Battle at Agincourt, while the Prince's little eyes just intently focused on

Henry as he spoke. He relished every aspect of his new healthy son. It could be argued that, at least for a time, Henry's son mellowed his vibrant personality and allowed him to revel in a good cheer at court, the like of which had not been seen since the very early part of his reign.

Anne recovered quickly and into perfect health. She was released from churching at the end of July, a full ten days ahead of schedule. This could have been due to having begun her "lying in" over a month in advance, though there are no records to prove or disprove that this was the case. Now that the Prince was born, she too was far more relaxed than at any time before. On July 16th, 1536, the Prince gained his own household, with the same Governess Lady Bryan, as his sister. He would join Elizabeth at Hatfield to be watched after and so that the two could grow up together; this was mostly at Anne's intense insistence, which the couple fought over.

3.4 . . . Portents of Danger

Henry's illegitimate son Henry Fitzroy, who had been suffering from consumption for several months, finally died at St. James Palace in early July 1536. His titles, revenues and all estates reverted back to the crown, including the Dukedom of Somerset. His death was covered up with unusual speed and Norfolk buried him at Framlingham Church in Suffolk, attended by only two witnesses. According to contemporary accounts, the King had ordered the Duke of Norfolk to dispose of the body as soon as possible. When Norfolk returned to tell his majesty that he had done his bidding, the King became overcome by grief.

Never again was the name Henry Fitzroy spoken in the King's reign. He was all but forgotten, except of course by his mother Elizabeth (Bessie) Blount, who retired to the country mourning the loss of her only son. The expediency and lack of public announcement on the death was particularly strange, especially considering that the King at one point had groomed Fitzroy as heir apparent. Conspiracies surrounding the nature of his death and what some believe were its cover-up still continues today, with no conclusive evidence to set the record straight.

As recognition for Anne having fulfilled her Queenly duty, Henry bestowed upon her St. James Castle, with an increase in her salary to the equivalent of a million pounds a year in current prices. Prince Henry was given the titles of Duke of Richmond and Duke of Somerset, along with a handsome sum of 500,000 pounds a year until his sixth birthday, at which point the sum would be doubled. Lord Rochford was given the Earldom of Hartford and Viscount Rochford received the additional title of Viscount Lisle. For all of Cromwell's efforts he too was advanced, elevated to peerage as the Baron Cromwell of Wimbledon, on July 8th, 1536. Not all nobles were so delighted. Many of the courtiers while claiming to be reformers remained secret Catholics and were still loyal to the Lady Mary. The constant advancement of the Boleyn's further aggravated them and spurred some to devise means of retaliating.

At the end of July, royal messengers received dispatches back from Europe. Francis I ordered bells rang at the time of birth, free wine for those in Paris and Calais, and sent cloth of gold along with plate and jewels for the new royal addition. Further, he sent a personal message to Henry congratulating his fellow brother on such a fine delivery. This was a genuine message of warmth and acceptance that appealed to Henry on various emotional and diplomatic levels and once again affirmed France as an ally. Germany, Portugal, and the Netherlands sent equally warm messages to Henry with gifts of gold plates, jewels, cloth of gold and silk from the East, spices from the Indies, and countless other rare treasures to celebrate the good news.

Spain was less celebratory, being that in her eyes the child was a bastard and not recognized by the Catholic Church in Rome as a legitimate heir to a renegade kingdom. Nonetheless, for the sake of political amity and keeping relations cool to avoid warfare, Charles V sent a standard message of congratulations—far less warm than Francis had been—and sent a single gold cup engraved with the Prince's title, date of birth, and encrusted with jewels. Anne too was delighted to receive it, knowing, it was sent with regret. With Henry's permission, she had the cup melted down and made into a gold necklace engraved with her logo "the most happy." While less than the flamboyant gestures made by the French, Henry accepted the Spanish tribute graciously, as England was not equipped to do battle with the Holy Roman Empire, certainly not with the Emperor, who was flush with wealth and power from its conquest of the New World.

The Italian city-states were cordial, but distant, mostly due to pressure from the Vatican, which lobbied staunchly against any form of recognition for this "bastard child of the great whore." As far as Rome was concerned, Henry was undone and not entitled to rule his own kingdom. For months, the Pope had been attempting to lure both France and Spain, the two most powerful militaries of the time, to invade and conquer England, returning its allegiance to Rome. Neither had any real inclination to do so, they both had their own internal squabbles to be concerned with.

Henry, conflicted at the mixed messages he was receiving from Spain and Italy, convened a Privy Council session to review the perceived slights. The Council judged that the gestures were not slights to the Prince, but rather, were responses to the status of the controversy over the Church of England. Recognizing that the difficulties of the new church had been bound to reverberate, but would not eventually bar his son from claiming the throne, Henry calmed in his anger. Meanwhile, Anne continued to advise her King in private and accepted the perceived public slights in exchange for growing private influence. In return for her loyalty, and still grateful to her for having borne a new Tudor king, Henry would come to rely upon her advice even more.

Chapter 4

Religion in England

The fading feudal system, invention of the printing press, and the growth in literacy that attended the latter, led to the spread of religious reformism to an entirely new class of people who would go on to become the primary sponsors of reform. These significant changes led to an evolution of society that was preparing the groundwork for a new age, leaving behind the long interregnum following the fall of the Roman Empire. Socially, culturally, economically, and politically, Europe was coming into an age of rebirth, or Renaissance; the power of the secular state was poised to rise and challenge the order maintained for 15 centuries by the Roman Church. What could not have been predicted was that this challenger would be a former "spare" to the throne, who had himself once been destined for life as a churchman.

4.1 Auditing the Church

As part of Henry's efforts to come to terms with the true scope of the power and wealth of the Church, and thus to plan on how to become its master, came the *Valor Ecclesiastes*. The *Valor,* a massive survey—or audit—of all the religious houses in England, and parts of Ireland and Wales, was instituted after Cromwell had been presented with evidence concerning the monasteries' corruption. Spanning the entire country, the purpose of this work was to truly understand the status of each monastery, both in terms of finances and whether or not they had embraced the reformation by recognizing the King as the Supreme Head of the Church. It would also allow the crown to determine how to proceed with additional administrative duties to complete the reformation. Henry authorized Cromwell to compile the—beautifully illustrated and bound—*Valor Ecclesiastes* in 1535.

The commissioners sent to do this assessment were unpaid agents of the crown, but they worked diligently to carry out their mission in only five months. The amount of information needed for these reports required that the commissioners be heavily dependent upon the local sheriffs, mayors, and other magistrates, who actually did the work of acquiring the data and passing it back through the commissioners. Those who appeared suspicious based on the reports found themselves visited either by Cromwell himself, or by his lead agents. These agents, Thomas Legh, John Price, and Richard Layton as the principal administrator, were hand selected by Cromwell for having proved themselves loyal to the new regime. Doubtless, the reports were not free from political and personal biases.

Richard Layton had diligently served Cromwell in the trial of Sir Thomas More by presenting questionable evidence for the state after interrogating both More and Bishop Fisher. Layton also served in multiple religious offices prior to his service in compiling the *Valor*, including the post of Chaplain of St. Peters, Dean of York, and Archdeacon of Buckingham. He also recommended Thomas Legh to Cromwell for the canvass. Legh was a highly respected, secular lawyer, who had represented Henry in his divorce suit. Along with Legh came John Prise, who worked directly for Cromwell and had served as Registrar of Salisbury Cathedral. A respected scholar with published historical volumes of King Arthur, he was well known at court for his literary efforts. These men held offices of theological vestments, but their works and beliefs were mostly secular. Perhaps this trio saw the value of serving the government in any capacity they could, be it for honest or manipulative purposes.

The construction of this survey also came to play a role in the continuing division between the Boleyn faction and Cromwell. Viscount Rochford was insulted that Cromwell did not consult him for his assistance in the survey and held it against him thereafter. George felt that he had made a great asset to the cause and was eager to begin surveying the King's lands, only to be refused by Cromwell. This decision was not without good reason, as Cromwell believed that far too many common people knew George's face, and thus that George's very presence would lead people to tailor their testimony. Nevertheless, George refused to relent and was further embittered by being passed over.

As the commissioners visited the monasteries, they found the sheer amount of wealth astounding. It was long thought, since the largest monasteries were established in the 12th and 13th centuries, that these institutions were powerful and had amassed great treasures; however, the scale of the treasure was remarkable. Marble statues of the Virgin Mary and the Apostles, solid gold crucifixes encrusted with rubies and emeralds, and rare pearl rosaries were just a few of the precious items cataloged. The treasures were worth many millions of pounds.

More troubling from the standpoint of the King and his men was that this wealth was insulated from the royal—national—treasury, and instead fed Rome. All men of the cloth paid dues to the Holy See to retain their titles, and these were inevitably monies raised in, and then diverted from, England. Alleged miracles were touted and holy reliquaries were paraded—even supposed bones of the Virgin Mary herself, which were found to be the bones of a former nun—all for profit. Naturally, there was also the raising of monies by means of that especially unpopular practice, the selling of indulgences. This money was kept on hand to splendidly decorate the Vatican and palaces of higher clergy with beautiful frescos, paintings, tapestries and magnificent sculptures and busts, including those of the Popes, Cardinals and Bishops, themselves. Even more shocking than the avarice seemingly at play in the church, was the prevalence of sins of the flesh, as well. Some religious houses displayed such licentiousness that nuns were pregnant, and monks and Priests held wives, mistresses, and quite often illegitimate children.

Not all of the 372 religious houses surveyed held to such vile standards. Some were in full compliance of the law and lived modestly and humbly, especially in the north where poverty and illiteracy were rampant. Regardless, Cranmer and Cromwell magnified the actions of the inappropriate houses to the King, leaving the suggestion that all almost all houses were living in greed and depravity. They advised the King to shut down these monasteries and immediately convert their assets and treasures into the King's exchequer. It was all part of Cromwell's grand scheme to make Henry the wealthiest King in all of England's history.

When the results of the *Valor* came out both the King and Queen were given beautifully illustrated copies that they both thoroughly combed through. Anne's careful review of Cromwell's suppressions and the results of the *Valor* led her to a central belief that Cromwell intentionally closed and converted even houses with excellent reports out of sheer greed. She was livid. After learning about the minister's activities, the Queen confronted Cromwell to understand why these houses were closed and to decide the course of action for those religious houses that were to be suppressed. This meeting did not go well and was quite awkward. Cromwell was highly cautious in his speech towards the Queen and Anne was careful to listen to his every word for any hint of disrespect.

She told Cromwell of her and Henry's plans to reform certain houses to become educational and humanitarian trusts, despite his efforts to the contrary. Cromwell did his best to reassure her that he had no intention to yield her plans, which was a direct lie, but he had to save face. She further let him know that she knew well of "his affairs and would be in touch." This mysterious comment has never been fully explained and it is highly doubtful that Cromwell understood its meaning to be anything but a veiled threat that the Queen was keeping her eyes on the minister, another indication that their relationship was far beyond repair.

4.2 The Ten Articles

Having secured his Queen and his heir, Henry followed his great audit by redoubling his efforts to free himself from subservience to Rome. For the Church of England to be successful, it had to have articles outlining the principal tenants of the faith for its followers. The chief means of doing this became a bill that Archbishop Cranmer who had been diligently working to complete, what would become known as the Ten Articles of 1536. Although most of the articles closely resembled that of established (Roman) Christian doctrine—including the belief that the communion Eucharist underwent transubstantiation into the body of Christ, observance of the saints and the special status of the Virgin Mary, and the sacrament of confession—three of the statutes would demonstrate a clear break from what had come before.

Presented to Parliament on July 11th, the Ten Articles were the foundation for the Church of England, decreeing the religious statutes that subjects were bound to obey in their worship. While civil law was now the legal system, a massive change from the cannon law system that the Vatican still practiced, the role of proper authority and the civil law was to be reinforced in society by altering how they were framed during worship.

What further distinguished these articles from anything that came before them was that they established several different reformist principles as key to the doctrine of the Church of England. Three key principles outlined the most dramatic changes to this new church that varied from the Catholic points of worship. One of the main tenants adopted was that through faith alone could one be redeemed and granted access to heaven. This doctrine held that without the intermediation of a Priest or any other clergy, a lay person had the power to directly connect to God. For centuries, lay persons had been told that their only route to heaven lay through the guidance of a Catholic cleric. To change such a key doctrine was not only a culture shock that would take time to absorb; it was a dramatic sign to the Pope that Henry meant business with his new church.

Another new article in the English church made baptism mandatory for all persons, including infants, as a prerequisite to any possibility of salvation, for any chance to be released from purgatory, and to prevent from being expelled from the community of believers and banned from worship. One of the last substantial changes was decreeing that redemption could also be earned through acts of charity. Good works by believers could be documented or simply be well known in their community, and so long as they were practicing reformers, these acts would make one eligible for God's redemption. Such acts included caring for the sick, feeding the homeless, and teaching children to read. Registrars would survey the churches around the country to ensure accurate recordkeeping of compliance with the Articles.

While many historians and laymen have acknowledged England as a revolutionary force during the Reformation, the actual doctrine of the church at its founding varied in only three key articles while retaining heavily Catholic influences in the other seven principles. The articles described above were reformist in nature and papist followers were highly resistant to these changes, however, the Church of England in doctrine would not become the Protestant establishment that modern historians think of today until decades later. Germany and other eastern European nations had taken far more Lutheran courses of religious policy than England was willing to take at this time. Perhaps history has remembered the intense effect the creation of the Church of England had on history and its own people; instead of understanding that its initial foundations still lay much grounded in Catholicism.

Cranmer would continue to keep his pledge to the King and follow up these articles with further guidance for the people with the publishing of *The Institution of the Christian Man* in 1537. Known as the Bishops' Book, it was developed by a committee of forty-six bishops, theologians and clergy; its entire premise was to not only support the Ten Articles but to be the official book validating the break with Rome. The book established *Ecclesia Anglica,* or Anglicism as it is presently known. Only later, as the monastery dissolution campaign continued, would the religious statutes be further eroded. Reformers were pleased that the King had embraced their cause and had structured his church around a few of their key beliefs. The articles would take adjustment for the whole of the realm including scholars who vigorously debated amongst themselves the impact this would have on the country. However, not all reformers freely embraced the Ten Articles.

One significant reformer risked his life to fight the principles of this new doctrine, Hugh Latimer. For such an important figure during the Reformation, little is known of Latimer's childhood and his early years. Even his birth date cannot be stated with specificity, but it is estimated that when he came into the Queen's service, he was nearly 50. By 1514 he had received a Master of Arts from Cambridge University, and the following year was ordained as a Priest. By the Queen's recommendation, Latimer had been appointed to the post of the Bishop of Worcester, nominated by Cranmer in 1535. His passion for reform came by embracing the ideals of a German reformer named Phillip Melanchthon, a contemporary of Martin Luther. It was Latimer's intent to spread Luther's principles into England by every means allowable. For his arguably radical views at the time, his appointment to the Bishopric was controversial.

Latimer's confirmation only enabled a larger spread of his ideals. Even before his appointment, he had already built a mass following of faithful evangelicals who praised his exceptional mind for persuasive arguments on religion. His strong disagreement to the Ten Articles was because he felt they were not strong enough. Latimer was what a person could call a radical at this time for enhancing the spread of reform. His books were among those that Anne had given Henry to read in the early years of their courtship. For a time, on Cromwell's advice, Henry had Latimer arrested, until Anne sought his release. His arrest was on technical grounds, since the law from Wolsey's time on possessing heretical material had not yet been overturned. Latimer technically committed treason by openly resisting the state's religious policies and Cromwell said he had no choice but to arrest him. Latimer did not spend long in jail and after his release continued his relationships with both the Queen and Cromwell with no ill feelings. Instead, he focused his anger on eradicating the papist heretics from the clergy.

For the common people who could barely read and write, it's understandable to recognize their difficulty in adapting to the changes in their faith. Prior to the Anglican movement, sermons were heard in Latin, and parishioners trusted their Priest to instill divine guidance without understanding what was actually being said. This very manipulative approach allowed the clergy who were educated in Latin to devise sermons to fit their own unique brand of Catholicism. With the Articles now in place, and what seemed to be only few changes, the embrace of the people was at first a mixed reaction. The changes that were made at this stage were certainly dramatic.

The crown would shape people's belief using a campaign of fear, primarily requiring the oath of Henry's supremacy, public burnings of heretics, imprisonment, and torture. The monasteries were also still being shut down, so in addition to awaiting dissolution, they were to be teaching the new Articles. This allowed Cromwell a convenient excuse to imprison long time political enemies within the clergy. Still, with little surviving evidence beyond the official accounts, opposition to the reforms would soon enough make their presence known. The current way of business, and the tactics by which the state dealt with perceived political enemies, truly bothered Latimer. He strongly believed that people should hear and know in their own language what they were to learn, what they were being accused of and why they were being held. In essence, though a radical for his time, he was a crusader for peace and for justice in a time that did not allow his rare brand of activism.

Despite the Catholic Church's massive following, it had surprisingly miscalculated how little real power it had to counter such intense attacks by so popular a king. Rome had arrogantly relied on the power it had previously accumulated to protect it from scandal, just as it had for the centuries during which it had deemed itself untouchable. Notwithstanding the vows of poverty enforced by some orders, to enter the clergy was generally one of the most financially rewarding career paths a person could take, provided one was politically savvy enough to maneuver through church politics. Unfortunately this possibility of riches also attracted the most devious, corrupt and deceptive persons. In an age without any but the loosest type of "background check," anyone with sufficient intellect, charm and enough acting ability to put on a devout façade was welcome into the organization.

Parliament had already been securing indictments for closing monasteries, claiming to be cracking down on the corrupt abuses of the Catholic Church; but really it was as a disguise to build up the royal treasury, which had been much depleted. English currency had been debased once already in 1526 because of the expense of maintaining the lavish court. In the face of this desperation, the wealth the monasteries held appeared limitless. Realizing that the monasteries held the solution to the country's financial problems, Cromwell put forth the results of the massive survey, with the support of Anne and Lord Rochford, and followed by sending out agents to visit the churches and monasteries to regain millions of pounds in recompense. If church fines alone were still not enough to replenish the royal coffers, the King's simply taking back ownership of all lands and then leasing them back to their former owners or new renters at a higher price would be an even more lucrative plan.

Anne had done her part in private to persuade Henry of the abuses of corrupt churches and monasteries, but she balanced the calls for fines with a call for mercy on those houses that received good reports. While Anne supported closing corrupt monasteries, her true purpose was to reform them. She did not believe that simply shutting down the corrupt monasteries was effective, and became deeply involved in drawing up her own designs on how to re-indoctrinate the houses into the new order. Reports that Cromwell had sought to shutter the monasteries to confiscate all the wealth did not please the Queen.

Anne would get wind of this and immediately put a stop to it. She yelled at Henry in person, setting him on the defensive, demanding to know why he was allowing his minister to make him seem such a fool by not using the monasteries as they should be, to re-educate the poor in accordance with their new church doctrine. This argument was one of the worst fights between Henry and Anne, recorded by courtiers down the hall, and lasted for a good hour. By the end, perhaps tired of his wife's awful nagging, Henry convinced Anne that he would take at least half the monasteries and convert them to educational uses, while the wealthiest ones would be forfeited to his control to sell off their goods for the benefit of the treasury.

Based on their only partial listing of the houses surveyed, Parliament had to pass legal summons before the King could properly act on closing monastic houses. To adjust for this, the *Valor* was used as absolute evidence to warrant such a wide legal proviso as allowing his majesty to shut down monasteries at will. The final *Valor* findings encompassed some twenty-two volumes of record. Henry ordered that Parliament review the report and take appropriate action.

On February 4th, 1535, Parliament passed a controversial Act called the Dissolution of the Lesser Monasteries Act. This would be the first of two suppression Acts passed in the realm. This Act specifically enabled the King to seize the revenues from those monasteries that were making less than 200 pounds per year, and that all of these deemed "lesser" monasteries for that reason were to be closed within one year. All assets would revert back to the crown. The monks, Priests, nuns, and other clergy that filled those houses that were to be dissolved were now effectively homeless. To avoid another tongue lashing by the Queen, Henry further ordered that any poor who were being housed at a closing monastery be moved to other monasteries to be cared for until further accommodations could be found for them.

Despite the real impact on the monasteries being seized, in one sense, Parliament's passage of the law was merely for show; Cromwell's agents had already started closing down these buildings months earlier, before the final verdict from the King even arrived. In a desperate attempt to placate the King, some monasteries attempted to bribe the King's ministers, offering thousands of pounds and priceless goods to save their stations. Such ploys were unsuccessful, and the attempts were used only to further document corrupt behavior.

Due to the overwhelming amount of goods and money passed from these houses to the crown, Cromwell had authorized special courts to distribute property and authenticate values. Though Henry had made clear to Anne he supported and even valued her cause, the truth was that the royal exchequer was near empty due to their massive cost of maintaining his court, and he wanted his wealth back. There would be times where he would have to sacrifice the pledge made to his wife to fill his accounts. The Court of Augmentations was established in 1536 and heard cases mainly on behalf of Cromwell and royal agents for the transfer and remittance of goods. The court was fully functional with its own staff of legal advisers, lawyers, clerks, and accountants.

For his part, Cromwell had, over-optimistically, or foolishly, assured Henry that the reformation was going well, despite some discontent, especially in the north. In so understating the threat, he failed to estimate just how great that discontent was, particularly with the new order's dispensing with various holidays (chiefly the feast days for observance of Catholic saints). The previously loyal subjects in the north were heavily Catholic and clung deeply to their faith, its traditions and its Holy Days. Holy Days were a long-held and beloved tradition. On these days all work ceased, and subjects were free to worship and spend time with their families. Meanwhile, as minister, Cromwell saw only the economic disadvantage brought to the realm by even one day's lack of productivity. It was sheer greed that motivated this momentous decision.

Cromwell recommended to the King that he declare these days invalid. Historians have judged that these actions were chiefly done by Cromwell, which is certainly partly true, but not wholly accurate. The King's minister would never have acted so boldly without his master's permission; to do so, especially with such division at court, would risk death. The express command for the injunctions came from Henry, with Cromwell merely the initiator and executioner. The decree from Henry stated that all subjects would work on these Holy Days, and that they were to be treated as any other day. With the elimination of the Catholic Holy Days, so too went those days off during which the faithful common people had previously been able to rest from their backbreaking, ill-compensated labor.

When Anne heard of the removal of the Holy Days she was livid. Contemporary reports from Cromwell's groom show that Anne physically struck him about the head for what he had done, and she repeated her threat of having him removed from his post. She fully intended to make good on it. The elimination of the Holy Days the people held so dear would not be tolerated. The people's anger was collectively gathering far more than either Cromwell or Henry could ever have imagined. In fact, the angriest among the people had already started to discuss the possibility of an uprising against the King.

In addition to heated political rhetoric based on religious reform, there were also practical considerations for the people to be restless. The wheat crop harvest of 1535 had been hit hard by lack of rain, and the scarcity of the staple crop led to high inflation. This, in turn, led again to the devaluation of English currency, a reduction in the labor force, and a continued downward economic spiral. Even royalty had difficulty obtaining enough rations of wheat to feed the massive court, and in most cases these were limited to the use of the King, Queen, and their children. Henry had decreed that workers found to be stealing rations of wheat would spend days in the stocks and/or pays a fine; however, the Queen insisted that such offenses not lead to executions. She refused to put her subjects to death for trying to feed their families in a difficult harvest year.

Farmers and other agriculture workers were some of the hardest hit by the season, but many religious houses also held farms or other businesses that were hit twice as hard. Farming provided year-round crops to feed the Priest, nuns, monks, clerks, and servants, along with the ability to sell extra crops for a profit. These properties would now be diverted to the crown. The state could manipulate prices and reinstate economic controls at will. One catastrophic downside to the closing of the monasteries was the termination of charity towards the poor.

With the wheat shortage, the dejected state of the country's poor, starving, and sick became more obvious. They came out in record numbers, protesting in front of the palace gates begging for rations of food—even simple bread—just to feed their families. Many died right before the gates from illness due to starvation, and other illnesses such as consumption (tuberculosis). The Queen, while fearful, also genuinely grieved at the suffering of her people, and immediately called for Elizabeth and the Prince to be brought to her, where she could watch them herself should a riot break out. Though the Yeoman Warders were on heavy guard, with additional troops keeping watch, it was still better to be safe than sorry. It would take close to three weeks to cautiously bring the royal children to Anne using back roads and an additional contingent of guards, but they would eventually make it so the family could weather the food riot together.

The religious houses were the only structured entity within the kingdom that fed, housed, and cared for the sick, dying, and the poor on their own income. Cromwell highly disagreed with the King's measures towards the rioters and thought that the sick and dying at the monasteries should be left to their own devices to die, as they were burdens on English society. He continued to enact reprehensible reforms, allegedly at the King's request. With the elimination of their income, those houses that were allowed to stay open could no longer afford to offer critical services to the poor, leading to violence, chaos, crime, and continued talk of revolution. Those who relied on the church to provide daily sustenance found none and searched for any means to survive the brutal living conditions. Crime became rampant, especially in the larger cities.

Further contributing to the poverty rate was the difficulty families had in providing for their large numbers of children. Large families were the norm due to lack of understanding of contraceptive methods, and the heavily religious Catholics favored many children in the home. Orphanages had been in operation around the realm, again run by mostly clergy and nuns who took pity on these children. Without revenue, these children were forced onto the streets to beg, steal, and commit petty theft. Many were arrested on charges of petty theft for stealing food, and in some harsh districts put to death to be made an example of to the others.

Henry, for the duration of the crisis, dismissed his court, ordering all courtiers in residence to return immediately to their own estates to feed themselves. Only the Ambassadors, doctors, and preferred clergy such as Archbishop Cranmer (and Henry's servants) remained in residence. Anne also begged Henry to provide some meager rations to the people if they could at all afford it. Henry, for a time at least, ordered his kitchens to prepare daily feasts of leftover mutton for distribution at the gates, which kept the kitchen busy all day. He refused to see his people starving. This generous gesture used all the mutton the court had, but Henry was seen to have done right by his people, who chanted praise to their King at nighttime vigils, along with prayers thanking God for Henry's mercy in helping feed them. His response to the crisis, guided by an insistent Queen Anne, helped turn the tide of public opinion.

The following harvest season was blessed with significant rains that overcame the drought, leading to the suspension of rationing; at the order of Queen Anne, any and all prisoners arrested for having stolen wheat were released. Henry was livid when he found out and once more the two argued. Eventually he came to understand her cause and the two reconciled.

While dining one evening with the family, including both children, Anne thanked Henry for his generosity and gratitude in the kindness he had shown his subjects during the wheat shortage. She told him this was one of the many reasons she had fallen in love with him, and felt he really knew his people well, and they too loved him. She highlighted their candlelight vigil that evening praising his name and recounted to Elizabeth how her father had been the brave hero of the day, comparing Henry to his own favorite hero, King Arthur. The ploy worked and Henry was in a very loving and generous mood with both of his children and with Anne. After dinner he dismissed the children with their Governess and spent the evening with Anne. While no official documentation exists regarding the conversation between Henry and Anne that night, the following day, Henry had notified Cromwell that, beginning immediately, only twenty percent of the smallest houses would be diverted to religious, educational and philanthropic causes.

The following day, while walking in the gardens with her father, Anne privately declared war on Cromwell and committed to bringing him down. She asked Lord Rochford to keep aware of his movements and affairs in the Privy Council. She had long felt Cromwell was out to usurp her position, but it was more than that. She felt he was hiding something and she did not know what. She feared that his loyalty had swayed, but could not tell in what direction, which is why she tasked her father to find out, albeit discreetly. He advised his daughter to appear as if all were normal and to continue to get on with the Minister, at least in front of Henry, so as not to arouse any suspicion; she would have her chance later to reveal her real feelings, but now was not the time. Rochford would provide the best intelligence he could on Cromwell's dealings, which for a while at least, were nothing spectacular and only routine official state business. They would have to wait until a time came to bring him down and replace him with someone far more suited to their interests. A candidate such as this would be hard to find, but it could be done.

On other matters, Cranmer and the Queen met several times over the summer and came up with a pre-planning strategy for formal re-indoctrination. This would include dedicating some houses strictly for educational teaching, providing basic services such as reading and writing, and teaching the Bible, services to be free for all people, regardless of station. They discussed and debated how tutoring services would be carried out, the cost, and the source of these funds. Anne was preparing to set in motion the largest change to education Britain had ever known.

In August Cromwell followed up Cranmer's work with enforcement of the Ten Articles. He issued injunctions to the clergy that they were to have the English Bible in every religious house. Anne fully agreed with the measure and even thanked the minister for his diligence in ensuring their reforms were coming full force. All appeared well, at least for a time.

This small meeting of the minds between Anne and Cromwell was to be short lived. Despite his previous generosity, Cromwell convinced the King to sign an official decree that any persons caught stealing food would be immediately put to death. The Queen would not find out about this policy until much later; it was intentionally kept from her as a vain attempt by Cromwell to usurp her cherished authority with the King. It was now more obvious than ever that the two competed on matters large and small for the King's ear.

4.3 Domestic Bliss

By late August Anne had lost the baby weight from earlier in the year and went back to the slender frame she was known for. She continued to dance with her ladies, and even created two new dances that she planned on showcasing for the French Ambassador's visit later that year in September. Henry and Anne continued to lie together, and by the end of summer she began showing signs that she was once again with child. She would wait to tell Henry, just in case the symptoms were false or should she suffer a miscarriage.

The summer sessions of the Privy Council, in addition to the religious reforms underway, had two other matters of state to be discussed. The Prince's household management, including the topics of servant wages and rank and recognition of the Prince's jointure estate payments, were all to be discussed. The other agenda item was the marriage ceremony of Sir Henry Norris and Lady Madge Shelton. With the King's blessing, the two courted for quite some time, and were finally betrothed in 1535. The King cherished Norris as a dear friend. They had hunted together many years previously, and he had planned to personally give a sumptuous gift to the new couple, as well as personally attend the ceremony, which he decided should be held at Hampton Court, one of his more magnificent palaces.

The councilors worked tirelessly for the next week until the council met again, with the clerks doing their due diligence to provide Henry the list of palaces to choose from for the Prince's dignity, and to announce the status of the wedding proceedings. Archbishop Cranmer, a close friend of the couple, was selected to officiate at the ceremony. The Shelton and Norris families were en route to Hampton Court, and would be lodged there for four days to enjoy the ceremony and festivities. All other attendants would have to find lodgings and the number of servants allowed to court was limited, to make room for the nobles themselves, their retinues and all their baggage. The palace had its own staff of servants to wait on the every whim of the families. The couple was delighted by the King's bounty, and thanked him for his graciousness.

The ceremony was to take place September 13th, 1536 at 2 P.M. The clerks had determined that this would be the best date for the wedding, to allow the proper time to prepare. Any time a wedding is held at a royal palace, it presents a load of opportunities for merchants in a variety of expertise. Wine merchants, fabric and textile traders, tailors, florists, stablemen, etiquette coaches, lawyers for the marriage contracts and land divisions, clerks to track the dowry and other wedding gifts, chefs and other cooks, butchers, fisherman, gardeners and various other roles showed a high increase in demand for several weeks leading up to the event, and the increased commerce greatly benefited the royal exchequer, which received taxes on those goods and services. Cromwell was indeed pleased to inform his majesty of such welcoming news.

Madge and Anne almost daily reviewed wedding fabrics, designs, floral arrangements, discussed housing arrangements, attendants, and generally relished in the wedding planning. Madge was not only her cousin, but Anne's closest friend among her ladies-in-waiting. The two women sat for hours through the night talking about how far they had come together, reminisced on happier times, and discussed Madge's fears and joy about the next phase of life she was about to enter. Anne gave her the best advice she could, without overstepping the bounds of royal marriage, and expressed adulation at the match, noting Sir Henry's worthy qualities and that he was a good man.

Hampton Court was a circus of people scurrying about on the day of the ceremony. The Bride dressed in the Queen's privy closet with the rest of the ladies-in-waiting, and Anne herself attending to her every whim. The dress was of white damask, with a square neckline, and a string of pearls sown into the top connecting both sides of the dress. The back laced up, the laces containing the arms of the Tudor crown on the fabric. Anne's account books show that she paid for the fabric and her personal tailor had custom made the dress, one of the highest signs of royal favor. The Queen had the royal jeweler create a golden ring of rubies and diamond clusters for the bride's right hand, as a sign of affection. The guests were seated by 1:45 P.M., with the King arriving a few minutes late to stand as the best man, an honor he insisted upon.

Archbishop Cranmer, Sir Henry and the King were joined by the ladies and the Queen to welcome Madge down the aisle. Walking with the utmost grace, she joined her fiancé and the entire court knelt for a prayer of blessing in English, another reformation ritual. The couple exchanged vows written by Archbishop Cranmer, praising their majesties and God for the blessing of this union, placed the rings upon one another, and kissed nervously to seal the deal. Cranmer pronounced them man and wife and the happy couple then made their way back to the palace to await the feast inside. The King and Queen shared an embrace before making their way as the guests of honor to the feast and toasting the couple. The happy couple retired back to Norris' estate to spend a joyous honeymoon. With Madge's departure, there was a now an opening in the Queen's household, a competitive spot. Anne would also make an announcement of her own; she was indeed pregnant once again.

4.4 Reforming Education

William Tyndale had been hiding for years in Germany after fleeing from England after his arrest, fearing for his life. To make a life for himself, he continued his scholarly and translation work, and took to mentoring pupils to earn wages, but his true passion remained reversing centuries of religious ignorance. Archbishop Cranmer had been careful to bring up Tyndale's plight during a private audience with her majesty towards the end of September. Cranmer greatly sympathized with the author, and felt that his talents would best serve the reforms. Now that the changes had begun in England, and royal attitudes were more tolerant and favorable, he advised Anne to summon Tyndale home. Anne had her reservations, but decided it was best to listen to the Archbishop. It was certainly true that Henry's changes in the kingdom had brought about not only tolerance of Protestant beliefs, but the enforcement of their principles. Perhaps now would be the perfect time to bring Tyndale back and encourage his works at home, where they were needed most.

By allowing Tyndale back into the kingdom, his influence and work could truly provide the catalyst for change the reformers had been seeking. After much deliberation and further meetings with her chaplain, Matthew

Fox, and with Cranmer, the Queen put in motion the summons that would be presented to the King. Cranmer shared his reservations with Anne about the possibility of rioting or further upheaval, especially in the north. Anne thanked the minister for his discretion and caution, but ordered him to proceed ahead with Tyndale's recall, albeit discreetly. At some point over the next few days, Henry signed the order to bring Tyndale back. Before the summons was to be delivered however, Anne and Henry wrote a personal letter to Tyndale, assuring him of his safety and praising his honor, virtue and courage. The letter, dated September 30th, 1536 also went on to express many thanks for his bravery in adapting the Bible to their native tongue so that all Englishmen might better learn of God. They also promised him a post at Oxford as a royal agent and co-chair of the theology department, with a handsome salary of 2,000 pounds per annum. Enclosed with the letter was 1,000 pounds, as assurance of their intentions, and a miniature portrait of their majesties. A copy of the letter has survived and still resides in a private collection.

Several weeks later Tyndale received the letter. In his diary entries he recorded a mix of both anguish and excitement that it had taken his banishment abroad to be summoned back with such gifts. The monies he received eased his discomfort and also paid for his travel back home. He was able to buy his fare on a German sea vessel headed to Calais, which agreed to drop him off at Dover where he would have to make further arrangements before heading to London. Tyndale notified his pupils he would be returning to England, and finished his affairs in Germany before setting for home in mid October.

He was most looking forward to the post at Oxford. It was there that he would go on to create some of England's most magnificent works. As co-chair he would be able to set lesson plans for the students and shape some of the brightest minds in the country. From this prominent post his influence would spread across all realms in the kingdom, through government, economics, philosophy, and the arts. It would also provide the perfect venue for him to distribute his completed translations and introduce them into his unique teaching style. He would finally have the opportunity to enhance real change, not only in the monarchy directly, but with the future generations of leaders. He could not resist such an offer of safety, with such a lucrative and influential post.

When Tyndale and Anne met face to face for the first time it was an awkward encounter. Sitting in the Great Room at Hampton Court, Tyndale was out of touch with customary royal greetings, which had seemed only to get more elaborate with this Queen. Cranmer did his best to brief him before he met Anne, but he became so nervous in her presence that he forgot most of what he had been told. Mostly he remained nervous that this homecoming was some sort of setup, and he was preparing himself for the worse. Just the opposite occurred. Anne made him feel as welcome as possible, even offering to share tea with her, a rare honor, before they got down to business.

Anne made it clear that she expected Tyndale to draft up a plan for spreading the English Bible across the land and also for establishing a curriculum for children and adults, regardless of their station, to learn it. Tyndale had not expected such a large task, but he embraced it with honor. She had expressly given him permission to stay at court so he might be available at any notice. Few practical matters were discussed, as this was only the initial meeting; he thanked her majesty and parted. After retiring for some personal reflection, Tyndale set about the task at hand. During this period, he and the Queen would continue to develop their plans for religious and education reform; the King would find his time occupied by a far more immediate danger.

Chapter 5

"And the Heads Did Roll . . ."

Strong, competing senses of nationalism, and what it meant to be both English and Christian were brewing both on the part of loyalists to the crown and those staunchly opposed to the new religious order. The rebels viewed the Reformation as a period of disgrace, seeing their beloved churches and relics destroyed and the King's ministers profiting from their plight. The commons had a regimented and harsh life. The church was one of the few comforts available to them and when it was taken away, simmering complaints began to rise to the surface. The grievances forced upon the people by the crown were becoming more than enough to bear silently anymore. The new and ever increasing tax rates, lack of proper, nutritious food, lands being taken away from the gentry by the rich, and now the plundering of church treasures, had pushed the people to their breaking point.

5.1 The Rebellion of the North

On October 1st, 1536, just after mass in Louth, a town in the Lincolnshire province, a group of commoners gathered together to rebel against Tudor rule. Lincolnshire was the first town to rebel against the crown. They placed blame, for the persecution of the church directly on Anne, Cromwell, Archbishop Cranmer and the rest of the King's councilors. In the month of August alone, 27 houses were suppressed, with their clergy being harassed, beaten, and in some cases arrested without cause. There were also two incidents where monks were reported missing after an alleged altercation with one of the commissioners. This made for the perfect storm and it was not long before a much heavier, more orchestrated threat was to emerge.

The King sent commissioners to Lincolnshire, one of the poorest regions in the north, to investigate abbies and monasteries and validate their conformance to the recent reforms; this mission would be mislabeled and turned into a provocation. Agitators spread the word among the commons that the men sent by his majesty intended to take their jewels, destroy their relics to the Saints, and take their silver crosses of Christ, replacing them with cheap tin. They were angry and had every reason to be on edge. A majority of the corrupt, land owning nobility took severe advantage of the people whenever possible. In addition, the north had been one of the most put upon in the whole of the realm. Because it shared a border with Scotland, it was often on security alert in case of an attack, and such an invasion was often a constant possibility. The people also paid high taxes to fund the King's massive court, and its frivolous spending, although these taxes also paid for the King's domestic agenda. Additionally, the nobility were appropriating more farm land from the gentry and turning it into grazing land—exacerbating the region's poverty and lack of food—to maximize their profits from the prosperous wool industry. The commons bore the brunt of those seizures by lacking land to work.

Since these many grievances had already created a dangerous environment, the commons were incensed to the point of action by news that Cromwell's henchmen had been tasked to enforce the August injunctions by removing their anti-reformation relics. Those who chose to rebel not only refused further obedience to the King's reforms; they called for the repeal of the Ten Articles. Precisely who was to make such a call, however, was made complicated by the class politics of the time. The nobility, naturally, sided with the King and his reforms, being dependent on his Majesty's good graces for their status. In between the poorest commoners and the nobility, stood the local gentry, whose status was more complicated.

The gentry were the modern equivalent of a sort of middle class; people who typically lacked the wealth, titles, and lands of the nobility, but who could acquire such positions faster than commoners because of ties to the nobility acquired through military service, connections at court, or recognition for significant achievements. Typically, the gentry shared some blood ties with nobles and could call upon them for favors. They were also more highly educated than the commons, but tended to remain low level merchants and businessmen. In these troubled times, the commoners' calls for lower taxes and to reinstate the suppressed monasteries appealed to many in the gentry, but ultimately, most joined forces with the nobility, if only begrudgingly, because the feudal system remained the basis for the possibility of advancement. Tension between the gentry and nobility led to strained relations throughout the period of the uprisings, but for a while at least they tended to maintain harmony.

Five of the King's commissioners had been captured in the town of Caistor Hill. These men were documented to be Sir William (last name unknown), Sir Edward Madeson, a Mr. Booth, Sir Robert Tyrwhit, and Thomas Portington. One of the servants, a man named Nicolas, was not so fortunate compared to previous visiting commissioners from the state. His master watched as the crowd beat him to death. Should there have been any doubts about the intentions of the angry commoners, this violence made it very clear.

The rebels that gathered together in these small towns used force to coerce their betters into joining them. As the uprising had been gathering steam, several of the royal taxmen, lawyers, and commissioners had been sent to the north to fulfill duties for the King or to suppress religious houses. When word arrived that these men were in town, the rebels sought them out. In the town of Bolingbroke, a lawyer named John Rayne, who served as the Bishop of London's Chancellor, arrived to conduct a suppression inquiry. Edward Dymmoke and Captain Cobbler, the initial leaders of the uprising were present as Rayne was taken from the monastery to Horncastle and was stoned to death by the crowd as the mob called for his head. He had pleaded, even attempted bribery, to save his life, but the crowd wanted blood, and they got it. After his death, the mob robbed his person. Rather than satiate their desire for violence, the crowd responded to this bloodshed by gathering more arms. After the murders, the rebels were certain that royal forces would be coming. At the direction of their leaders they continued to march on other towns, and made known their threat to eventually get to London, hang Cromwell, kill the Queen and hold the King at ransom until he agreed to address their grievances.

By the following week the King had been made aware of the uprising in the north and the deaths of his agents. The news both frightened and enraged him; this was the first time in his reign that he had faced a serious rebellion. These rebels violated the sanctity of Henry's divine right to rule by rejecting him outright. It also put the monarchy in great jeopardy of losing control of its subjects, which if left unresolved, would mean an end to the Tudor line. Even more than the theoretical loss of the crown, Henry knew well the torture these rebels meant to subject him to, should they ever succeed, and the rebels were threatening death to his Queen as well. Indeed, this karmic retribution was unwelcome and had to be prevented. Instead of embracing a role as general of his own armies, Henry assigned Brandon as the leader against the rebels, with a fraction of his forces, a mere 5,000 men. The King's father, Henry VII, had met a similar rebellion during his own time in person with a great show of force. His son, on the other hand, had chosen the cowardly path of least resistance by assigning a still-recovering Brandon to listen to the rebels' demands and act as General.

Brandon probably was not the wisest choice, given his previous injury. It was only recently, over the summer, that he had learned how to handle a sword again, and he lacked the quickness and vigor that he had once shown in battle. Further, his wife was pregnant for the fourth time, and he wanted to stay at home with her instead of risking his life. He also had his doubts about the mission that lay before him. He knew that these rebels must be stopped, but these were also his countrymen, with women and children that he would be responsible for putting to death. Unfortunately for him, he would have to go and obey his master's order. Henry attempted to reassure him that he would be overseer only, and was there to act in a diplomatic capacity, to negotiate the terms of peace that the rebels sought. Still not convinced, Brandon accepted his charge, if not from genuine desire than out of friendship and loyalty, and went home to inform his wife and prepare to be away possibly at battle for several months, should diplomacy fail with these rebels. Cromwell had advised the King that it would take at least three-four months before this uprising was quelled, so the King ordered enough reinforcements for his agents to last that long; should it take longer to restore order, the royal forces would be at a disadvantage.

Sympathetic historians have painted a picture of Henry as being wise for assigning other men to take control of the army on the ground, while he maintained control of the government miles away from the danger. By doing so, he would be able to direct his government from the palace, protect his family and his heir, and be distant enough to avoid being personally charged as oppressing his people. This was not, however, a careful plan by a wise and shrewd King; it was a selfish attempt to escape unscathed. Despite his prowess in many areas, Henry displayed a lack of core values such as honor and courage, especially on the battle field and by not engaging these rebels directly. He very easily could have left Cromwell in charge of the country's affairs and led his men to the fight. There is a legend that, as a child, Henry VIII and his mother were forced into the Tower of London by rebels while his father fought them off, and won his family's safe release. Perhaps Henry VIII, now as King, never forgot this moment of valor, and knew he could not live up to the strength it took his father to execute such a daring feat.

In any event, when it became Henry VIII's turn to suppress a rebellion, he instead sent his wounded friend Brandon to battle, and stayed in London. This tasking of others to do his work caused controversy among more than one council member at court. Going with Brandon was Thomas Howard, the Earl of Surrey. The Earl was the son of the Duke of Norfolk and had extensive experience in military campaigns; however, he had fallen out of favor with the King some time previously due to lewd behavior at court. The Earl had quite the reputation as a womanizer, gambler and fighter, acting more like a commoner than an esteemed member of the peerage. Many of his fellow courtiers disliked him immensely, but in matters of battle he was highly skilled and was one of the few the King could count on to perform violent acts others would refuse to do, such as crimes against women and children.

Cromwell had been completely caught off guard by the rebel uprising and was fearful of his status with the King, now that he had not only failed to anticipate the serious opposition to their reforms, but had actually downplayed their intensity and possible effects to his master. Knowing full well that his very life was already in jeopardy with Henry, he was even more keen to keep his eyes open for all areas of gossip that could potentially help him out of his mess with the King. Henry held Cromwell responsible for not informing him of the discontent in the north with the reforms. His minister's failings now put his entire reign in jeopardy. He also was well aware that Henry never warmed to him personally, as he had done with his predecessors (although both Wolsey and More would, in their own ways, fall out of the King's favor and die either indirectly or directly as a result) and so he could not fall back on that relationship to appease an angry sovereign. Worse yet, with the Queen out for blood, she now had all the ammunition she would need to seek his destruction.

Though the minister was far too clever to let this unfortunate situation get the better of him, he had to think of a way out of this. Henry was known to publicly beat Cromwell about the head when angry, and on the occasion of the uprising, he did so in his own chambers, calling Cromwell a knave and threatening his neck if he failed to resolve the crisis. At Henry's command Cromwell drew up the terms the King dictated for presentation to the rebels. It was the equivalent of a modern day cease-and-desist letter that demanded that they disperse or face his wrath.

With both of their majesties now angry at him, the only relationship of value Cromwell managed to develop and keep was a private one with the Ambassador Chapuys of the Spanish Empire. Politically, these two were on opposite sides, with Chapuys a strict Catholic and Cromwell a reformer (if not atheist). The two had no reason at all to be friends. Nevertheless, the two got along quite well and found they had much in common. On a personal level, the two shared a fondness for drink, tapestry, and intellectual conversation. Cromwell found the Ambassador stimulating and enlightening, a welcome change from the typical matters at court. The minister and the Ambassador shared many a drink together and Chapuys met Cromwell's son Gregory, his daughter-in-law and his new grandson.

Cromwell played on the Ambassador's keen knowledge of Spanish trade, being a former merchant himself. The King's minister was sensible enough to realize the potential of realigning with Spanish interests. Spain, with its new territories in the Americas producing unheard of wealth, and with the Spanish King also holding title to the territories of modern Germany and central Europe as Holy Roman Emperor, was the most powerful country in Europe, affording Madrid access to the finest fabrics, spices, jewels and food varieties on several continents. Building these ties would help the Ambassador's position as well, as the majority of these goods were frequently demanded by the English people, and the English nobility would pay handsomely for them. Chapuys and Cromwell could indeed use each other.

More than anything else, Chapuys was interested in any news of a rift between the King and "his whore." Cromwell told his foreign confidante that he feared having lost any affection from a Queen who no longer cared for him at all and that, in fact, his Queen hated him and wanted to see his downfall. This was quite pleasing news for Chapuys, who would later share it with his master, but the Ambassador also wanted to advise his new ally of how best to play the matter, so as to survive this dangerous monarchy. Cromwell, understanding that his relationship with Anne had changed and was reaching out for new allies, had received surprisingly warm counsel from Chapuys, who (as a foreign minister) was the only noble at court who could fill that position without risking his own status.

Of course, Cromwell's association with the Ambassador also held a potential danger for the minister, as it could be manipulated into charges of treason, should Henry or the Boleyn faction decide it was time to push him out of the way. Nevertheless, if his efforts were to be successful, Cromwell would have to secure a powerful ally, and he chose Chapuys. It can be reasoned that he took the lessons of Wolsey's foreign relationships and attempted to repeat his methods. That, combined with his general lack of friends among the English nobility found him little social comforts at court. He had told Chapuys, who later documented this to his master, that Cromwell trusted in the King and thought himself protected from any harm from Anne. Cromwell was also aware of Spain's animosity towards Anne, so for a nearly fallen minister seeking powerful new friends, he was heading in the right direction; at least, so he thought.

In November 1535, at Emperor Charles V's request, Chapuys offered to Cromwell the same relationship he had once had with Wolsey. They would trade inside information and it would pay very handsomely. No surviving evidence suggests Cromwell took the bribe, and thus might have formally committed treason, but all accounts of their continuing and deepening personal relationship suggest that the likelihood is high that he did. The minister also certainly realized that to ensure his political survival, it was not good to entirely alienate and create enemies where potential opportunity existed. Beyond being well compensated, he probably would have had the opportunity to temper his master's anger by uncovering vital information about Spain through Chapuys' unique connections. He would have been a complete fool not to take the opportunity presented him, given the set of circumstances. Chapuys as well understood the situation all too well. The understanding was probably that information of potential use to their masters would be exchanged, in return for a generous sum to Cromwell.

Unconfirmed reports allege that during the uprising, Cromwell confided to Chapuys that he grew ever fearful of Anne's hold upon the King, and that he feared his own standing in his master's graces. Such a tip would have provided valuable information to Charles V on Anne's affairs, status with the King, the King's status with regard to his people, and the strength of his monarchy, and thus more broadly on Spanish interests with regard to England. It was, indeed, a mutually beneficial relationship. Nevertheless, the accuracy of this account of Cromwell's espionage cannot be validated as the source was one of Cromwell's own grooms, a servant known for furthering his own ambitions at court at any price and so whose allegations could be interpreted as seeking favor with those who sought the minister's downfall.

The rebels sought the cooperation of Lord Hussey, a member of the nobility who lived in Lincolnshire, and had supported Henry's cause against Rome to marry Anne. Despite this, the rebels needed Hussey's support. For the gentry, the joining of any nobles to their cause was essential. By securing his support they could add to the weight of their threat against the crown. Hussey, by his position, also had powerful friends in the nobility, especially the Lord Darce, another Northern resident. By gaining his majesty's trust, Hussey had been given a privileged position as Lord Chamberlain to the Lady Mary, an interesting choice given his role in the removal of her mother only a year prior. Anne Hussey, during her husband's time serving the Lady Mary, had been sent to prison in the Tower only weeks before the uprising, merely for calling the Lady Mary by her old title of Princess.

Certainly, Hussey had cause for divided loyalties, and when the commoners called upon him to join them, his answer was mixed and he was initially not trusted. The people's instinct turned out to be correct. When they arrived in person to persuade him to join the rebellion, they found only his wife home, with no knowledge as to Hussey's whereabouts or even when he had fled. In fact, he had left her to face the rebels alone. By the time the rebels arrived, their numbers were close to 30,000 and included people from several neighboring towns including Worcester, Leicester and Stafford, to name just a few. The rebels forced others to join their cause by burning and pillaging their villages, beating to death those who refused, and other vile acts of duress.

On October 12th the group received a message from Brandon. This insolence would not be tolerated. Interestingly, these rebels were not only more numerous than the troops dispatched to suppress them, they also had more passion and commitment to their cause, and a much better knowledge of the landscape. Still, the rebels needed more support if they were to stand a chance of winning their demands for the long term. By order of the King, they were to cease this rebellion and, if they failed to do so, brutal force would be used against them. The King also demanded that 100 of the rebels, presumably its leaders, be turned over immediately to face swift punishment, making it clear that for their very unnatural act of rebellion they would face his wrath. Anne was kept well informed of the actions and only further encouraged Henry's wrath against the traitors. Regardless of the validity of accusations waged against her involvement in religious persecutions to that point, the Queen would be well blamed for encouraging a harsh response to threats against her and her husband's reign. She was fearful, but remained resilient in the face of opposition, never missing an opportunity to chide her husband to send the rebels to their doom even quicker and far more harshly than even the King had probably intended. The Queen would not hide her displeasure over the rebel's intransigence and would openly damn them, condemning them for their treason at court, to while dining with Ambassadors and Henry. His brutal response to the rebels most likely did come at Anne's insistence.

Soon after attempting to persuade Lord Darce as well to join their cause, the Lincolnshire uprising fell apart due to lackluster management, but the rebel movement, which had spread across the north, was replaced only days later by an uprising in Yorkshire that was gathering strength. This Yorkshire uprising would be called the "Pilgrimage of Grace." The gentry, as well as commons, in Yorkshire were up in arms that only three of the closed church houses had been converted to educational trusts, none of which were in the north.

In the same month, Cromwell's agents added another provocation by visiting a monastery at Hexham in Northumberland seeking to impose the suppression measures, even though its revenues far exceeded the thresholds set by the Acts that justified confiscatory measures against those houses considered small. In this instance, the King's minster was attempting to supersede Henry's orders, allegedly on behalf of his master. Whatever the claim, he disobeyed the King and should have faced severe consequences, but he never did. The King seemed all too willing to forgive Cromwell upon realizing how much money the crown stood to gain by closing this monastery down. In fact, in time, the King would reward Cromwell for enhancing his much depleted treasury.

This new, broader uprising would, as with its more chaotic progenitor, seek as broad a basis for support from all three classes, but do so more successfully. Of all the noble families in the north, none were sought for recruitment to the rebel cause so heavily as the Percys. Henry Percy, the eldest of the family, had fallen onto difficult times, and to seek favor at court. He had signed his entire estate to the King upon his death. He was childless, his wife had left him, and he had fallen into bad health. His brother Thomas, however, was the complete opposite and not only embraced the rebel cause, but took to the leadership of one of the rebel factions. The Percy family held vast tracks of land in the north, which were looked upon to protect the crown and to warn against Scottish invasion, should it occur. It is interesting to note that, although various local towns gathered together under the cause, the leadership of these commoners was often done by men with no formal military experience, and was frequently subject to change. A different noble, Lord Dacre, was coerced to the commoners' side using threats of violence, but only after hiding from the rebels and leaving his young wife and child to suffer the consequences on his behalf. A Parliament Member from Cumberland named John Legh of Isel had also joined the rebels.

During this uprising, the figure who would become most valuable in negotiations on behalf of the rebels was Robert Aske. Aske, a law student, was with his nephews on his way to Gray's Inn for instruction, when he was met by rebels who demanded that he either let the nephews come with them as attendants, or that he come himself. He persuaded the rebels to accept the latter alternative, and his nephews fled home on foot, telling the town what had happened along the way. The rebels took him to listen to their complaints and coerced him into representing them against the King. For Aske, even to have heard their ideas was considered treason under the Act of Supremacy and meant instant death. Mindful of the circumstances in which he found himself after hearing their cause, Aske realized that they shared similar ideals for the management of their kingdom.

Reluctantly, Aske joined, and became leader and spokesman for, the rebellion of what would be nine total parishes in a northern alliance against the crown. Aske's joining the Lincolnshire cause was of enormous significance as he could use his considerable talents to aid in drafting a formal petition to the crown, which offered an air of legitimacy to what might otherwise have been portrayed by Henry as a mere uprising of illiterate northern peasants. More than that, Aske had gained the trust of the commons despite being a member of the gentry and was well educated; he was down to earth, with a friendly disposition that led them to believe he could—and should—be the official face of their movement.

The petition he drafted to the crown railed against the corrupt abuses of the council, such as the destruction of the monasteries and high taxes, concerns that went well beyond the northern counties, and were shared by the poor throughout the country. Aske determined that the local groups should not send a call for battle until after the response to petition had been received. He managed to provide a sense of calm leadership for an increasingly angry group of rebels from different towns, backgrounds, and ranks in society. Now that the movement had its key leaders in place, the march was getting underway.

5.2 The Lady Mary

With the rebel forces now numbering near 35,000 from villages and towns all across the north, the uprising had become a very serious threat to the crown. Decrees from the King to cease their rebellion or face lethal consequences went unheeded. The council briefed the King on rebel movements, troop supplies, and how long they estimated they could hold out with what resources they had. They also advised him to show no mercy and take full advantage of the rebels' weaknesses; should Henry decide to be lenient it could have disastrous consequences. The council painted for him the very worst possible picture: the rebels marching upon London, burning down famous buildings as they went, holding nobles hostage, and, in time, overtaking the King himself. With such detailed and brutal imagery in his mind, the King grew angered and felt he had no choice but to act tough. This, along with Anne's persuasions in private, only ensured harsh action, albeit it would come after a feint at dialogue.

After reviewing the best course of action, against the advice of counsel, the King sent through Brandon an offer of general pardon, in exchange for their dispersal. When the rebels reached Doncaster in mid December 1536, they found Brandon waiting there with a small army of men, along with the King's decree and a regiment just shy of 5,000 royal soldiers. It was here that a major turning point occurred. Brandon had been charged with negotiating means of diplomatic resolution with the leaders of the rebellion, provided they met the conditions demanded by the King.

The initial visit was cordial, with Aske taking a white flag to the center of the field to meet Brandon to discuss the terms of a peaceful negotiation, along with listing their demands. It was decided they should visit the nearest fortification to review such details, and the two sides rode together, with their leaders at the helm, towards the nearest fort, nearly twenty miles away, and a solid day's ride at a good pace. When they finally managed to arrive, all the men of both sides were starving. After an initial meal, the leaders met across from one another to review the terms of Henry's decree and the rebel demands.

The Duke of Suffolk presented the King's terms first. He read aloud a letter that Henry himself dated December 9th, 1536, in response to an earlier rebel letter. The terms included that the rebels cease their rebellion, that those rebels gathered disburse back to their homes, and that the leaders voluntarily turn themselves over, along with four unnamed persons who the Privy Council may have thought were co-conspirators, but who were yet unknown.

The King's letter bore a hostile tone with mixed messages. It told the rebels they had no business interfering in matters of state, such as whom the King chose to appoint to positions within the government. As divine head of the realm, only he was qualified to make such decisions and he would not be pressured by the influence of common subjects, whose obedience they owed to him and God. However, to extend an olive branch and make a vain attempt at reconciliation, he agreed to hold a session of Parliament in York to address their grievances, with the understanding that this session would include a general pardon. Then, in the same letter, Henry went on to threaten them all with death should they not comply with all of his requests to cease this uprising.

After reading the King's demands, Brandon was careful to sound as a friend, advising the leaders to heed to the King's will, and that His Majesty would have their compliance in the end, whether by voluntary means or by bloodshed, and instructing them that the King was making no idle threats. The leaders listened carefully and peacefully to the terms that Brandon had presented, along with his heed of caution.

Then it was the rebels turn to present their demands and they would show the King's agents the same respect. Aske was the primary speaker for the group, with occasional outbursts of typical cynicism from another rebel leader (with the ironic name of) Robert Constable; however, for the most part the negotiations went off smoothly. As the rebellion took on new members, it evolved in its leadership with Aske, Robert Constable, and Lord Darce at its helm. Aske told his Graces that the leaders, including himself, Lord Dacre and Constable were all seeking peaceful means of resolution, but they also advised Brandon that the rebels demanded action. They were angry and it would be difficult for them to stand down without some assurance that their terms would be met. Brandon then agreed to hear their list of grievances assuring the King would come to judge on the matter.

Aske then read out the official list of ten grievances the rebels laid out, and that they insisted be addressed for a truce to be agreed upon. These demands were as follows: declare and restore the Princess Mary as the rightful heir, restore the monasteries and suppress no more houses, repeal recent Acts of monastery suppression, remove Queen Anne, provide a general pardon for all involved in the uprising including its leaders, remove Lord Privy Seal Cromwell from all of his posts, recognize allegiance to the Pope, remove heretics, and punish two persons they considered to have taken advantage of the commons in the north. The basic goal was to undo all of the changes enacted by the Reformation and restore England back to its original Catholic faith. Should their demands be enacted it would reverse all of the reforms Henry fought so hard to enforce, and would invalidate his divine right to rule, hitting the very core of such an egocentric ruler.

Brandon and the other nobles were taken back by the clarity and the number of demands the rebels held. At best they had figured on the reinstatement of the Lady Mary to the succession and the removal of such high taxes, but their list clearly extended far beyond that. In concession, Brandon assured them that, should the rebels agree to Henry's demands and turn back their course, in exchange the King vowed to set up a formal court at York to hear their grievances and he would decide on the matter himself. Further, as a sign of favor, he would bring the Queen and his heirs, along with food, wine, and clothing for the poor, and pardon all the rebels—minus the leaders and the four unnamed persons—in an official ceremony at York. Brandon graciously allowed the rebel leaders to take a few moments to discuss these terms of conciliation in private, before rejoining them at table half hour later to come to a final resolution.

As the leaders excused themselves to another part of the fort to review the King's terms, they began a massive argument, which Aske attempted to mediate peacefully. He was able to flare down Constable's temper and convince the rest of the leaders to take the King at his word and accept the terms of the condition. This meant that none of the rebel grievances would be addressed that day, but if the King's word was to be believed, each would be decided by the King himself at York in only a few weeks time. Choosing to take His Majesty at his word, Aske managed to persuade Constable, Lord Darce and the rebels to trust the King. It was not, however, without some heartburn.

Aske further argued to Lord Dacre and Constable that if they had waited this long to get their issues heard, another few weeks of waiting could little harm their cause. Aske spoke so eloquently that he managed to succeed in persuading the others to accept the terms of Brandon's deal. Constable was the initial hold out, who took a lot of convincing, and eventually chose to agree to the terms admitting that it was against his better judgment and on Aske's word alone. He made it plain to the other leaders that he had no trust that the King would keep his word and believed the promises to be false. Regardless, he eventually conceded, and Aske was able to answer Brandon directly with a universal front of agreement. The other leaders had serious doubts about Henry's intentions, and for good reason. The very letter promising clemency also assured certain death, and they had all just agreed to sign their own death warrants.

When Aske, Lord Dacre and Constable rejoined Brandon and the Earl to redress the King's decree, they agreed universally to its terms but noted its key demand of a swift trial at York to specifically address the rebel grievances. They would also need to be allowed sufficient time to alert the rebels to stand down, and that they were in talks with the King's agents to have their demands met, to which Brandon agreed. Upon the rebel leaders having signing their names to the King's decree of a—nearly—universal pardon and accepting the terms, Brandon outlined the key exception, which he had intentionally minimized until that point. The leaders of this movement, including the four unnamed persons, would be taken into custody immediately to serve their sentence for treason, while the others would be granted full pardon on behalf of the King.

They agreed, with Brandon giving Aske leave to alert his stable groom to spread the word that all of the leaders were off in good faith to speak to the King directly to continue negotiations, and ordering that the rebels stand down before their leaders would head off to London. Overall the meeting had been a success. Brandon then told them that, as another sign of good faith, the leaders would be attending the Christmastide festivities as His Majesty's guests of honor, a rare privilege. Each leader thanked Brandon for his professionalism, chivalry, and courtesy in executing negotiations with them and treating them as men. He may not have enjoyed it as much as facing battle directly as a General, but Brandon had a real knack for diplomacy, and his disposition suited it quite well.

The leaders left with Brandon and the Earl, feeling fulfilled that their meeting had been a success. Aske embraced the terms, but the other leaders left feeling that the King was making false promises he would later reverse, once he had them in their grips, and that ultimately they would never escape the Tower's walls. Their instincts turned out to be right. Aske's only request in accompanying Brandon to meet the King in person was that his dispatches, allegedly to his family, be sent along their way, so that his wife would know of his health and the King's good will in their cause. Brandon agreed without hesitation. It took them nearly a week, through murky water, heavy bouts of desperately needed rainfall, livestock herds, and other obstacles, to reach the court.

While this visit had been successful, in the back of his mind Brandon knew he would soon have to return to the north to execute his duty and dispatch the traitors to death. He would do his best to enjoy the Christmastide festivities that awaited him and attempt to resolve their grievances with his wife, but a small part of him always remained plagued at the future duty the King would shortly come and order him to commit. In private, Brandon had conflicting feelings on his King's orders.

On the one hand, he understood well that these rebels, now seeing their numbers and organization in the flesh as it were, indeed did seek to do the realm harm; however, he also was of strong Catholic faith and found it difficult to do his duty, knowing that in doing so many young subjects, even children, would be dispatched to death as traitors to the King by joining in this rebellion. These young boys could have been his own sons and he would have to look in the faces of these children knowing that any of them could also have been his own unborn child, as his wife Catherine was nearly four months pregnant before he had left to confront this "Pilgrimage of Grace." Rebellion.

Upon his return, Catherine also never let Brandon touch her again, although they nevertheless named the child to come after the father, hoping that the son would never have to know nor share Brandon's fate at being so near the crown. After telling his wife of his true mission, Catherine was deeply distraught and would never look at him the same way again. Brandon's journals reveal how conflicted he was as he escorted prisoners Aske, Robert Constable, and Lord Dacre back down to London to meet the King, who would sentence them for their Acts.

Out of good faith, Aske in return privately asked Brandon if he would carry his dispatches to his family to ensure his safety. Brandon's kindness obliged him, and with his other concerns so weighing on him, had led him to make a very basic blunder. Rather than merely sending Aske's dispatches "to his family" along their way, he should have known well enough to open them and review their contents himself. However, as a gentleman, he had not. Had he done so, proof of treason would have been found on the spot and Aske and others might have been hung the very day of their negotiations; however, his sympathies with some of the rebels' goals, and his trust in the eloquent Aske, and Brandon's own desire to return to London to make things right with his own wife, led him to take Aske at his word. One of Aske's letters was simple enough, an additional petition to the King. The other letter was far more dangerous. It was a single note, in Aske's own handwriting, dated December 4th, 1536. This letter was delivered to the Lady Mary by Brandon's own private messenger, telling her of their great plight, and telling her of the rebel leaders' goal to restore her grace's true honor as Princess, and praying for her in the way of the old faith.

He reassured her that all would be done well and quickly for her sake, and that she was surely the innocent Lamb of God that the usurper Queen wished to slaughter. He saw himself as the savior of the lamb; a very poignant biblical metaphor with which the Catholic Mary would have been very familiar. The Lady Mary received the letter at Hertfordshire, where she spent the majority of her days in seclusion after the death of her mother in January 1536.

Upon receipt of the letter, Mary retired to her private chambers to read it without the presence of servants, and immediately upon discovering its contents should have turned it over to the King's agents. Instead, she held onto the letter, re-reading it several times with joy, shock, and surprise, and even went to her desk to draft several handwritten letters in return to Aske about how to respond. In his letter he professed, that he would love to make her acquaintance, for he had so longed to do so. Perhaps she kept it because it reminded her of her previous life, one where she was the rightful heir and Princess, and to hear that other followers had now taken up her cause gave her validation that her cause was just, and this letter, this treasonous letter, was just too difficult for her to part with, regardless of the consequences.

As an additional symbol of Queen Anne's generosity, Archbishop Cranmer had persuaded a reluctant Anne to allow the Lady Mary to attend court, if only to keep a watchful eye on her. Especially during such dangerous times, the Lady Mary's presence in good faith with the King and Queen might bode well with the sentiment at court. Even a façade of family bonding could be interpreted, at best, as a sign that Mary had made peace with her accommodations and reduced status. It might also enhance Anne's image at court, with those who still held a grudge against her. Further, it would prove in front of all the court, that the Lady Mary would have to accept her as Queen, a personal goal of Anne's. Because Mary graciously accepted the King's demands to swear to the oath in June of that year, and fully acknowledged her bastard status, Henry warmly embraced her and would look forward to seeing her. This was a ploy by Mary to gain favor and perhaps enhance her lowly status, or at the very least, her station as a servant by finally bowing to her father, but not at any time was she doing it for the pleasure or sake of her step-mother.

For the first time in years, the Lady Mary was being shown royal favor, and courtiers were attempting to gain her honor; a privilege she had not felt in quite some time. It made her feel like a Princess again. Thankfully, for her comfort after her mother's passing, and much to Queen Anne's dismay, Henry allowed Mary to grieve in private at Hertfordshire, and rarely left the residence unless summoned, or it was absolutely necessary. His generosity was kind, but he did not leave her alone without spies, just in case she meant to cause him harm. As with the mother with whom she shared the old faith, she would enjoy hours of mass, and might take a walk in the gardens, but this letter from Aske revitalized her in a way she had not felt in years.

The Lady Mary kept the contents of the letter private, and trusted Brandon's own courier not to betray her honor, by disclosing his dispatch to her. In truth, couriers were notorious for their silence, and even if Brandon's messenger had uncovered the contents of the letter he dare not, as a matter of honor, betray his master by notifying him of its purpose. She lacked a plan as to how to respond and was mostly content to revel in the little bit of power that she held on to, and in knowing that the rebellion had all started in her name and to restore her true title as Princess. She was overjoyed.

Mary hid the letter within the folds of her mattress, between several barbs of both wire and wood, ensuring that it could only be found if searched for. Even the laundress servants who regularly changed her linens would be unable to find them, this she was certain of. Confident in her own charge, that very same day, ironically, Mary received an invitation to attend court at Christmastide from the King and Queen, to serve as their guest of honor for the week of seasonal festivities to begin the evening of December 21st, 1536.

At the time, both of which events were quite separate, with the King having no knowledge of Aske's treason in communicating directly to his former heir the rebels' desire to restore the former Princess to her prior glory. With no reason for Lady Mary to offer up such information to her own detriment, she ordered her servants to gather her finest garments and accoutrements to prepare at once to head for court. In a rare show of honor, perhaps in an incredibly good mood, she would even wear the liveries that Queen Anne had spitefully sent her months before, when the former Queen Katherine, Mary's mother, shortly after her own mother had died. Where Anne had previously rejected Mary and her mother entirely, this irony even sarcastic showing of generosity had perhaps been meant to show some little respect for the prior order, knowing full well that the rebels could possibly succeed in restoring Mary to her prior role as the rightful heir. In such tumultuous times, she did not mind pretending to pay homage to a "fake Queen," even if it could as easily be interpreted as a complete slap in the face. Mary longed to be reunited with her father and to be blessed again back at court.

Mary thought that, perhaps, her prayers had finally been answered in Robert Aske. She would seek him out as soon as she got to court, hoping that not only had he and the other rebel leaders been welcome but also to find out if there was any hope in his rebellion, and learn how it was coming along; most particularly, she surely sought more information on what their plans were for restoring her. While she loathed having to wear Anne's liveries, even for an instant, she kept reminding herself that she had been forced to do much against her conscience on behalf of "this whore," and that with the appearance of a legitimate change of bringing down the Queen; this outward display would be a small price to pay to manipulate her enemy. In packing her things, Mary found a beautiful, uncut, six-carat diamond that her mother had acquired and given to her. Mary decided to give the gem to Aske when they met, for him to sell to use for his cause. She knew that, especially in the north, her followers were strong.

Perhaps, with this new development, she could at last convince Ambassador Chapuys that the internal strife they had been waiting for had arrived, and she could prompt him to advise the Spanish Emperor into an all-out invasion of the island. All her actions had been treason, but Mary had waited long enough for the crown and was eager for anyone who seriously took up her cause, such as had Aske. She would seek out Chapuys when she got to court to seek his counsel on Aske's motives, but until then she held the rebel's intentions near her heart and believed it with every ounce of her faith.

After arriving at court, Aske and the other leaders were bathed, fed, and sufficiently groomed by the King's servants to make themselves appropriate in the King and Queen's presence, which included a brief lesson on royal etiquette. Naturally, Lord Dacre was not required to attend the etiquette lesson. Once made ready for the event, the festivities were to start promptly at 6 P.M. on December 25th, 1536, with Henry and Anne coming in first to massive cheers, followed by the nobility, and then their retinue. After Henry gave a toast to the health and happiness of all his subjects that year, followed by a short toast by the Queen, the court joined in. It was customary for guests to bring presents of good will at this time of year, which would be kept in the "gift room," minded day and night by four Yeoman guards.

The King dressed in royal blue liveries featuring his own emblem of the Tudor dynasty, encrusted with gold, rubies, pearls, and diamonds, about his neck. On his left arm he carried the *Henrycus Rex* logo, and on his right, the Tudor white and red roses. On his front piece, he had his family arms, and below it, he had Anne's initials of *AB,* naturally making the Queen proud. His leggings, codpiece, and shoes matched his outfit, and his crown this day weighed nine pounds, heavy, but which Henry wore with pride. This piece was custom made for this occasion, to match his outfit, and was one of the only Tudor crowns that did not come from the Tower of London. Anne and his private jeweler and tailor helped assemble the crown for Henry's head.

Not to be outdone, Anne was allowed her own custom crown for this occasion, matching her dress as well. She chose a royal purple velvet gown with amethysts, diamonds, and pearls sewn into the square neckline and bodice. She chose a custom made cross of pure diamonds and amethysts, held to her neck with a piece of purple velvet from her dress, and her amethyst and diamond earrings truly made her stand out. Her dark hair was swept up into a bun within her custom crown, made of only diamonds and amethysts for her small head. This crown was made of a lighter metal and was only about five pounds, so she could wear it throughout the ceremony with the least amount of discomfort possible.

The pair looked radiant, and Anne decided they should have Holbein paint them in these very outfits at a later time. Anne's dress had to be pulled out slightly since she was several months pregnant at the time, although with her small frame she was barely showing. Henry had planned to announce the pregnancy that night. The two were very affectionate and in love with one another, and before the ceremony they played cards, flirted as though they were teenagers again, and in generally excellent cheer.

When the Lady Mary entered court wearing Anne's formal liveries assuming her kneeled appropriate greeting to the King and Queen, the entire court was shocked even her own admirers; it also provided discomfort to her enemies. With her and her servants now at court, Cromwell's search of her chambers and household went far smoother than imagined. At this time, the King was not informed that a search of the Lady Mary's houses and possessions was taking place, the minister felt it was best to gather evidence against her first and risk presenting it later. Cromwell had started the search in hopes of regaining favor with Henry, if he could uncover evidence she was in any way involved in the plot with the rebels. He had long suspected the Lady Mary and her followers of attempting to bring down the reforms, and now with the rebellion, he had even more reason to be suspicious. Some courtiers were convinced it was nothing more than play acting, and then others wondered if Anne really had gotten to her and thought of Mary as a traitor to her own cause. The real truth, none of them knew. One dinner party was hardly enough proof to speculate on Mary's motives, even if the gesture was significant.

Was her showing of attire truly the recognition of Anne's legitimacy that for so long she had resisted? The only time she had publicly acknowledged Anne as Queen was when she was visited by royal agents in July, under threat of imprisonment and death. Now this sudden change of heart caused at least Queen Anne to immediately embrace her, shocked as she was to see, in public court, her now lowly servant, the Lady Mary, bowing in recognition, wearing one of Anne's own liveries. Mary was now having the ultimate revenge, at least for now. Her wearing these garments would force Anne to bring the Lady Mary up from her knees and formally recognize her title and position at court, a sign of good will that was common at the time. While it greatly pleased Henry, Anne was a mix of confusion, paranoia, and suspicion. While embracing the Lady Mary, Anne invited her to dine with her and Henry in their chambers later, meanwhile seeking to use the dinner to discover Mary's intentions. Anne graciously played the consummate host, even to the point where Chapuys could agree to Anne's generosity by inviting Mary to join in dancing as the evening ensued. At dinner, she sat the Lady Mary beside her as her own personal guest, although this was perhaps mainly so she could keep an eye on her.

For a time before the meals had been served, Lord Rochford and Anne had disappeared, perhaps so he could advise her to sit Mary beside her despite her personal feelings. Anne's father had it on good intelligence from his own agents that the Lady Mary may not be around at court to entertain for long, so it would be wise to embrace her presence for as long as Anne could bear it, with as much enthusiasm as she could muster. It was here possibly when Anne asked her father to investigate the Lady Mary's suspect actions before returning to adjoin her guests. Anne did love a good intrigue, so without asking questions, she rejoined her table and in a dramatic gesture in front of all the court, she asked the Lady Mary—to mass applause—to join her. Anne was puzzled at Mary's behavior towards her after the invitation, but did not let her guard down. She knew something was going on, and would look into the cause behind it when she had the time. This evening, she was going to enjoy. Graciously, the Lady Mary accepted, and even Chapuys, while commenting on the lewdness of the gifted liveries, did provide Anne with a compliment for treating Mary so graciously.

All the court was gossiping. Here were two former arch-enemies, now seeming to get along as though great friends. It was quite a show, even for the Tudor court. After dinner, the two women engaged in a dance display for the court, which everyone applauded. Even cynical courtiers remarked that perhaps the English court truly was changing for the better. Anne grabbed Mary by the shoulders, calling her 'dearest friend' and kissing her on each cheek in the French fashion, although it is doubtless both women cringed equally to do so. Henry and Lord Rochford could not have been more thrilled with Anne's maturity and political acumen. After the Queen excused herself to her chambers, there she found her drunken brother George, waiting to berate and mock her for her performance with her foe. When she tried to calm him and explain that it was all for show, he refused to believe it. She had her ladies call for her father, had him removed from her presence, and sent back to his chamber at once.

It was custom for after dinner guests either to continue dancing or to retire to their chambers, but only after the King and Queen had done so. The Queen had been the first one to leave to her own chambers to undress for the evening, and later the King motioned for Brandon to join him in the study. The Lady Mary followed suit and retired to her own chamber within Hampton Court, but first she had a servant she trusted with her life to bring Robert Aske to speak to her for a few moments in private later in the evening. She urgently expressed her wish that no one know of their meeting, especially the King and Queen.

Brandon immediately briefed Henry on what he had seen and experienced in the north with the rebel movements, answering questions on whether or not they could cause serious damage and what should Henry's next moves be. Brandon was very diplomatic about the entire affair and first pointed out the enormous greeting the people had given to the armistice once the rebels realized Henry's forces had approached on a diplomatic mission. Brandon related how Aske, as the leader, had greeted Brandon as a gentleman, along with the Earl of Surrey, and asked for all of them to come into their makeshift camp at Lord Dacre's castle to negotiate. Once inside, they were treated to every kindness, including ale and fresh meat, so they could all dine before getting down to business. Brandon told his King how the negotiations went off peacefully; although the Earl of Surrey let his own disposition and ale get the better of him and finally had to be removed from the interactions after passing out. The King enjoyed a good laugh at this it was this very type of behavior he found so amusing in the Earl, although it made it extremely difficult for the Earl to conduct serious affairs.

The King grilled Brandon for nearly an hour while the festivities continued in the dining hall late into the evening to ask specifically about each of the leader's inclinations in the rebellion. Did Brandon feel they were guilty? If so, what was the extent of each of their guilt, what was their level of activity, and would it be viewed as too generous to host these rebels at court at Christmastide this year? In typical Brandon fashion, he gave the appropriate diplomatic answer that, indeed, Henry was right for inviting them to court, if nothing else so that the nobility could see their enemy face-to-face, and for them to engage with an educated man, Aske, who was not the mere barbarian most of the courtiers had made him out to be. It would also show the King as a reasonable man who could put aside personal differences and even welcome hostility in an environment of neutrality.

All these elegant speeches were meant to play on the King's ego, and it worked. Relieved with Brandon's answers, they rejoined the dinner festivities. The King would announce that his guest of honor was Robert Aske, and ordered that he be treated to every kindness while he was in residence at court. The King returned to find Anne had once more rejoined his fellow courtiers in revelry, laughing at a final joke Anne was busy telling to entertain them, and immediately ordered the servants to start serving more food.

Henry then rose, followed by his guests, and on a serious note he raised his glass in a toast to Robert Aske, praising him for his courage in leading the rebel movement to a series of gasps and sighs at the tables. Henry then announced that Aske was his personal guest of honor for the evening and to be treated to every kindness by all. Before he sat down, he toasted to his wonderful queen, telling the court that she was once again with child. This announcement was greeted with mass applause and Anne waved with a smile. With that, they all continued to enjoy a great feast, followed by lavish gift-giving. Anne approved of the show Henry was putting on for the guests; she had advised him to make light of the situation in front of the court to show all his mercy and goodness. In time, Henry would have the opportunity to punish these rebellious traitors as God would see them punished. Henry played his part perfectly.

The custom after dinner was to join their majesties in the gift room to receive the guests' fine pieces, humbly thanking each one. This could be exhausting and take hours, which is why at least this year it was decided best not to invite Prince Henry and Princess Elizabeth, and subject them to the long excursion, especially at their ages. After the gift giving ceremony, which took some three to four hours, the royal guests of honor (usually there were two, although this time there were five, the three rebel leaders the King and Ms. Isabel Astley and (the Lady Mary for the Queen) gave short speeches of thanks to their majesties for allowing them to be present. After the gift ceremony, the King and Queen lead the court back into the great hall chamber for dancing, card playing, and conversation that would go on for hours, late into the evening.

During the gift giving, Henry and Anne had some of the finest pieces given out. To the Lady Mary, from the King and Queen, went a fine gold challis engraved with a Latin inscription of the Book of John, 15:10-12, as a stern message from the King: *"If you obey my commands, you will remain in my love, just as I have obeyed my Father's commands and remain in his love. I have told you this so that my joy may be in you and that your joy may be complete. My command is this Love each other as I have loved you."* The beautiful inscription was circled around the top exterior of the challis. Henry's jewelry maker had custom made this piece at his behest specifically for Mary. The message was meant to be more than inspirational. The Lady Mary in return gave their majesties a beautiful solid gold Virgin Mary with the hands extended and eyes of pearls. Mary wept at receiving her father's gift and in presenting her own to their majesties. It was an intense moment for all at court who witnessed it.

As a gift to the King and Queen the orphans of the St. Mary's Church put on a play. The theme of the play was kindness. Its main characters focused on noble children who treated a local common boy very meanly until they discovered his family truly was rich and chose to live modest means because of their faith. The boy never retaliates and, through his acts of kindness to his bullies, he manages to teach them humility and repentance. The children's performance was met with a standing ovation, tears and shouts of an encore.

The Duchess of Suffolk had helped finance the children's present, a beautiful, brilliant rare four carat sapphire from the West Indies, to be presented to the monarchs at the closing act. The main actor, an eight year old boy named Nicholas, presented the gift. With tears in his eyes, Henry graciously accepted the gift and welcomed all of the children and their sponsors as permanent guests of court to thunderous applause. The King also returned the sapphire to the children and ordered it be sold to supply their needs, and ordered 5,000 pounds sent annually to manage the orphanage.

Anne gave a beautiful speech following Henry's decree, thanking the Duchess, the orphanage staff, and inviting them all to spend the entire week as her guests in the palace, to be treated as royalty. The gestures from both of their majesties were magnanimous, yet cruelly recorded by Ambassador Chapuys of Spain. He wrote to his master that it was a mere act to impress their subjects, pathetically executed and without warmth or sincerity; it was another mischaracterization meant to slight the Queen's involvement. In truth, in the midst of the seriousness of the rebellion, this show of pageantry and graciousness uplifted everyone's spirits. After the emotional performance, Henry and Anne retired to his chambers to spend what remained of the evening together.

The Lady Mary dismissed her servants, which was odd, and retired to her chamber instead of joining in the dancing, claiming a severe migraine from the evening's activities. She told her trusted maid servant that it was now time to bring the rebel leader Aske to her chambers discreetly. It was vital that no one know of his presence in her chambers. A few moments later Aske arrived and dropped to his knees, as if he were greeting her as the true Princess she was, to which she smiled and humbly raised him to his feet. She thanked him for his kind letter, even though it was dangerous, and for his own safety she cautioned him not to write to her again, in case it might be intercepted, putting them both at risk. She did admit to him in private that she was hopeful that he would succeed in his plight and restore her, but she dare not think it, for that alone was treason.

Aske replied that it was his primary mission in bringing a true Catholic England back to its rightful place in Christendom, and that could only happen by restoring her to her true place in line for the throne. He also reassured her that no one, not even an earthly King, could make the truth treasonous, which brought Mary to smiling tears. He prayed with her, offering her a blessing. Out of fear of being caught, she told him their meeting could not last long but thanked him for his cause and prayed that he might be successful, stating that he truly had been sent by God. All her faith and hopes at restoration to her former titles now lay in his hands. Then she placed the six-carat raw diamond in a pouch in his hand with discreet instructions to tell no one of this meeting, nor where he got the diamond, and to sell it for the supplies his groups would need. Aske dropped to his knees, again calling her Princess, and thanking her for her generosity, giving her his word that what they had discussed would die with him. With that, Aske was dismissed and left her in peace. The meeting would last no more than ten minutes, but would be enough to damn Mary.

Unfortunately for the conspirators, Anne's father, Lord Rochford, was paranoid of Mary's visit to the court in general, and had her followed. Mary stood no chance. She was being watched by spies of both Cromwell and Rochford. Her slightest movements were reported to Rochford first, including her midnight rendezvous with Aske. Cromwell's agents were elsewhere enjoying the revelry instead of their charge, and missed out on this vital opportunity to catch Mary so brazenly in the act of treason. The following morning Rochford told the Queen at once so they could strategize their next move. While Rochford admitted he was not present in the room to hear exactly what was said, he advised the Queen to have Mary's chamber searched immediately, for he felt she was a part of the activities to bring down the Lady Mary for years; only she could not figure out how. Now with the rebellion going on, her enemy may be eliminated all on her own. He and Anne strategized throughout the morning on the best way to bring this news to Henry's attention. Nonetheless, Anne considered Mary to be the final remaining enemy who could ruin her, and decided Mary had to be dealt with accordingly. She railed against the outrageous display of loyalty Mary had pathetically shown. She often fantasized that if Henry were to leave her as regent she would do away with Mary entirely, imprisoning her in the Tower, or having her permanently banished to a nunnery like her mother, or poisoning her in a variety of horrible fashions. As a final twist, when Mary's fate could be proven Anne wanted that chalice to be enclosed in her prison cell so that she might contemplate on her wicked ways; it was clear of Anne's intentions.

This proof of Mary's traitorous ways, by meeting with the head of the rebellion in the King's own palace, would do away with Anne's enemy for her. Best yet, Anne had nothing to do with setting it up. Her only role now would be to convince the King to do the right thing, and order the potential rival heir to death. A common metaphor in 16th century England was the image of nurturing a snake in one's own bosom; Anne would use the phrase by repeating it to Henry in private, describing how, after all he had done for Mary, by giving her own estates and allowing her to keep her household and servants despite her bastard status, she nevertheless proved herself to be in league with traitors.

First though, for all her plotting, Henry would have to be notified. Anne and her father had both grown weary of Cromwell's involvement in such machinations, and they debated the benefits and detriments of having Cromwell tell Henry of Mary's treason. Because the two factions were not working together any longer, each had no idea that the other was investigating Mary's actions. Ultimately it was decided that, because it was

Lord Rochford who directly learned of the treasonous meeting with Aske, he would be the one to go to the King.

Anne prepped her father on the best time of day to approach the King with news so, when Henry's mood would be highest and most receptive, such as before or after the hunt that she would take him on the following day, ensuring that his spirits would be heightened by the prospects of having caught game. Anne instructed her father to Act humbly and humiliated even to have discovered this, and even more so to tell his majesty that all he could prove was having witnessed Aske entering Mary's chambers at midnight. That would be all it would take for Henry to grow outraged and demand that action be taken. From there, Anne would play her part well in private and exercise that prowess she was well known for. She would have Mary's head if it was the last thing she did.

The following day, true to her word, once Henry had finished his Privy Council meeting, he was told by Edward Seymour, Keeper of the Stables, that his and Anne's horses had been made ready for a hunt, as a surprise by the Queen. Confused he took the bait, as he always enjoyed a welcome distraction from the business of court. Since Henry had already been briefed by Brandon about the meetings with the rebel leaders, he wanted his Privy Council to be notified and asked that Brandon keep him abreast of their discussions. On such an important day, when he should have been present, Anne's surprise intrigued him, and he found it hard to say no to her, especially while she was with child.

As he was preparing to head to the stables to meet Anne, Lord Rochford burst in at the appropriate time, delivering the most unnerving news in private. He played his role of humility and embarrassment to perfection. Naturally the King was enraged at Mary's insolence, but with Anne waiting he had to hide his temper and thanked Lord Rochford for his discretion in the matter. He advised his father-in-law to keep this matter private until further measures could be taken.

Anne was waiting at the stables, already aware that Henry would know of the Lady Mary's meeting the night before. She played the unassuming Queen with dignity and poise. Whatever bad mood Henry was in, he could always count on Anne to uplift him from it. True to form, after several hours of hunting and demounting from the horses to take a walk holding hands, he confided in her and tried to be as gentle as he could in "informing" his Queen about the actions of the Lady Mary. Anne appeared to act shocked at her betrayal. She carefully listened and waited for the right opportunity to discuss Henry's next steps regarding the Lady Mary.

While the King and Queen were out attempting to enjoy the hunt, the rebel's demands had been delivered via Brandon to the Privy Council, who were undertaking a thorough review before coming to consensus. The restoration of the Lady Mary hit a particular nerve with more than a few members. They all had sworn to the Oath of Succession and the majority at least outwardly supported Anne. Back at the Privy Council meeting that same day, Brandon remained silent while Lord Audley read aloud the rebel grievances for the group to debate. After their careful review, they were to decide the most appropriate steps to advise His Majesty on taking against the rebel traitors including the leaders. Most were incensed that the King would even entertain holding a formal grievance court at York. They already had Parliament, which was established for such matters, but any member who spoke so boldly against the King's design was quickly reprimanded by Cromwell, who kept them all in line.

Cromwell suggested that, while the rebel leaders were in residence, they all should be taken to interrogation at the Tower. The minister firmly believed that only under further interrogation would they truly uncover all they needed to know. The council members did not dare disagree publicly with the minister, but Brandon still held his reservations to himself. The rebels had been more than forthcoming about their movements and resources, and besides their openness at parley, the entire rebel management was there to agree to a peace treaty under false pretenses. Despite their success at rousing the people and gaining an audience at court, they were yet a dysfunctional and unorganized group at best.

Cromwell's harsh proposal was seen as purely an act for the minister to save face before a King he knew he had fallen out of favor with. Brandon also held the paranoid thought that there were evil advisers in the council who agreed with these traitorous rebels. Regardless, Cromwell persisted. He would privately take this matter up with the King. The rest of the council agreed that the King was doing the right thing by having grievance hearings held at York, and none spoke out against it. There was not a single member who agreed with Cromwell's plan to arrest and torture the leaders of the movement, (at least not in public) any such decision should be Henry's alone.

Upon leaving the council meeting, Cromwell ordered private investigations of the council members he suspected of any potential involvement in the rebellion. While Cromwell investigated the Privy Council members, Lord Rochford ordered his agents to further investigate the Lady Mary's residence, discreetly, for any evidence of treason against the King, especially any evidence regarding Aske or communications with the rebel movement. Their primary instruction was to search her residences and the belongings of all of her servants for any evidence, specifically regarding the rebellion, her letters with Chapuys, Aske and any other Acts of treason against the King or Queen that they could find. Their investigation would take a deliberate and shocking turn.

An urgent dispatch sent to the Rochford—in the late evening hours of December 27th revealed evidence of Mary's contact with the rebels. It was during their search at Hertfordshire that Rochford's agents uncovered the damaging evidence. The search was conducted in the late hours with her servants being barred from the premises, under pain of death. The intruders quickly suppressed the little security detail the King had allowed for Mary and entered the castle having their way of the grounds. Mary's household were not informed who these men were, but were most likely scared within their lives to give them any information they wanted; they were unnamed henchmen who destroyed most of Mary's property in their search.

Rochford's agents tore the place apart leaving it to appear as though the entire palace had been robbed, although in truth nothing had been taken but the evidence to bring Mary down. The men were not dressed in the any royal liveries, in order to disguise their identity, and they most likely frightened the poor servants greatly. Guards assigned to watch the palace were put under the same threat at knifepoint and ordered to stand down. They ransacked the lodgings, breaking fine china and crystal gifts. They destroyed tapestries worth a fortune, which ironically were owned by the King himself and were not Mary's property. The few remaining servants were questioned thoroughly, and while no direct notice of torture was given, the agents stressed in their report to Rochford that the methods of interrogation were "deliberate" and revealed that the servants knew nothing of their mistress's affairs.

Despite the Lady Mary's precautions, a laundress maid, perhaps too thorough in her duties, discovered Aske's letter reassuring Mary of her restoration to power and Mary's many draft responses; the discovery was the proverbial smoking gun. At knifepoint she revealed all, and the location of these letters, which Rochford's agent's quickly snatched up.

These letters validated not only that Mary was in direct contact with the rebels, but that she understood their entire cause to be one of replacing her in the succession, and that she had even drafted thanks and prayers for their success. Nevertheless, while the drafts alone were incriminating, they could not find evidence of a final dispatch actually being sent in return to Aske. In fact, within the trove of evidence was a draft thanking Aske for his cause, but urging him and the rebels to stand down and obey the King. She revealed that she too could not reconcile her conscience to the King's Acts, but that he remained her true Lord and Master, ever appointed by God, and she had advised Aske to obey their King. Still, her many drafts prayed for the rebels' health, blessed them with good tidings, and vowed to keep them always in her thoughts. It was in the last line of a particular draft, written in Latin, that Mary met her downfall. The simple phrase: *"ego voveo vestry prosperitas multiplex super quod dues mos rejoice in vestri causa"*: "I pray for your success many times over and God will rejoice in your cause."

The agents rode through the night to report the evidence back to Lord Rochford. Shortly after 2 A.M. the agents returned, detailing the treason they had uncovered with what they claimed was little force. It was far too dangerous at this time to brief Cromwell first, so Rochford was the one they left the Actual evidence with. It mattered little as Cromwell was aware that Rochford had agents who had broken into Lady Mary's residence. He knew not what they were looking for, but this gave him all the proof he needed to know that he was no longer welcome as a trusted ally and associate of the Boleyns, which was a very dangerous place to be.

True to form, Cromwell notified Henry immediately of the break in, unaware that Henry already knew of Mary's private meeting with Aske. With the proof in hand, Rochford had beaten him to the King's chamber and when Cromwell came in, Rochford had already briefed Henry of Lady Mary's treason. Rochford woke him, apologizing profusely, but saying that there was the most urgent business to inform his monarch about. Cromwell listened as Rochford began recounting all of the evidence in its utmost detail, handed Henry the documents that Rochford's agents had uncovered and awaited further instruction from the King.

As Henry began to read, he grew angry, and because he was already tired, he was even more livid than usual and so ordered Cromwell to begin immediately drafting up the Bill of Attainder that would essentially list out Mary's crimes against the King. Before he left, Cromwell also suggested that, now that they had Mary's crimes in hand, they draw up additional bills against the rebel leaders so they could interrogate them further while they were still at court; Henry agreed. Cromwell immediately left to discharge his duty and prepare the bills. Henry thanked Rochford for coming forward with this most unwelcome news, but that he needed his rest to determine what steps next to take; he so ordered before dismissing Rochford to make certain the Queen was aware of the evolving events. Henry would go back to sleep and would comment the following day that he slept remarkably well, all things considering. Per the King's command Rochford briefed his daughter immediately afterwards of Mary's treason. Anne rejoiced immediately calling for George and told her family that it had been divinely ordered that the wicked daughter, the Lady Mary should fall. Anne wanted to celebrate immediately. Rochford left his daughter to enjoy her good fortune in private as he went to ensure his agents were unharmed and remained anonymous.

Cromwell woke his clerk and, despite the late hour, immediately called for his staff to start preparing the necessary notices of Mary's crimes to Parliament. Treason or not, it was the King's daughter they would be acting against. Cromwell spent the remainder of the evening drawing up the Bill of Attainder against Mary per the King's wishes to be presented to him in the morning. The minister was certainly grateful that the Lady Mary's crimes had been uncovered, but he wanted to know how and why Rochford had his own independent agents investigating her first. He would in time have his own agents answer that question. He also debated how or if to even share this most upsetting news to Chapuys. For the time being he made a wise decision to keep this information to himself.

When Henry awoke the next morning he got ready for the day, went to see Anne, and kissed her good morning while she was still asleep, along with their growing child. He eventually woke her and detailed the events from what had happened the night before with Rochford and Cromwell along with the evidence found against the Lady Mary, to which she acted genuinely shocked, another exceptional performance. The actual extent of Mary's treason was surprising, especially given how only a few months prior she would finally taken the oath against both her faith and conscience; she did so to not risk death, and turned out only to have delayed it. The girl was apparently not quite as wise as her admirers often professed.

Either way, Anne kept these thoughts to herself. Henry assured her that Cromwell was drafting up the Bill of Attainder for Mary that very morning and that she would be arrested and taken to the Tower within the hour. The verdict was as good as made. Naturally, he was sullen about the entire affair and his conscience, he admitted, was genuinely stricken about having to put his own to death, although in Anne's presence he was extremely careful not to use the word daughter. He left Anne's chamber that morning and went off to sign the warrant.

Within the hour of 7 A.M., Cromwell brought all the Bills of Attainder. Once they were signed, Henry summoned the head Yeoman, William Forsthgate into his chambers and ordered him to carry out his duty by arresting the Lady Mary for treason in aiding the rebels. In accordance with the Queen's wishes, Rochford, knowing full well that Mary would be arrested within the morning hours, got to Forsthgate and gave him Mary's chalice from her father to place in her cell at the time of her arrest along with 50 ducats for his charge to keep the matter discreet. Back in his own chambers now, the King signed the Attainder for Mary and further ordered the arrest of Robert Aske, Lord Dacre and Robert Constable for their parts in leading the rebellion in treason against the crown. Henry spent the rest of the day out riding, without notifying anyone but some close servants who would accompany and attend him. Forsthgate would be the man responsible for seeing the Lady Mary to her cell in the Tower. As Lady Mary lay sleeping, the Yeoman barged into her chamber and ordered her awake, whereupon Forsthgate read out the list of charges against her.

Dropping to her knees immediately, confused and half asleep, she begged to speak to her father the King and pronounced her innocence repeatedly. She prayed to God and begged the guards to let her explain that she was not guilty. She became hysterical and began shouting that she was no traitor, she was the most honorable and humble of the King's servants and never had she betrayed his majesty. The pleas went unanswered. Legend has it that her screams for mercy can still be heard in the morning hour, passing the west side of the manor, where the remains of her chamber stand today.

Rochford delivered breakfast to Anne around 9 A.M. that morning to review the events as they were unfolding. They both were pleased; all of their political enemies were falling according to plan, at least for the time being. Her pregnancy was progressing relatively well, although in the past few days she had been experiencing mild cramps and spotting, which her midwife assured her was normal, but she worried regardless. Anne had always been known for her anxiety. Even when things were going her way, she could not help but worry about the most trivial matters. She shared her concerns with her father about the baby, but he managed to cheer her up by telling her that both the rebel leaders and the Lady Mary would soon be put to death, and she would never again have to worry about the threat they posed to either herself or her heirs. Lord Rochford ordered ale to celebrate. After the celebratory ale, Anne's father left her to attend the Lady Mary's interrogation and, as he put it, *"allow her to hang herself,"* kissing her forehead before going. Anne and her ladies-in-waiting did needlepoint the day of Mary's arrest and finished several quilts for the children of the orphanage.

Lord Rochford headed straight to the tower, arriving shortly after 11 A.M. to find a devastated, confused, and despondent Lady Mary pacing back and forth in her cell. Her golden chalice lay on its side in the corner, as if it had been thrown. This was not what he had expected. He expected to greet the epitome of coldness; she had always shown the utmost class, dignity, and an almost cruel grace that bordered on snobbery. This Lady Mary was hysterical, crying, and still genuinely confused, yet warm. She had no clue why she had been arrested, proclaimed her innocence repeatedly to Rochford, and begged to know what she had been accused of. After all the harm the King had done to his own daughter, he would not even allow her the dignity of knowing her own charges, beyond being a traitor to the crown and in collusion with the rebel forces. Rochford even went one step further to say that she was the sole motivation behind their entire rebellion, encouraging them and inspiring them to remain strong despite their difficulties until she was restored to her true place. Rochford also accused her—falsely; she insisted—of attempting to poison the Princess Elizabeth while she was at Hatfield serving as her attendant. This was a completely baseless accusation, but anything he could say to make Mary even more of a wreck he enjoyed.

During the interrogation, due to her fragile mental state, Mary denied everything and gave away little of value to him, even after the threat of torture. She did know that at least this accusation was a complete lie. Women of Mary's status, and generally all women, were immune from torture in the 16th century, to protect their fragility. Considering her status as a Lady, she was placed in rather common confinements, a stark reminder of her loss of royal prestige. After several hours of repeating the same questions with no hope of solid answers, Rochford left, satisfied in the knowledge that it would only be a matter of days before this hysterical lady would be dead.

Cromwell showed up as Rochford was leaving. The two exchanged only minor banter to relay that Mary was too emotionally fragile to get any useful information out of; Rochford wished Cromwell better luck. And so it was that on December 27th, 1536, Cromwell formally read the Lady Mary all the charges against her. Like Rochford, the minister would leave with nothing but a headache from Mary's hysteria; he notified her that she was to be tried in the "Star Chamber"—a special, secret court established to prosecute the powerful—in the early hours of December 29th, 1536, once the court had returned from a holiday break. As a final request, she asked that a cross be placed with her so that she may pray for mercy; the minister acknowledged that request, and after that evening's supper, the Tower Constable, Sir William Kingston, brought it to her and even prayed with her.

That evening, Cromwell chronicled in private dispatches to his wife that he had never before seen his majesty in such a strange state. First the King hunted alone all day, returning only late at night, demonstrating incredible rage, then intense grieving, and at times sullenness with no speech, as if his renegade daughter were already dead. The Queen did much to reinforce his conscience during these troubling times and proved a great comfort to him. She reminded Henry of Mary's refusal to take the oath until threatened with death, and warned that Mary, like her mother, would do everything in her power as she grew older to take power from him and his future heir, the Prince. Unlike her manner with Henry during the Brandon affair, she fully manipulated her husband over Mary.

Although Queen Anne hated Mary, she was still his daughter and Anne had to reinforce that his own flesh meant to cause him harm and actually take his place on the throne, even replacing his true divinely appointed heir. This continuous reinforcement was mistaken by Henry for genuine affection, when in reality it was a shrewd political play by an advanced player of the game. Anne knew full well what she was doing, and she would not cease her manipulative tactics until the Lady Mary's blood spilled from the scaffold and she was dead. To some extent it can be reasoned that, although Henry reacted out of sheer emotion to have his daughter arrested and tried, it was Anne who was taking pleasure for being indirectly responsible for Mary's plight.

The truth is that Mary's own treasonous actions are what resulted in her arrest and trial. She was well aware of the law, and of the rebellion, and she knew full well that communicating in any way with the rebels would be viewed by her father as treason, even if she may have viewed her words as inherently harmless. Henry had a choice of whether to keep Mary alive or kill her, but after several failed attempts at a real heir, now that he finally had a Prince, his own dynasty was at stake by allowing Mary to live. It was both a combination of Mary's own treasonous actions and Henry's succession fears that brought about her downfall.

As much as Anne's supporters would have loved to have her and her faction alone take credit for this momentous act, the truth is that it was not just her. She just helped speed Mary towards her ultimate end. Her final warning to Henry was what put him over the edge. She warned that if he should let Mary live it would only further inspire her supporters to free her and lead a rebellion to his majesty's very door, until all of their own heads were posted on spikes in London, including that of the Prince. With that, Henry made the decision to execute his own daughter. The court had not yet even been informed of her arrest. Cromwell, previously a man without high regard for faith, felt a mix of both sadness and guilt for his feelings of joy at Mary's situation.

The entire week of Mary's ordeal was somber for Henry. While the court had just thoroughly enjoyed the feasting and entertainments of the Christmastide celebrations, they were also painfully aware that a rebellion was still being waged and Henry's first child was considered a co-conspirator in the overthrow of the new Tudor heir. Both Henry and Anne were preoccupied with how both of those issues would play out. After a few days, Henry's conscience would grow even more genuinely stricken that he, who had fathered her, should now be he who condemned her to death. This trial was the first true test of her new status. If Henry honestly believed, as he had previously proclaimed to all who would hear him, that Mary was a bastard, could he now treat her as he might any such maid and put her to death so easily? Anne reassured him that he was pursuing the divine course of providence and that his judgments came directly from God. This play on his ego worked well, and within a few hours, his conscience had made a miraculous recovery to his original thought. Henry thanked Anne for her consolation and remarked in front of several servants who took down the words, *"how blessed am I to have one such as you!"*

When the Star Chamber jurists returned from holiday on the morning of December 29th, the first case to be heard was that of the Lady Mary. Most of the court, and certainly the people, had not even heard about the arrest and impending trial. When the legal system was reformed earlier in the year, Lord Rochford had made certain the removal of certain "papist-biased" judges from their posts, ensuring to stack the court with Boleyn and reformer-allies. These jurists were solely in Boleyn's pockets and he paid them well that they would remember his family's advancement. Henry made it clear what verdict he expected the court to find by subtle means when they had rejoined. By the time Mary appeared before them, shortly after 8 A.M. that morning, she stood little chance of a pardoning.

The state sanctioned the death of the one person whom, in the eyes of Europe, was the true and legitimate heir. Thankfully the news had barely begun to spread in noble circles beyond pure unconfirmed rumor and speculation. The Lady Mary's Attainder had been delivered to the jurists early on the morning of the case with strict instructions from Cromwell that the case was to take precedence over all other activities on that day's rolls and remain as confidential as possible, upon pain of death for the jurists, themselves. Members of Parliament were not notified of the case, unless they were to sit in judgment, until after the proceedings had actually occurred.

Henry did not want to risk that the members of the House of Commons might relay to their subjects—and those traitorous rebels—that their idol was about to be put to death. The last thing he wanted to do was risk making her a martyr. In a closed session of court, the jurists received the Lady Mary to stand against her charges. She arrived wearing a simple garment of blue and brown damask, with bell sleeves and a white maid's cap. She wore a signature ruby and gold cross around her neck. The yeomen, as was custom, brought her into the courtroom, bringing with them their axes, turned away from her until she was pronounced guilty.

The Lady Mary arrived at her defense table alone, as defendants in those times were not allowed defense counsel and had very limited rights, and listened as the clerk of the court read out the initial indictment against her. Lord Rochford, despite a clear conflict of interest, served as a jurist and would later tell the Queen that the Lady Mary could barely keep her composure. She was nervous, anxious, and had cried as soon as she entered the chamber, protesting her innocence as the charges were read. The state presented the evidence against her, the Aske letter and those draft responses written in her own hand. Since prisoners were not allowed a defense attorney she was immediately found guilty of her crimes once the crown's Solicitor General Richard Rich presented the evidence on Henry's behalf.

A full jurist panel found her unanimously guilty of corroborating with the rebel leaders and for treason for attempting to overthrow her father. They threw the book at her. The evidence was damaging. Even if some evidence was taken out of context, her very contact with the rebels was treason, regardless of her message. When the court asked her what her response was to their evidence, she replied that she had been forever a maiden of Christ, and a true and loyal subject to the King, but that only Christ's judgment should suffice in her eyes. That she had been falsely accused by wicked servants about her person, over whom she had no control, and that she would not rest to clear her name with his majesty if so given the opportunity. *"If it appears that I shall die, I say this to you all: Christ in his mercy has determined it is by his will alone I shall perish from this earth, I believe in him and wish you all to pray for the King, for he has been surrounded by evil council."*

She could barely get the words out through bouts of heavy sobbing. Without a change in her unstable demeanor, the High Constable of the Court, George Kilroy, pronounced the predictable verdict and found her guilty as charged, to be beheaded or burnt at the stake, according to his majesty's pleasure. After the verdict was pronounced, it was acceptable to spread the word that she had been found guilty and would await sentencing at the Tower. There would be no further trials or hearing, simply a letter in the King's own hand, read to her aloud by the Tower Constable, pronouncing her method of death, along with the date and time.

Cromwell immediately dispatched the verdict to the King who, after his hunt, had gone to his estate at Whitehall to be with his family. Cromwell would have to wait for Henry's decision on what to do about Mary. As Mary struggled through her trial, the King spent the remainder of the day after his hunt with Anne and his (other) children. Perhaps this was his own unique way of making peace with putting an old part of his life to rest while focusing on his future.

Mary left the courtroom that day hysterical. The Yeoman's axes were now turned towards her, signifying a guilty verdict, as she was escorted back to her cell at the Tower to await her father's decision on her execution method, date, and time. When the response did come, several hours later, the King ordered her to be beheaded by the next available executioner the following morning. His only orders, given sullenly, were to get it over with quickly. The following day Cromwell delivered the message that Henry, in his mercy, had granted that the relatively merciful sentence of a quick beheading was to be carried out that day, December 30th, 1536, at 7 A.M. in the morning. A local, experienced executioner, highly recommended by Cromwell and trusted by the King, would do his charge. Cromwell gave her a purse of 18 ducats to give the executioner for his duty, as it was customary for the accused to pay the executioner as they were about to die. She requested the Bishop Stephen Gardiner to come and hear her last confession and administer the last rites.

Bishop Gardiner attended Mary around 7 P.M. the evening before and stayed with her until midnight, in prayer for a majority of the time. They prayed for hours refusing to allow him to leave her presence. She confessed that she had been an innocent maid and a faithful servant of the King. She admitted she hated the Lady Anne, but was letting that go for the betterment of her soul. Should she meet her maker the following day and wanted to go to God with a pure heart and a clean conscience. She dictated to the Bishop her last will and testament, along with a personal letter to the King:

"My dearest and most gracious Father and Majesty,

I solemnly beg your highnesses forgiveness for any impediment I may have caused to your majesty's humble heart. Please know that I am only a woman and beg for your majesty's earnest mercy as your true faithful servant. You were the only father I have ever known and my heart loves you as a daughter, though I no longer acknowledge I am as such. I would beg of your majesty's humble forgiveness for referring to myself in an improper fashion but my soul commends I do so before I pass. I beseech your majesty to be good to Prince Henry and Princess Elizabeth. To love them as a father to a child as they are only small children with large hearts to love you better with. I beseech your majesty to spare my life, but if you cannot find it in your person to recompense my sentence I beg humbly that you beseech me to a swift death so that I may not suffer unjustly prolonged [unreadable] for your better conscience.

Your true, humble and loyal servant, the Lady Mary."

Historians have debated whether this letter was actually written, but forensic testing of the parchment and the carbon dating of the ink used does match the time period between 1530s and 1550s and Mary's unique signature was on the paper; however, the rest of the handwriting was not her style at all. At the very least it could have been written by Bishop Gardiner as, considering Mary's emotional state, it could be debated that she would not have been able to write so clearly and easily. On the other hand, given her delicate, modest personality, and the protocol of the time—which would have made a condemned prisoner's writing to the King quite uncommon—to be so intentionally brazen towards the King, even in her last letter, would have been out of character for Mary; the letter was thus more likely written by a revisionist fan after her death. The only contemporary account of the drafting is Bishop Gardiner's statement that he did, indeed, take down Mary's last will and testament, along with a personal letter to the King, but both of those letters have been damaged over time. Notwithstanding these factors weighing against Mary having written the Actual letter, under the stress she was facing she might have had a mental break and penned the note to relieve her conscience and make peace before she was to leave the Earth. This debate has continued for centuries and most likely will proceed without resolution.

When questioned by Rochford and Cromwell the following morning as to the Lady Mary's state of mind, Bishop Gardiner reported that she had made her peace with death and took responsibility at the end for her own disloyalty towards the King, but that she vowed upon her very soul that she had never betrayed him in the charges upon which she had been accused. She lamented the loss of her relationships with both her mother and her father, and had often wished that the good Lord had chosen to take her back far sooner, but she had come to terms with the time and method of her returning to wait upon her God, and wished the King nothing but good will and Godspeed.

By the following morning it was fairly public knowledge that the Lady Mary was to be put to death. Most of the King's subjects refused to believe it and labeled it vicious gossip by Anne's cronies. The news had failed to make it to the north where the rebels were still gathered. Interestingly enough, neither Aske nor any of the other rebel leaders were yet to be brought upon charges for their parts in the uprising, or for Aske's own letter to Mary. This was not merely an oversight by the crown; this was an intentional delay tactic by Cromwell, who had failed to provide any counsel on bringing charges so quickly on Aske. Aske's being in residence for the Christmastide festivities bought the minister time to further investigate him and make him an easy capture when the time was right to bring him to trial.

At 7 A.M. on December 30th, 1536, Constable Kingston escorted the Lady Mary from her cell in the Tower of London to the scaffold on the Tower Green. She denied herself a final meal and seemed nervous and faltering on her way to the platform. According to contemporary reports, she was wearing a rather plain dress of blue fabric with a white and black damask overlay and a ruby and gold cross necklace about her neck, said to be her mother's. She wore no headdress and her hair flowed loosely down her neck. Spectators commented that you could see she had been visibly upset and her face had shown the effects of prolonged crying, with red puffy cheeks and streaks from the tears visible about her face. She was shaking rather nervously and more than once had to be held by a guardsman as she slowly made her way to the scaffold. She appeared to be trying to hold her composure as she made her way through the small group of people who had heard about the impending execution. She was trembling on her way to the scaffold. Then, the limited few assembled people began to chant a call of encouragement for the Lady Mary, and their shouts and applause started to roll through the group. She collapsed into tears and fainted, having to be revived by a guardsman, taking another few moments to bring her up to the scaffold.

When she made it to the scaffold she gave her executioner his purse and when he asked for forgiveness, she readily thanked him for his duty, tears running down her cheeks. Next she was greeted warmly by the Priest, who blessed her and asked for her last prayer and if she would like to make a final statement. She nodded and approached the end of the scaffold, turned to face the crowd, and began to speak:

"My fellow Christian people, I proclaim that I have been ordered by his grace, the most High Majesty King Henry VIII, to stand my justice this day for my crimes against him and my sin against Christ. I beseech you to ask Christ in his mercy to receive my soul, and I humbly submit my will to you and to my most gracious Lord, and ask of you all that you bless and pray for his majesty. With this, I leave you now to join my rightful place, as the lord our God commands. I beg you to be good to one another and faithful subjects of his majesty. I pray forgiveness for my sins upon this earth and for having

offended my master so. I beg you all to pray for my soul as I take my leave of you."—Lady Mary

It was common for prisoners at the scaffold to thank their King for his service and say nothing ill of him. It may seem strange today to hear of prisoners giving such kind words for being put to death; however, in the times of the Tudors, those who had not done so would have their loved ones suffering for their insolence after their deaths. The family members of those who spoke out of turn about their sentencing before their execution were often subject to imprisonment, removal of titles, lands, and income. This tradition of silence and obedience continued in Mary. Although she had no immediate family left to burden, she did have her supporters and she did not wish them harm. Due to the speed and secrecy of the trial and execution, only around 25 people were there when she met her end, mostly servants at the Tower. Tears were strewn from nearly all in sight at her declaration. A few short moments later, with a single stroke, her head was struck from the block, and the beloved Princess Mary was pronounced dead. Her body was buried with her mother at Peterborough Cathedral. Her ruby and gold cross was delivered back to Henry later that day with a note from Sir Kingston that read: *"the Lady Mary begged for you to cherish this token, with her love, as both a parting gift from a dutiful subject, and as a loving daughter."*

5.3 The End of the Uprising

At the next session of Parliament, Cromwell would introduce an Act recommending to the King that all papist heretics and their families would now face even stricter penalties for refusing to recognize the King as supreme head of the Church of England. It would be illegal and punishable by death to be considered a heretic, not only for the individual so pronounced, but also for the entire family of the accused. Given the rebellion and Mary's intransigence, it was not enough for Henry to go after the traitors; Cromwell wished to send a dire warning to *all* Acts of sedition or treason by anyone—or their associates—would not be tolerated. To prove it, he intended to use every weapon in his arsenal. Anne was blamed entirely for this measure, but while it is certainly true that there was insecurity on the part of the Queen about the Catholics, this measure was entirely Cromwell's doing.

After Mary's death, Henry took full advantage of his ability to go back on his word to the rebel leaders; he had them removed from their comfortable guest rooms at Whitehall Palace and placed in the Tower where they had been languishing since their own arrest on Bills of Attainder two days after Mary's arrest. Cromwell read them their charges at their arrests, and they had all been thoroughly interrogated but not tortured; however, the investigations produced no solid intelligence, other than to corroborate the other conspirator's stories that the rebels were waiting for word from their leaders upon their, still presumed, safe return with the King's demands. With this in mind, the King met directly with Aske and agreed to let him alone head back to meet the rebels, with Brandon and royal forces not far behind, to assure the rebels that their grievances would be addressed in good faith. Henry had no intention of keeping his word after the incident with his daughter, but to suppress the active rebellion and prevent any marching upon London, Aske had to be released to convince the other rebels to stand down.

It was a risky move, one that Cromwell and Brandon had to orchestrate together heavily to ensure that Aske would not be clever enough to run from view only to then attack them from another angle. This risk was heavy, but nonetheless one that had to be taken. Aske would have to provide a cover story for the absence of the other leaders, Constable and Dacre, to tell other townships to stand down and hope for the best for compliance.

To help anticipate and answer questions by the rebels, the King—in his own handwriting—agreed to draft a fake proposal of peace and pardons for all involved. Aske was not informed that this offer was fraudulent. In fact, Henry privately revealed his true intentions to Brandon during the first week of January, ordering his military commander to hang all of the rebel traitors: men, women, and children. The King was out for blood and he wanted the death of every single person involved, whether for actively participating in the rebellion or for merely aiding the rebels with shelter or food. He wished to set a prominent example and this was the best means to ensure that no future uprising would threaten his realm.

Brandon visibly cringed at what his King had asked of him and began to disclose his own scruples against hanging what he considered to be innocent women and children. Henry reassured him that, in his dreams, he had a vision that God wanted him to seek justice for these traitors. Henry felt, with all of his conviction, that this was the only way to secure his kingdom and all the honorable citizens in it. He openly admitted that this was a terrible favor to ask of his oldest, closest, and truest friend, but confided that he could trust no one else to ensure that his orders would be executed.

According to the memoirs of a servant who was present, Brandon's only response was to hang his head; he told his King that his wife Catherine was pregnant with their third child and asked, how could he . . . drifting off before he could finish his sentence. Henry could relate. Anne too was pregnant with their child. By bringing up their wives pregnancies, Brandon was attempting to get Henry to realize the magnitude of what he was asking. His King was asking—in fact, ordering—him to take the lives of innocent children; souls who had not yet fully lived. Henry did not fully comprehend his friend's meaning.

Henry was focused on vengeance. He only congratulated Brandon and Catherine on their expectancy, increased Brandon's annual jointure salary, and asked him to do this service as the King's dear brother, for all the love he bore his sovereign. Brandon reluctantly nodded his head in agreement, but every part of his being resisted the stomach-turning duty. Before dismissing Brandon, Henry also demanded that Aske be brought back safely, so that he could later be formally charged with the capital offense of treason.

Despite his recent prison stay, Aske returned to the north feeling fulfilled that Henry would keep true to his word in the end and grant most of the rebels' demands. He had no idea that these "promises" were merely lip service. Brandon and the Earl's forces stayed at least a solid mile behind the proceeding caravan, while Aske rode, unbeknownst to him, with one of the King's own trusted groomsmen. This servant of the crown had been disguised as a rebel follower to provide Henry with extra insurance of knowing the rebels' intelligence. Aske carried in his satchel the King's pardon decree and all appeared well. That is, until the group neared Doncaster, where a second uprising was starting under the leadership of Sir Francis Bigod of Settrington, a smaller part of Yorkshire.

With the Pilgrimage leaders away celebrating with what Bigod viewed as the traitors of the crown, Bigod had stirred up sentiment amongst the rebels for the same demands Aske had originally sent to the King, but Bigod used the length of time it had taken for the leaders to return as proof that the King was incapable of keeping his promises and that another uprising was essential. Bigod led this second uprising at Cumberland and

Westmoreland and intended to go through Yorkshire once more; however, for his campaign, Bigod wanted to be successful where Aske, Constable and Dacre had apparently failed. Furthering his potential for success, Bigod had a talent for rhetoric that rallied the remaining rebels to pick up where they had left off back in October.

When Aske came across deserters from Bigod's Rebellion, heading back home to feed their families, they informed him of Bigod's activities. Aske was devastated. His entire belief in what the King stood for was now in jeopardy because the people had failed to achieve their goals fast enough to satisfy the rebels who were left. When Aske had met with them in October, he found the group as a whole to be reasonable and understanding that these negotiations would take time. With this new information he found nothing but an angry, tired, frustrated and starving group of rebels being fed rhetoric from an inexperienced leader seeking fame, fortune or some other benefit unknown to Aske. After his meeting with the deserters, he turned back to Brandon and told him of Bigod's Rebellion and sought special permission to go on ahead with the King's groom to learn their demands and attempt to peacefully resolve the latest uprising. Unfortunately, Brandon had his own private orders and denied Aske's fairly reasonable request. For all of Aske's work on the rebels behalf, Bigod had single handedly assured their destruction. There would be only one outcome of this, unimaginable bloodshed.

Aske and the groom were kept back behind Brandon and the Earl as they marched ahead, now nearly 10,000 strong; the King had been wise enough this go around to provide additional reinforcements, enough to be able to slaughter Bigod and the rest of the rebels. Brandon planned to strike at night, after the rebels had set up camp and would have been sleeping for at least several hours, this would not only ensure his own men would be able to get some rest and use some of their food rations, but also that Bigod's forces would be completely unprepared and vulnerable. The lack of formal military training in this instance would work to Brandon's benefit. In this harsh winter, temperatures at night dropped into the low teens would cause sword blades to stick inside their scabbards, like a tongue to a pole. This would effectively allow the King's forces to strike when the rebels were not only vulnerable, but practically disarmed. Brandon also ordered that his forces proceed in silence, so as not to alert the rebels that they were coming, preserving the element of surprise, as well. His attack would focus on a campaign of fire, torching the tents as the Bigod rebels slept and were killed if they tried to exit.

Brandon's plan turned out brilliantly and nearly 400 rebels were killed while still sleeping or in their tents. Those who attempted to run, were instead run down and the King's forces slit their throats or killed them by gunfire in a short battle. The rest were gathered up by the massively superior force and hung systematically. In total, the King's forces suppressed the entire rebellion in less than three hours, with over 790 rebel bodies to result, and dozens more unaccounted for. Aske became physically ill at the sight of the carnage, especially at witnessing the killing of the women and children. Several times he tried to intervene and begged Brandon stop the slaughter, especially after the first one hundred or so surrendered, but Brandon knew it would not be enough to please the King and continued his duty. Of these casualties, no distinction was made for rank, there were men of the nobility, men of the cloth and commoners alike, all sharing the same fate. With their blood Henry had secured peace through tyrannical means. Their bodies languished, hanging from the trees as a fearful reminder to prospective rebels of what crossing the King meant. With his duty done and the victims' blood on his hands, Brandon ordered his forces, along with Aske in chains, to return to London to report back to the King. It was reported that Aske shed tears on the battlefield at the loss of his fellow countrymen and for what was to come for England. Reportedly he had asked Brandon as a fellow gentleman to give him a proper soldiers death instead of taking him back to die at the hands of a tyrant. For all that Aske had started; Brandon felt for him and respected his honor and dignity in his request. Sadly he replied that he had to take him back to the King as per his direct command. Privately, Brandon suspected he would have requested the same if he were in Aske's position.

Although the Pilgrimage leaders had nothing to do with, and even attempted to suppress Bigod's rebellion, they too were captured and put on trial. Thanks to Brandon's strategic military planning, the only official uprising in Henry VIII's reign ended in January 1537. Among the leaders captured were Lord Darce, John Hussey 1st Baron of Sleaford, Robert Constable, and Robert Aske. Hussey and Darce were beheaded and Aske was taken to the Tower to stand trial for his involvement.

Aske was tried at Westminster and found guilty of treason. As part of his sentencing he was to be taken back to York and chained in prison, languishing for seven months before finally receiving his execution date in July 1537. The reason for the length of time between Aske's trial and sentencing remains a mystery, especially in light of the Lady Mary's extremely expedient proceedings. Lord Rochford's accounts show liveries and accommodations charges made for his presence in York when Aske was hanged. He was most likely present on behalf of Anne, who could not formally be present, but to ensure that the justice she so desired was carried out. Anne's direct involvement in the events of the Pilgrimage and resulting crackdown has not been proven with any substantial evidence, beyond dispatches by scrupulous sources. Nevertheless, Aske was to hang at Clifford's Tower in York and on July 12th, 1537 his sentence was carried out.

The Duke of Suffolk returned home after the suppression of the rebellion to attempt to reconcile his broken relationship with his wife Catherine. Returning home took a significant amount of adjustment for him, as a result he stayed away from court, pleading that he was tending to his affairs. In reality, his conscience was so stricken with his involvement in the slaughter that he could barely function. He slept and ate little, and would stay alone for hours, practicing his archery or riding. It was also rumored he had ulcers that left him in constant pain and that the court was too much an excitement and irritant to him, especially considering his other wounds as well. The Duke was undergoing a significant course of depression. He despised Anne for her involvement in turning Henry's mind to this course, first with the death of the Lady Mary and now this. He never forgave the Queen and sought every opportunity to bring her to ruin. His only real comfort came in being a father to his children, with hope of reconciling with Catherine now that he was home for a while.

At the end of the summer of 1537 Ambassador Chapuys finally received a reply to his letters to his own court, detailing what was taking place in England. When the word spread shortly after the Christmas season about the death of the Lady Mary and the senseless murders of hundreds of northern rebels, it solidified Henry as a major force to be reckoned with. The Catholic people of England, as well, had reacted with genuine shock, disbelief and grief. A significant number of refugees had fled to nearby France and even Spain to escape not only the religious changes afoot in England but the possibility of being killed for those beliefs as well. Since record keeping was in its infancy at this time, there are no clear figures for the number of English refugees, but testifying to the number is that Henry never had another rebellion to contend with during his reign.

Charles V had finally had enough, the senseless murder of his cousin was more than he could bear, and he had finally grown concerned that if Henry had too effectively been able to consolidate his power. If Anne's power had been doubted after the Wolsey affair, it was definitely solidified with Mary's death. She was now untouchable. The Emperor told his Ambassador, through coded messages, that he was preparing for "alternate means of compensation" and would be in touch with Chapuys in due course. The Emperor could not have known how true his words, promising vengeance, would prove. While the people silently suffered the loss of their great, pious, Catholic heroine, the Lady Mary, the English royals too would come to suffer a loss. Anne suffered a near fatal miscarriage in August 1537.

5.4 Personal Trial

In August 1537 the Queen was practicing her dancing with her ladies-in-waiting when she felt intense cramps; suddenly, blood rushed down the front of her gown. Anne collapsed in pain, screaming for her ladies to get help. The guards outside her chambers rushed in as her ladies yelled for a doctor. The King's primary doctor was out at his estates visiting family, but another physician, Dr. William Tate, examined the Queen. Within only a few minutes he had diagnosed Anne as undergoing a severe miscarriage. He ordered her gently moved and that supplies be made ready for instant delivery of a stillborn fetus only a few months old. He also called for any midwife that was at court, and that the King be alerted as to the emergency.

He would try to deliver the child, but the situation was delicate. Anne was losing large amounts of blood very quickly and the doctor feared that her placenta was beginning to come lose. Should that happen, in combination with the blood loss, it was very likely that Anne could die; especially given her previous history with miscarriages.

The child, a girl, was instead delivered smoothly, but was stillborn. From contemporaneous descriptions it appeared to be about 7 or 8 inches long, and quite formed, making it about 24-25 weeks old. After the delivery the doctor delicately placed white linen inside the vaginal canal to slow the blood loss. The Queen was nearing passing out, a dangerous sign as death could be near if she lapsed into a coma. Her ladies kept her talking as the King entered the chambers demanding to know her status.

He went straight to her bedside to hold her hand and keep her talking and focused. Due to the heavy blood loss, she was incoherent and speaking gibberish. The situation was perilous.

Thankfully, the doctor and her ladies-in-waiting Acted quickly and were able to prevent the placenta from coming out faster than it should. They were able to finish the delivery and within the hour the blood flow virtually stopped, thanks to the doctor's quick thinking. Afterwards, Anne successfully answered questions as to her name, marital state, and the names of her children, testing her faculties. When he felt that the bleeding stopped and she was now safe, the doctor ordered a 48 hour watch on the Queen, and prescribed only fruits, no meats, and light breads for her stomach. She had just made it through a harrowing ordeal, and had nearly died.

The King was shown the stillborn girl, which he named Anne, and had the child buried immediately. Queen Anne refused to see the girl. After the experience, the Queen lapsed into a depression, taking months to recover, both emotionally and physically. Dr. Tate told her she stood a good chance of never being able to give birth again, after the damage this birth had caused.

While the Queen stayed in her chambers, the King plunged himself into work, as well as other diversions. This miscarriage severely rocked the marriage, at least for a time. Both parties were unable to come to terms with what had happened and return to life as normal for several weeks. Henry attempted to keep himself busy by having ordered the construction of five new warships and then the refortification of the country's naval defenses, intensifying a worsening iron shortage. He also upped his hunting schedule, spending hours a day in riding away his cares in pursuit of game. Anne meanwhile spent her days locked away between bouts of sobbing and sleeping confusing her days and nights.

He also sought the temporary solace of a common courtesan, named Janelle, who was visiting from the French court. The affair did not last long; Janelle was not the most beautiful woman at court, but apparently she was the most skilled at using certain talents "to alleviate the woes of the powerful," or so it was rumored. She was also allegedly the one time mistress of Charles V, but this rumor could never be proven. The affair with Janelle lasted less than a month.

Henry's relationship with Cromwell, delicate at the best of times, now became tenser, causing Cromwell to rely more on his private friendship with Ambassador Chapuys, from whom Cromwell sought advice on how best to handle the King. Without Anne, his principal advisor, Henry was difficult to deal with and frequently shifted his purpose, often without explanation.

The Queen finally recovered from her physical ailments the last week of October, leaving her chambers to see her husband and apologize for being away from him so long. Naturally, he forgave her. She would leave court the first week of November to see her children and then she would be off to make good on her word to Ms. Astley at the orphanage. Henry had a tiara custom made of amethysts, gold, and Princess cut diamonds, to welcome Anne back upon her recovery. He wanted to show her that she had already done her duty with their son and he still loved her, despite their brief rift. Anne loved the tiara, it becoming her favorite accessory to wear that winter season.

5.5 Lessons at Home, Lessons for All

Her visit with the children went very well; in fact, she brought the Princess with her to the orphanage, encouraging her to play with the other children. This would be the first time the young Elizabeth had been around common children her own age. Elizabeth embraced many of the children quickly, often forgetting her place and asking to play with them, to which the Queen agreed, so long as she did not soil her dress. Anne and her ladies-in-waiting delivered blankets, clothing, and brought their entire royal kitchen staff to serve the orphans meals of thick breads and heavily salted game birds that would easily last a week. Her ladies also bathed them so their hygiene would be appropriate in Anne's presence.

The Queen also made good on her promise to visit the children of St. Mary's to oversee their education. Anne read to the children and taught them biblical stories such as that of the battle of David and Goliath, and—no doubt with deliberate intent—the story of Esther, who was chosen to replace a stubborn Queen and went on to save her people. After the reading lessons were complete, she met privately with the headmistress of the orphanage, Ms. Isabel Astley, as the children continued to play.

Ms. Astley, a former nun who had renounced her habit in order to run the orphanage, was from Paris and taught for nearly fourteen years in the French monasteries. Hers was a sad story. As a youth she had often moved from house to house, attempting to escape an abusive father in an unstable household with a mother powerless to stop him. She had fled her home on foot, at night, with neither food nor other resources, and left her three siblings behind to start a new life for herself. At her most desperate, she had discovered a monastery in the dark of night that came to shape her future.

Anne sympathized with the plight of the headmistress and the two women got on well, perhaps due to the Queen's caring nature and her youthful affections for France. Anne pledged to return every month to visit with the children and ensure their lessons were proceeding as usual. She also pledged a monthly tour for the children to visit the palace to play with Elizabeth. This gesture alone, for a Princess to play with such lowly commoners, was quite unusual, and when she told Henry he immediately shut her down, railing at her about her place; the two did not speak for several days. It was quite a row. Anne attempted to stand her ground that they were children and should be allowed to play. As far as Henry was concerned, he was busy trying to reinforce Elizabeth's legitimacy throughout Europe, and here Anne was, sullying her image by having her the playmate of the commons, a rumor certain to delight the Emperor and the Pope regarding her bastard status.

Anne saw the situation very differently. While she had not been raised a royal, her family had been one of status and she fondly recalled playing with local children without distinction. She did not wish to impose restrictions on her own children, believing it important to her daughter's development to be around children her own age; being that there were so few other children at court, Anne thought the orphanage plan could prove an excellent outlet for the Princess to be around her peers and grow socially and emotionally. Additionally, the story of the headmistress's own turbulent childhood and—literal—salvation by the church and proper education, sparked in Anne ideas of a broader effort that might use the new Church of England or strengthened state to bring greater knowledge to the people.

While designed with the best of intentions, this scheme to mingle the royal heirs with the lower classes certainly proved her critics right in one respect. Anne's greatest difficulties as Queen stemmed from her unwillingness to recognize and respect differences in social station—having been quite the social climber, herself—putting herself at odds with entrenched power structures. Her vastly different life experiences led her to view things extremely practically, at the expense of respecting customs and traditions upon which others depended. Meanwhile, her King husband's role had always been tied to protecting these same institutions by fulfilling his duty to preserve the state and the existing social order. His desire to preserve his own supremacy allowed him to overturn the existing religious order in the name of his higher goal, but to throw out all tradition and overturn the feudal system itself, which relied upon strict class distinctions, was quite beyond him.

To come to a compromise with his wife Henry ordered that more of the courtiers' children brought to court so that Elizabeth, and eventually the still infant Prince, could bond with fellow children as playmates. Anne, however, remained stubbornly committed to her cause, and pressed for her children to grow up better knowing the people they would someday rule by learning, first, as children. Ultimately, Anne would win the day, but the orphan children Elizabeth was allowed to directly interact with were hand chosen by Henry, and the visits were allowed only in a private room, with only Anne and her Lady Governess in attendance, to reduce the likelihood of a scandal.

Anne's plan for the betterment of her own children, now executed, she refocused her thoughts on improving the education of the masses as well. Archbishop Cranmer, Tyndale, Henry Clifford the 2nd Earl of Cumberland, and Anne were all diligently working towards outlining a plan for the spread of educational reforms. The Earl was a trusted friend of Cranmer and an avid reformer, one of the first to embrace its principles. The first groups to be re-educated would be the children of the Kingdom, as these subjects had the least to un-learn (chiefly about the need to obey the Church of Rome) and thus who would be most easily taught. So soon after the recent calls for rebellion and revolution, however, this effort would require some acceptance and buy-in from the people. As popularizing an education program would take time, at Anne's insistence, the orphans at St. Mary's were used first as subjects upon whom to design their program. If successful, they could then alter their lesson planning for the nobility, the gentry and finally the commons.

Cranmer employed four of his clerks out of the basement at Westminster, John Elthsman, Leonard Davoy, Richard Mandigle and William Taylor, to begin reviewing all the technical, administrative and operational logistics involved in determining the costs involved to develop course content, textbooks, to select instructors, and to pick venues for instruction. Cranmer would focus on ensuring that content met the religious criteria outlined previously in the Ten Articles while Tyndale worked on developing standardized lesson books—written in English—that would be the most useful for both illiterate adults and for children.

It might seem surprising to learn that Cromwell had not been included in these sessions, but Anne's official reasoning was that the minister was far too pre-occupied with his affairs running the country and he would be well informed in due course. The truth of the matter was that, after their falling out, she no longer trusted his counsel and feared that he would get to the King and possibly sabotage her plans before she could get to Henry and plead her case.

The nobles would prove to be the most difficult group to convince. Their entire power base relied on the ignorance of the commons and Anne feared that they would think her plan threatening to their entire way of life. Lord Rochford would keep his spies on the lookout for any mention of uprising so he might deal with each member of the court sufficiently. Bribes would be enough to ensure the temporary quiet support of most of them, so he secured a sufficient portion of his own fortune to be made available for such a purpose. He also suggested that the nobles' children be the first to receive such education publicly, to win over the mothers of the upper classes, who heavily relied on their sons' titles to ensure their own status.

Anne and Lord Rochford worked behind the scenes preparing the political maneuvering that would be essential to ensuring the success of their plan. Several drafts of their proposals to Parliament and the King were drawn up, two of which still survive. Meanwhile, Anne would advocate for the scheme directly to Henry, in private. Henry overall was receptive to the idea, but he too shared the nobles' sense of concern that so instructing all children, especially the commons, would put at risk the current separation of classes. Anne knew how to bring lessons from home to the aid of supporting lessons for the people. She invited the children from the orphanage to serve as test subjects, and ask Henry to watch their reactions to the material and their eagerness to learn.

Children had always been a soft spot for the King and she knew how to play to his affections. She managed to convince him to hold the trial lesson for the orphan children at court, so long as the exhibition met his condition of privacy away from gossiping courtiers. Anne agreed and sent urgent dispatches out to Ms. Astley for the children to come to court the following week to begin their lessons. Her dispatch was delivered by two of her own ladies-in-waiting, along with a purse to pay for suitable clothing for the children to wear before the presence of the King. The ladies would also bathe them, fix their hair, and instruct them on their manners before they would be allowed in the royal presence.

Anne expressly commanded that the children were to arrive at the back palace gate, where the food and supplies were brought in, under cover of darkness. This would reduce the likelihood of gossipmongers among the courtiers noting the new arrivals. Should the nobles hear that the education plan that their own children were to undergo was designed using mere commoners, there would be an uproar and Anne's entire plan could be placed in jeopardy. Archbishop Cranmer disguised his true purpose by preparing to claim that any orphan children at court were being hosted for charitable purposes, a plausible enough excuse given the King's well known sentimental reaction to plays by such groups at events like Christmastide.

The first lesson was set to begin December 3rd, 1537, and Anne and her father met privately several times before that day to begin reviewing how they could use the program to better her people, and further inoculate themselves and their heirs against future enemies. Anne was excited to have the first group of children taught her version of Reformation principles. A dry run of the course was completed with Tyndale, Clifford, and Cranmer one final time before the lesson commenced. This lesson would consist of how to read and pronounce the letters of the English alphabet. The second lesson the following week, with practice in between, would consist of how to write one's name. The third through sixth weeks, after the children had mastered their own names and the basics of the alphabet, would simply teach the principles of the Ten Articles and why their King was appointed by God to be both head of the state and of their Church. At Cranmer's insistence, each lesson would end with an open forum for the children to ask questions, to ensure they all understood the material. The instructors also offered to make themselves available for private tutoring for those who needed additional training.

As they were not adults and did not understand the controversial, dangerous times they lived in, the children were even afforded more of a freedom to question and speak than their elders might have enjoyed, although they were of course strictly told to refrain from using foul language in front of their majesties. Since they were children, toys and other forms of propaganda were used to illustrate what was right and wrong. They would be allowed to play with the toys, touch the relics and other objects. All parties reviewed the lesson plan one last time and all were prepared for a moderately successful venture for the initial course. This set of orphans ranged in ages from four to fourteen, so they would have to try to find a delicate balance between how much to tell and when to hold back. Tyndale would teach this lesson with their majesties and Cranmer observing the children and his performance.

The Princess Elizabeth, per Henry's express command, would not be attending this trial session, and depending on how he viewed it, he would then decide if she would be allowed to attend from that point on. To keep her from getting upset by seeing the children without being allowed to meet with them it was thought best to send her back to Hatfield with her Governess until the lessons had been concluded; in the meantime, she would continue her own tutoring with some of the brightest scholars of the day.

True to form, the astute and precise Ms. Astley brought the orphans in strict accordance with the Queen's orders and they were lodged in additional servants' quarters, away from the nobility. The instructors and their majesties would meet them later in the day, after they had sufficient time to be prepared by the Queen's ladies-in-waiting. Just in case there should be any outward opposition, Lord Rochford sought to eliminate it before it could cause true damage.

The initial lesson went off without a hitch. After getting over some nervousness at being in the presence of their King and Queen, the children quickly became excited by their lessons, particularly so when it came to learning how to use the letters to make their own names. Naturally, because they are children, at times they proved difficult for their tutor to corral and focus them back to their lessons. At one point Henry reached over to hold his wife's hand as he looked on in sheer amazement, watching these common orphans embrace learning. Towards the end of the lesson their majesties played games and even took turns reading to the children and answering their questions. Overall it was a complete success. Henry eagerly agreed to let Anne have free reign over the educational plan. From that point onward she took full control.

5.6 Ensuring Support for Change

Various notes from the Boleyn's private meetings on the education plan, and how they sought to implement it, still survive. The majority of these documents came from Lord Rochford's estate and contained key background information on each Member of Parliament and all of the courtiers. They also outlined the entire strategy on how to overcome opposition to Anne's agenda. Because the lessons were held in the servant area, where nobles rarely went, it was hoped that the lessons had little chance of being discovered. Still, it was better to be prepared than not.

The main surviving volume is a secret journal of each courtier's private activities. Did the subject keep his tithes to the church, pay his taxes on time, was he a gambler, a drunkard, did he frequent whore houses or have secret bastard children? Was the subject committing fraud of office, or was he a suspected papist, and could it be proven in court? Most of all, even though all had had to swear the oaths of Supremacy and Succession, was the subject thought sincerely loyal to Queen Anne and the new Prince, or was the subject deserving of further investigation for possible treason? These records were meticulously kept, and contained every lurid detail—detailed back several years—about every member of the court and Parliament, including even the Star Chamber jurists, the groomsmen and ladies-in-waiting to their majesties, the Tower Constable, Members of Parliament, local sheriffs and mayors and the Yeoman Guards.

While those who gathered this intelligence have never been confirmed, it is highly probable that Viscount Rochford did much himself, with the aid of Sir William Bryan, who was known for conducting such operations for Rochford. Bryan's involvement in the plot is significant. His loyalties had previously lain with the Seymour family, perhaps earning his reputation for playing both sides of the political aisle to suit the current winds. Regardless, he diligently performed espionage and regularly met with Lord Rochford. As an evident reward of his services, Rochford generously granted him a salary of 1,000 pounds a year, recorded only as *"for his counsel."*

Gradually the information started leaking out only when it suited the Boleyn's purposes. A clear example of how this trove of information was put to use took place early in the effort to find support and funding for the reform effort. In February 1538, the Privy Council met to discuss imposing new beard taxes on barbers, for use by the crown in paying for the upkeep of shop supplies at a discount. The barber merchants would obtain their materials, chairs, razors, semi-clean water, lotions, herbs and oils at a generously discounted rate and in turn would voluntarily submit over 60% of their profits back to the crown. This arrangement, primarily with the barbers in London, managed to grant the exchequer a continuous, albeit small, source of revenue. With the increase in court spending by Henry and Anne, not to mention Henry's various military expenditures, the crown's coffers were running dangerously low. Anne desperately counted on additional resources being available to spread her reforms of the English Bible and education plan.

During the Privy Council session, Henry Grey, 3rd Marquis of Dorset rose to vigorously oppose the tax resolution, claiming that this would be more than a modest inconvenience and would jeopardize the provision of vital services to the community; he called it deplorable and demanded the resolution be dismissed. It was certainly true that barbers in Tudor society played a critical role, they not only cut hair but also performed basic medical care and even some surgeries, but it would have been a good exercise of Lord Rochford's "Black Dossier" to use the information to deflect the Marquis from his opposition.

Henry Grey had received his title upon the death of his father, Thomas, in 1530. He held a close friendship with the King and the Duke of Suffolk and as a result was granted permission to marry Lady Frances Brandon, the daughter of the King's late sister Mary Tudor and Charles Brandon, the Duke of Suffolk. Their union produced three daughters, the Lady Jane Grey, Lady Catherine Grey and Lady Mary Grey. During his time at court he had managed to make the most of his surroundings and quickly became known for his good fortune at card playing, his love of the minstrels, and his charm and ability to win and retain useful friendships. Grey was knighted by Henry as a member of the Order of Bath, a very prestigious order of chivalry, and one of the highest honors a courtier could hope to achieve.

Nevertheless, Grey also had a knack for drinking and frequenting houses of ill repute. Contemporaries would remark that he had a violent streak with his wife and struck her about the head quite often. Should there have been any visible truth to such speculation; the Duke of Suffolk, his father-in-law, would have dealt with Grey accordingly at the time. Most likely, these rumors were falsehoods spread by enemies Grey had made at the gambling tables. Rochford had managed to record an extensive tally of Grey's gambling debts to a local merchant named Charles Shrewsbury, an up and coming but still low level courtier who custom made cod pieces for the King.

On one such evening in April 1536, Grey had incurred a debt of nearly 25,000 pounds and had ever since been unable to pay it. Shrewsbury, drunk himself, attacked Grey with a sword leaving a deep mark on Grey's left forearm before being pulled away by other gamblers. Shrewsbury never forgot or forgave the debt and would blackmail Grey for favors at court in exchange for his silence. This may have been about the time that Shrewsbury became the King's private tailor, for that most delicate accessory.

Although Shrewsbury's tailor shop was known for catering to noble and royal clients, no specific mention of the merchant had been made until early 1537 in Henry's privy expenses, a recording of a New Year's gift, meaning that Shrewsbury would have been in attendance at Christmastide that year. Grey's debt would have been a most convenient one for Shrewsbury to have obtained.

At the conclusion of that day's session, Lord Rochford pulled Grey aside and spoke to him privately. The next day, Grey recanted his prior objections to the barber tax and vehemently reversed his course, not only rising in favor of the tax, but of increasing it further. When Cromwell questioned Grey's sudden change of mind, he modestly declared he had been persuaded of the barbers' debauchery and had come to realize the true nature of these beasts' depravity. He quietly sat for the remainder of that session, very out of character for such a robust, boisterous man. However it was that Rochford had managed to persuade Grey, he would be the first of many such opponents to step aside.

Another well respected member of the nobility, Henry Bourchier, 2nd Earl of Essex, had bypassed Cromwell and appealed to the King—vaguely—for permission to remove peasants from his lands in the manner he saw most fit. Those reading between the lines could understand that he sought to use severe and brutal force. Otherwise, he had no need to seek royal approval; however, if word was received back to the King about the tactics he wanted to use to remove them, he might risk losing his own head. Only the King could grant permission for such methods. Like most of the nobility, Bourchier hated Cromwell and avoided dealing with "the despised little clerk." The King denied his request and told Cromwell to write back to the Earl sympathizing with his plight but making it clear that no brutal force was to be exercised. The Earl's request had been denied. Bothersome peasants were a common occurrence at court; Henry could not see a reason why their deaths should be had over such minor inconveniences. Cromwell did as the King commanded, but would not forget the slight that the Earl had done him. He brought the matter to Lord Rochford and wanted to know what information, if any, his agents had been able to uncover about the Earl's activities.

The Earl was on the surface a clean man. The faction could find no evidence of treachery; he had taken the oath without objection and had always paid his taxes on time. Further, he sent beautiful gifts to the King on both his marriage to Anne and at each of the royal children's births. The only scandal that had ever touched him was being a judge at the former 3rd Duke of Buckingham's trial for treason back in 1521. At the time, it was rumored that he secretly favored the Duke's cause and that he privately grieved at Buckingham's death, but outwardly he passed a verdict of guilty. The rumors were started by jealous courtiers with nothing to corroborate them, but Rochford was not satisfied. A cynical view to be certain, but he could not believe that the Earl had led such a clean life and made it his personal mission to ferret out anything unscrupulous in his affairs. The Earl had managed to slip by Rochford's agents because of how outwardly clean he appeared to be, but mindful of the possible advantage in winning some gratitude from Cromwell, he sent George to Essex to find out more about the Earl. George was to visit local merchants, the clergy, close friends and associates of the Earl, and find out any information he could.

Anne was also hiring and engaging her own agents where possible. She had received numerous requests to fill two new vacancies in her household as ladies-in-waiting and she was diligently going through each of the applications to uncover the potential candidates' loyalty and appropriateness. One such lady was Lady Audrey de Vere, daughter of John de Vere, the Earl of Oxford. The Queen knew her well. She was a beautiful sixteen-year-old girl with an outgoing personality and a charming disposition. She was incredibly devout in her studies and known for her beautiful dancing and singing. She was one of the most sought after ladies in the land and several offers of pre-contract for her hand had been presented to the King. Anne wanted such a lady in her inner circle and sent for her immediately. Anne could certainly exploit the talents and connections of such an in-demand lady.

The last week of February 1538, Tyndale was ready to present his translation plans to the Queen and the Archbishop. This massive work was to be executed in three parts. First, not only Bibles but all approved religious and reformist secular works for distribution would need to be translated and for a time be made available to the public at the expense of the crown. This would be done with paid tutors available to teach people how to read and interpret the reformist documents. If adults were to understand it, she understood that they needed to be given the tools to do so and most of the English commons could barely read or write their own name, much less understand complicated religious texts. The translation work in itself would take several months, possibly close to a year.

Secondly, Tyndale recommended giving the people a national Holy Day in exchange for their participation at court, where they would be invited in heavily guarded sessions for the Queen to personally read highlighted scripture, and hear a sermon and receive a blessing by the Archbishop. It is on this day that the people would receive their free English Bible and associated texts, in addition to wine, food, and any other items to bring them closer to the crown. Tyndale fully admitted this objective would be the most difficult upon which to gain approval, but that it was the most critical to ensure that all of their efforts could succeed; they needed to make it in the people's benefit to embrace Reformation, and—so soon after an attempted rebellion—not be seen to be imposing the reforms solely through fear.

Finally, Tyndale thought the people should be permitted regular, ongoing dialogue with the Archbishop and the Queen, to reinforce reformist principles. One day of festivities would not be enough, there would need to be continuous cultural outreach by the heads of state, and the tutoring lessons would have to continue for several years at the expense of the crown. Tyndale understood the gravity of what he was suggesting, but he was very persuasive and confident in his approach.

Anne excitedly embraced his plan but expressed reservations about getting Henry to agree. The Archbishop was outwardly nervous and felt the plan might be perceived by both the King and the people as too Lutheran in its elements, causing the opposite of what they had intended. He warned that pushing the people beyond what they were ready to accept could lead them to repeat the series of uprisings and hostilities that the Pilgrimage had brought only a year earlier. He also feared, knowing Henry's religious scruples all too well, that his Majesty would never allow these reforms to extend this far. For the King's entire outward embrace of Reformation, he privately reserved some Catholic sentiments and

Cranmer understood that. Paying little heed to the Archbishop's warning, Anne thanked Tyndale for his and Cranmer's continued works and vowed to persuade the King to her cause. The timing of her message could not have been more critical.

Henry had spent most of the spring hunting with his nobles. The Privy Council had been busy preparing an increase in ale taxes, a bill that would certainly not be popular. Diplomatic affairs had been uneventful; the latest news was word of a wedding in the Netherlands that did not attract much attention. Charles V continued his campaign against the Ottoman Empire, making significant advances against the enemy. Chapuys received a request from his master to return home immediately, pending further developments.

The Ambassador formally requested to take leave of England to attend to his affairs and promised his replacement once his master had chosen a suitable successor. The request was made for only three months, just enough time not to arouse suspicion at court and to truly attend to personal business at home. Seeing no impediment, the King temporarily gave him leave to leave, making great cheer with the Ambassador before he left. Before leaving for home, he and Cromwell dined at the minister's estate.

As it stood England had only enough supplies to withstand maybe one or two solid attacks from enemy forces, whether in Scotland or from the Continent. Reinforcements, if they were available, could take weeks to reach certain parts of the country and would be unarmed. A shortage of iron had not just affected Spain but England, and while new mines were being uncovered, it took significant time to conquer logistical challenges. The majority of the weapons confiscated from the Pilgrimage were melted down and made into other goods without foresight. Continuing food shortages also heightened anxiety about war. Although domestic policy concerns were the focus of the English Court, to quell any potential flare up of public opinion leading to rebellion, these concerns had to be carefully cultivated to ensure that threats from abroad did not also rear their heads. Little did Henry know how great a threat was, indeed, looming.

Figure 1: Anne Boleyn, 1534

Figure 2: Anne Boleyn Wax Figure
Copyright Lara E. Eakins, www.tudorhistory.org

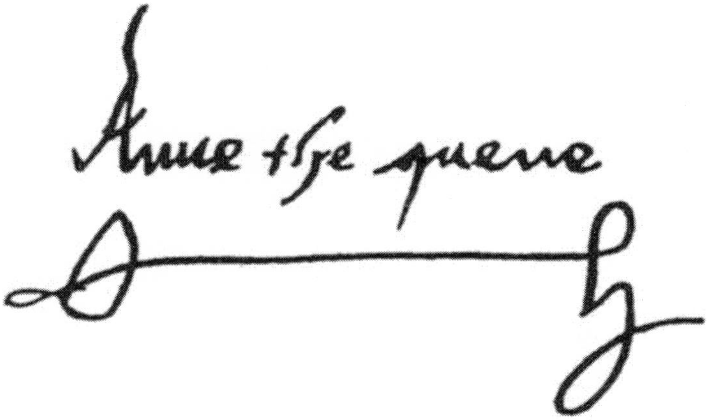

Anne the quene

Figure 3: Anne Boleyn's Signature
Copyright Lara E. Eakins, tudorhistory.org

Figure 4: Anne Boleyn Falcon Badge Crest.
Copyright Lara E. Eakins, tudorhistory.org

Figure 5: Henry VIII, Portrait from the 1520's

Figure 6: Westminster Abbey

Figure 7: Tower of London. Copyright Dave Hogue, 2009

Figure 8: Hampton Court Palace, Main Entrance Exterior

Figure 9: Thomas Cromwell,
Lord Privy Seal and Earl of Essex.
Painted by Hans Holbein the Younger.
Copyright The Frick Collection

Figure 10: Drawing of Anne Boleyn, 1520's

Chapter 6

The Pope Strikes Back

The Pope who would most seriously challenge the revolution Henry and Anne would institute in England would begin as a favored member of the Italian gentry. Alessandro Farnese was born in 1468 to one of Italy's wealthiest families in Latium. On his mother's side he was distantly related to a previous pontiff, His Holiness Pope Boniface VIII. The Farnese family made connections with senior nobles at the court of Lorenzo de'Medici. As a result of these connections, he studied at the University of Pisa under the generous support of the elite Medici banking family.

It was here that he shared the study of humanist principles with Sir Thomas More and Cardinal Wolsey. Humanism studied the variety and depth of ethical theory, with its principal application in scientific reason, logic, and rejecting actions based on the belief of a deity. They believed that actions should be based on rational logic, placing faith in their understanding of the world in its natural state, rather than basing conduct on the presumed understanding of the will of a supreme being. The irony is that so many brilliant scholars during the Renaissance period studied this system, yet ended up devoted Catholics, whose agenda often worked against the very humanist principles they studied. His diligence in papal affairs was noticed and in 1491 he was ordained as a Cardinal Deacon of Santi Cosma e Damiano by Pope Alexander VI. He remained in the church until several pontiff's later. Pope Clement VII promoted and ordained him as the Cardinal Bishop of Ostia and as Dean of the College of Cardinals.

In 1534, after Clement's death, the curia elected Alessandro Farnese pope by universal vote; he chose the name Pope Paul III. This Pope would provide the first serious challenge to reformers since the movement began. Pope Paul III began his reign less than a year after Henry's marriage to Anne. The Pope had railed against Henry's reformation since the beginning. It was no great secret he harbored deep inner resentment towards the Queen and publicly blamed her for all of England's problems.

One of the main criticisms of the Catholic Church by reformers had been the financial corruption within its own clergy. This was, surprisingly, one area that the Pope agreed on and diligently sought to correct. After the full scope of England's closure of the religious houses became apparent in 1536, Paul III invited eight papal legates to form the *Consilium de Emendanda Ecclesia* (Project for the Reform of the Church). This commission was set up to identify any truth to accusations of financial mismanagement. Seven of the delegates were Italian Cardinals handpicked by Paul himself. The eighth member was an Englishman, the scholar Reginald Pole, who had fled England at the start of the Reformation. To Paul's credit, its formation was the first substantive step in reforming the church.

Pole was the King's cousin, through the Plantagent side, and enjoyed wide influence with him when they were younger, until Henry split with the church. Henry personally paid for Pole's education and was highly insulted when Pole chose his loyalty to Rome over that of the King. It enraged him even further when Pole publicly denounced both the Act of Supremacy and the Act of Succession from 1534. He railed against both of these religious policies, inflaming Catholics across the land. He stood as a rare beacon of hope for the Catholic faithful; they looked to Pole as an Activist to restore England to its true faith. Given his rare connection to the King, his message was not only inspirational but drew an audience that irritated Henry. When the King had been told of Pole's insolence, he immediately sent for his arrest, but Pole also had valuable court connections and was given advanced warning to leave England immediately or risk losing his head.

Pole left in the middle of the night using friends to escape to various parts of Europe. When Henry found out that Pole had escaped and, worse, that the royal guards were unable to locate him, the King put a bounty on

Pole's head; upon an eventual capture, Pole would be put to death under the Treasons Act of 1535. For a period of time Sir Francis Bryan, another of the King's cousins who was known for his mercenary tactics, traced Pole all over Europe in an attempt to capture him and bring him back home. He was never caught. While on the run Pole found sanctuary through an extensive network of Catholic sympathizers throughout Europe.

Paul III declared him a true Prince of the church, making him a Cardinal, understanding the potential benefits Pole could bring to the church. The Pope saw Pole as a possible mediator between the church and the people of England, possibly even as a mediator to Henry, once the King's anger had subsided. The Pope disregarded Pole's fugitive status and instead encouraged him to continue his cause. Cromwell's agents were informed of Pole's involvement with the Vatican, yet English agents were not able to successfully apprehend him. Cromwell refrained as much as possible from detailing Pole's activity to the King, knowing it would well anger him.

Official findings of the papal commission were concluded in mid-1537 and presented to Paul III in the summer of that year. The results of the finding were not surprising. The church had squandered vast sums of money on building projects, namely restoration. The tithings of Europe and indulgence fees brought in most of the millions sitting on the books. The rest of the money came from wealthy benefactors of the church, with every coin desperately needed to avoid deficit and subsequent reductions of staff. Only a small amount of revenue came from vestments, licenses, and charges for blessings.

The church had been through financial hardships before, but the sudden loss of English revenue hit the Vatican hard. The church quickly found itself in deficit by the equivalent of over 450,000 pounds in current prices. For obvious reasons, the church needed to conceal the findings of this project, should it be released it would only fuel anti-Catholic resentment and validate the heretics' complaints. At the same time, the Pope needed an accurate representation of where his finances stood if he was going to make any genuine improvements. There were those in the curia who were against reforms of any kind and criticized Paul, saying that he was giving into the reformer's rhetoric by checking their books. Paul disregarded his own Cardinals' judgment and continued with the inquiry. Based on the findings, the Pope would order drastic changes to how income was spent including, if necessary, reducing palace renovations and the purchase of the massively expensive works of art and sculpture that the Vatican had became known for.

Although the work was ordered secret, a servant in the house of the clerk of Cardinal Cortese, one of the original commission members, leaked the document. It was rumored that Cortese himself had intentionally released the document, but an investigation would ultimately deem that rumor false. Cortese had strong inner convictions against the financial misbehavior of his Church, viewing it as the singular reason for the punishment of the reformation. His staunch views led to what amounted to administrative discipline for such carelessness with church property, but he retained his Cardinalship at the insistence of Paul III. Once the findings were made public later that year, Martin Luther publicly admonished them and used the results as vindication to his followers. Other reformers were conflicted about the findings and some even alleged conspiracy theories that this was nothing short of a stunt to entice followers that the church had changed. None of that proved to be accurate.

Unlike his predecessor, this Pope well understood that Henry would not be returning to the Catholic faith. Instead of extending the proverbial olive branch to Henry, the Pope would be confrontational with England. He was outraged at the harsh tactics the English monarchy had used in closing the monasteries, along with the executions of several high profile members of the Catholic faithful. Upon hearing of the dissolution of Bourne Abbey the previous year, and how the Priests there were mysteriously killed during the closing, Paul decided to Act. As a Cardinal he had visited Bourne Abbey and had retained a close bond with its staff. The reckless murder of a close associate struck him hard. On the heels of the financial report disclosure, Paul formed an advisory board, in the summer of 1537, to hear the case of presenting Henry with a Papal Bull of Excommunication.

One of Paul's predecessors early in the 1520s had threatened to do the exAct same; however that threat was never carried out. This Pope did not intend to be so lenient about carrying out a stated threat. Typically, this was a power that the Pope needed no support to exercise; however, given the prominence of the subject being so threatened, he wanted the personal satisfaction of the curia's full backing. Further, he organized with church leaders all across Europe, canvassing their support and ideas. Naturally, he excluded the Archbishop of Canterbury from the meeting, he only wanted the English representative to know in due time, once the final decision had been made. He intentionally also sent Archbishop Cranmer notice of the meeting, certain this would make it back to the King.

When Pole arrived at the Vatican he hit it off with his pontiff immediately. For months he had proved a valuable resource, helping Paul map the strategy of getting the English Catholics back. He possessed unique and intimate knowledge of the details of English facilities and the King's own state of mind, which put him in a rare position of favor with Paul III. By having an in-depth knowledge of the King he was able to clarify existing religious policy, speculate on the direction the King intended to go, and predict how much worse it might possibly become.

The situation had become precarious. The previous winter Henry VIII had maliciously executed hundreds for the rebellion, the Queen had birthed a bastard and the Lady Mary had been killed. The Pope also recognized the precarious financial position his Church was now in and needed to win back the support—financial and otherwise—of the English Catholics. Politically, England's withdrawal from the Church set a dangerous precedent for other nations to follow.

Meanwhile, Pole's favor by the Pope brought this exiled English cleric many opportunities to attend closed door sessions as a special guest of the curia, and also to be formally recognized by the Vatican as a Cardinal and also to have him blessed, the first step towards being a professed a Saint. This final step would never happen, but Paul III wanted to repay Pole's knowledge and dedication to the cause by whatever means possible; even if the other Cardinals could not agree. Instead of placating Henry, in September, Paul finished drafting the Papal Bull of Excommunication, with Cardinal Pole's assistance. They worked late into the evening, until the sun finally rose one day upon a completed document; they wanted to ensure that everything was proper in this most momentous of edicts.

6.1 The Delivery

At the Vatican, the Pope convened a series of council meetings in October 1537 with the Kings of France, Spain, rulers of Italian territories and Portugal convened for a conference to last the autumn in reviewing the state of Catholic affairs in Europe. The Pope acknowledged the official release of the Project Report findings earlier that year and vowed that the church leaders would make every effort to bring followers back to Christ, both spiritually and financially. The speech was intended to thoroughly convince European leaders of the church's dedication to positive reforms while, maintaining original Catholic doctrine, including the supremacy of the Vicar of the throne of St. Peter.

Practical matters were also discussed such as fees, papal application of canon law, exploration of scripture, and disbursement of what today would be called humanitarian aid, nationally organized aid to the poor. Paul set a quota system where each country was responsible for sending 1,000 pounds of donated clothing and non-perishable food items, such as cooking spices, salt, and elixirs for medication. Each country would be responsible for donating their share at least once a year to the Vatican, in exchange for lowered vestment fees, increased royal authority in spiritual matters, and personal audiences with the Pontiff.

The conference was judged a success and won massive approval by the people of Europe; treaties agreeing to the arrangements were drafted by the New Year and signed without complaint. After the final meeting, a lavish feast was held in the Pope's honor, where compliments on each of the European Kings flowed around the table, while all were cautious not to bring up politically sensitive topics such as the continuing French occupation of Milan, Italy. For at least one day, all countries invited were at peace; plotting and efforts at political sabotage would wait until the evening.

Later that night, the Pope reached out to Charles V's delegation and requested a private audience. The Pontiff and Holy Roman Emperor would be the sole attendees in the Pope's private bed chamber, a space few would ever be invited to, a real honor for Charles. He humbly accepted the Pope's invitation, but was just as curious as his delegation as to the reason for the unusual invitation. When they met, Paul thanked Charles for all his good deeds and for remaining a true and loyal subject of the Catholic faith. He praised him for being more than deserving of the title Holy Roman Emperor, and said that all of the Kings of Europe should reflect upon his deeds and emulate them in their own lands.

They discussed exploration, how the Emperor was continuing to fight heresy in his own kingdom, the War with the Ottoman Empire, and finally, the Spaniard's relationship with England. Charles explained that diplomacy with England had been strained for many years, mainly due to the current "Lady," clearly meaning Queen Anne. Charles insinuated that Henry had been one of the most difficult leaders to engage with because his policies on government "often came from desire in his loins." Charles blamed the radical religious policies on Archbishop Cranmer and Queen Anne, a regret that the Pope acknowledged.

Regardless, Paul corrected Charles, saying that the real power lay still with Henry and that if he should so choose to let his wife and a renegade cleric run his territory, then he was no more a King than a commoner; Charles could not help but agree. To the Pope, Henry's appointment as King was not divinely ordered, it could not be. No real earthly King could be so heretical and unforgiving of heresy in his own kingdom as Henry VIII had been in his. At every turn, whenever the Pope's predecessor's had attempted peaceful reconciliation, Henry's delegation had refused. They agreed that the only way to deal with what they both perceived as a common bully was to fight fire with fire (indeed, thought the Pope, knowing of his recently drafted Bull of Excommunication, with hellfire.)

Charles shared with Paul that his primary English Ambassador, Chapuys, had been encouraging him to invade England for quite some time, sending reports back of the high rate of fear, murder and disturbance in the realm. Chapuys had also made an exclusive friendship with the King's principal minister, Cromwell, and that this potential confidante was privy to state secrets that would be of great value, although he could not write them in his dispatches for fear of interception. These reports both troubled his conscience and alarmed him; the Emperor begged His Holiness for guidance on what to do. Despite the Emperor's great power and growing wealth from the New World, he had not the resources to invade England, at least not with his own troops spread so thin fighting the Ottoman Empire and in Italy and Africa.

Charles confessed privately that he barely had enough troops to defend Spain and should a large, more prepared, less distracted country (namely, France) invade, his own realm might be found without sufficient reinforcements and doomed. The Pope reassured the monarch, noting that resources for Henry's own armies, currently yet preoccupied by suppressing possible rebellions, were also being strained, and with good reason, as an iron shortage of several years in England had hit Henry's own forces hard. Henry's best defense had been to deploy the sword, but it was only at great cost that Henry could get his hands on the metal the King needed to equip his men. The Pope assured his most powerful, albeit overstretched, ally Charles, that their great adversary was deeply concerned about the future of his own realm, and that Henry doubtless had little time to think of foreign threats.

They then discussed Ambassador Chapuys' reports on the senseless killing of the Lady Mary, Charles's own cousin. The King confessed to the Pope that this single Act of murder, alone, led him to debate invasion, and brought forth in him a deep, profound hatred of his brother King. Paul urged to him to have faith and use caution. While stoking the fires of anger in Charles, the Pope maintained his aura of seeking only peace by continuing to advise that these were delicate times, and neither of the Catholic leaders should Act in haste, lest it be to their detriment, and that of their Holy Church. The Pope then asked Charles to join him in a prayer for the Lady Mary's soul, bringing the Emperor to tears with both gratitude toward the Pontiff, and fury toward Henry and Anne.

The Pope then asked Charles, if his conscience so required of him and if it were possible, would he have his troops and supplies on hand to begin making initial preparations towards an invasion of England, merely to inform himself of the possibility of such an undertaking? Charles shocked at the Pope's request, readily admitted that his troop supplies were low, at best, after his war with the Ottoman's and that he had maybe 40,000 men on hand to defend Spain. Most of those potential soldiers were the backbone of his labor force and he feared that if they too left their homes to fight England, the country would be left in famine, not to mention vulnerable to other invaders (again, especially France). He admitted that many of even these troops had died in the field from the flux (dysentery) due to poor sanitation and a lack of skilled surgeons.

The people of Spain had made daily pleas to their King, begging for sustenance, and he knew not what to tell them. Due to low rains that season food was scarce. He barely had enough to feed his own troops and, admittedly, he was hoarding for them what few supplies he did have, to expand his empire for Christendom. It was only a generation since his predecessors Ferdinand and Isabella had expelled the Muslim invaders and unified the country and he had spread his only just growing resources too thin in too rapid an expansion. His people were hurting and all he could do was to beg God's forgiveness for their sins and possibly increase taxes, never a popular option. His weapons depots had recently run into a shortage of iron of their own and he had no other means to procure of any of the simple, but increasingly vital, metal.

Charles thought hard and told his Pope that any plans to invade England would be a mistake. While England was an island nation, with resource problems of its own, Henry had done a thorough job of starting to build up a substantial navy defense and would see Spanish forces coming miles away, putting Charles at an immediate disadvantage. Further, he did not want to deal with the chaos that England was going through. Charles was interested in conquering the vast amounts of territories that the Ottoman Empire could offer him, along with their spices, medicinal trades, and fabrics. He was also exploring new territories and treasures that lay in Mexico and the Americas and wished to see those endeavors through, he fully expressed how much was on his plate. England had nothing but ancient practices and a harsh people with a rough tongue; he was already frustrated to the point of exhaustion with ruling the Germanic peoples in the territories of the Holy Roman Empire.

Paul listened closely to his ally's troubles before offering a resolution. His intelligence had already told him in advance of Charles' military troubles, but he had wanted to hear this assessment directly from the Spaniard, to judge both the King's honesty and the truth of the information he had obtained. He then decided to complete his play by removing Charles' constraints and reinforcing the wary King's resolve.

The Pope extended his hand for Charles to kiss, and comforted the Emperor for the pain his conscience must have been afflicting him with for being so eager to do right by God, but being so plagued with doubts as to his capacity to avenge his cousin and free their fellow Catholics from the heretics who would lead their brethren away from the true Church. Upon seeing Charles' shame and remorse, and further tears at the pronouncement, he then went the extra, required step.

The Pope's armies had done well in surrounding themselves with some of the strongest allies in all of Italy, making marital alliances with top Italian Houses that carried with them the military prowess, numbers, and resources needed to help Charles in his Ottoman and English wars. The Pope offered Charles food, clothing, stores of weapons, ships, the Pope's own military advisors, and any other materials Charles would need to set free the peoples of England—as a gift to a true servant of God.

Stunned by the generosity of His Holiness, Charles humbly thanked him and vowed he would take the matter under advisement, after hearing from God. *"Ah my son,"* said the Pope, *"God has already spoken, and he orders you to invade. He also says you are to give Henry, this."* With that, the Pope quietly passed Charles the papal Bull of Excommunication. Charles objected that he had not the right by God to deliver such a decree, but the Pope's insistence was not one to be refused. He explained to Charles that, after much reflection, God had answered his prayers, and decreed that Henry was unworthy to serve England any longer. His people needed freedom from spiritual tyranny and political oppression at the hands of wicked rule by a wayward King and his whore. Charles quietly accepted his duty before bowing and leaving the room.

6.2 Spanish Decisions

The Emperor took his time arriving home surveying progress and overseeing military strategy against the Ottoman Empire before returning home in January 1538. His first order of business upon returning home was to order his English Ambassador Chapuys back home in January 1538. Chapuys delegation returned home under the pretense of family need, to which Henry readily agreed with the understanding that his absence would be six weeks at most depending on weather and travel accommodations. Upon his immediate arrival back home he was immediately summoned to Charles great room for a private meeting with his master. In truth, Charles notified him of the Pope's Bull of Excommunication and the possible invasion plans. Chapuys replied, carefully, that England was a broken nation and that by invading as soon as the seas would allow (later that spring and summer of 1538) the King would no doubt have God's blessing. Further, Henry had been strengthening his naval defenses and where possible attempting to develop his fortifications against possible invasion. The King was in private concerned about being attacked over his religious policies though he was adamant genuinely he was right, and would never openly confess to such high concerns.

Nevertheless, he cautioned, the Emperor should not underestimate the possibility of meddling by the French forces, whose full support Henry had, mostly thanks to the great whore. The French were well prepared thanks to the shrewdness of King Francis. French arms in the region far outnumbered those of overstretched Spain and, although the Ambassador was confident in the skill of his country's generals, Spain lacked in foot soldiers, and their knowledge of vital details concerning French supplies was based on information nearly a year old and from spies whose information was shaky at best.

In private, the Ambassador was torn. His loyalty lay with his own land but he had doubts about taking on the burden that invading and occupying the English could become. Under Spanish rule they would prove poor subjects and would most assuredly rebel, even if promised a return to Catholicism. The country had only just recovered from the rebellion a year before and was in no mental, physical, or economic state to revisit the past, as much as the rest of Europe desired it. His post had taught him a lot about the English people and, the way he saw it, they were pretentious, ostentatious, and haughty, but could also be generous and kind, as well as very resolute. This perception had changed at the Spanish Court once Anne became Queen, but his extensive service provided valuable outlets of information from both English and French agents. Charles would come to count on these reports heavily.

A formal war meeting was held to discuss logistics. Strategy was critical if their mission was to be successful. Out of fear of interception, Charles ordered all messages to his Holiness coded before delivery. If they were to invade, they needed at least another 20,000 troops and all the weapons and food supplies his ally was willing to provide. His advisers urged him to take caution in delivering the papal edict to Henry. The never-ending war with the Ottoman Empire had all but exhausted Spanish troops and supplies; they were doing all they could to hold their own at the borders of Europe.

Taking on the English would represent an entirely new series of challenges. England was an island country and Henry had wisely invested his inheritance (the part he did not manage to blow on court revelry) quite heavily on building his naval forces. The reality is that Spain did not have the resources available for so massive an undertaking. Even if Charles wanted to invade and the Vatican could support them, they were unprepared, at best.

Despite this, the council drew up the Declaration of War; all that it awaited was Charles' signature. Chapuys remained consistent and cautious; he urged patience and prayer on the matter. After three days of restless contemplation, Charles decided to carry out the Pope's order; however, so as to minimize the risk of an extended campaign, he considered also sending along an entire ship of gold plate, jewels, and a contract of an annual sum of 1 million pounds in current prices, to persuade Henry not to retaliate and to instead step down peacefully, in the interests of serving God. He could not afford an additional war with his already overstretched portfolio.

Upon further reflection on the matter, he then decided to have only the Papal Bull delivered, and not yet to formally declare war. He ordered a new peace treaty with the English, as a sign of good will. After all, he rationalized that God Himself must surely have mandated this decree, so how could a King, presented with so clear a papal edict, go against the will of God? Charles had managed to build up a vast empire with resources—though limited—that could be sucked dry if he were to proceed, but it would leave him vulnerable at a time he could little afford to be. Each council member was awoken and discreetly notified shortly thereafter. His advisors were able to breathe a sigh of relief for not being immediately overburdened with a second theatre of war.

The Papal Bull of Excommunication against Henry would be delivered by none other than Chapuys himself. Charles had ordered the Ambassador back to England on the next available ship, in late February 1538, cutting short his personal leave. It would take at least a week for the ship to reach England and possibly another three to four days to request the audience with the King to deliver the Bull. Henry had not been expecting the Ambassador back until sometime in the summer. Chapuys arrived at court, in session at Whitehall, two days after an exhausting journey. He had slept little, ate poor food that had left him in great intestinal distress, and his foot was throbbing from the early stages of gout. Despite all this, he changed in chambers set aside for his replacement and immediately went to Cromwell's clerk to request an audience with Henry. Always the consummate diplomat, he refused to disclose the content of his visit, but insisted that it was urgent. His Excellency was told of an opening in the King's calendar the following morning at 9 A.M. With that, Chapuys thanked the clerk and departed back to his chambers. He spent the remainder of the evening in prayer, both for his own country, and for the English people.

The morning of February 20th, Chapuys and his delegation greeted the King and Privy Councilors as they were discussing business. The chamber was generously decorated with lavish tapestries the King had received from all corners of the world, many of which remain today worth millions of dollars. Henry appeared to be in a genuinely cheerful mood, which only unsettled the Ambassador further. In his entire career, spanning close to thirty years of service, he had not once delivered a Papal Bull to a sitting King. He had known other diplomats who had had that "privilege" and recalled their reluctance and fear, which he now himself felt. Standing before the English, Chapuys removed both papers, and read the Bull of Excommunication. As he read aloud the words on the document, he could see Henry's cheerful mood change rapidly to anger. Unsettled, he continued:

"Your most gracious and high majesty King Henry VIII of England, I do hereby declare the following Papal Bull of Excommunication from his Holiness Pope Paul III delivered to your person and council. His Holiness has asked that my master, the most gracious and high King Charles V, Holy Roman Emperor, deliver this Papal Bull to you. You are hereby officially excommunicated from the Roman Catholic Church in all its rights, entitlements and distributions thereof, and separated both in this life and the next from the fellowship of Christendom."

6.3 A King's Response

After reading out the Bull, Chapuys paused for a brief moment; and then was shocked as Henry burst into hysterical laughter, all the while cursing the Pope. He grabbed the Bull out of the Ambassador's hand mockingly reading it aloud in Italian tone of sarcasm and using abusive language about its creators for his courtiers to laugh over. Shouts and laughter from the council members present, damning the Pope, were heard from around the table. Chapuys had expected a far more solemn and humble a response. He—again, mockingly—asked why the Pope could not have delivered it himself, and far sooner, and why did he feel it necessary to involve his "dear brother king, Charles"? After more laughter, Henry belittled the Pope's masculinity and referred to him as a cowardly hyena, daring to do battle against a lion. Chapuys only replied that the Pope had directly tasked his master. He then went on to inform the English council of Spain's intentions to renew a peace treaty and deliver the document to the King as instructed, to show the continuation of Spanish goodwill. After reading out the Bull, Chapuys was quick to tell Henry of the massive plate of gold and goods that Charles had sent reassuring his love for his majesty and their dear friendship with the English and he hoped that this delivery would not interrupt that continuing good faith.

With that, Henry thanked and dismissed him. He even made light of the situation, telling Chapuys to return that evening for a drink. The Ambassador graciously thanked the King, and left confused. Lord and Viscount Rochford at once departed to inform the Queen what had transpired. Neither of them found this funny, but instead rejoiced at Henry's reaction to such a potentially damaging document.

Chapuys was right to have been conflicted. For years he had generously enjoyed Henry's goodwill, far more so than any other Ambassador at court. He had been invited to seasonal festivals, christenings, and summer progress more often than any foreign diplomat had in their tenure. Perhaps most importantly, Henry had appeared to honor him with implicit trust. This rare honor allowed him to engage the highest levels of English government and society. Now, with Acts far beyond the realm of his control, he had in the course of less than ten minutes destroyed nearly thirty years of respect and admiration.

Later on the evening of the recital of the Bull, Chapuys had been invited into Henry's private chambers to dine with him and discuss matters of "Spanish friendship" and a possible renewal of a trade treaty. The Ambassador managed to convince the King that his master was sincere about renewing and securing their alliance once more against the French. Charles was concerned over the continued occupation of French forces in Italian territory and wished to seek the English cooperation on the matter. Henry told him that he would take the matter under advisement but seriously asked why the Pope had not dealt with Archbishop Cranmer directly?

Why use an intermediary? Had not Henry appealed directly to him when his Great Matter was ongoing? Why the run-around? These were questions that the Ambassador was not privy to answer for he was not in attendance in the meeting between his master, the other Kings of Europe and the Italian Territories along with the Pope. Henry told the Ambassador before dismissing him that he would contemplate on the matter further and call for him in a few days after he had made a decision regarding a renewed alliance. Chapuys was cautious to tread lightly with the King when discussing matters of spiritual reputation regarding England and the rest of Europe. After a rather intense meal, the Ambassador was dismissed and he immediately requested a private audience with Cromwell in the minister's chambers.

This meeting was highly irregular and should not have happened, given the official capacity both men held; however, their fondness for one another allowed this to be overlooked. The two men had an unstated understanding of one another's convictions and confidences. The implications of that meeting, no matter what might have been said, would reverberate far more than either man might have expected at the time.

Henry was to take a few days to contemplate what actions to take in regards to Spain and its recent delivery of the Papal Bull.

After the King realized that Charles lacked the manpower and weapons to engage in another war while he was fighting the Ottomans. Should Henry decide to enter into Europe's wars, Spain's vast Holy Roman Empire would almost certainly be destroyed and broken into pieces. On the other hand, his own people had just overcome a rebellion, changes to ancient religious tenets, had an increase in taxes to deal with, and he longed to secure their affection for the Queen, and thus further secure his own heir. Upon careful review and after a heated meeting with his Privy Council, he decided against going on the offensive against Spain. He had matters closer to home to attend to, but there would yet come a time when Spain might reap what it had sewn.

Chapter 7

The Fall of Cromwell

The Queen, after recovering from the surprise of the situation, also laughed and reveled in the declaration. She ordered that Archbishop Cranmer and Tyndale be sent for immediately so the four could dine together to discuss how to turn this development to their advantage. The Boleyns sat down to discuss business after the servant left the room. While they enjoyed an extravagant luncheon together, the group was concerned over extended implications for the succession with the Queen in particular concerned that with this excommunication, would her children not be recognized by European Houses for marital alliances?

Cranmer believed there would be room for religious negotiations to take place to ease European comforts but it could pose a serious risk as the children grew older and these alliances became a concern. Tyndale was a little more pessimistic and expressed concern over the dynastic implications this would have on the House of Tudor and for the start of the Church of England. He posed how the group should handle the educational reforms now that Henry and effectively England itself had been excommunicated, what implications if any would this have? Boleyn as the experienced diplomat in the room posed both the pros and cons emphasizing more on the pros of the delivery. He took a different route ensuring the Queen that this only strengthened England's positions in matters of state affairs by not bending to a corrupt tyrant and there were other refined countries who were recognizing spiritual awakenings in their own kingdoms that England could still do business with. They also still had France as a major ally due to King Francis intense hatred of Charles, so England would still continue to be a dominant European player, excommunicated or not. Anne felt genuinely relieved after their luncheon and thanked them all for their company as she took to walking and reading in the gardens afterwards with her ladies-in-waiting.

Henry's excommunication had little, if any; substantive effect on religious reforms. On the domestic front, Cromwell continued closing monasteries at the King's behest and in November 1537, the Cluniac House monastery, one of the larger monastic houses in the realm, had voluntarily handed over its lands and property to the King. This was viewed as a major victory to the reformist cause, but was done primarily out of an attempt at self preservation. It did however, set the voluntary standard for other monastic houses of ill repute to follow.

The house, located in Lewes in East Essex, decided it was better to give its property to the state rather than to see it being callously destroyed. The Cluniac Order, a Benedictine order from France, dates back to the early middle ages period, around the 11th Century. The order's monasteries were commonly called Cluniac in Henry's time and there were thirty-eight of these monasteries in both Scotland and in England.

After its deeds were handed over, Cromwell ensured the property itself was utterly destroyed and that what did remain was renovated for his son Gregory to use, which he called Lord's Place. At the time of the confiscations, Anne had questioned Henry on why the house was targeted for dissolution when the *Valor* findings showed that it was one of the houses in good standing and that it had readily adapted to the Reformation. Henry told her to check with Cromwell, which she did. Initially the Queen was very puzzled and concerned, fearful that there had been a grievous oversight or mistake by one of the minister's clerks, and she was very conciliatory on the matter. When she asked Cromwell about the abbey she was genuinely shocked to discover that, indeed, no oversight had been made and that it had been Cromwell's decision alone to submit the house to Henry for dissolution.

Enraged, Anne lectured Cromwell about the true cause for their reforms and warned him not to interfere in "her affairs" again. She passionately viewed those religious houses in good standing as adhering to the true principles of Christ; she not only wanted to keep them intact, but to promote them to the rest of the realm as models of compliance. Cromwell was attacking that very foundation. He had to be destroyed.

Thomas Cromwell was one of the most powerful Secretaries of State in England. His rise to power had been swift and methodical. By putting forth his friend Archbishop Cranmer's theological resolution to the King's Great Matter through his social network of reformist-minded friends he had secured his favor with the King. Cranmer suggested that the Great Matter was a matter of both theological and historical factors, in search of a solution based as much on legal and historical understanding as on clerical, and advised surveying the Universities in Europe to have them judge the matter instead of waiting out the Papal courts. Cromwell rejoiced that this simple solution would have Henry answerable to no mortal man, only his own understanding of God and his own logic and prerogatives as a secular ruler. Further, Cromwell helped design England's break from the Catholic Church, allowing Henry to take complete and absolute power. Cromwell's rise to power came with much envy and scorn from fellow courtiers who viewed him as unfit to be the King's closest minister.

Cromwell was considered to be of low birth, the son of a general tradesman named Walter Cromwell, who dabbled in cloth making, brewery and blacksmithing. His mother was a commoner; the daughter of a Yeoman guard who had given her husband two other children, daughters Katherine and Elizabeth. Thomas was born around 1485 and little is known about his early life. Of what we do know, he and his father did not get along well and Walter was known for causing disturbances in the city. He was often drunk and abusive. His father's frequent shift in occupations left a strong impression on the young boy, who would try hard not to repeat the same mistakes as he grew into adulthood. Unfortunately, his early career found him working as a mercenary, and he spent time in jail before fleeing to Florence, Italy, where he secured a clerkship under the patronage of Francisco Frescobaldi, a prominent banker who felt sorry for the wayward youth. It was here, before 1512, which allowed Cromwell to pick up many useful skills including Latin, Italian, bookkeeping and the merchant trade.

In 1513 he returned to England to marry Elizabeth Wykes, the daughter of an acquaintance of his father. The couple married in London and settled down to family life as Cromwell secured a position through his father-in-law's contacts as an assistant to textile makers. This proved to be quite a lucrative post and within a short while he had his own house with servants off of Fenchurch Street, in a busy part of the city. By Elizabeth he had a son Gregory and two daughters, Grace and Anne.

Playing on his accounting skills he Acted as the equivalent to a modern loan shark to a wide variety of clients and his reputation spread as being an intelligent, affable, and shrewd businessman. This reputation helped him gain the attention of Cardinal Wolsey in late 1520, when the Cardinal sought Cromwell's acumen on a land dispute; this proved to be the ultimate connection that brought him into royal service. Wolsey had secured for him a position as his clerk. While not glamorous, it afforded him the opportunity to advance politically and socially. His clerkship and cunning ability brought him in contact with numerous patrons, with whom he used his many talents to acquire favors, estates, and additional business.

Politics seemed to be a natural fit for a man of his talents; his increasing reputation and wealth could only be enhanced by having the power and prestige to accompany it. By 1523, he had become a Member of Parliament in the House of Commons and was well known for his invigorating speeches. Without formal legal training he served the crown as legal advisor in property disputes. His efforts won him election to Gray's Inn in 1524; one of the four top law associations in the realm.

Under Wolsey, Cromwell learned that, to be successful at his post, he would need to not only adopt that approach to making himself indispensible to his King, he would need to perfect it. Cromwell served the Cardinal as a clerk in the Blackfriar Trial and even assisted him in overseas dealings, spying on the Lutherans and creating his own network of valuable European associates. His only concern over Wolsey's fall was for his own neck. While he had no direct links to the causes of his predecessor's ruin, he easily could have been viewed as a complicit accomplice of the Cardinal. Thanks in large part to the Boleyn family's patronage—when they were still seeking allies for their rise—he was saved from the slaughter thanks to their association and friendship.

When Thomas More briefly took Wolsey's place as Chancellor before retiring from public life over religious disagreements with the King, Cromwell was deeply concerned that he might never ascend to the post he had so bent himself to winning. More was a staunch Catholic, Cromwell a hidden reformist. Amazingly, he survived his clerkship under the new Chancellor and continued to thrive virtually unscathed. By January 1531, he had become a member of the Privy Council, a trusted position of the

King. From there the titles and offices continued to come, especially after More's resignation in 1532. In 1534 Henry would finally reward Cromwell for his services by bestowing upon the one-time-clerk the position Cromwell had so craved, Chief Minister of the realm. Due to his administrative genius, the King would continue to reward Cromwell with titles and eventually elevating him to the nobility as a member of the peerage.

At its start, before word would come of the Papal Bull and the coming of crisis with Spain, 1538 appeared to be relatively calm for Cromwell. The King and Queen held court at Windsor Castle and were looking forward to a peaceful year there. The King was in the process of renovating this palace with new kitchen equipment and upgrading the plumbing to allow hot and cold pipes into additional chambers among the grounds making it easier to water the gardens and maintain the stable houses. Prince Henry would welcome his second birthday and the Princess Elizabeth was thriving in her studies. Already she was fluent in the English and French alphabets, and could read short stories in each language. Anne personally taught her French when she visited Elizabeth's estate which was frequent at Hatfield. The Princess would also see her 5th birthday this year with her mother spoiling her with lavish new wardrobes and a grand party she planned most of the spring. The court saw only its usual rivalries, with nothing out of the ordinary, and everyone was attempting to make it through what had already proven to be another brutal winter. Cromwell would become a grandfather for the first time, embracing his family again for the first time since he became Lord Privy Seal.

Religious reforms continued at full speed with January seeing the destruction of relics and shrines to saints. Cromwell ordered destroyed monasteries that had failed to comply fully and speedily with the reforms, along with those that had willingly volunteered their financial assets to the King. He would follow up with each monastery by sending royal agents acting on behalf of his office to collect revenues for tithings and to ensure progress on reforms for those houses that were newly converted. To see through those houses which mandated destruction, Cromwell hired foreign mercenaries to carry out the destruction at a cheap rate. One of the first and most controversial monasteries to experience this type of devastation was Bisham Abbey.

In July 1537 the monastery was dissolved, but only partially. A series of Benedictine monks moved in and did what little they could to renovate the property to make it habitable. The partial dissolution removed vital rooms such as the kitchen, galley, and worship halls. The monks did what they could, but aside from the removal of these rooms, the remainder of the structure was in a horrid shape of disrepair and was due to be completely destroyed in May 1538. Upon receiving notice from Cromwell, the monks wrote to the Queen in urgent desperation for their plight and to save the monastery.

When Lord Rochford discovered the monks' letter, he informed Anne and she immediately confronted Cromwell, yelling at him in the middle of a council meeting with his tax advisors. She berated his sense of honor, threw a series of hostile questions at him and meticulously scrutinized his every answer. No matter how carefully crafted his words, or his poor attempts at flattery, she would have none of it. She had not forgotten their previous encounter concerning the improper closure of the Cluniac house, and reminded the minister of all of her and the King's good charity works and his deep sense of caring for the well being of the impoverished.

Before departing the room she threw Cromwell's seal of state at the window, cracking the glass, before calling him a knave and a coward and vowed to see his undoing. Cromwell later recorded to Chapuys that he had never seen Anne so enraged towards him and that he feared her vengeance this time especially, that she would bring about his destruction. He saw a different side to Henry in the months since the last miscarriage and he no longer trusted his master's good will towards him. Chapuys advised him that he was right to be cautious; the Queen could easily have him removed. With his options limited, Cromwell attempted to assess his remaining available political maneuvers.

Anne's intense argument did not end with Cromwell. According to the King's groom William Buxton, Anne stormed unannounced into Henry's chambers and demanded Cromwell's removal. When he questioned for what cause he should do so, she lashed into a somewhat confusing tirade about his grand abuses of power, his intentionally disobeying Henry's will, and his deliberate cruelty towards the poor followers of Christ. She then fell to her knees, turning from anger to intense crying, and begged Henry to rectify the situation, out of fear for Henry's own safety. She claimed that she feared only for his kingdom and that, like Wolsey, this minister was now becoming far too powerful for their own good. Through her tears she told Henry that Cromwell's thirst for blood, his eagerness to do cruel Acts without mercy, and his ambitious nature, would only lead him to seek his next conquest—Henry's throne. Enraged, Henry shoved Anne aside and left the room fuming, booming as he departed not to bring up the matter again.

Whether or not Anne's anger was genuine, or a mere manipulation tactic, remains unknown. Their fight did not end there and was one of the more heated that court followers documented. Her dedication to charitable trusts has been documented by her generous Privy Purse expenses, but even to political insiders the Queen and the minister had appeared to be allies for years. What is certain is that Henry confronted Cromwell on January 28th, 1538 and demanded to be shown the exchequer expense accounts, how the revenue from the monasteries was being spent, and a record of the placement of those persons evicted from dissolved monasteries. That meeting apparently left Henry feeling satisfied that Cromwell had his best interests in mind and he returned to Anne's chambers afterwards to correct her opinion of the minister's activities. Anne remained silent and changed the subject abruptly. She apologized for her outburst and begged the King to forgive her womanly foolishness, insisting that if she had been led astray in her opinion of the minister, it was solely out of concern for the King.

Anne realized that if Henry was angry at her treatment of Cromwell, she would need to change the subject until his mood had softened, before she could accumulate more evidence and again bring criticism of the minister. She stormed off to see George to cool her temper until she could find a means of ridding herself of her problem.

7.1 A Successor Stands By

The following day, Anne had her father and brother meet in her chambers to discuss their next strategy; Lord Rochford told Anne of his deepening relationship with Lord Thomas Audley, 1st Baron of Walden. He briefed the Queen on Audley's success at accumulating wealth in commerce, and of his intense hatred of Cromwell. The Baron despised Cromwell for the same reason the rest of the nobility did, they felt he was an imposter who never should have been able to reach his post, being of lowly birth.

Audley had never been a fan of the minister and the relationship was even further damaged at the falling through of a lucrative land deal the Baron hoped to own by the end of 1531, that Cromwell instead had directed to the crown. Audley remembered the infraction against his wealth and honor. He also had been one of the first to support Anne's marriage and take reformist views. For all of the Boleyn's intents and purposes, Audley would make the perfect successor to the minister. He was a loyal Boleyn supporter, a reformer, got on quite well with the Queen, and could be counted upon to exercise discretion in his dealings. Rochford called him to attend their sessions and the four of them first met February 6th, 1538 in the Queen's Chambers, under the rouse of playing a game of cards.

It is unclear when Audley's loyalty to the Boleyns came about, but it had been solidified in a separate land deal in early April 1534 where Lord Rochford leased part of his Norfolk estate to Audley at a discounted rate. The estate contained a farm that produced several crops, including wheat, which was a highly valued commodity for the period. The arrangement brought prosperity to both men, Audley gained a cheap rental and Rochford earned a share of the profits in return. No formal record exists outlining how close the two courtiers were aligned in religious affairs, but their political aspirations no doubt were adjoined. Baron Audley had been in favor of Anne's marriage and was present at the trial of Thomas More.

Like many of the nobility, Audley resented Cromwell's rapid ascension to royal favor and his involvement in the King's affairs, particularly when Cromwell's interference would lead to Audley's detriment. One of the principal transactions Cromwell halted involved an attempt at a fishery contract with merchants along the southern coastal city of Portsmouth in 1531. The Chancellor had solicited various marine merchants for a percentage of their business and in return he would provide necessary materials and supplies, some of them desperately needed for the fishermen to sail their vessels.

The seamen were at a sincere disadvantage in this deal, they required the netting, canvas, salt, and other items necessary to capture and transport the fish, and now they were at risk of being extorted for an exorbitant share of their profits to maintain access to essentials for their trade. Cromwell's agents received word that Audley was proposing this deal, excluding any benefit to the crown. This oversight was not without reckless abandon and, had his majesty been notified, Audley would have had a lot more to explain than a mere fishing contract. Cromwell halted the deal and immediately imposed a tax on seafood arriving from the Portsmouth ports. He also notified Audley in a letter dated March 17th, 1532, that his business arrangement with the fishermen had been ceased and he was advised to desist in the matter. This deal would have brought Audley a few thousand pounds a year, instead, those revenues now passed to the crown. Ironically enough, the amount of the tax imposed on Portsmouth fisherman was the same amount Audley had proposed in his scheme; however, Audley would see not a farthing.

When the Boleyns had in 1535 sought to investigate Cromwell in anticipation of future struggles, Audley was one of the first members of court Rochford sought out. Fortunately, the Baron was at court at the time to petition Henry. When Audley had learned of the September 1535 death of fellow peer George Nevill, 5th Baron of Bergavenny, who had been master of vast holdings throughout the realm, Audley had travelled to court to seek parts of the estates that had yet to be divvied out. By the time, in 1538, those relations between the Boleyns and Cromwell had truly soured and Anne sought to finally bring down the "cursed clerk," Audley agreed to a meeting.

Cromwell was a careful, calculating minister and so their strategy to counteract his measures had to be meticulous and inscrutable. The Queen was adamant about discretion and consistency. If Henry refused to hear Anne directly on this matter for the time being, they would have to find a way to make a very strong case against Cromwell through other means. She knew that, for Henry to believe it, their case had to be rock solid. She directed George to obtain and scrutinize copies of Cromwell's books and any and all records related to the King's Privy Purse, reformation progress, state policy, and diplomacy.

The Queen wanted Cromwell's blood. She railed against his abuses of power and the King's trust while he was stealing from the poor right in front of the crown. Anne and Cromwell had at one time been close allies of reform, so she viewed any deviation from her path as a deliberate betrayal. She also believed Cromwell was using Henry's coffers as a means of covering up his own vicious attacks on the righteous, just as Wolsey had once done, and she made many comparisons of the current minister to the former Cardinal.

Anne reasoned that if she could somehow explain away to Henry the domestic abuses in Cromwell's execution of royal reformist policies, she might succeed in bringing him down by linking him to foreign enemies. She was suspicious of the well-known close relationship between Cromwell and the Spanish Ambassador and wanted solid proof of a traitorous relationship with Spanish interests; in particular she sought any evidence of Cromwell promising Charles assistance with the Spanish war against the Ottomans.

7.2 Setting Maid Against Minister

Rochford insisted on evidence from their spies in Cromwell's service. Since time was of the essence, a majority of this information was unrealistic to obtain. George was able to view Cromwell's handling of the treasury and managed to find only a single questionable transaction, a shipment of precious metals to the East Indies placed in a Spanish vessel. There were no further details, but given the tense relationship with Spain—even during this plotting, before word of the Bull of Excommunication—this alone could provide evidence of entanglement with Spanish interests. It is questionable whether or not this sole action would have been tantamount to treason, but it was enough to justify further questioning when the time was right.

Anne also wanted the chambers of the Duke of Suffolk and Chapuys searched, but carefully and only when it would arouse no suspicion. Lord Rochford interjected that the Duke maintained a retinue of security whether he was out or not, so his would be quite impossible, but the Ambassador's chambers were subject to routine monthly cleanings, as were all palace rooms, giving them the perfect opportunity to slip in one of the maids as their mole.

They would have to find such a spy, a maid who would be trustworthy and well-compensated to maintain discretion. Fortunately for their purposes, the cleaning crews were managed under the household, which was strictly within Lord Rochford's duties. The down side was that they were all so distracted by the ever shifting political alliances at court that they rarely bothered to befriend any of the servants, and were not certain who they could trust. This was a wrinkle, to be sure, given the short timeframe available, but not such a serious challenge that it could not be overcome. Rochford would seek out the most discreet and lowly maid, bribe her with a substantial sum, offer her an acre with a small cottage on it in the country, and immediately remove her there after her service to him was done.

The maid was Susanna Caley, a longtime servant of the crown, going on twenty-three years. She had a very gentle nature, was a grandmotherly type, and for the most part made sure to keep to herself. She had four sons, three of which were serving in Henry's army, and one who was a blacksmith apprentice in Wales, about thirty miles outside Cardiff. This son, Matthew, had two little girls, ages four and seven, and Susanna's first grandchildren. Her husband Gregory was in his late sixties and very ill, Susanna was the main income earner in the family. With her husband ill, she would have to work for at least another decade for even the possibility of earning enough for a small piece of land to sustain them, if she managed even to live that long. The palace household accounts show that she received a regular paycheck and outstanding performance reviews when they occurred, and on several occasions had been offered advancement or replacement to the kitchen staff, a prestigious position within the palace. She turned them all down, claimed she was content with her duties and did not want the added responsibility. A shrewd move, considering her responsibilities in caring for her ailing husband, but given what she was facing she needed a safe job with a steady check. With just the two of them at home it would not be difficult to place her far away and from the sounds of her unfortunate circumstances she would welcome a chance to be paid off.

Typically, Rochford's manner had been one of intimidation and threat, but given Susanna's nature and situation, this would not be necessary. He would approach the maid with a handsome payoff of 1,000 crowns a year with a two room cottage two miles away from her son Matthew. She would be able to retire in peace, take care of husband and be near her grandchildren. Being a grandparent himself, Rochford appealed to this emotional sensibility and met with Susanna on the 9th to discuss the arrangement.

He explained that all she would have to do is her routine duties, but with the utmost care smuggle out any documents she could with Cromwell's name on them. He then showed her documents bearing Cromwell's name and signature to memorize the appearance of, in case she was not literate. Susanna vowed to do her duty and Rochford told her that as soon as she had briefed him, she would immediately be taken to her new home in the country with the first three monthly payments with her. He would arrange for her non-essential belongings to be moved immediately so that they would be there waiting for her when she arrived. Hearing that her last day of work was upon her and with such a lucrative offer waiting, Susanna graciously and repeatedly thanked Rochford and vowed that upon her death she would take the arrangement with her to her grave (we only know about this arrangement today because of Rochford's own later accounts). The documents she would deliver would establish that the first minister to the King had maintained a close, even intimate, correspondence with the most important representative of England's greatest enemy.

On a morning in late spring 1538, not long after the Papal Bull had been delivered, Henry and Anne had gone for a hunt, the perfect venue for her to subtly attempt to again place doubts within him about the minister. During this visit she asked Henry about his concerns over their worsening relationship with Spain, carefully suggesting that his minister could help him redress the problems because of his *close relationship* with the Spanish through their Ambassador, trying to plant the seed of distrust in Henry by continually linking Cromwell with the Spanish. She also noted Cromwell's cleverness and ambition, likening his capacity for subtlety and secret-keeping to that of Wolsey—quickly noting, of course, that she was sure the King was right that Cromwell was unlikely to turn out as disloyal as his disgraced predecessor. The King grunted at the thought and grew silent.

The hunt was a success on two fronts. Henry killed seven birds and two deer, and Anne had found Henry—himself—raising the idea that he might do well to look into Cromwell's affairs. It was a shrewd move to catch the King in such a great mood, and Anne would return to the palace thinking that, perhaps, she too had struck a blow at her own wily game.

George and Lord Rochford continued to gather evidence to solidify their case. They were pleasantly surprised at the King's request, upon returning from the hunt, that they look into Cromwell's affairs (smiling at Anne's obvious success). Several weeks later, when it would not appear they had actually been long at work at the task, The Boleyns were granted an audience where Henry heard about their "preliminary" suspicions about Cromwell's running of the royal treasury, and his foreign activities. They encouraged the King to investigate further and he signed an order that they get started right away. So ordered, they left the room to do the King's bidding.

Select members of the Privy Chamber and Parliament who resented Cromwell were also notified and many were eager to participate in providing evidence against the minister. Many who sat on the bench had similar reasons to Audley in seeking Cromwell's downfall and when potential evidence arrived speaking to his transgressions, belief in his guilt rather than Actual truth was all that was required. Most of the jurists had been waiting a long time to get Cromwell in front of their bench.

On June 13th, 1538, with concerns over Spanish influence at a new nadir following the Papal Bull incident and evidence gathered and witnesses were standing by ready to testify that Cromwell had held a secret meeting with Ambassador Chapuys on the very night that the Bull had been delivered, the Oyer and Terminer Court was set up for hearing evidence against Thomas Cromwell, Chancellor of the Realm.

Lord Audley had interrogated Ambassador Chapuys at length about his relationship with Cromwell, asking if the minister had divulged state secrets, what were his intentions, etc; he gave up little evidence. The only thing Chapuys confirmed was that they had conversations on many occasions and had socialized at his estate with his family, but he declined to comment further on anything of a political nature. Given Chapuys' diplomatic status, Audley refrained from pressing him any further, for fear of exacerbating the tense relationship with Spain. He let the envoy go about his business, but he fully intended to recall him as a witness at Cromwell's trial.

Rochford was cautious not to alert any of Cromwell's agents of the investigation. In order for this to be successful, they would have to be discreet. Anne took her ladies-in-waiting with her and left to visit what remained of the Bisham Abbey, so the Queen's involvement could not be questioned. The purpose of her visit was to bring with her some of the English Bibles Tyndale had translated, along with wine, breads, money and clothing that she and her ladies had personally knitted. She planned on attending services and hearing what their next plans were for keeping their establishment together. The *Valor* report fully absolved them from any wrongdoing towards the crown and documented that they had in every instance obeyed the changes in the law. Notwithstanding an understandable time lapse between a law being changed and word reaching the parish, their compliance was above reproach.

When Anne arrived she was treated with the utmost respect and found nothing but a genuine group of clergy and parishioners who wanted nothing more than to retain the little bit of faith they had clung to. She offered any service she could and vowed to make it her personal mission to save the parish. It was by all accounts a welcome change from the hostile and cutthroat environment happening back at court.

The day after Susanna the maid had cleaned both Cromwell's and Chapuys' chambers, and delivered to Rochford all that she had found, George and his father woke early and spent the entire morning going through the exchequer reports, Cromwell's and Chapuys' dispatches—including to each other—and reviewing interview notes from the minister's clerks and grooms. Audley joined them later in the morning and began reviewing the minister's diplomatic dealings. Their review of the expense accounts did not find very much to condemn the minister.

In fact, Cromwell had kept good on his promise to make Henry the wealthiest King in all of Europe. For the year 1536 alone, the minister had diverted the equivalent of millions in modern pounds from the monastery closings to the King's exchequer—an astounding sum considering that the initial asset estimates were valued at less than 800,000. The crown had also gathered tens of thousands of weapons from the suppression of the Pilgrimage rebellion, aiding the army's badly in need weapons depot. For all of their digging, they could not find, at least on paper, any evidence of misconduct regarding the King's finances or the running of the military.

The interviews and documents from Susanna did, however, uncover damaging evidence of meetings between Cromwell and Chapuys on several occasions over the past few years. These meetings took place both when court was in session for official reasons and privately in either man's chambers or at Cromwell's estate. One groom recalled Chapuys meeting with Cromwell and his wife and son at the latter's family estate, although the groom had not witnessed any state business discussed. None of the other attendants was able to detail these conversations, but Rochford did not believe that Cromwell's main clerk would truly have been absent, and ordered the man to the Tower for holding until he could be dealt with later.

Susanna had handed over seven documents where she found Cromwell's name, but only three of them were of value. She told them that Chapuys had hidden these in the bottom of his chest, inside a Bible, and that he most likely would notice that they were missing; she advised that the group copy these papers and return them before the Ambassador returned. She was not certain what time that would be but stressed that they were all she was able to find. Rochford thanked her, assured her that they would be put back in time and, true to his word, his servant took her to a Boleyn family coach to take her to her new home. The coach was already packed with the last of her belongings and she immediately left court. Rochford ordered copies of the letters be made so they could be returned to Chapuys' chambers before he could examine them.

The contents of the letters astonished Rochford's group. The letters were coded, but from what their own code experts could make out, it appeared the minister was attempting to secure a rapprochement with the Emperor on trade policies to benefit England, but Spain was hesitant given the radical religious policies that Cromwell was implementing. Spain accused the English of promoting heretical ideals and Cromwell was promised that Spain would be more flexible in its dealings with England if Cromwell would assure the Emperor that no further radical reforms would be implemented at the minister's hand. Cromwell had returned the proposal and attempted to assuage Spanish fears by promising moderations of religious policy to secure their friendship; that promise, alone, was enough to hang him. The Boleyns had finally uncovered the smoking gun.

Rochford and Audley presented their findings to the King, who was horrified to find that Cromwell had been conducting treason under his own roof. Henry ordered Audley to draw up a Bill of Attainder for treason against Cromwell and bring it to him immediately. He further ordered a continuous round-the-clock surveillance of Chapuys and his agents while at court. Anne had been notified of the pending investigation and checked in from time-to-time on how it was going. Once she heard the King not only had been told but had ordered his arrest she was delighted. She was notified after the fact only due to expediency reasons; they needed to review the evidence privately and quickly in order to ensure that a thorough investigation would be conducted. He ordered his guards to take Cromwell to the Tower where Audley would meet him with the Attainder that evening. The sheer speed of how quickly the group had been able to maneuver the minister's arrest and downfall was astonishing. Cromwell protested his arrest that he had been no traitor and obviously some type of mistake had been made. Lord Rochford had been present at his arrest and smiled at him as he watched guards take him away.

7.3 A Chancellor in Chains

Around 4 P.M. on June 17th, 1538, several days after the quickly assembled court was presented with the evidence the Boleyns had obtained, Thomas Cromwell was arrested at Windsor Castle in his office. The head

Yeoman, William Forsyth, read his charges for treason according to the Bill of Attainder and ordered his immediate detention and transport to the Tower. Cromwell was shocked, protested his innocence and demanded to speak to the King, kept repeating this was a misunderstanding and told his clerk to get his lawyer and to tell his son Gregory. He would admit nothing, he had been guilty of nothing no matter how much his former ally Sir Richard Rich had tried to convince him for the crown that he was guilty. Rich only watched out for himself and when Audley had told him that the King wanted him interrogated he treated him as any other prisoner, as if their past meant nothing to him.

By the time Anne returned to Windsor the following morning Cromwell was already arrested. She called for her father to brief her on the latest developments in her chambers. The Queen was delighted to hear of his arrest. Rochford advised her to appear naïve and careful with the King, he had not seen Henry's mood since Cromwell's arrest and it was possible the King had not fully had time to process the impact of the arrest. She thanked him and headed to see Henry. The King was happy to see her and lovingly sat her down to inform her of what had been happening while she was away. Pretending to be shocked, she comforted her husband. She supported his actions and encouraged him to be relentless until he was able to find the truth of the minister's activities.

The Queen had an excellent way of cultivating Henry's moods and managing his shifting political alliances while keeping the King in line with her family interests. Anne questioned the logic of having the Oyer and Terminor court meet after an extended absence when they had the evidence they needed now to punish Cromwell. She reasoned that if Henry's true purpose was to keep the kingdom running successfully and to embrace the nobles, he should order the court hearing be held quickly to avoid additional scandal and speculation. She proposed they go on the offensive and let the public know about how devious the minister had been towards the crown, assuring her King that the people would embrace Henry further for his actions.

Having had his ego placated, the King agreed with his wife and called for Audley right then. Shortly after, Audley appeared in front of the couple and Henry ordered him to hold Cromwell's trial, at the latest, by month's end—and to ensure that the trial resulted in the correct verdict. Before dismissing him, the King made clear that Audley was able to use torture and disregard Cromwell's formerly high rank; he was now but a common prisoner accused of treason. The Lord Privy Seal was now officially undone. Audley later recorded how thrilled Anne was to hear of this news and that she did her best to conceal her glee; he had no doubts this entire effort to arrest and execute Cromwell was her doing.

Audley took his charge and on the evening of the 25th of June, 1538, he visited Cromwell in prison to read to him his charges. He further read the order removing Cromwell from his offices and titles, and notified him that his estates were now the property of the King. He interrogated the minister for hours, well into the following morning, receiving no hint that Cromwell would plead guilty. Having enough, he ordered the minister to the rack to "rethink" his positions.

The rack was a medieval torture device that strapped an individual to a plank designed with a break in the middle. The ropes holding down each of the person's limbs were tied to a rolling wheel that tightened each of the ropes, stretching the limbs until they would be slowly pulled out of socket. The device was incredibly painful and was one of the more popular choices for the crown to use to secure the "right confessions." Cromwell would have been very familiar with this device, he had been so bloodthirsty he had subjected hundreds to the punishment; now he was to experience it himself.

George took great pleasure in drawing up the public notice of Cromwell's arrest and charges; he personally delivered the notices to Chapuys and other nobles who were friendly towards the minister. As expected, the public rejoiced at the humiliation of the man so many blamed for the ruthless persecution of even compliant churchmen and many of the nobles celebrated his downfall. Further, it was not yet made public who would succeed him in his post, so many of the senior nobles felt they were being considered.

Cromwell's torture yielded nothing more than what was already known in the letters to Chapuys. He did admit to his conversations with Chapuys and attempting to make peace with Spain, but he was adamant that it was only in Henry and England's best interest to do so. He knew that trade was at an all time low and claimed only that he sought to secure England's greatness. When the King heard these report, he grew enraged, breaking items about his chamber. Cromwell was formally charged with Treason by right of *Praemunire* for attempting to make treaties with foreign powers and usurping the King's rights.

Cromwell was tried before an open public gallery that was filled with booing when he walked in and cheers when the court found him guilty on July 2nd, 1538. It took the jury only a few minutes to pronounce sentence. The court ordered him to be executed at the King's pleasure, which Henry let stand. When the verdict was made public nearly all of London rejoiced. His execution was set for July 6th, 1538, at 9 in the morning. The Yeoman turned his ax towards Cromwell and led him back to the Tower to await his death; he was not allowed to defend himself and said nothing upon leaving the court. Upon hearing the verdict the Mayor of London ordered free wine for the city's citizens to celebrate the downfall of the wicked. Cromwell's family, in attendance at the trial, wept heavily, but the intense rejoicing of the crowd drowned out their sobs.

The evening before his execution, Cromwell called for Archbishop Cranmer to visit him. He had introduced Cranmer to Henry and considered the Archbishop of Canterbury and Queen's personal chaplain to be his friend. Cromwell wanted Cranmer to read him his last rites and take his confession. He then confessed only to having secret dealings with Spain but denied usurping Henry's authority, calling the evidence against him false. He blamed Lord Rochford for planting it, and admitted to sympathizing with the plight of Wolsey, his predecessor in so many ways. He lamented his role in Wolsey's downfall and admitted to God that he had sinned against his fellow man. He insisted that he had been a devoted servant of Henry, but not of God or his family, and said that had he to do his life over again; he would certainly repent and lead a morally righteous life. He was not at all prepared to die.

While imprisoned, Cromwell had written several letters to the King, begging him for mercy; all the letters went unanswered. He also prepared several drafts of his speech for the scaffold, one filled with repentance and praising Henry's justice, in keeping with his desire to spare his family further retribution. According to Cromwell's biographer, Robert Hutchinson, he spoke these words at the scaffold:

"Good people, I am come here to die and not to purge myself, as some think that I will. For if I should do so I would be a wretch and a miserable man. I am by the law condemned to die and thank my Lord God that he has appointed me this death for my offence. For since the time that I have had years of discretion, I have lived as a sinner and have offended my Lord God, for which I ask him heartily for forgiveness. And it is not unknown to many

of you that I have been a great traveler in the world but being of a base degree was called to a high estate. Since the time I came thereunto, I have offended my Prince, for which I also ask him for hearty amnesty. I beseech you all to pray to God with me that he will forgive me. O Father, forgive me, O Son forgive me, O Holy Ghost forgive me, O three persons and one God forgive me. And now I pray you that be here, to bear record that I die in the Catholic faith not doubting any article of my faith, no nor doubting any sacrament of the church."—Thomas Cromwell

If Cromwell could have at least hoped for a swift and smooth execution, then it was not to be the case. Henry, enraged at Cromwell's collusion with the Spanish—and through them with the Pope who excommunicated him—chose not to commute the usual sentence for treason to a simple, quick beheading. Cromwell would be hung, disemboweled while yet alive, drawn on the rack, and quartered, with his limbs sent to the corners of the Kingdom, a brutal and dramatic warning to any who would dare to commit treason.

The crowd was both horrified and intoxicated by the spectacle, and blood was everywhere. Most of the realm was glad to see him go. Cheers rang out each time the executioner performed a different part of his charge, especially loudly when Cromwell's genitals were cut off. Contemporary accounts claim that it took only ten minutes for him to bleed to death while still hanging, suggesting that whoever cut him open had severed a femoral artery. At least for that unintentionally quick death Cromwell may have been grateful in his last moments.

Pamphlets were printed hailing the King for ridding the realm of such a vile traitor. One popular one was called the *Ballad of Thomas Cromwell.* Anne threw a celebration banquet where she declared her public support of Henry's actions. Universities began debating on who the next minister might be and, with three successive such ministers having been arrested on treason, if one should seek that post at all. Cromwell had made no repentance of his intransigence, he had only asked for forgiveness by his Prince, whom he must have viewed as the ultimate authority in the realm. The pieces of his body were hung on the four posts of London's city entrances. Three days later, his head was stolen from its post, never to be recovered. After several weeks, his remains were taken down from their posts and their final resting place is still one of debate.

Anne was able to breathe a sigh of relief at the execution of her former ally and later adversary. Now responsible directly for the fall of not one but two of Henry's most trusted ministers, her position was solid. Cromwell had proved his usefulness and, now that he was gone, she would need to set about making new powerful friends at court. Several names had been put forward to the King for selection as a new minister. Conservatives saw this as their opportunity to advance one of their candidates with a Thomas Writothesley and a Stephen Gardiner mentioned for the post; however, Baron Audley officially replaced Cromwell in his duties. As Audley had been was Lord Chancellor before Cromwell became Lord Privy Seal, the Privy Seal's duties were transferred to Audley after Cromwell's downfall. The title Lord Privy Seal was not used again in Henry's reign.

7.4 New Security at Home, New Danger Abroad

Anne had delivered the first editions of Tyndale's English Bible in February 1538 to the Bisham Abbey attendants, but additional changes at Henry's request had been made that summer. With the second edition, the Ten Articles were even further emphasized with the banning of worshipping false idols. After the Cromwell execution, a spiteful Henry ordered gold-embellished versions of the English Bible to be custom-made and sent to Francis I and Charles V. This would prove to be a provocation that unintentionally aided Charles in what had been the Emperor's concerted effort over the summer of 1538 to remove the threat from France while incorporating the Pope's promised aid to his men-at-arms.

In addition to the Bibles, confident at having rebuffed the Spanish and consolidated his control over England, Henry personally wrote a letter to each of his brother kings, letting them know that he was intimately involved in the domestic affairs of his kingdom and encouraging his brothers to do the same. This was a too obvious implication that Spain and France should both keep to their own affairs and not dare threaten England. To Francis, at Anne's behest, Henry sent along a gold plate filled with jewels and a 17-carat sapphire that the Ambassador from the Venetian States (France's rival in Italy) had gifted to the shrine of St. Beckett. The Queen also signed the letter with her husband, calling the King of France her dear and beloved friend, wishing him fair health, and pleading with him to visit England soon. The gesture would be too little (or perhaps too much) too late.

Part of this diplomatic effort was to get a feel for the climate towards England. By the end of the 1530's France and Spain were rumored to have started peace talks and to be working towards a treaty together, which would have permanently put England on the sidelines as a major European player. Although this was not necessarily a bad thing—after all, the country had enough major items on its domestic agenda items to keep them occupied—Henry was an egocentric ruler who pathologically craved respect and recognition from other nations. This possible peace treaty was a direct insult to Henry's status, one he would not tolerate.

Anne did her best to encourage Henry to keep his mind focused towards domestic affairs and press for further religious changes, but he kept his thoughts on France and Spain. In January 1539, the two nations made good on their peace treaty, which stipulated that neither nation was allowed to enter into foreign alliances without the advanced approval of the other country, effectively binding the two largest European powers on the same side. This "Peace of Toledo," as it was so named, was one of the singular diplomatic events of the 16th century.

The two powers boasted the largest populations of Western Europe, but also held between them the largest land-based military prowess in the entire Continent. Henry had a right to be fearful, but the reality was that Spain was still heavily engaged in its war with the Ottoman Empire for control of the eastern Mediterranean and was seeking to recover from recent losses in Hungary. France was doing its best to maintain adequate food supplies and hold on to lands it had occupied for several years in Italy against Venetian forces. Neither country was in any real position to engage in a full scale war with an island nation, especially one as fully equipped as Henry's, yet both Francis and Charles, despite the former's loose friendship with England, were increasingly upset with Henry and Anne's religious reforms, and Charles certainly had every reason to attack, but no means of capably doing so. At least, not yet.

Chapter 8

The Mistress

Lady Frances Hastings was born in 1525, the first of eleven children to Francis Hastings, 2nd Earl of Huntingdon, and Catherine Pole. The Earl had been granted his title of nobility November 3rd, 1529, for service to the crown. A healthy girl with a yielding and pleasing disposition, Frances was educated to the standards of her day in sewing, household management, cooking, and child rearing.

She had developed a fondness for reading a variety of subjects from her father's libraries in their Leicestershire estate. As a child she was often caught sneaking books by the creek to read in private, some several times; she simply adored the written word. When she was caught, her mother would scold the servants for indulging Frances and often times garnish their wages for influencing the impressionable youth.

Frances excelled in her studies and developed a great talent for knitting, but while well educated in secular matters, she was not particularly trained in religious affairs. Her mother focused mainly on the practical aspects of life and while her father was secretly a committed Catholic, he was emotionally absent from his daughter's upbringing and often away at court. Her tutors taught her the new faith, but Frances did not take much to piety; her preferred means of reflection came in self-expression and reading, rather than in devotion to God. As with most children, she found religious lessons boring and was unable to concentrate.

Her introduction to court came in the spring of 1540 at a diplomatic ceremony honoring the Ottoman Ambassador. Her father sent home the invitation with a letter saying that her training had sufficiently prepared her to be introduced at court. The remaining children would be attended by his mother-in-law and the servants while Frances and her mother came to London. The Earl had been aware of a vacant position in the Queen's household for quite some time and that the latest front-runner for the spot, a Lady Anne Hastings, had recently failed to meet with the Queen's approval. Francis would speak with Lord Audley about recommending his daughter to the household.

Her first experience at court allowed her to showcase her dancing skills, education, and to finally experience a world of excitement and culture. Only fifteen, Frances had already developed womanly curves and was often mistaken for being older than she truly was. Her features were also above average, based on the beauty standards of that day: standing 5'4", she had fair skin, green eyes, and dark blonde hair. Her manners were impeccable, because of her mother's strict training, but she was still unprepared for life at court.

Despite the pretense of chastity among young ladies of the upper classes, the court was a place where nearly none of the women long retained their virginity. Hardly a moral training ground, the court had quite a way of exciting this impressionable, amiable young lady, and she reveled in it. Nevertheless, her potential competitors for the position with the Queen did not consider her a threat because her youth and vitality combined to appear as naiveté. They would come to regret so quickly dismissing the young Lady Frances.

Not long after bringing his daughter to court, Frances' father was sent on a mission to Italy, leaving his family alone. In his absence, her mother and her father's trusted advisors continued to lavish Frances with advice on court behavior, grooming, and making herself stand out from the other Ladies while yet appearing demure. To be at court was expensive and exposed her to an entirely new standard of living where shopping for new dresses, glittering jewels, and other accouterments commonly took place on a daily basis. Spoiled by these extravagancies for the first time, Frances felt a new sense of value and happiness. She also had more time to spend with her mother and for the first time began to form a genuine connection with the woman who had given birth to her.

Her mother had watched the court reactions carefully and quickly understood how easily Frances could bait men of wealth and power; indeed, the Earl had not informed her of his private ambition that Frances might catch the eye of the most powerful man in England. Lady Pole cultivated her daughter as a potential prize, training her in the rituals of courtly love. Correspondence between her parents during this time shows that the girl was progressing quite well.

It was not long before Frances caught the eye of the conservative, anti-Boleyn faction as well. The faction now consisted of her father, Henry Howard the Earl of Surrey, the Duke of Norfolk, the Seymour family, and Bishop Stephen Gardiner. Attempts to persuade Ambassador Chapuys to join failed; while the Spaniard would have made one of the strongest allies the faction had, after the Cromwell affair he became understandably disengaged from English affairs. He was waiting to be recalled by Charles and looked forward to retirement.

While away in Italy, the Earl had been in contact with the faction. Frances' father had initially been the hardest to persuade to start associating with the conservatives, but his fierce jealousy at the skill and speed with which the Boleyns had risen and his deep Catholic faith had finally swayed him. Francis was raised a devout Catholic even though he was not home enough to ensure his wife enforced this principle in their children. When the Reformation happened he conformed, like many papists, under threat of loss of life and property. Given his rank in the peerage he ensured that and he and his family were among the first to swear the oaths of Succession and Supremacy, as not to arouse suspicion; however, privately held to the old ways and resented the influence of Anne in pulling the King away from the Roman church.

As for the other members, the rest had suffered at the hands of the Boleyns. While all but the Seymour brothers were of the nobility, and had suffered little financially from the Queen's influence, it was the power to influence the King that they most desired to take back from the Boleyns.

As this faction reviewed every avenue that might benefit them in attempting their own rise, Norfolk suggested Frances as a possible candidate for Anne's open lady-in-waiting position, which would give them a pair of eyes and ears within the royal chambers, and perhaps to entice the lusty King. The rest of the faction agreed, provided that Francis could guarantee his daughter would do her duty. The faction had attempted to lay low since the Jane affair went sour but with Frances, it was a renewed chance for them to Act. With this Queen, ensuring the placement would not be easy. Such positions were highly competitive and the ladies-in-waiting already chosen were of very prestigious families and exceptionally educated.

Bishop Gardiner viewed the Lady Frances as a mere tool to be used in helping his allied anti-reformists win back power. He was primarily concerned that her religious background would pose a serious obstacle and that Frances, herself, might be a reformist. The faction attempted to persuade Gardiner that Frances was the means to their eventual restoration, and they needed his aid because by virtue of his position in the church he would be a critical player in getting the lady appointed to the Queen's chambers.

Without Gardiner's input, Lord Audley was certain to reject adding more servants to the Queen's chambers during such difficult financial times. The success of this planned infiltration was far from assured; but the faction was convinced that the King would take a liking to the striking young lady, so great a contrast she was with his wife. To prepare her to catch the monarch's eyes, the group pooled resources and showered the young lady with the most extravagant gowns, and jewels, an already star-struck young woman's wildest dreams were coming true.

They took advantage of her ignorance as to how she should court a gentleman. Instead, they played to her youthful passions and reinforced the values of chivalry. Prizing her as their latest meal ticket, they acquired the best tutors and etiquette coaches, and taught her a great deal about the social graces expected of a lady at court. It is questionable whether her father had grasped her knowledge of relationships but it is known that he conditioned her to treat her virginity more as a commodity to be used as bait than as a matter of virtue. He reinforced the value of using one's advantages to achieve position and wealth and managed to manipulate Frances' good nature, innocence, and intoxication at the luxury and attention of courtly life.

Anne, so skilled thus far in climbing to power and consolidating her position, was yet finding it difficult transitioning her role with the King she had so long sought to win. Throughout their marriage Anne had struggled to maintain the quiet dignity befitting a Queen. As a mistress, it had been acceptable, even enticing, for her to continually assert her independence, intelligence, wit and political savvy. As the royal consort, by contrast, her duties had become drastically different.

As a wife, obedience, submission, and loyal servitude were meant to be her strengths. She was to serve as the silent partner behind the throne, her only responsibility being to bear a male heir, which she had already accomplished, along with her surviving daughter. Over time, despite her success in moving her husband to her side during instances such as the Cromwell affair, she found her interactions with the King to be growing tenser, mostly over religious matters. She could feel strains on her marriage building with every time she gave the King her views, but her nature would not allow her to consistently hold her tongue. The King's eye was again poised to wander.

8.1 A New Lady-in-Waiting

In early 1540 an application was filed on Frances' behalf for a position as a lady-in-waiting to the Queen. The Earl's recent successful diplomatic ventures between England and Italy saw an increase in trade and revenues due the crown. He returned in the spring to join his wife and daughter at court. These events provided the perfect platform to advance the standing of Frances. Intelligent but still young and naïve, the Queen was seen as certain to be insufficiently impressed with the lovely but inexperienced young maid. Anne had typically preferred her servants to be affable but intelligent, reform-minded, and most of all obedient and humble. Frances was far too young to be any of those things and while she did her utmost to impress her majesty, she never measured up to Anne's standards.

To assure his daughter's placement, Francis arranged for a beautiful gold and onyx broach to be made for the Queen, with a French inscription on the back reading "Her Royal Majesty Queen Anne." Later accounts by one of Frances' nephews indicate that the Queen received the gift favorably and asked to meet Frances again, before making judgment. The ploy worked and by March of 1540, Frances was officially a lady-in-waiting to Queen Anne.

Each lady was given room and board—not to mention access to the royals and invitations to the many feasts and official events being held at the palace throughout the year, and the generous Christmas gifts bestowed by their majesties. The ladies also received gifts of favor from noble families hoping to use the ladies' access to the King and Queen to influence them. Some of the ladies formed lasting relationships, had illicit affairs, and either married or birthed bastards (or both!) using these connections.

Frances served with women from the best houses in the realm. Elizabeth Blount, also the King's former mistress, Anne Basset, Lady Jane Denny, Jane Rochford the Queen's sister-in-law, and Margaret Taylebois were among the ladies in the Queen's household. She also struck up a great friendship with Lady Norris, one of the Queen's existing ladies-in-waiting. Norris provided Frances with an opportunity to hear gossip about the royal couple's affairs, much like a verbal version of the tabloid papers of a future century. Ladies were removed chiefly for demonstrating "unseemly" behavior, such as being indiscrete about scandals, pregnancy or if the Queen felt they were becoming a threat to her. A position as lady-in-waiting did not exactly offer permanent security, but it did have its advantages, which allowed the aristocracy to replenish the blood of the royal court from time to time.

Serving her majesty had its advantages, but it also had more negative consequences. The wardrobes each family was expected to provide these ladies were outrageously expensive, and with this Queen's constant changes in fashion, some found the cost too high to bear. Some families even spent time in prison for the debts they accumulated in attempting to acquire these robes. It was a fact of the time that the more money one had, the more one spent to keep up appearances and show one's status. At court, one's clothes said as much about a person's position and rank in the feudal system as any chain of office.

When those of lower rank sought to wear such beautiful fabrics (when they could afford them from the same merchants and tailors who catered to the nobility), the aristocracy considered it a direct threat to their entire establishment. As a result, the King passed the Sumptuary Laws, or "the Statues of Apparel," actually describing the ranks of each social class and the types of fabrics they were allowed to wear, based on that rank. Only those with titles were able to wear finer fabrics such as damask, velvet, and taffeta. While appearing frivolous, even arbitrary, such laws came about to protect the social order during a time of a rising class of merchants who could afford to dress as nobility, but might thereby confuse the commons by appearing to be of a different social status, or might even deliberately seek to masquerade as nobles, claiming rights and privileges they were not privy too. Those found in violation of this law were subject to time in prison.

The influences around Frances made a lasting impression. Lady Norris outwardly was a staunch reformer, to keep up pretenses with the reigning power base, and as such no one suspected that privately, she was a very pious Catholic. Norris continued to secretly practice mass according to Roman rites and was cautious in exercising her true beliefs. Frances felt the tensions at court, even by those who were closest to the King. The efforts they undertook to hide potential controversies from their King's attention were astounding.

As they began to become deeper friends, for hours, Frances would pester Norris to explain the reasons for the dissention that existed, and how these problems could be remedied. In her youth and inexperience with court politics, she simply could not understand how people—even these rich and powerful courtiers—could be made to completely suppress their own beliefs, just to align with those of an even more powerful person. For her, this alone was sin. She longed to make sense of a chaotic place like the court, which still poses complications to modern historians today, much less contemporaries of its own time. Despite this fact, Frances looked up to Norris in all matters and considered her not only her closest friend, but also a mentor in her new life.

As Frances was getting settled in to life at court, in autumn 1540 her mother was recalled back to the family estate to care for the rest of her children. Her only comfort now was her friendship with Norris, which continued to develop, even when Frances returned to the country with her mother to make further arrangements for the care of her siblings. Frances and Lady Norris exchanged weekly letters and came to enjoy sharing each others' bits of news and thoughts a great deal. It was great comfort to Frances to finally have a friend and companion whom she could trust. Over time and because of this trust, Lady Norris shared with Frances her true faith, her private rituals, and her understanding of the inner workings of the Catholic faith.

In kind, Frances shared her own secret: before she had returned home with her mother, Frances had made a secret pre-contract engagement with the secretary to Ambassador Chapuys, Don (the equivalent of the English "Sir") Miguel de Valez. The two had struck up a courtship after dancing together during the festivities to honor the Ottoman visitors. In a few months time they promised each other that they would seek to become betrothed to each other.

A young, vibrant man of twenty-three, Don Miguel had been dispatched to replace a previous secretary who was retiring from the Ambassador's service. With Chapuys facing a recall and subsequent retirement, a flood of new clerks and diplomatic aides were heading to the English court to learn what secrets Chapuys had uncovered over his years of service.

Considered an up-and-coming star in foreign relations, Don Miguel was fluent in Italian, French, Latin, German and English, in addition to his native Spanish. He was also quite handsome, tall, athletic, and proud. As a child, his father had sent him to study under the great Italian artist Titian. Don Miguel showed remarkable promise in the arts as a child, which initially his father had embraced, but as he grew older, his father forced him to join the ranks of the diplomatic service to earn international prestige. His father, a cousin of Charles V, by marriage had arranged for his son's placement at the age of twelve to court to learn under Chapuys' own former mentor.

Henry liked to engage Don Miguel on matters of sport and often asked for his accompaniment during hunts, especially once Chapuys began to more frequently decline the invitations due to failing health. When the Queen attended these events as well, along with her ladies-in-waiting, it provided a perfect opportunity for Frances to publicly meet with Don Miguel. What had initially began as courtly pursuit was quickly turning into something far more serious.

In early November of 1540, soon after having returned to court from her time with her mother, Frances revealed to Don Miguel her recent interest in the Catholic faith, a factor perhaps more greatly endearing her to the dashing young Spaniard. In Catholicism she increasingly adopted from her friend and mentor Lady Norris, Frances had felt a sense of devotion, purpose, ancient ritual, and unexplained miracles that gave her a feeling of comfort that the constant politicking and luxury of the court failed to arouse. Although the intensity of the pious sometimes put Frances at a loss, it also provided an allure of stability not present in Protestantism. The more she came to understand the tenets of the papacy and the history of the church (and of her own King's prior support to the church), the more she felt it truly was her calling to practice as a Catholic.

Further, the young girl also shared a strong desire to become closer to her lover by sharing his interests and it was well known at court that Don Miguel and most of the Spanish retinue were devout Catholics. He shared with her materials on the old faith that had been banned in England, and that he had smuggled in with textile shipments. The more she learned from both Norris and Don Miguel about the suppression of their faith, the more enraged she became.

By that time, the young Spaniard was not the only man at court to have noticed the comely young lady. The French Ambassador, Antone Jervais, wrote to his master of Frances as early as the preceding June. He slyly noted, of the skills her dancing hinted at (his King adored such gossip) and *"that should a master seek her company, she would make a most eager accomplice, by her movements."*

Plenty of men at court had lusted over this beauty; however, although she had been at court for most of the year, Henry rarely paid her any notice. The Queen had a way of monitoring her ladies' conduct and she employed spies about the court to report back the most minor of infractions, any bad comportment would be considered a serious reflection on her ability to manage her servants.

The Conservative faction was becoming unhinged and was more anxious with each passing day that the King had not made his move on their bait. Every possible effort was made to promote Frances to his attention, to no avail. Meanwhile, although Henry paid the girl no attention, Anne certainly had. Anne was cautious of the girl and would converse with her late into the evening, to keep her within her sights (a tactic her predecessor Katherine had employed). Outwardly, Frances she seemed very fond of the Queen, and perhaps she truly was, even if conflicted because of her deepening Catholicism. The summer, fall, and winter had all passed without any requests for the girl, at least not from the intended party.

In late November of 1540, Don Miguel de Valez paid a formal visit to his love's father, the Earl of Huntington, to seek permission to establish a formal pre-contract for marriage. The Earl was enraged. Realizing that this courtship had progressed to the point at which it threatened the plan to use Frances to entrap the King's affections, Hastings railed against the Spaniard and ordered the romance ended immediately.

The Earl then notified his fellow conspirators, and sought about planning how possibly to turn this series of events to their advantage, perhaps by informing his Majesty that he had blocked an new attempt by the dishonorable Spanish to insinuate themselves at court; such a plan might serve to bring Frances to the King's attention, and in a favorable light. They called an emergency strategy meeting, concealing their purpose as being a discussion of tax proposals. Bishop Gardiner was ready to pull Frances from her position and banish her from court. Unfortunately, any retaliatory efforts against the secretary would have proved futile and revealed their ultimate aspirations, landing them all in an unfavorable situation. The others were able to persuade Gardiner to let Frances remain at court a few weeks longer, to see how events progressed. Her father reassured the Bishop that he would see to it that his daughter succeeded in becoming the King's mistress.

Frances' father railed at her in private, telling her that her silly game was over and forbidding her from speaking with de Valez again. Frances was devastated and in one of her later letters vowed to run away to Spain when Don Miguel's appointment was over so that she could be with him there if she could not do so in her own land. She became almost inconsolable and lapsed into a serious depression over the next few months, but remained at court, under the greatly increased supervision of her father.

With ironic timing, Henry finally began to notice Frances that very December, 1540. Most of the older ladies of the court began to take their families back to their estates to prepare for the Christmas festivities, leaving the young woman more obvious in the Queen's shrunken retinue. He had long been aware of her beauty, but political affairs had kept at bay his lustful desires. In the meantime, the relationship between Frances and Don Miguel had continued, albeit more discretely, with passionate letters being exchanged frequently. Lady Norris Acted as their messenger, concealing the messages or pretending to be carrying correspondence from her own family. The faction finally achieved a long-sought victory when the King requested a private audience with Frances in his chambers. Fearful, she was anxious and fumbled her words when in his majesty's presence. She was also unclear as to why the King had summoned her and, with her father away, she did not have the time to gain his counsel on how to attend to the King. They had intentionally kept the girl in the dark about using her as bait.

Sir Anthony Denny, a groom of the privy chamber and close friend of the King, witnessed the two supping together, Frances nervous and the King doing his best to impress the lady. It was clear to the servant that the King had been swayed once again to take a mistress. Chapuys would report that the lady's intellect was suspect, but her motives pure. Nothing could have been further from the truth, as the attractive young courtier was fiercely bright, and secretly becoming ever more committed to causes that would count as sedition against the crown. Indeed, Frances' silence stemmed not from her lack of wit, but because she was still devastated at her father's decree banning her contact with the young Spanish diplomat.

Nevertheless, however nervous she may have been, she apparently made an impression on the King. The following day, December 19th, 1540, the royal register shows expenses for a "Lady Hastings" for a bracelet of gold and sapphires, engraved with the King's "Henrycus Rex" initials. This gift was a sure sign of favor.

The gifts Henry presented that Christmastide were among his most extravagant yet. It was now clear that Henry had his eye on Frances. For Anne he had a gold book casing made for her Bible, inscribed with their monogram. He also granted his Queen an income worth 2,000 pounds a year. Typically, such a large salary was due to a jointure but none was given; for the time being, Anne could be relieved. The King was careful in public to present Frances the same gift he had given each of his Queen's ladies, but he had Lord Audley draw up her salary payments in private, and notified the Earl directly. Still, this charade did little to ease Anne's conscience. In private, Frances was given a bracelet encrusted with rubies, with a note likening her to the jewels, and to the fire burning within him waiting for their next encounter.

Frances sought the advice of Lady Norris on how to proceed. Still ignorant as to her fathers' plans, she had no intention of becoming Henry's mistress; her lover's was the only attention from a suitor that she wanted. Furthermore, she had set in her mind to remain a virgin until her marriage to Don Miguel. Norris was less confident about the discreet relationship and strongly urged her friend to distance herself at all costs from this affair and be cautious with the King.

Anne was a cruel mistress when she needed to be, and certainly, a threat from a young potential mistress was what it would take to set her on a path of war. The Queen already had doubts about her; when she received word of Henry's interest, the girl could be in serious danger. When her father had returned he advised Frances to forget her lover once more and embrace the King as his replacement. Her father persuaded her that if she played her cards right she may very well be Queen one day. Frances wanted no part of it, but also knew of the fates of those who had come before and offended his majesty in any way. She made very clear that the very thought repulsed her. The Earl attempted to persuade her of the benefits of this potential romance, but to no avail. Instead, his scheming evoked the opposite reaction.

Frances was distraught. Several factors, including her secret relationship with Don Miguel, her growing Catholicism, and her now facing the prospect of becoming the sexual plaything of a King, all contributed to her downward spiral. When not attending the Queen she spent her days writing drafts of letters she was now fearful to send to Don Miguel, and countless hours crying. Lady Norris was her only source of release, and this friend encouraged her to maintain a level of outward enthusiasm for life at court, as if nothing had changed. Anne was incredibly perceptive and had her agents about the court keeping an eye on the King's activities. The Queen already suspected Lady Frances as a potential mistress, so any noticeable mood change on her part could land her in the Queen's sights.

8.2 Being Courted by a King

Henry was 50 when he started courting the young lady-in-waiting, and he was hardly the man he had been even a few years before. Henry still jousted and hunted, but he also had a staggering appetite, and the feasts prepared for his meals were enormous. His metabolism had slowed with age, something not well understood in his time, and his gluttonous feasting on heavy meats and sauces had started to add appreciably to his frame. He was obese at this time, but not morbidly so and was still able to function and get around on his own; he just embodied a protruding gut that his tailors had to adjust his wardrobe. He had lost the handsome vigor of his youth, but he was still King of England and thus still quite a prospect for a potential mistress.

Frances had gone from being an obscure juvenile to captivating the attentions of the most powerful man in the realm. The only time that the two were able to spend together was in his private chambers when the Queen was out with her ladies or away tending to other affairs. This new part of her life had the potential to be the most exciting, and yet she wanted none of it. She longed for a life at court on the arm of her true lover. The next several weeks, from the festivities leading up to Christmas and extending beyond to the New Year, saw Frances showered with gifts and signs of affection. These obvious signs of favor also bore a significant downside.

The Queen, who quickly became well informed as to the affair, now daily abused Frances in any way she saw fit, exploiting every possible opportunity to humiliate and denigrate the young Frances. Now, it was Anne who was the aging Queen, and Frances reminded her of the actions she had herself undertaken a decade before to supplant her predecessor. Anne had secured the dynasty, to be sure, but although she had done her duty, the people never warmed to her; they never forgot their beloved Katherine and held Katherine's dismissal and death against Anne for the whole of her life.

As the relationship with the King began to develop Frances found herself caught in a terrible position, she was the highlight of the social season's gossip circles at the same time as she was secretly conflicted over her lover. Rioting had broken out in her home town of Leicestershire when a monk had refused to acknowledge Henry as head of the Church and prayed instead to the Pope. The monk's name was Thomas Pete; he had led a life of poverty, and was considered no great political threat during the initial break from Rome, in fact, he had not even been asked to swear the oath as, at that time, he had not taken his vows. Once the matter of the public denial of the King's supremacy was made plain to the city's magistrate, Frances' father was notified and brought the matter to the Privy Council.

Pete was interrogated and most likely tortured, with rumors spreading that he had been racked and burnt with hot pokers, but that he would not deny his faith. The monk was quickly tried for heresy and sentenced to be burned alive on June 13th, 1541; in front of the church he so loved, to be made an example of. Interestingly, few attempts were made to make him recant; it is believed that the King felt this case could further reinforce his authority by serving as a reminder of the penalty for denying the King's supremacy. At the burning, Pete maintained his faith until the end, urging those witnessing to be obedient to God, above all others. After the burning, Lord Audley ordered pamphlets be released and spread throughout the realm to showcase the result of having lived such a vile, seditious life. Archbishop Cranmer attended the burning begging him to recant, to which Pete did not answer.

Catholics and Protestants alike were outraged; especially Anne, the reformation was never meant to silence the opposition by death, rather, the people had been told there would be peaceful re-indoctrination, unless rebels took up arms against the King. With the death of this monk, along with those of previous martyrs, it appeared that the crown was waging a campaign of fear to silence critics at any cost. Many devoted Catholics, especially in the north, kept their true faith hidden, and kept a watchful eye on their neighbors, lest they themselves become the next "example."

The burning of a heretic in this part of the kingdom was significant for a number of reasons. First, a majority of subjects had previously sworn to the oath and, under strict guidance from the mayor and magistrate, had converted voluntarily all their monasteries into reformed houses. Only a select few were found to be disobedient and these few holdouts were imprisoned. The economy of the region was stable, but not growing. Agriculture was the main source of revenue for the town, although there were also skilled laborers in the blacksmithing trade. The area was also a critical producer of wool. The Mayor ruled the town with an iron fist and everyone learned to publicly refrain from acting out. When the Reformation came, the people went along quietly enough, but there were still those who privately clung to their faith. The death of a poor and simple monk angered far more than it frightened.

Hearing news of Pete's treatment further convinced Frances that the Catholic cause was just and she privately began seeking out those of like minds. Her father would come to know nothing of his daughter's newfound beliefs. She wept over the torture of Pete and became interested in self flagellation as a means of sharing both in the poor monk's torment and that of the Lord Jesus. Hearing of a man being tortured to recant his most deeply held principles frightened and angered her, and made her loathe her time with Henry. A letter to Don Miguel, intercepted by Chapuys' agents and in the Spanish archives, reveals her hidden angst.

Frances had managed to obtain miniature wooden relics for use in praying according to Catholic rites, and concealed them in the bottom of her clothing trunk. Rosary beads, presumably obtained from Lady Norris, became her most prized possession. These items were considered relics and as such were banned in the kingdom; even to possess them risked being tried for heresy. These secret observances were an even greater risk to her because of her still developing relationship with her king.

In June had come a turning point in the King's affections. Late in the month, he paid an unannounced evening visit to Frances; while the details of that meeting are unknown, it can be accurately presumed from what is said in a letter from Frances to Lady Norris that there was a romantic encounter. However, the extent of this encounter was not known. This new relationship had energized Henry. He felt as he hadn't since he had started courting Anne a decade before; in fact, she behaved much as Anne had, playing with his feelings, showing some interest in him on one occasion, only to turn it off again on another. Except with Frances, her feelings of contempt for him was genuine and not just sheer manipulation, as Anne had previously done. This back and forth uncertainty only proved to drive Henry's lust further.

With distance from the forced separation from her Don Miguel, Frances came to be flattered and even partly enjoy the attentions her King showered upon her, but she was overwhelmingly annoyed at the pretense of having to appear genuine. Her refusals to bed the King completely were not done with the cynical intent employed by Queen Anne so many years ago, Frances genuinely loved another, and sought to save her virtue. Nevertheless, these differences in intent were of little consequence. Henry loved a challenge and in this young girl he once more had found one.

The following week, the Earl was granted land in Nottingham worth 1,000 pounds annually, and Frances was showered almost daily with new jewels, dresses and accoutrements from the King. There was a noticeable change in his previous routine, he was rising earlier and hunting more, perhaps in a vain effort to keep himself young for his new mistress, or at the very least to appear to be doing so. He appeared to be attempting to get into shape for his new lady to make himself more physically appealing to her.

To anyone at court not completely blind, Frances was clearly now the King's mistress. Anne was livid and tasked George to investigate the lady. Lord Rochford had been keeping a close eye, but the health of the Queen's father had started to turn over the spring and was starting to become a serious issue. Having Frances still in her service allowed Anne to keep a watchful eye on her lady-in-waiting and keep her as much as possible within the Queen's own chambers. George's searching had turned up nothing of note, only a note of an outstanding debt to a tailor. Not satisfied, Anne persisted in the investigation.

Meanwhile, Chapuys was keeping a watchful eye over his secretary, who had been told to continue his duties in England. The Imperial Ambassador was aware of the romance between Frances and Don Miguel but he had not discussed it with his secretary (he had long since learned that it was occasionally wise *not* to know details) and while he suspected the lady to be a Catholic, he had no direct proof. Realizing how valuable the King's pawn could be if she were on the Spanish side in the religious dispute, he had his own agents at court looking for any trace of her sympathies. Don Miguel was intentionally kept out of these affairs, better to preserve his ability to genuinely appear sincere, were he to become a pawn in the great game.

Anne also grew increasingly cruel with Frances physically, often times slapping her for minor infractions of her strict rules of conduct. On one occasion in July, the Queen went so far as to question Frances harshly about her interactions with Henry in front of the other ladies, to the young woman's great humiliation. At a summer feast accompanying a jousting tournament, Anne partook of too much wine and even publicly shouted from across the feast hall that the young Frances was the palace's "great whore"—forgetting that the insult had been associated with herself for over a decade.

This increasingly public conflict did not temper Henry in his pursuit of the lady. A woman had not refused him since Anne. When he became aware of his wife's harsh treatment towards his mistress, he admonished Anne not to do so again. His command would fall on deaf ears. When Anne was not tormenting Frances, her other ladies would fill the role, especially the Queen's favorite, the Lady Audrey de Vere. Audrey would put strange herbs in Frances' food at meals and would spike her drink to make her sick. She also Acted as the Queen's spy and would follow Frances' movements as often as she could.

Panic rang out in the Queen's chambers and her mood swings grew more dramatic, pronounced, and threatening. Her behavior was erratic for long periods, flipping between stretches of sullen quietude and sheer mania. She could not bear to see her husband fall for another. Unlike her more calculating behavior towards her previous rival, Jane Seymour, she could not hold herself together this time. She was older and, although she had a son, she knew she could no longer capture the King's attentions the way she once had. This young girl was more of a threat to her because she appealed to Henry's true lustful nature; one that Anne well knew could be powerful.

Frances attempted to smuggle letters to Don Miguel, but nearly all of them were intercepted by an unknown agent, presumably working for Chapuys, and destroyed. Both grew frustrated that the other had not been true to their love, not realizing they had been duped. By August, Chapuys had his secretary banned altogether from attending celebrations at court, on the pretense that the Ambassador alone should represent the Spanish throne at such gatherings. This dramatically reduced the encounters Frances and Don Miguel would have.

William Buxton, the King's groom, reported Henry's whereabouts to Lord Audley; how often he would visit with Frances, what types of gifts he bought her, and what if any influence she attempted to exercise with Henry concerning his marriage. Naturally these were reported back to the Queen who wanted continuous surveillance on the King and his affair. There were no such statements to report as Frances was ignorant of such political manipulations and sought only to remain in her monarch's good graces and maintain the level of gifts Henry was showering upon her. Other concerns were irrelevant to her; she was neither mature nor cynical enough to understand fully that these gifts could be perceived by others as signs that the King was preparing to divorce Anne replace her as Queen.

What did not go unnoticed by the Queen was that, based on the reports of her spies, Henry's gifts rivaled the total sum cost of those he had spent wooing Anne those many years before. He bought Frances prized horses, pearls from the East, nearly 200 yards of damask and silk for gowns. Of all the gifts he bought her, Frances was careful to send most back to her family estate, to keep them from the grasp of the Queen who might destroy them. For as much as she disliked the role she was now in, she did appreciate the finery she was being bathed in, and wished to keep the tokens safe. Even Frances so otherwise free of guile, realized that they would be of great financial importance to her were she to someday leave court. She maintained appearances as the King's mistress and met with her father regularly to report on her progress. Her father, in turn, reported his daughter's successes to his allies in the Conservative faction, who were pleased with how well she was managing and encouraged the exploits. None more so than Gardiner.

Over the summer months Henry continued his pursuit of Frances. The two were often reported dining together in his chambers, playing at cards and discussing courtly games. Buxton, the King's groom, continued to keep Audley informed of Frances' movements and how the affair was progressing. Henry occupied the majority of her free time and her visits to Lady Norris significantly slowed during this period. Nonetheless, with Anne's eye ever more watchful, the visits became shorter and virtually no talk of religion or Don Miguel was possible. The King showed the beautiful Frances off to foreign dignitaries and, according to correspondence from the French Ambassador to his king, she was formally introduced as Henry's official mistress to the court on August 3rd, 1541.

Anne was furious. The French Ambassador wrote mixed reports of his majesty's intentions with this mistress. On an official visit to England, King Francis I greeted Henry's lady with the standard approach given an official mistress, but he remained cold and distant. Francis and Anne shared a genuine warm embrace for the King of France was very fond of the Queen. He remembered her and her sister Mary well many years ago when they were serving at the French court. Later that evening Francis refused an invitation to dance with Frances, claiming malaise, and retired to his chambers. Francis personally wrote the Queen of his continued support for her marriage to the King and his deep and unending affection for Anne and appreciation for the support she had always shown for France. He went on to say how sad he was to hear that Henry had chosen to take a mistress but reassured her that Frances possessed none of the superior qualities that Anne had. He concluded with his confidence that the affair would be short lived.

It was clear to everyone at court, except Anne, Frances herself, and the hopeful anti-reform conspirators, that Frances was nothing more than what we would today call a "midlife crisis." Anne made the mistake of treating her as a genuine rival, and her cruelty towards the girl had driven Henry increasingly to the suffering girl. Anne banished Frances from her presence and refused to allow her in her royal presence. Henry and Anne had massive fights over Frances. In one of their more intense fights, Anne threw things at him and he shook her and threw her on her bed. These fights only separated the couple further. The court gossiped about Anne's fate and the Catholics continued to plot the Queen's eventual overthrow. Few courtiers were upset about the new mistress. Previous Boleyn supporters were now found talking with the ranks of Bishop Gardiner and his associates.

In private, the royal couple's fights included public reprimands with Anne using such abusive language towards his grace that some thought her words alone were enough for the scaffold. She scolded him as one would a child, and reminded him of the son she had borne him. Anne's inability to accept his affairs was becoming dangerous to herself and those who supported her. She had done her best to put up with the occasional dalliances during her pregnancies, but after having suffered her near fatal miscarriage, she would not stand for his infidelities any longer.

Buxton continued to report on Henry's movements, but George thought it wiser not to strike just yet. One point used continually to argue that Frances was unfit to be a royal mistress was her age. During her tenure as his mistress, she had comported herself quite well, all things considering. Buxton went on to continue reporting to Audley that there was no sign that Frances was using her influence to threaten the Queen. She was either not wielding such influence, or was perhaps even ignorant of the possibility. It is interesting to note that had the Boleyns' agents not been so fixated on the matter of the affair and signs of Anne's position being threatened, they might have noticed signs pointing to Frances' Catholic faith and the affair with the Don Miguel.

The only information Chapuys could find of potential conflict between the King and his mistress was an account that Frances once spoke disapprovingly of a monastery in Lambeth. Henry immediately shut her down and warned her not to speak of such matters; it was his will that the monastery be freed from corruption and abuses and that she should not concern herself with this or any other affairs of state.

Increasingly realizing that their success in creating a rival to Anne was not resulting in an Actual threat to the Queen's position, the conservatives gathered to plan their next strategy. For the better part of a year, Frances had been keeping the King's company and while many found it hard to believe that she had not yet shared his bed, she constantly professed at having maintaining her virginity. It was uncertain that Henry would tolerate the sort of behavior from the young Frances that he had tolerated—even welcomed—from Anne; apparently all that Henry wanted from Frances was the promise of recapturing his youth, not a politically charged mistress; he already had that sort of council from his wife. Henry instead saw Frances as a beautiful plaything, and thought it surely only a matter of time before he would bed the enticing beauty.

In private, Henry would still visit the Queen, with one particular incident, on the night of September 12th, 1541, recorded by Anne's sister-in-law, Lady Rochford. The account can be taken as accurate, as Lady Rochford had great animosity for her husband and his family and it is believed that she was working with the conservative faction to bring the family down. She was a staunch Catholic and believed God surely would smite those who had betrayed the natural faith. She saw herself as the perfect tool to help assist in the reformists' ultimate demise.

More than that, it was rumored that Lady Rochford had grown to despise her husband and the Boleyn family because of George's own philandering eye, which apparently wandered equally to both sexes.

According to rumors, Lady Jane Rochford had caught her husband in the throes of passion with one of his grooms, a young man named David Matterson. She watched the encounter, unnoticed, for nearly an hour as they consummated their Act until Lady Rochford lost her nerve and fled. Later, after vomiting several times, she reported the incident to the Queen in a fit of hysteria in the Queen's chambers, with Anne's other ladies within earshot. Anne was livid. It is not known what knowledge the Queen had of her brother's affairs at the time, but to have his wife so intently denounce him was a step too far. Most likely this humiliating episode would cost the Boleyns if word spread to the rest of the court.

Anne called for her father that night to discuss next steps. For a while at least, George would need to retire to the country until rumors of his actions had calmed a bit. They would do what they could to reduce the damage at court, but, surprisingly, there was little. The Queen's ladies were terrified of spreading rumors, both because of Anne's wrath and for fear of her lady-in-waiting Audrey. The following day, Jane was removed from the Queen's service, not to be replaced, and George had retired to his estates in the country, allegedly to tend to business affairs. Jane never returned to court and had a nervous breakdown the following year. She was placed in a nunnery, where she later hung herself.

George would finally return to court, to little scrutiny, but he would find that the young groom, Matterson, had been removed, as were another two of his grooms, just in case. His father kept him on a very tight leash from that point onward. Anne's relationship with her brother from then on became slightly strained, but not enough to distance her completely, as she had done with her sister Mary.

Relations between Anne and her brother were not the only ones strained. She and Henry had been at odds since the affair with Frances began, although the Queen sought desperately to win back the King's affections in any manner she could. According to Lady Audrey, during one evening's visit in September, when Henry had been drinking heavily, he rather roughly forced himself upon the Queen, proclaiming she would once again do her duty for England, much as she had done before. Anne did not resist and once it was over, he stayed with her at her table, playing cards. As he came to sobriety through the evening she described how painful it had been watching Henry's affairs play out, and how embarrassing it was to her. She cried and dropped to the floor, kissing his hand and beseeching his majesty to show her favor. This attempt to rekindle his affections, however desperate, was met with tenderness, as he kissed her on the lips, told her he still very much loved her, and that he had not forsaken her. It was with this small comfort that the Queen insisted on spending the next few days with Henry on a hunt, playing to another of his passions.

Henry then solicited her advice on how best to deal with his cousin James V, the King of Scotland, who had been causing trouble on the northern border. Sex and politics were still very much alive in the royal bedchamber. Henry kept true to his word and rising at six in the morning he prepared his retinue for a hunting excursion with the Queen. They were gone until the late evening, and then dined together privately in his chambers. While Anne was on the hunt, she had ordered Frances to her estate to await their return. In their absence, Frances was finally able to get a letter to Don Miguel by way of one of Lady Norris' associates.

The letter was filled with longing and passion; clearly the absence had done little to diminish her feelings. She desired above all else to see him and meet him—at any time and place he could manage—just to catch a glimpse of him. This dangerous correspondence was delivered about a week later to the secretary's own hands and is one of the few letters that went unread prior to delivery. The letter is now on display in the National Archives in the United Kingdom.

Their majesties' hunt went for the next three days, Henry spending time with Anne and virtually forgetting Frances; however, he did manage to write her a letter before the hunt. Frances' mind was filled with nothing but Don Miguel; Henry was out of sight and out of mind. When she finally did answer the letter to the King, she was vague and demonstrated no pain at his absence. It had become very clear to the court that still Anne remained very much in control of the King's ear on political affairs, and that his young mistress was not.

Optimistic still, Norfolk—through Frances' father—advised her to retire to the family household, instructing her to take longer than usual to reply again to the King. Their strategy was to tempt Henry with the young maid's absence, but exercise caution in doing so. The same tactic had been employed by Jane Seymour years before, to no avail. Frances was also advised that, upon her return to court, she should step up her sexual acceptance of the King, while yet withholding the main prize. The boundaries of the Acts she could engage in were implied.

It is still unclear when Frances yielded her virginity to the King, but rumors to that effect were flowing around court. If they were true, this would have changed the game dramatically. The behavior of other courtiers was mixed between loyal supporters of Anne and new blood seeking whatever favor they might gain should Frances replace the Queen. Henry had a custom-made gold necklace, with rubies and diamonds, send to his mistress at the end of April, along with a purse of gold and letter declaring his unending love and seeking an answer that she felt the same. Her only reply was to thank him for such wonderful gifts, and not answer his feelings at all.

8.3 Challenging a Queen

The late summer of 1541 was one of the hottest in recorded history up to that time and the heat and the drought it caused brought pestilence upon the larger cities that, after suffering again through the sweating sickness, had not even attempted to reconcile their unsanitary conditions. The heat and lack of rain dried up crop fields and famine spread to some parts of the realm. Rioting broke out in smaller towns and a crime spree had heated up due to the lack of food and treacherous conditions.

The sweat had broken out five times over Henry's reign: first in 1508, then 1517, again in 1528, in 1541 and 1542, and lastly in 1551, according to the New England Journal of Medicine. One contemporary account was made by a John Caius, a doctor at Cambridge, who wrote the best record of the disease of the time in a 1552 dissertation entitled: *"A boke, or counseill against the disease commonly called the sweate, or sweatyng sicknesse."* His pamphlet described the incubation period of the disease, timeframes of death, and all the symptoms. Due to the filth and overcrowding of the cities, it is unsurprising to uncover that lack of sanitation allowed rodents and other animals—even humans—to become vectors, or carriers, of the disease.

While food supplies were low, the sweat was spreading and overall discord was taking place on a massive scale; yet outsiders would not have known it by visiting the palace. The court of the time consumed food at one of the highest rates on record, and had nearly depleted one of the neighboring forests during their prolonged stay at Hampton Court. Henry's physicians, who kept him updated on the sickness, advised him to stay put and eliminate as many possible contaminants from his person and the Queen and heirs as possible. This included servants who had contact with the outside, especially the forest; those responsible for the hunting and preparing of meats. The Prince and Princess were safe at their respective estates and no mention of the sweat had been noted with fifty miles of either palace. Nevertheless, Henry took the utmost precautions and ordered their nursery staff not to leave the grounds and all meats, wine, and bread to be thoroughly inspected by a physician prior to consumption. He also ordered that the children's living quarters were to be cleaned three times a day with only their Lady Governess and one other servant attending at all times. Neither of these individuals was allowed near any of the servants who had been outdoors recently, and those who had left the indoors without permission were to be removed from the palace immediately.

When news of the sweat hit the rest of Europe, the Pope declared Henry an incompetent ruler who God was now punishing with pestilence, as he had the Pharaoh of old. He told his loyal flock that only if the King were to divorce Anne and turn back to the Church would these series of plagues in his lands be abated, and that he would be welcomed back into the fold. Henry rejected these pronouncements outright and Anne labeled the Pope a heretic. She had Archbishop Cranmer, who was in residence at court, write up a pamphlet denouncing the Pope's arguments. Tyndale would translate the works into Latin and draft a personal letter for the King and Queen to submit to His Holiness directly. These documents were to be distributed once the sweat had left.

The House of Commons was contemplating action against the nobility for taking lands without cause to further their own profit and for displacing thousands of the poor. Lord Audley was drawing up plans to submit a law for Parliament to vote on regarding the nobility's property rights. He had engineers working on re-zoning certain parts of the north, lands that were hotly contested and in high demand. The purpose was to eliminate a free for all land grant that was difficult at best to tax and even harder to collect against. The nobles felt they were entitled, per their jointures, not to invest in the King's coffers like the rest of the subjects. The nobles resented what families like the Bendici's had been doing encroaching on their abuses and territory and routinely struggled against them both in court and out. Lord Audley would soon rectify this. Yet despite all of these events, the court continued to engage in lavish feasts and dancing. The country was in a complete state of disarray and Henry's main preoccupation was with his young mistress.

In October of 1541, Lord Rochford died from a massive stroke in his chambers. He had suffered a minor stroke only weeks before, and only his groom and physicians were made aware. His children were not notified of the minor stroke so as not to burden them with unnecessary stress. The physicians had advised him to take care and be at ease with his person, but for the sake of appearances he accompanied the King on a hunt only three days earlier. For two weeks his body laid in state as an honored servant of the crown and the father of her majesty the Queen. He was buried at St. Peter's church in Hever, near the family estate. Anne took his death particularly hard, as the two had become closer in the last few years. On top of her already fragile constitution dealing with an unstable marriage, her one true ally was now gone. His lands and titles were passed to the Queen to disperse at her will and Henry showed genuine concern at the death of his father-in-law.

While she grieved, Henry fully supported his wife and, for the first time since the affair with Frances began, it appeared he was turning his course. Frances requested permission from Anne to leave court for personal reasons, without providing notice to Henry, fully taking advantage of her mistress's distress. The Queen merrily granted her leave. Neither the conservative faction nor Frances' father had any idea that the young woman was headed back to the family estates. Frances was thankful for any opportunity to be away from her eager suitor and possibly closer to a rendezvous with her true lover.

Chapuys reported the passing of Lord Rochford to his Master Charles with glee, remarking that God was now making his presence known, and seeing it as a sure sign that Anne was soon to be undone. The Earl of Hastings and Edward Seymour were fearful that a repeat of Anne's previous performance during Brandon's injury would occur and bring Anne firmly back into the King's trust. They and the rest of the conservatives, perhaps justly, feared that this emotional turmoil would yet again place the King in a fragile state and turn him back to his wife; but it was not to be so. He only spent two days with Anne before sending for Frances and leaving Anne alone to grieve. To his surprise, Frances was nowhere to be found, she was already en route to her home estates. Henry erupted with fury. He sent for Lord Audley, demanding to send royal agents to bring Frances back, kicking and screaming if necessary, he sought the girl's comforts and did not care about her wishes.

The stress of recent events was more than Anne could bear and she suffered a nervous breakdown. She confined herself to her chambers, drinking heavily and refusing the company of all but two servants and her brother. She missed church, public appearances and all audience requests, including even those of the beloved children of St. Mary's Orphanage. If she had hoped that her husband would hear of her distress and return to her, she would be disappointed. Henry showed no interest in her condition. He instead spent greater periods of time Audley attending to matters of domestic policy, while awaiting his lover's return. A relieved Frances arrived home two days later enjoying spending what little time she could with her mother and siblings. She read by her beloved creek and wrote many letters to Don Miguel and Lady Norris updating them on her happiness at being back at home. This was not to last.

She was home for scarcely three days when Henry's agents came knocking one suppertime. They sought to return her to court, on the King's orders. Frances, for the first time, boldly refused. In her anger, she burst into tears, saying that she could no longer stand to be at court and would die if she had to go back. As the men grabbed her by the arms, she begged for her mother and brothers to help save her and asked repeatedly "why are you letting them take me? Please, dear God, don't let them take me!"

While Frances was returning to court, malicious rumors circled that she was pregnant with Henry's child. Her sudden unannounced departure had sparked gossip and the whispers appeared confirmed when it became known that her tailor was owed money for the letting out of two garments. Although, at only 15 years, it was very likely Frances had merely outgrown the frocks and sought them altered to inexpensively maintain her wardrobe, such alterations were typically done for women that had gained weight due to pregnancy. Given the circumstances, word quickly spread that the King had fathered another bastard.

George refused to let Anne be aware of any of this. She ultimately discovered it from Lady Norris, who had sought any opportunity to add to the Queen's stress while yet appearing a friend. The conservatives were thrilled to hear of her breakdown and Henry's lack of concern towards his wife. Their plan was working after all; perhaps not perfectly, but in accordance with their desires. Frances was in full favor and, just like a decade before, the palace was realigning as ambitious courtiers sought to position themselves to gain from a new Queen's patronage.

When Frances finally did return to court on September 3rd, she was tired from her long journey and emotionally exhausted. She was taken to Henry's chamber where her King, instead of scolding her, warmly embraced her. He shared his feelings for her, again begging his mistress to answer him with some kindness; all she could reply was that she was very fond of him, but confused and needed time to sort out her feelings and how exhausted she was from her long journey. She begged Henry to be understanding of her worries, especially because of the difficulty in continuing to serve the Queen, who was growing ever more angry and harsh. He was disappointed but did his best to comply with Frances' wishes. It would be weeks before he would receive any answer from her at all, but that did not stop him from courting her openly.

December 1541 brought a nervous Christmas season to Whitehall. The sweating sickness had finally abated in November, with the changing weather (which saw the insects carrying the disease begin to die off), but continued fears of another round were everywhere. The King would go back and forth between the two very different women, which caused confusion and concern at court on both sides of the political sphere. Spain and France were still enjoying the benefits of the Peace of Toledo, but this allowed them to marshal ever more strength without fear on their shared border, potentially threatening Henry's England; Rome was still seething from Henry's insolence and Henry feared its cooperation with the Spanish; now, the Queen and Frances shared one roof. It had been a very chaotic year.

The King celebrated by lavishing Anne with expensive presents. One such gift was a necklace of diamonds and pearls that bore his "HR" logo, with a heart of gold enclosing her initials. He had given her a similar gift when they were betrothed. His devotion belonged to Anne for all she had helped him to accomplish, but his affections, attentions, and lust, were directed at Frances. Perhaps his generosity to his wife was a "guilt gift," in recompense for his affairs and her emotional distress over the past few months. Or at least a vain attempt to keep the Queen silent. Whatever the motivation for the present, his attempt to placate his wife with expensive jewels did little to put her at ease. She was completely drunk by the end of the proceedings and attempted to lure Henry to her bed, but he failed to yield to her desires; some thought her actions were more desperate than ever before.

As far as the tense court was concerned the writing was on the wall; the royal marriage was approaching its end—or so it appeared. Dancing at the center of the floor—after the King had left the room—was the woman who would soon replace the Queen, and everyone knew it. Rejected, humiliated, and abandoned, with nothing to lose, Anne made her way over to Frances as the court came to a quick halt. The French Ambassador noted in his later report to his king that he could make out the drunken, boisterous Anne very clearly, but could quite hear the response made by the shy and nervous Frances. The Queen admonished the King's mistress:

"You think you dare replace me? You think you ought to be Queen? You know nothing beyond your youth and vulgarity. I know he has had you thus, and now you are ruined. You are no more a lady of this court, than I a commoner. Flaunting yourself as some play thing, do you know what you are? You're nothing more than a passing affair, a whore for jewelry and he will tire of you; I will destroy you as I have done your betters, Lady Frances."—Queen Anne Boleyn

The situation was frighteningly tense; a direct and public threat by the Queen of England was no laughing matter. Anne had (less publicly) done away with several former enemies—Cardinal Wolsey, the Lady Mary, and Thomas Cromwell—who were much more wily and experienced than this young maid. Rising only after the Queen had left the room, Frances was very much shaken. She ran out of the room in tears, fleeing to her chamber. Understanding well the fate that had befallen others who had angered the Queen, she cowered in fear and collapsed into hysterics. Only a visit by the King, reassuring her of his love, finally put her mind to rest. Anne, by contrast, went to her chambers, even while drunk, contemplating her next move; the lady had now been warned.

Word of the incident quickly spread and was taken to show—not Anne's strength and ability to intimidate, but rather—that Anne had grown desperate and was losing control, both of her King and of herself. Norfolk and Gardiner resumed plotting against Anne and successfully persuaded one of her ladies to report on the Queen's mental state. Initially she had tried to dissuade his affairs but this was different. By all accounts she was undergoing a sense of mania, shifting for no reason from hearty laughter to severe melancholy, and sometimes taking to her chamber for days. She hunted less, prayed often, and would speak only to her brother, and only about how to win back the King's devotion.

While her behavior may be understandable considering the severe strain she was under, it was concerning to both her friends and enemies. Her violent temper was well known, but this was something entirely new. By the time word of the incident at court had reached Henry, he laughed at it, commenting that "the Queen knows no boundaries" and took Frances to his bedchamber. It surely must have boosted his ego to have such women about him, competing head to head for his affections.

As the spring developed, Frances remained very much in the King's good graces and the two attended several public events and festivals together, while the Queen was secluded, claiming to be in prayer. In reality she was plotting new ways to bring down the "wretched whore" who was seeking to steal her husband. Buxton the groom, meanwhile, was remaining in the background of the King as much as possible, so he could continue his attempts to spy on behalf of the conservative faction.

Anne fastidiously attended to preparations for the Easter holidays of 1542. For hours she sat and decided what biblical passages she might preach with the aid of Archbishop Cranmer and John Skip, her almoner (a chaplain whose primary duty was disbursement of charity). This year's message would be one of hope and finding salvation in Christ. She had Prince Henry and Princess Elizabeth brought to her to assist in the preparations, along with the children of St. Mary's Orphanage. The previous year her family and her people had encountered many domestic and foreign obstacles, this sermon was meant to reinstall in the people their faith that all would be made well by God, through the person of the King. Pamphlets were drawn up depicting the religious idolatries of the old faith and praising instead those who sought redemption under the reformers. The previous editions of pamphlets responding to the Pope, such as after he had blamed the sweating sickness on Henry and the reformers, were redistributed, but the new ones were highly persuasive and illustrative. These were not to be the only arrangements made for the services.

Following the death of Anne's father in the winter, she had seen her sister Mary for the first time in years. It is not exactly known why the sisters fell out, but it is likely that Mary desired a quiet life away from the pace at court, and it was too awkward for them to maintain close ties after Anne had replaced Mary as Henry's mistress, only to go on to become

Queen. With Frances mother ailing and near death, the King granted her leave to go home to care for her and if necessary prepare for her burial.

Mary had married Sir William Stafford in 1534 and by him she had two children, Anne and Edward. Stafford was Mary's second marriage; her first marriage to William Carey also produced two children, Henry and Catherine Carey. Their father had never approved of Mary's first husband, perhaps because William was not a man of high status. Initially he had shown promise as a courtier, but after he married Mary and her sister became Queen they had both desired to leave court and lead private lives.

Anne and Mary rarely spoke, except for an occasional note to borrow money or announce a coming child. Unfortunately, the sisters did not have long to rekindle their childhood bond. In July 1543 Mary died at the Boleyn family estate in Essex of Rochford Hall. It is not known what impact if any her death had on Anne. There are no recorded visits of the Queen visiting her nieces or nephews. The only family she had left was her brother George and she would come to count on his counsel greatly.

In the mean time, Henry continued to shower gifts of jewels upon Frances. He sent expensive gifts to her family estate and short letters reminding her to be true to him whilst he was away. Frances disposed of most of these letters and when strapped for cash allegedly sold one of the fine necklaces he had sent her. Her mother's health was failing daily and by the fifth day of her return, the Lady Catherine had died. Burying her mother had been more difficult than Frances could have imagined. The pair had not been close in life, but her death permanently ended all ties she could have had. The closest their relationship had been was when the young girl had first arrived at court. Her father was away in the Netherlands at this time, negotiating a trade deal, and was not there to bury his wife or console his children.

Frances, the eldest and now lady of the manor, appealed to the King to allow her to stay at home long enough to see her father return to care for her siblings. The request was denied and she was ordered to return to the court before the fall. The King had gone long enough without his toy, and he wanted his affections answered. In an attempt at consolation, he sent her a purse with 500 pounds, to ease her disposition. Her younger brother recorded years later in his private correspondence that she threw the money into the fire pit upon receipt. The accuracy of her brother's report is questionable, given that Thomas Hastings was to go on to be known as a fraud and extortionist, but the story cannot be dismissed out of hand.

8.4 Scandal Erupts

Frances could no longer stand her separation from Don Miguel, neither could she stand to keep up the charade of adopting the Protestant faith or pretending to love Henry. In essence, she was being someone she was not and it was taking its toll on her psyche. It had been months since she had seen her true love; she did not return the deep feelings Henry felt for her and was still often repulsed by his advances. She wrote Miguel, pleading for his presence, detailing her grief for both her mother's loss and their absence from each other. Eventually, another letter was able to find its way directly to his hands, through Frances' good friend and confident the Lady Norris.

Don Miguel appeared by barge late in the evening of August 2nd, 1542, and was shown to Frances' chamber by her closest servant, Emily Waterston. They spent hours enjoying one another's company, and perhaps even consummated their love, despite their earlier promise to each other. It is difficult to say for sure whether or not they took that step, but things had surely changed in Frances, given how increasingly intimate she appeared to have been growing with the King. Don Miguel vowed never to forsake her and pledged eternal honor to her as his husband. She detailed her dealings with the King, and according to his diaries, at one point even damned Henry to hell.

Miguel understood her frustration, yet was powerless to move against the English King. She begged and pleaded with him yet again to take her to Spain with him where they could be happy with one another. He pleaded with her to reconcile herself to her post in life for as long as it pleased the King. She must endure, for both of their sakes. He urged her to stay strong and assured them that, in God's good time, they would someday be together. Unfortunately this was not a realistic option for either, given his status at court if he were to leave abruptly. If his intentions were uncovered it could lead to an international showdown, when relations were already strained between their two nations. Not only that, Chapuys was in failing health and he was only waiting for Charles to send a replacement that would be along shortly. The situation was precarious for both of the lovers. Tokens of their affection were exchanged, Don Miguel gave her a modest gold necklace with a simple cross on it; it would be the only necklace she wore thereafter.

While it is not known when Don Miguel left her home, a letter from Frances dated August 18th, 1542, described to him her most intimate thoughts. In the letter she vowed that she was forever his servant and longed to be nothing more than his to be his wife and a true Catholic. She explained how she eagerly awaited their wedding day and when she could bear him children. She also described her true feelings towards Henry, nicknaming him the *"fool,"* and her hatred of Anne.

The letter was intercepted by the Queen's agents. There is no record of how they encountered it, but most likely, one of Frances' servants betrayed her by turning over the information, whether from being threatened or for profit. Regardless of the source, it is believed Anne hired agents to thoroughly dig into Frances' past, hoping to ruin the girl. They did not have to dig very deep. At this time, Lady Norris' involvement was not suspected. What is not clear from the evidence is why Anne waited so long if she had indeed decided to look into Frances' past. Either way, such serious evidence changed the situation dramatically in the Queen's favor. With Frances at her estates, the Queen hired agents to search into the girl's affairs. Once she had returned to court they were to search her estates.

Frances returned to court on August 27th and it was not long thereafter that Anne's agents had uncovered proof of Frances' affair with the Spaniard, her pre-contract of marriage promising herself to only him, and her devout Catholicism, constituted treason and heresy, all within one piece of paper, written in her own hand. Anne immediately sought George's counsel on how to proceed. George advised her to send the letter in secret to Lord Audley, leaving them for him to uncover and tell Henry when the time was right. By leaving the evidence anonymously the Queen could not be found to be tampering with the evidence. Later that evening, George disguised his handwriting by writing a note in broken English, dated September 13th, 1542, and forwarded the evidence damning Frances. He left it on top of the evidence of her crimes in Audley's palace office, upon his very chair, in the dead of night.

The following morning, Lord Audley returned to his post. Waiting for him was George's letter, and proof of Frances' betrayal of the King. The Chancellor could hardly believe what he was reading. The letter from George warned that he should take the evidence very seriously, for the royal mistress meant the King such harm the likes of which had not known before. It also warned that Audley should speak of the letter's contents to no one but the King himself. Audley was puzzled as to who would leave such damning evidence, and more importantly, if it was true? Audley followed his anonymous spy's instructions to the letter. Upon finding another letter from Frances so as to confirm the signature on the incriminating letter, he immediately headed for the King's chamber. This was the first time that the Chancellor would deliver devastating personal news to his master, and he was not certain how the King would react.

Upon hearing Audley's news of Frances, Henry was outraged and refused to believe it. He immediately summoned Frances into his chambers for an explanation. As reports of the incident tell, she humbly attempted to confirm that the letter was indeed hers and she meant every word of it, while half-heartedly apologizing to the King and throwing herself on his mercy, and asking only that he not hold her love accountable for her duplicity. Buxton reported later that she seemed almost eager and relieved to be rid of these secrets. Audley could hardly believe that this girl not only wrote the letter but was actually confessing her actions. A rational person could venture that she was either incredibly brave or incredibly naïve about what awaited her, if she thought honesty in this situation would save her from the gallows; perhaps it was a bit of both.

The fury that swept over Henry was terrifying to all those present. He struck her twice and ordered her sent to the Tower at once. According to Buxton, the King shouted *"I'll show you what torment I can truly inflict! Get her from my sight NOW!"* After removing Frances, the King began to weep at being made such a fool. He spent the remainder of that day in his chambers refusing admittance to everyone. Audley informed George of the day's events, ignorant that it was he who had forwarded the damning letter. Afterwards, George's first action was to tell the Queen.

A Bill of Attainder for Frances, on charges of heresy and treason, was drawn up within hours of her arrest, subject to the uncovering of additional evidence. The King took Anne away from Whitehall by barge the following evening, to escape his humiliation. In rare form, he told his Queen everything about what he knew Frances had done. Anne listened in silence, comforting her husband, and received several genuine apologies from his majesty for his conduct at so long having chosen this "wretched whore" over his true and ever faithful wife.

Although she listened comfortingly and humbly, inside she yet seethed, and she chastised him for his actions. She had been deeply hurt at his betrayal and was not sure when, if ever, she could or would forgive him. He vowed to her that, on his honor, he would never again take a mistress, so long as he lived, and re-instated the pledge he had made during their courtship to love only her. He admitted that he had betrayed Anne's trust and had treated her as if she were no more than the lowliest maid in his Kingdom, actions the foolishness of which had now been made abundantly clear. He thanked Anne repeatedly for the children she had borne him, her fierceness of spirit and in helping him to secure his Kingdom as its supreme master, and for the gracious love she bore him. In true humility, Anne graciously accepted his apology and both shared tears of joy, the husband and wife were now also, friends again. The Queen once again proved to provide great comfort to his majesty, and he was grateful to have his truest ally back on his side.

On October 17th, 1542, Frances trial was held in the Star Chamber. The court date was delayed so that royal investigators could search the Hastings family estates for further evidence. It was there that they had found the relics and rosary that Frances had hidden away, confirming the charge of heresy, along with other letters from Don Miguel that confirmed treason.

Due to the sensitivity of the circumstances, which were an embarrassment to the King, all means possible were used to keep the Lady Frances quiet and outside of the public eye. Lord Audley had even been given the strictest orders to maintain the girl's silence and under the laws of the time Frances was not allowed a defense attorney, nor to defend herself from the charges. She would only be allotted the right of a brief statement once the court had passed judgment. Heresy alone was enough to make the trial a charade and its verdict a foregone conclusion, but given her status, it was the scandal of the decade, perhaps of Henry's entire reign. The conservative, anti-reformist faction was in absolute panic, although some knew of the affair with Don Miguel, none—including Frances' father—had known about Frances' religious beliefs.

Frances was found guilty after a hearing of less than twenty minutes and sentenced to be burned at the stake, at a date and time of his majesty's pleasure, at Tyburn. It was then that Frances' famous words were finally spoken at court:

"I tarry not for the Tower, at the King's pleasure, and yet it was not so long ago I tarried on the voyage of my soul to hell, also at his majesty's pleasure."—Lady Frances

The words were outrageous and unrepentant that they infuriated the chamber. During her stay in prison Frances came to realize that she was pregnant, only by a few weeks apparently, but the signs were there. In the early morning hours of the 21st of October, a physician was summoned to her chamber to examine the matter more closely and concluded that she was, indeed, with child. This element dramatically changed the situation. It is still unclear whether she was carrying the King's bastard, or that of her lover Don Miguel. No conclusive evidence, beyond rumor and assumption, validate whether Frances ever actually had intercourse with the King, or with the Spaniard, or both.

Either way, when the Queen was informed it was in the presence of Lady Norris, who immediately asked permission to validate these rumors for her majesty. Anne agreed and four nights later the Lady Norris was privately escorted into Frances' cell. Left alone, the two women reminisced of fonder days, and Norris slipped the prisoner a poisonous vile before leaving the Tower.

Reporting back to the Queen that evening, Norris detailed the dejected state that Frances was in, reported that she was suicidal at the news of her pregnancy, and prayed constantly that God would take her before his majesty would; also, that if not, she would seek to remedy the situation herself, as her soul was already destined for Hell. The following morning, on October 26th, Frances was found dead in her cell. The physicians confirmed that she was dead, but no cause could be found, the cell was searched for weapons and none were found. Poisoning was suspected as the suicide method, but no means of it were discovered. Lord Audley ordered an investigation into the cause of this apparent suicide. The scandal caused a sensation not only in London but throughout Europe.

The Pope used this chance to again denounce Henry calling the events following the Excommunication, from the sweating sickness to this scandal, certain proof of God's disapproval. Beyond Frances having made Henry a cuckold, her suicide made evident her true feelings toward the King. Further, Henry had so corrupted a young maid that she preferred Hell—suicide is a mortal sin in Catholicism, from which there is no absolution—to staying an English subject.

Historians have speculated that Frances' traumatized emotional state, and woeful circumstances overcame both her reason and her faith, allowing her enough a lapse as to permit this dramatic final Act. Here was a woman who had risen to the highest place in society, and hated every minute of it. She was now imprisoned, with no hope of again seeing her true love; all told, she would have felt that she had been left with nothing. Understanding Frances' state of despair, it is entirely possible that she consumed Lady Norris's parting gift in her friend's presence, only for Norris to remove the evidence. The truth may never be known.

No public notice was made of the suicide. The only public mention of the sorry events was that the Lady Frances had died of natural causes. The mode of death shamed Henry and fueled Catholic anger, leading to claims that he had been proven unfit to be God's messenger on Earth. No record of Anne's response to the matter survives, but it can only be speculated that she was overjoyed. Frances' death came swiftly and quietly. The young maid remains one of few political prisoners whose crimes were left unexploited by the crown, for obvious reasons.

Adding to the turmoil, Prince Henry came down with smallpox in November. The King's personal physician, William Butts, attended the child and, while he made a fully recovery by the spring of 1543, the renewed sense of crisis over the fate of the only male heir to the crown caused severe tension in both family and government. Lord Audley kept a close eye on the Prince's condition, even seeking advice from European doctors on new cures. As it happened, the Prince suffered from a mild enough strain of the disease that he survived, indeed, to modern understanding, he would even have gained immunity to the pox. Nevertheless, based on this illness, the King ordered that the Prince would ever afterward be moved every few months among various palaces. Further, the King ordered his son to begin an intensive study of military, political, and foreign affairs, to prepare him for the crown.

Chapter 9

A Queen's Influence

If the conservative faction had hoped to drive Anne Boleyn from the throne with a mere teenage girl, they were woefully disappointed. They would not only quickly see proof that the Queen's hold on the King had not only survived, it had been enhanced. In matters both foreign and domestic, Anne remained the Mistress of her own house, and would be an even more important adviser to the King than before.

9.1 A United Kingdom?

In late 1542, tensions between England and Scotland rose to an all time high. The two nations had a tenuous relationship as King James V—son of Henry's sister Margaret, and thus the English King's own nephew—resisted Henry's attempts to divert Scotland from its religious ties to Rome. The previous year Henry VIII had instigated negotiations for an amicable resolution of the two countries' differences in religion, taxation, and other policies. James V had failed to show, sending Henry into a fit of blind rage. Henry ordered his council to figure out a means of finally resolving the "Scottish problem." After much debate, and with the Privy Council torn about how to proceed, they remained at stalemate.

Without resolution, and while the controversies in the English court were playing out, in October 1542, Henry ordered his troops to invade Scotland and use any means necessary, including the burning of villages and farmlands, to force the Scottish into obedience. The English destroyed Scottish lands, rendering them useless and forcing many families into destitution. Their raid was brutal, but quick, with the English leaving early in the month as their supplies began running out.

Upon hearing news of the English invasion, James V gathered over 15,000 troops to retaliate. Lord Robert Maxwell volunteered to lead Scottish forces south and fight at the border. They met only 3,000 English troops, led by Sir Thomas Wharton, and by sheer numbers alone Scotland should have emerged the victor; however, the Scots lacked a skilled commander and a unified army.

Instead, this skirmish, known as the Battle of Solway Moss, saw the better organized English victorious. The English had superior understanding of the landscape of the battlefield, allowing them to capitalize on tactical advantages that won them the day. Wharton even captured several Scottish nobles and sent them back to Henry for questioning; these prisoners would prove highly significant.

Meanwhile, James V had not been present at Solway Moss. He had instead fallen ill at the same time, finally dying of a fever on December 14th, 1542, with his daughter Mary—born only days before James' death—as his only heir. The new regent of Scotland was James Hamilton, Duke of Châtellerault, who held the next legitimate claim to the throne.

The Scottish regent was in a difficult position. The Scottish crown remained Catholic and had planned for the Princess Mary of Scots was to be wed to French nobility; however, the Duke, himself, was Protestant. Further, Henry loomed on the Scottish border, seemingly more powerful than ever. The Duke was desperate for a way to secure the Princess and their entire line, which remained fragile so long as a mere infant was on the throne. The question was how this could be done.

Henry surprised everyone with his own solution. Although he had hoped someday to see his son married to European royalty and secure a permanent role for England amongst the most powerful Kingdoms on the globe, the birth of a Scottish Princess presented him with an opportunity to unite the whole of Great Britain under a single crown. He could gain without war what he had so long wished for, complete dominion over every speck of earth before him, to the water's edge. Since the captured Scottish nobles were still at the English court, Henry ordered Audley to begin talks with the "delegation," with an eye towards arranging for a pre-contract of marriage between Prince Henry of England and Mary, Princess of Scots. Henry VIII would seek to forge a "United Kingdom."

Anne was livid. The last thing she wanted was for her son to be betrothed to what she viewed as a "low class" bride. Anne wanted a cultured, refined, and sophisticated bride for her son, and her time in France had led her to prefer the idea of a marriage with a French Princess. Despite their continuing Catholicism, Anne thought of the French as far superior to the provincial English and Scottish courts in matters of etiquette, fashion, and respect for the ideals of the European renaissance. To her mind, a son of Henry's blood was certainly worth more than to be married off to the "rough and barbaric Scots."

Henry initially disregarded his wife's concerns and made all haste towards a treaty that would unite the island. Aside from forever removing the need for costly garrisons along his northern border, a unification with Scotland would add more followers to the Church of England, allow him to purge the whole of Great Britain from Continental influence, and bring in a new stream of revenue for the royal coffers by expanding his tax base and access to (still) Catholic church properties. With their backs against the wall, the Scottish delegates initially agreed to take the proposed treaty and marital contract back to their regent for his decision.

Henry and Anne fought vigorously over the issue both in private and at court. The Queen openly spoke against the marriage and damned the Scots to hell at a feast for their Ambassador at Christmastide that year. Such outbursts did not endear the English to their Scottish guests. After three days of not speaking, during which time Henry had grown ever more sullen, the couple made up and Anne's objections won out. Despite all that the King had done to convince Anne of the value of the unification, the Queen refused to budge and would not have her son marry "that Scottish peasant."

Henry rescinded the offer of a pre-contract with Scotland on December 28th, 1542, sending his new message while James the Scottish regent was still considering the original offer, and formally freeing the Scottish to find an alliance elsewhere, namely, with France. This put England and Scotland in direct competition for a marital alliance with the court of King Francis.

The reaction at court over the potential Scottish match, along with its almost immediate collapse, was the talk of the season. There were plenty of courtiers who saw the advantages that alignment with Scotland could have brought and equally as many who saw it as a saving grace that it fell through. One unexpected reaction was that Anne saw a newfound surge in courtiers seeking her favor. These potential new allies saw the Queen as the ultimate power behind the throne. She was petitioned daily on all matters. New and ambitious courtiers were advised that, for better or worse, Anne held the King's ear. If one wanted to ensure a favorable outcome to a petition, it would be necessary to obtain her favor. To sort through and prioritize all the new requests she was now receiving Anne even had to hire two more clerks.

Elsewhere in Europe, the Peace of Toledo had proven short lived, and Charles V was again fighting Francis (alongside his continuing battles with the Ottoman Empire), due to continuing conflict over their holdings in Italy. This "Italian War" was to last from 1542 to 1546 and brought destruction and chaos all over Europe. The war drained vital food and materials resources all over the continent, leaving most of Europe in some phase of food shortage, or leaving vast lands vulnerable to attack. Henry had been nervous about the conflicts' effect on England. He was right to be concerned as many of the goods that the court relied upon, such as luxurious fabrics, exotic spices, and rare gems, were now at risk of having their imports disrupted. This had serious implications to the nobility, as clothing and jewelry were the very essence of a person's social standing.

Many of his council felt that the King, while appearing to be wary, was truthfully more inclined to inject the country into the middle of the European wars. By interjecting England, he might be able to add a chair for England at the negotiation tables and create a renewed sense of international prestige. Additionally, English involvement would make plain to his enemies, mainly the Pope, that Henry deserved to be listened to, which would validate his country's reforms. His advisors failed to see it that way. They were aware of the stark realities England was facing. With the continuing wheat shortage in the north, persistent shortage of iron for weapons, and low seafood harvests that year, it would be near impossible to feed and equip an army.

Knowing that he would have trouble sustaining a large army in combat, Henry instead chose to focus on developing his Navy. Although the royal coffers were still lower than Audley desired, with monastery income coming in at a regular pace Henry ordered that eight new ships be commissioned and outfitted with the best war-fighting equipment of the day. He also ordered a survey of current naval affairs, including how many men were Active, what resources they were lacking to repel an attempted invasion, what reinforcements were needed along England's coast and ports, and the status of their current vessels. England's naval defenses were already strong, but Henry wanted to ensure that his defenses would be strong enough to block any potential invaders before they could reach English shores, and so compensate for his smaller army. It would become the linchpin of England's defense strategy for the next 400 years.

9.2 The Power to Forgive

The food shortage remained a serious concern, and not only for its effect on military affairs. Wheat was the critical ingredient in making bread and ale, two staples of Tudor times. This important crop had been dramatically reduced when the typical rain season failed to yield the high volumes of water necessary for growth. Irrigation systems in the north had not yet been remodeled even to the standards of the technology of the time. Ironically, many noble landlords who owned these vital crops failed to improve their farmers' materials and lands, citing the high cost of such investments. In defense of the nobles, cost truly was a significant factor; however, greed to squeeze every penny of existing profits (accentuated through the shortage) may have been the main catalyst to the otherwise short-sighted policies.

The majority of agricultural experts of the time came from the English Midlands, who charged enormous rates for their labor, often times many landlords refused to pay for such advice on principle alone. This unique skill set was not widespread in England at the time, so until the knowledge spread to farmers the landowners were at these experts' mercy.

These agricultural experts came mostly from one family, the Bendicis. The Bendicis, of Italian heritage, had a long lineage in the agricultural trade, profiting enormously and owning vineyards, rare works of art, and building ties to some of the most powerful people in Europe, including the Pope, Kings, and senior nobles across the continent.

Antonio Bendici, the head of the family, had been a shrewd businessman. Realizing the profits to be made as, what we would today call agronomy or even general consulting, he expanded his business in 1473 from Verona, Italy to Antwerp, the Auvergne Province in France, and finally to Newcastle in England. Antonio and his wife Marla had six children, although she had also suffered a number of miscarriages.

Antonio's eldest son, Silvestro, was groomed to succeed as head of the family business. In order to secure his empire, he arranged exclusive contracts with blacksmiths in the West Indies and Asia, for which he paid handsomely. Should other potential merchants come seeking their services, Antonio had them removed from the competition. His tactics were ruthless and effective.

Several of the other children, Marco, daughters Marla, Eva, Sylvia and Clarisa, also entered various forms of the family business, which was mostly spreading the family's influence throughout society. Marco initially served as the family salesman/mercenary. Where he could not bend minds through his charm, he did not hesitate to use force. Eva was known as one of the most beautiful women in all of Newcastle. Several times over, suitors from afar had vied for her hand and she had been sent to the court of Naples for nearly four years as one of the Queen's ladies; it was also rumored in Naples' social circles that she had become mistress to the Pope. Sylvia married at sixteen to a local merchant and had lived a fairly quiet life in a remote village away from the city, raising three strong sons; all of her children joined Henry's army. Clarisa worked as an assistant in the court surgeon's shop and witnessed barbaric Acts of torture conducted in the name of medicine; before she turned thirty-three she allegedly had a mental breakdown from the horror.

Marla was her father's favorite; he desired for her a similar path to privilege as had been found for her sister Eva. He had petitioned Lord Audley for a spot in the Queen's household once he learned of the vacancy left by one of Anne's ladies-in-waiting, who had recently become pregnant. Marla was not gorgeous, compared to her sister, but she had charm and wit. Having her as a member of the royal household would further enhance the family's credibility. Her application was forwarded for further review by Anne herself and was accepted around July 1543.

The Privy Council may have been appalled at the rough tactics of the Bendici family and their apprentices but many members themselves perfected these tactics on both political and familial fronts. These nobles had built fenced-in properties, enclosing their lands not only as a matter of security for their livestock, but supposedly to keep squatters from their lands. In reality, the practice was to ensure that less labor was needed to run the farm operations. This practice, known as enclosure, all but eliminated the need for labor. Human capital, in other words farmhands, were now replaced by security guards to ensure that neighboring farmers could not go onto their property and attempt to harvest their crops, or steal their livestock or other materials. In essence what these clever nobles had done was all but eliminate economic rivals in their areas. What they considered competition, however, were merely poor farmers and their families attempting to carve out a living for barely enough to obtain food.

When word spread to Parliament of these abuses, the non-land owning politicians were furious. Not only had the nobles refused them a share of the profits they were hoarding, but they also had not been paying any taxes into the royal coffers on a formal basis. Often they misled the crown about the amount of taxes they owed and many attempted to hide their large profits from the crown. Granted, these nobles had been paying out handsome bribes to the King to keep their arrangements ongoing. Still, it mattered little when riots broke out the summer of 1543 by northern farmers protesting their continued oppression by the nobility. They torched Sir Robert Southwell's lands in Newcastle, with nearly ten acres destroyed by the rebels. What was not destroyed was stolen.

Sir Southwell was Master of the Rolls of the Court of Chancery and one of the key members of the enclosure pAct. Upon receiving notice from Lord Audley that his lands and property had been destroyed he immediately demanded satisfaction. When he appeared at court three weeks later to obtain compensation for his loss, Audley failed to satisfy his demands. Southwell began striking Audley about the head, disregarding the King's express command of no fighting while court was in session. Audley responded in kind by throwing him in prison at Tyndale until he had better learned control of himself. While Sir Southwell was in prison, Audley used the opportunity to further his own interests and get closer to the crown. He formally requested an audience with Henry and Anne on August 17th, 1543, while the court was in residence at Sudeley Castle, to review the matter of the northern riots.

While dining, the Chancellor informed their majesties of the northern uprising but also cautioned against the abuses not only of the clergy, but in the King's own Privy Council. He claimed to have in his possession evidence of lechery, abuse of power, and treason from several government officials and Privy Council advisors. Naturally this peaked their interest and they demanded to know exactly who these persons were. Audley handed them a list of names containing mainly his and Anne's political enemies. This list has not been found in any contemporary account and it is also not known if Anne was aware of the list ahead of time. Nevertheless, actions were taken shortly after against those on the list of names and it is plausible that these actions were taken by the crown at the implication of either real or perceived threats.

This brilliant move was enabling the Chancellor to get one-step closer to binding inner-circle loyalties to him. Exposing these alleged traitors to the crown—as they were enemies of Anne as well—would build trust with a powerful advocate to the King and almost assuredly promise his own advancement. After all, he was merely following the path of his moderately successful predecessors Wolsey and Cromwell, while seeking not to share their fate. The alleged evidence he brought forth included the well-known back-door deals of the nobility, and implicated some of the most prominent and longstanding members in the peerage. Interestingly, he had been keeping a private record of these dealings for some time without acting on the information, most likely waiting for the right opportunity to present his case. It was one thing to be aware of such activity, it was quite another in these times to formally document it. This list, true or not, would damage the lives of all those named on it. Audley felt confident that what he was bringing to light was going to keep him safe and earn their majesties' trust.

One of the names was Henry Clifford, the Earl of Cumberland. Tyndale and Cranmer had been working with him to recruit tutors of reform principles in Cumberland. Audley had accused the Earl of stealing from the King's coffers, extorting the monastery in Cumberland, and having an affair with the sheriff of Cumberland's wife. If these allegations were true, the Earl's actions were enough to hang him. An unfortunate reality in Tudor times is that mere accusation was often sufficient to find one guilty, and when the head of state was accusing you, it was not a far cry from mere accusation to manufactured guilt. Evidence and a guilty verdict could be easily bought by the wealthy and powerful.

This news came as a genuine shock to the Queen. Anne had worked with the Earl of Cumberland to spread reformist practices. This allegation was a betrayal on a personal level. She genuinely enjoyed the Earl's company and he had been invited to dine privately with her and Henry on many occasions, as well as joining them in hunting excursions. Clifford had a very charming demeanor, he served as an intelligent aide in domestic affairs and for quite some time was one of the most eligible bachelors at court. He made powerful friends very quickly and had a way of ensuring loyalty to him. He was one of those rare few at court who had no need to bribe his fellows for support, most everyone genuinely liked and respected him. He had also been selected by the King to serve as a royal agent. Anne was outraged. Her initial inclination would have been to confront the Earl directly, but seeing as he was not at court at the time this was quite impossible. To satisfy her immediate desire for confirmation, after dinner she barged into her Brother George's chambers seeking counsel on how to proceed.

Along with the Earl, one of the members accused of treason had been one of the King's dearest friends, Sir Richard Greyson. Greyson was now in his early sixties, with extensive ties to the Irish leadership. Court gossip had accused him of false loyalties to England, swearing that he would promote Irish interests ahead of those of the crown. In addition to his Irish connections, he was thought by many—who had remained silent due to his close ties to the crown, to be a secret papist. Given his financial position among the nobility no one dared to challenge him. Thanks to the careful planning of his father he, like Henry, had been granted a massive inheritance, which he used to its fullest extent to build a lavish palace to house him, his wife, and two eldest sons Gregory and Richard the younger.

Richard the son was serving in the King's forces as a Lieutenant at Dover. His father had afforded him a first class education in military strategy alongside other noble sons tutored by former commanding officers from the War of the Roses, and even from surviving veterans of the 1512 "War of the League of Cambri," a victorious English naval battle over French forces. The family had been politically cautious, tending to sway with whichever party held the reins of power at the time. He gathered intelligence by paying court servants generously with additional coin and food.

George advised Anne to proceed with caution on Clifford; she needed to be moderate in her approach and advice, which Henry was bound to ask her for. George feared that Clifford's influence was far too powerful to make a potential enemy of him until they could be absolutely certain of undoing the King's confidante. Further, George reasoned that Audley had to have an ulterior motive to present a list of names alleging these crimes. Most of those on the list were high-ranking officials, many of whom were close friends or associates of either the King or prominent nobles. George urged caution and to investigate the minister before immediately jumping to conclusions that everyone on that list was guilty. He also advised them to outwardly proceed with the investigations into the alleged activities of those persons on the list, but to privately look into Audley's own affairs and why he would present such a list.

Anne listened contently and agreed with her brother's assessment of Audley, but when it came to Clifford she vehemently disagreed; she let her temper get the better of her. News of this particular alleged treason, this particular betrayal of her reforms, reignited her anger and hatred of dissenters. She had genuinely cared for Clifford, as did Henry, and just the notion that they had been betrayed set her into a fury. At one point she had exercised tolerance, but the policy of abiding scheming by the nobility silently, for the sake of their titles, had endured well past its expiration date. The familial argument hit a high point when Anne broke a mirror out of rage at her brother's advice. George was able to calm her down but only after an hour of convincing her to investigate first before acting. After finally being able to leave her brother's chamber calmly, she called for the Earl to be brought to her immediately, despite his post. All she could do at that point, was wait.

After leaving George's chambers Anne went to see Henry regarding Audley's allegations. The King was just as troubled over them as she was. Together they reviewed the list and Anne repeated the words of her brother, questioning the minister's motives for coming forward with this information at that particular time. What was his true purpose? How did they know that the names on that list were not mere political enemies of Audley that he was attempting to do away with by manipulating them into action? Henry had not considered this possibility and had taken his minister's allegations at face value, but Anne's reasoning did make sense.

She was incensed that here again was the case of another minister attempting to usurp his authority, but this time, by trying to fool the King into acting first and asking questions later. True to the form that had developed since the Lady Frances affair, Henry heeded his wife's counsel on how to proceed. She advised him to continue the inquiry so as not to arouse Audley's suspicions, but that they needed to be certain that the minister was not simply using the power of his office to urge the King into doing his subject's personal bidding. Henry agreed and told her that he would employ two of his best investigators to look into his minister's dealings. Anne returned to her chambers that evening satisfied that the best outcome would be sought.

Later the same evening, the King recalled Audley to draw up a formal inquest into the allegations. In an unusual move, he also recalled Parliament into an emergency session for August 22nd, 1543, to announce the inquest. Politically, it was the equivalent of extending an olive branch to those members who were guilty of crimes against the crown to let them confess early and have a chance to plead for mercy. After the Lady Frances affair, not so long ago, perhaps Henry felt it was better to ease the court into potential scandal, rather than reveal such controversy all at once. He had a remarkably fragile ego, even after thirty-plus years on the throne. On the outside, one can judge that Henry was being honorable by allowing these nobles to come forward early; on the other hand, it can be viewed as him lacking the will to expose the truth if it meant harming his image and self conception as a "good judge of character"; the latter assessment would paint Henry as too vain to courageously meet the truth head-on. This would be in keeping with the cowardice and selfishness he showed in such circumstances throughout his reign. Further, this inquest announcement did not include any formal offer of leniency for those who might come forward.

The mixed messaging did not work as well as he may have hoped. There are no contemporary records regarding Henry's mindset towards releasing this inquest to his council, but, given the facts, it seems quite remarkable that he would have done this for any other reason than to soften any blow to his own reputation at having tolerated so many traitors, so near to his own person.

When Parliament reconvened to hear Audley's briefing, gasps and shouts of outrage reverberated throughout the chamber. One of the jurists walked out in protest. Sir Richard Rich, who had been so integral to the purge of Bishop Fisher and Sir Thomas More, attempted to regain control of the chamber and passionately promoted the King's argument. Audley provided the closing speech, letting them know the inquest would be ongoing, beginning that day. When the crown had gathered enough evidence they would be presenting a formal case against the guilty parties and referred all questions regarding the proceedings to Audley's office. They quickly exited the chamber to a loud chorus of boos and shouts of anger.

The Earl of Cumberland had finally managed to arrive at Sudeley on August 30th, 1543. By this time Anne had gathered her composure and arranged to greet the Earl in her chambers, along with her brother. Anne immediately began questioning him, before he could even take his seat. No pleasantries had been exchanged and Clifford had not been briefed on why the Queen had called him in. Her series of questions came off as an interrogation and the Earl immediately became emotionally distressed. He adamantly denied treason of any account, from the alleged extorting of the Cumberland monastery to keeping revenues from the crown. He pleaded with the Queen to remember that, by her very side, he had helped the monastery to keep its religious status, and even paid for the renovation of the building himself, including the refurbishment of the lecture halls. He said he had no reason to extort a building that had cost him a handsome sum (although in fact this could have provided him motive to recoup his expenses) and offered Her Majesty the records of his private accounts, detailing all of his financial dealings, including his tax payments to the crown. George accepted the offer and Clifford said he would order them immediately dispatched.

As to the affair, he confessed about his indiscretion with the Sherriff's wife, but proclaimed that he wanted her for his wife and meant not to use her as a common whore; he said he truly loved her. Anne asked about his wife, the Lady Clifford, and he admitted that he had never loved her. His father had arranged for this marriage to unite their families' lands, and to gain the sizeable dowry of nearly 300,000 pounds her family had offered. He found his wife in nearly every manner repulsive and could tolerate her company as little as possible. He met the Sherriff's wife, Lydia, several years prior during a town festival and was immediately enraptured by her beauty, intelligence, and grace. In courting her thereafter, they both vowed to keep their relationship a secret, but as with any excellent scandal, at some point it was discovered. On one occasion Lydia's husband, who was a drunkard who beat her often, received the reply of Clifford's own anger, out of impulse motivated by love. That incident instilled a long resentment towards the Earl, who doubtless had vowed vengeance. The Earl apologized for the affair, in that such adultery was breaking God's law, but he did not apologize for the love he felt in his heart.

In hearing his account, with such genuine sorrow, Anne felt sorry for Clifford and changed her approach. He was nearly in tears recounting his lost love and feared he might never see her again. He provided intimate details of their letters, tokens of affection, and places they had consummated their union. He apologized on his knees to Anne repeatedly, before she took him up by the chin telling him it was understandable, but wrong. She told him his actions could have left him harmed, but that she would personally see to his protection. She finally asked what reason Audley would have to accuse him of such evil deeds. Clifford confessed that he had often spoken out of turn against the minister during Privy Council sessions, which George verified, but insisted that he only ever spoke only out of love for his country and not for personal gain. He felt that Audley was only out to pave the way for his own further rise.

It all finally made sense to the Queen. Audley was doing just as George had suspected; attempting to use the King to shield himself from his own political enemies. She vowed to do all she could to aid Clifford out of this situation. The Earl was extremely grateful for her help, kissing her rings repeatedly. As he would soon learn, no debt to the Queen would be without repayment. Nevertheless, Clifford returned to his chambers at court thankful that he had not lost the Queen's favor.

Meanwhile, Audley thought he had his enemies exactly where he wanted them. Greyson and Clifford had been two of his most prominent critics. Both men had wronged him by speaking out against his attempts at council to enforce controversial actions, such as increasing taxes, his pro-war policies, and on a personal front, they had insulted his taste in food and sophistication. Greyson in particular insulted his honor by telling Henry that the Chancellor had ulterior motives, contrary to Henry's own, in running the country. When Audley found out, he never forgot it and had vowed to seek Greyson's ruin. Since Clifford was at court, Audley ordered the Earl's arrest; he was taken to the Tower the same day of his arrival back from the Queen's audience for further investigation. Audley further ordered Greyson taken to the Tower as well, which took at least a week to bring him back to London from his estates.

When Anne found out, she went to Henry and asked for Clifford's immediate release (she remained uncertain as to Greyson and remained silent as to that accused traitor). She recounted the story of Clifford's confession to her and begged His Majesty to let the Earl go; arguing that they could use the enhanced loyalty Clifford would freely give them to aid them in other purposes. She convinced the King that Clifford was genuine in his confession and that his record books were on their way to either confirm or give the lie to his protestations. Giving into her, Henry released Clifford later that day and brought him to hunt with their Majesties.

Henry himself expressed regret over the arrest and the confusion surrounding it. Trusting Anne's judgment he told the Earl of serpents in his court that meant to take him for a fool. He put his hand on Clifford's shoulder and told him he was glad he could confide in him. The Earl was understandably shaken from the events, but was overjoyed to, in the circumstances, have been afforded the honor of a personal invitation to join the monarch on the hunt, and played cards with the King that evening. Henry asked for the Earl's views on domestic affairs in the kingdom and his opinion of the inquest. The Earl expressed concern over the damage to honor and reputation that could follow from false accusations, reminding the King of his own plight, but encouraged that the inquests should continue if they be genuine in finding traitors about the realm. He advised Henry to *"squash real [traitors] as one would a beetle."*

Audley visited Southwell in prison later that week, initially questioning him about the persons on his list and their alleged crimes. Southwell spit in his face and failed to yield any information. The only thing Southwell said was to warn that Audley would end up just like his predecessors. After leaving Tyndale prison, Audley sought and received permission from Henry to further interrogate these nobles and other government officials yet in prison to uncover the extent of their depravity and scheming. Reading between the lines, Audley had clearly been seeking authority to torture, which Henry fully understood, and told him to use any method he saw fit to hear the truth before dismissing the minister. Audley sent a dispatch to the Constable of the Tyndale Prison, stamped with the King's signature (given the frequency of such writs, such a stamp had been in use since the 1530s) authorizing and encourage the use of "further interrogation methods" for the noble prisoners. Constable Robert Eckland was well aware what the Chancellor meant and later that week had his guards and the crown's investigators take Greyson and Southwell to the torture chamber. Greyson died on the rack from heart failure before giving up any information. Southwell talked, and talked, and continued talking before scalding wax was poured in his eyes.

The court, and Audley, noted carefully that where the Queen sought to intervene, mercy would be forthcoming. He would pull back on his attempted manipulations and seek to delay any further overreach, so as not to anger again the Mistress of the Realm.

9.3 The Healer Queen

As the investigations into the minister and other members of the nobility were underway, the Queen managed to keep herself otherwise occupied with charity work. This is perhaps most evident in her personal expenses, which show not only the usual monies paid to St. Mary's Orphans, but also to several reformed monasteries, to assisting court petitioners that had been turned away, and some 4,500 pounds of her own funds (a massive amount for the day) to open up a hospital in London. After her second miscarriage, which had nearly killed her, she became immensely interested in the medical arts, and would become the chief patron to a revolution in medicine that would affect all of Europe. Closer to home, she would continue to fund the facility that became known as "Queen Anne's Hospital" until her death, along with anonymous donations to many other charities for the commons.

Medicine in Tudor times was barbaric. Surgeons, at least for those not in the nobility, were usually also barbers, with limited if any practical training. No anesthesia was available, apart from forcing patients to drink themselves into a stupor with quantities of alcohol that were dangerous in and of themselves, before even the minor surgeries known at the time, and "surgeons" relied heavily on concepts of treatment involving the use of leeches or direct bleeding to "remove poisoned bodily humors." Any layman or merchant could sell medical treatments with the proper permissions from the state, which knew no better than to approve of whatever treatments were in vogue.

The Queen successfully petitioned the King for a change in the law such that to portray oneself as a surgeon one would need to pay for a license and be accredited as understanding "accepted medical practices," with the fees for such licensing of course going to the crown. Under the new medical laws, any persons or facilities operating without such license would be shut down and their operators imprisoned until their fines could be repaid. This reform was intended to ensure the safety of the citizenry.

Of course, despite the King's desire that Anne be seen as legitimate by the people, the credit for the reform would go to Henry. Official records do, however, show that the instigation of the reforms followed a petition to Henry by Queen Anne. Although the practices of the day remained far below modern understanding of how to properly fight disease, this early revolution in state regulation of the medical trade can be traced to Queen Anne and her interest in medical care.

For weeks leading up to the Medical Licensing Act, Anne had been in talks with some of the best physicians of the time. She met regularly with a council of doctors from Oxford and Cambridge, the King's personal physicians, and invited the leaders in medicine from Paris, the German territories, and even from the Ottoman Empire—under leave of the Caliph now known as Suleiman the Magnificent—to participate in discussions as to how medical standards might be raised. The leading advances of the age were so brought to England. The Ottoman ruler, aware of the Protestant King's hostility to the Catholic powers constantly threatening his own conquests, was pleased to share signs of his doctors' superiority over his enemies' physicians with a King equally hostile to Rome.

Henry gave his blessing for her to hold such meetings, and even attended one or two himself. True to his earlier reputation as a Renaissance King, Henry was so impressed with what he heard that he would go on to periodically invite leading physicians from throughout the continent to court to teach English doctors their discoveries and their art.

The Ottoman delegation had been the first to be received at court. They were invited in August 1544 and arrived with a team of their top three doctors. Medicine from the Islamic Caliphate in the 16th century was far more advanced than in the rest of Europe. After dining one evening, the Ottoman Ambassador met privately with the King and Queen to discuss the latest medical achievements. He told them of new techniques, beyond the standard bleeding of the time, and stressed the use of compressed herbs, exotic spices, and ground metal complexes to heal a variety of common ailments such as ulcers, skin rashes, and various types of fevers.

Anne became convinced that bleeding a person was not only barbaric but that there had to be a way to improve medical care. At the conclusion of that meeting, the Queen asked Henry to task the Ambassador with providing her hospital with some of these new techniques. In the interests of his Caliph's desire to find potential European allies, the Ottoman Ambassador assented. England would thereafter be among Europe's leaders in medicine.

In the fall of 1544, Henry and Anne went on a three-week progress from Sudeley to visit her hospital in London to give alms to the poor and show Henry's desire to heal the sick. At the time it was thought that the touch of a King could heal the sick because he had been ordained by God.

Due to the city's size, Anne's hospital saw a large number of patients each day. When word spread of the hospital opening, patients from far across the realm sought its remedies for a variety of ailments. Henry took an avid interest in his wife's project and wanted to visit it to see for himself all she had done. Anne checked on the progress with the nurses and after listening to their needs she decided that a Nursing College would be needed to improve medical treatment. To reduce costs and combine medicine with the religious reforms she decided this new program would have to be a part of her continuing education reforms. With Henry's blessing Anne called Tyndale and Cranmer to meet to review their progress and to propose a new college for nursing.

Impressed with Anne's work, Henry approved her college program and ordered that the surgeon licensing mandate be put in place as soon as they had returned from London. The fee for each surgeon would be set for the first year at 10 pounds, until the crown could assess the impact of the cost. True to his word, that October he had Audley draw up the licensing mandate, bypassed Parliament with little fuss, and was spreading the decree by courier that autumn. One immediate impact was that the majority of back door surgery shops closed down and their operators went back to cutting hair and other grooming services.

Most of those practicing medicine at that time assented to the cost of the licensing fee with relatively little negative impact. If a patient was unhappy with the level of pain, scarring, or overall care that he received, there was no recompense for his injury. The surgeon still was paid and the patient had to deal with their lot. Nevertheless, the licensing program led the commons to favor licensed physicians as having the skills a mere barber lacked. This licensing fee ensured that only dedicated healers to the craft, with the ability to pay for their own supplies, would stay in the industry. The King's personal physician, Dr. Butts, highly commended the King and Queen for this new license practice and sent their Majesties a fine scalpel, made of gold and inscribed with a verse from the Book of Matthew, 10:8 *Heal the sick, cleanse the lepers, raise the dead, cast out demons. Freely you have received, freely give.* Henry gave Anne full credit for this and she kept the scalpel on display in her chambers until she died.

Dr. Butts was invited as a member of the council, along with his recommended doctors, to create the curriculum for the nursing program at Oxford. The council did not come to an immediate consensus and worked diligently throughout the fall, winter and into the spring of 1545 to address solutions to complex medical questions. The main concerns were being able to put these theories into solid practice, and not everyone agreed on the standards to agree upon.

Additional experts from Europe were summoned to advise as to the program's content. The curriculum would finally be presented to their Majesties in early 1546. They both eagerly approved and ordered its adoption to start enrolling students that fall. Henry also ordered that the program be adopted by the other English universities. He also requested that the top medical experts of the day be brought from places such as the Ottoman Empire, France, regions of Italy, and even Spain to help assist in a medical knowledge transfer. Anne had managed to convince him that a doctor's oath to heal would persuade these experts to spread their talents where they were needed the most. With that, he ordered Lord Audley to begin making the official requests. When these doctors arrived they would train skilled professors who could further spread their knowledge at universities across the land. Thanks to Anne, he could now count this medical program as the first of its kind in the country.

9.4 Henry VIII's Last Minister

Back in the end of 1544, the rioting over the policies of land enclosures had died down. Audley had sent out proclamations across the land that the nobles and gentry were being investigated by the King for their actions; this was enough to quell the enclosures and remove the motivation for uprisings without the need to use force. Before the proclamations had been distributed Parliament was briefed, but the minister wanted to ensure the commons that their oppressive overlords were being looked into. It did not hurt their case that massive rains came that autumn as well. Although the country was still overcoming that season's wheat shortage, they were able to make a moderate harvest in spring of 1545. The anger that had swept over most of the country over the nobles' activities had, at least temporarily, subsided with the peasantry's ability to once more earn a meager living off wheat profits. Although tempers began to subside, the government inquest continued.

Most of the people in the north were happy to hear that the crown was actually doing something to ease their plight and highly approved of the investigations. When interviewed by the crown's administrators they were eager to supply any information they could on their landlords.

This was seen as the common peoples' only chance to get back at their overlords, who for years had treated them poorly, often overcharging their families for basic supplies and tricking them into indentured servitude. This practice had been ongoing for decades and was well known, but little formal documentation existed proving the commons' claims about their plight.

While the Queen was receptive to Audley and had liked him well enough, certainly compared to her previous dealings with Wolsey, More, and Cromwell, she distrusted any future ministers the King would have. She also feared that perhaps Audley too would seek to supplant her own influence with the King. This she could not abide and personally began to keep her eye on Audley. She had George find out who Audley's grooms were and where the minister stored his files. It could be viewed that Anne sought to influence the King's actions regarding his minister. The past three had not worked out and Anne reasoned that her guidance and unending support during his reign had been invaluable.

According to modern historians, there was no specific incident that appeared to set the Queen to keeping a watchful eye on Audley, but it was rumored that after Cromwell's downfall she wanted to be her husband's sole advisor, and not only his principal counselor in private; she wished to be acknowledged the King's chief counsel publicly as well. Anne lacked the relationship with Audley that she had built with Cromwell before those two had come to be rivals, and so she was unable to view Audley as anything more than a political competitor.

She saw the position of the King's minister as one of doing the King's bidding and advising him on important matters of the realm, nothing more; yet previous ministers had sought to exert their own control over official matters. Audley thus far had kept himself in line, and was proving to be loyal, but Anne lacked the assurance that this minister held her best interests at heart as well. In addition to having George investigate Audley's activities she charged her ladies to keep their eyes and ears open. She also had not forgotten the Clifford affair, and remained wary because of Audley's empty allegations against a trusted friend to the crown. Anne saw Audley as a formidable opponent that nearly got away with the murder of a true subject merely for having spoken out against the minister's policies. Anne resolved to be cautious in her approach towards the crafty Audley. The King thus far had been supportive of her advice regarding the minister, but she was not privy to their intimate conversations and she had no knowledge of how he might attempt to persuade Henry to his cause. Anne saw this as a dangerous situation, which she needed to fortify herself against.

Southwell had revealed, under the "enhanced interrogation" tactics being employed at Audley's orders (approved by the King) scandals involving most every Member of Parliament and the nobility. Ironically, that included Lord Audley. He spared no one and at any cost was determined to save his own hide by casting allegations in most every direction. Some of the information he quite possibly made up completely, as no evidence was ever found to corroborate his stories. Despite this, a report was drafted by the chief constable detailing each of the prisoner's allegations. Southwell accused the Chancellor of inflating the cost of shipping supplies in the deal he made with Thomas Boleyn in the 1530s, and paying only those revenues to the crown that were based on the Actual cost of the products involved, instead of the appropriate tax for the inflated the price he actually sold the goods for. As an example, Audley was charging 20 pounds for 5 yards of heavy-duty rope for ship sails; the rope's Actual cost was a mere 6 pounds so the chancellor paid only 1 pound of taxes to the crown, instead of the 3 pounds he should have paid based on the profit he made. This was a damning accusation, indeed, for the man now charged with minding the royal treasury.

Boosting the credibility of the report, the constable had no direct involvement in any of the accused or accuser's affairs; he was simply doing his job. By all accounts he executed his duty well and stayed out of the political sphere. He followed Lord Audley's precise directions of interrogation to the letter. The original orders he had received from the Chancellor required that a formal report of his findings be compiled with one copy going to the King and the other to the Chancellery. Audley's own hand had ensured his destruction.

The King received the report the first week of November 1544, when the Constable felt that the interrogations had procured all the evidence available. He felt confident enough that the report detailed every aspect of the prisoner's confessions and implications of other associates. The King read the report and once more feared that he had been brooking serpents in his employ, in this case, with a third trusted Chancellor. Henry had never known the security and safety of a single state minister. He spent the better part of the day pondering what to do and called Archbishop Cranmer to hear his confession and absolve him of any sins he might need to undertake. Before Cranmer could advise him, the King ordered Audley's arrest. When the guards came for the Chancellor he was reading the report alleging his own criminal Acts. He said nothing during his arrest.

Cranmer paid a visit to Anne before heading out. He informed her of the King's heavy conscience and advised her to pay him a visit to bring him good cheer. She found Henry gazing out the window and he told her about Audley's arrest. Anne listened for a while before comforting him, assuring him that he had done the right thing in ordering the arrest. During Henry's weakest moments was when Anne's greatest strengths came out. She genuinely comforted him and listened with compassion and sincerity, while carefully noting any phrase that might help to serve her purposes later. Politics was a dangerous game with Henry and no matter how deeply she was in love with him, she had to be careful to maintain his love at all costs in the face of so many enemies at court who would seek to turn the King against her. For quite a while, Anne had felt that Henry needed to abolish the entire post of a state minister and take full and absolute power unto himself, and ultimately, to her.

Anne convinced Henry that this fourth straight betrayal showed that it was time to terminate that office of Chancellor entirely. She reminded him of his idol, Henry V, who had (temporarily) unified the English and French thrones in his crushing defeat of French forces at the Battle of Agincourt. She compared her husband to this earlier Henry, proclaiming that his forbearer would not have hesitated to take direct charge of his country. She went on to tell him how, like Henry V, he too had brought their enemies to heel, even while being betrayed by close advisors about him (some of whom had been implicated in an attempt to assassinate Henry V before he set sail to make war with France.

Finally, she advised him to keep Audley in prison while he contemplated his next move, but encouraged him to be deliberate, but swift and decisive. She convinced him that a King was born to rule and it was time that he took charge of his Kingdom. Her argument was so convincing that, had the necessary orders been before him right then and there, he would have. As a final thought before leaving she kissed him and urged him to ponder carefully on their discussion. She entreated that he let no other man take what should rightfully, by will of God, be his. She also reminded him that the beloved Prince Henry was coming to court the following day and they needed to secure the throne for their heir. This played on the King's ego masterfully, working like a charm.

That evening, Henry called Sir Richard Rich to advise him as to what documents he would need to formally abolish the Chancellor's post. Rich was shocked and advised the King that he could of course do so, but that Parliament would have to be notified and would need to approve such a move. Henry burst into anger, grabbing Rich about the throat, threatening him that if Parliament stood in his way they would all find their heads at the bottom of a basket. He ordered Rich and his chief Yeoman Warder to visit any Member of Parliament that might be troublesome, and rattled off a few names of those who should be monitored because they might attempt to override his command.

By removing the entire office of the Chancellorship, which had been in place since Henry II had entrusted the position to Sir Thomas Becket (another Chancellor who, as Henry would have noted, had betrayed his King) the King would be burdened with far more responsibilities. Still, this would also ensure that complete and utter power was in his firm grasp. By December 1544, Henry would have complete and utter control of his kingdom in all affairs. Parliament was dismissed, subject to his recall, and he relied on the Privy Council to swiftly enact his reforms, rather than entrust them to a chief minister.

Audley, Southwell, and four other nobles were tried on the same day, December 7th, 1544, and found guilty of treason and usurping the King's rightful authority. When asked if the prisoners had any statements, only Southwell made a statement, thanking his majesty's court for leniency; Southwell was informed ahead of time that he would be allowed the quick death of a beheading in exchange for graciousness to the King at trial, and thanks to having provided the information leading to the others' arrests. Audley remained silent not only at trial but at his execution as well. He and the other men were put to death December 10th. Audley was hung, drawn, and quartered. Southwell and the other nobles were beheaded. Three state ministers had now been killed in Henry's reign (with Wolsey having died of natural causes before he would have been executed). England would not have another state minister until his son's reign. Anne had gotten her way once more and Henry, with his Queen as his chief advisor, was now the unitary head of state.

9.5 The Spread of Reformation

Domestic affairs during this time revolved around the design of a second edition of an Anglican Book of Common Prayer. The Queen and Archbishop Cranmer worked closely together with various other theologians to develop and enhance their church's doctrine. Given the successful spread of the Ten Articles, the Book of Common Prayer was relatively easy to produce and distribute. Vital lessons in the production and distribution process had been learned and Cranmer also spoke often of how grateful the commons were to be able to embrace their faith in their own language. Whether or not this was the true pulse of the commons is questionable; most of the country, especially the north, had not genuinely adopted the Anglican reforms; however, the Archbishop remained optimistic and advised the Queen to speed and intensify the reforms, much to her delight.

Henry gave the revised book his blessing and introduced it to the English people in 1546, with a dedication to Queen Anne. She was invited, as a guest of honor, to the planning meetings that discussed doctrinal changes. This alone is significant; women in that time were not invited for high level meetings of state. They were deemed inferior creatures, with feeble minds. This Queen had changed that entire understanding. It may not have been Henry's desire to have his wife so politically able, but his grandmother Lady Margaret Beaufort was also a strong woman and he grew up understanding her impact in his own life, including how well his household was run under her strict instruction.

It is interesting to note that the original book had specific guidance on matters such as how the clergy should dress, while the new edition had more freedom for variations in dress while yet being sanctioned by the state. This lifting of various such ceremonial bans was viewed as a step forward, as strict regulation of things like Priestly garb was seen as hewing too much to Catholic tradition. A common complaint amongst the people had been the requirement that they ritualistically continue to dress their Priests and remove their vestments after mass; with this single Act the Queen was acknowledging failings to go far enough in the original reforms.

Anne was instrumental in determining both the changes in the prayer book and how it would be spread to the people. She had reviewed Cranmer's speeches with him so they could present a unified message concerning the new teachings. Her vision of educating the masses about the reforms also extended to children and included teaching the people how to read and write. This radical education plan was not popular amongst the nobility who felt threatened by the prospect of the rise of a new enlightened class. Anne felt very strongly, however, that for the people to understand their faith, they would have to be enabled to read it for themselves.

While religion was the central tenet of daily life in Tudor England, commoners could barely afford either the required tithing or, when rural, to travel long distances to attend services. One of the main changes in the second book was to this mandate that all persons attend mass weekly. The more obvious change was the use of the English language, so that the masses (at least those who were literate in their native tongue) could study the Bible themselves, without need to know Latin or Greek. It was under Anne that the first Bible was printed in English, with the Book of Common Prayer following that example.

Further, the very design of churches was changed, so that the hardworking commons could focus on their worship and even come to look forward to a time of peace and reflection. The modern church design, with rows of pews and pillows for kneeling in prayer, was also a concept that arose during this time. The pillows came later of course, but the pews themselves were introduced and allowed for a semi-comfortable place for families to be as one group when hearing the gospel. These slight renovations seem standard today, but in that time, the ideas were revolutionary. Henry had to be brought on board with these changes and was hesitant to implement them at first, but a few weeks of Anne's careful nudging ensured that the improvements were executed.

When the news of the new prayer book was delivered to the clergy, a near revolt erupted, led primarily by Bishop Gardiner. Cranmer attempted to argue that the reforms were Actually quite small and to rationalize them, but the Bishop was not having it. Dissention erupted among the clergy and only when her majesty was brought into the discussions would the angry clerics tone down their disagreements (if only on the surface). Once it became clear that the clergy were largely on the verge of an outright revolt, Anne saw it necessary to put down the imminent rebellion. The Queen publicly reprimanded Gardiner and threatened him with the loss of his position if he did not mind himself.

A few short days later, presumably because of her threat, Gardiner lost his lucrative post as Bishop of Winchester. He was also stripped of his assets and his rich robes were directed by Anne to be sold to help finance her education plan, with Henry's agreement. He retired the day he lost his bishopric on November 1st and died within the year. The cause of his death was never known and his estates were quietly returned to Henry.

Cranmer appointed as Bishop Gardiner's successor a cleric named John White. White would turn out to be just as much of a papist as Gardiner had been, but not as vocally Active and far more willing to collaborate with the crown. He could also be bought. Cranmer felt his education, his meekness, and his reputation for virtue would serve the clergy well. Previously vulnerable, the reformers at court had at last landed the final blow to the entire conservative faction. The crown had done such an expedient job of removing political opponents, while simultaneously spreading their reforms, that the influence of papist sympathizers was all but eliminated—at least in public. Those who did remain devout to the old ways were harassed, humiliated at court, and their business interests all but eliminated. Henry had become, at Anne's coaxing and with her counsel, the most singly powerful monarch in English history.

Chapter 10

Unifying a Kingdom

The early 1540's as England was occupied with executions of traitors, dramatic shifts in domestic policy and further religious reforms; these would also contribute to the King becoming estranged from his dearest friend. The last of the monastic houses, Dunstable Priory, had been dissolved, and all its possessions had become property of the royal treasury. In the House of Lords Abbots had lost their seats, with Bishops and Archbishops retained only as advisors on religious policy. These Bishops represented the only voice of the clergy in government affairs in the chamber. For the first time in Henry's reign, secular authority dominated Parliament, and with that came swift changes. In 1540 the King had officially sanctioned the destruction of shrines built to honor Saints. This action was meant to reinforce that England was wholly its own realm, beyond the grip of Roman rites and beholden to God alone, and to show the people that these shrines were a continued reminder of the papacy that would no longer be tolerated. This religious policy change was not without controversy.

In spring of 1545, the King's closest friend, Charles Brandon, retired to his estates with his fourth wife Catherine Willoughby. His sons were Prince Henry's playmates and he would often reminisce about his own days as a child with the King. He often wrote Henry, telling him of his deep affections for his old friend, his memories of the many hunts they had shared, and came to inform him about his ill health, and his will. Of all the courtiers who tried to take his place, none ever managed the feat.

Charles truly was Henry's closest and lifelong friend. He could anticipate the King's mood better than almost anyone else, including his wife.

Brandon' health had also become an issue; he was no longer the young robust man he had once been. His injury from 1536, along with his involvement in the Pilgrimage of Grace rebellion, ruined him both physically and emotionally. Due to the exceptional care he had received, he had fully recovered in body from the shoulder wound he had suffered that morning of the joust, so many years before, but had ever afterwards suffered from debilitating migraines and severe mood swings. As he aged, he also suffered from arthritis and possibly had contracted dysentery. It remains unclear what combination of old wounds or new illnesses led to the event, but Charles Brandon, Duke of Suffolk, the King's closest friend and brother-in-law, passed away August of 1545 at his estates in Guilford. He willed his personal library and all of its effects to the King.

Towards the end of his life, Brandon's friendship with Henry had waned, mainly as the King grew to rely ever more upon Anne for counsel, but also, Henry's continued religious reforms went beyond what Brandon could embrace. He was a true Catholic at heart. He knew well where the boundaries of his faith lay, and Henry pushed those to the extreme. When he sought leave to retreat to his estate and leave court, Henry gladly dismissed him. That would be the last time the two saw one another again. The King mourned the loss of his once-dear-friend greatly; he paid all of Brandon's debts and paid for his burial in St. George's Chapel at Windsor. Brandon, the one man who had always been true to him, was now gone. No one would remain who could restrain the King from pursuing even wider reform.

Court was changing in other ways as well, with foreign affairs being altered by Anne's survival on the throne. After years of waiting, Chapuys was finally recalled back to Spain in January of 1546. He was replaced by Cristobal de Castillo, from Madrid. With the new Ambassador and a final Spanish acceptance of Anne's status as Queen, Charles once more reconsidered the possibility of an English alliance, particularly given his ongoing competition with the French over their contested territories in Italy. Charles also factored in his realization that English naval power had made the prospect of invading Britain unappetizing, at best. By aligning with England, the Emperor could have a serious advantage over Ottoman trade routes, and all but eliminate the Caliphate's ability to transport troops and supplies through the western Mediterranean. Nevertheless, despite the logic in approaching the English king with the prospect of a treaty, the injustices Charles suffered at Henry's hand could not be easily dismissed.

Early in his tenure Ambassador Chapuys had advised hostility to England, and maneuvered to weaken the English court from within, but over years of being bested by Anne and her fellow reformists, he had come to reconsider his initial and instinctive opposition to friendship with England. Chapuys, as he aged, had longed to go home, and had become more familiar with the English people than he had first desired. His very close friendship with the Lady Mary and Queen Katherine perhaps clouded his initial objectivity. With the coming of a new, ambitious, and young Spanish Ambassador, and the prospect of returning home and no longer remaining in London, where Chapuys needed to balance his advice to Spain with the necessity of preserving his access to the English court, his old prejudices had fallen away.

Charles, too, was aging, and with the concurrent failing health of his adversary King Francis, Charles came to acknowledge his own mortality and seek more peaceful days. The 1539 Peace of Toledo had nearly collapsed on more than one occasion, and only survived through both signatories ignoring flashes of conflict on their borders. Tensions remained high through the 1540s. Even in old age and failing health, these leaders could not let go of their animosity for one another.

Meanwhile, the English had sought to bolster their sometimes strained friendship with France. King Francis had been unwell, suffering from syphilis he had caught when still a youth. It had been clear to the French court that Francis was preparing his son to take over the French throne. By 1546, Francis could barely get out of bed. The disease that had so ravaged his body did the same to his mind, so much so that he often forgot who or where he was. He finally passed away on his son Henry's birthday, March 28th, 1547. It is said that upon hearing the news of Francis' death Queen Anne wept for hours, remembering fondly when she served as girl at the French court. Despite his continued Catholicism, she considered Francis her strongest European ally. Henry sent the new French King, Henry II, a plate of gold and jewels, with a letter of condolence and an invitation to visit as soon as he was able. While the gesture was diplomatic, England and France had tense relations during Francis' reign. He and Henry were similar in age and were both gifted in multiple areas. Henry viewed him as a rival but called him, affectionately, his cousin.

Francis was the first of the powerful European trio of leaders to pass, leaving only Henry VIII and Charles V, and both of these were increasingly ill, themselves. Henry had been going bald, was overweight, developed gout, and suffered from frequent bouts of indigestion, especially after heavy meals of meat. Anne and his doctors did what little they could to persuade him to alter his diet, but he remained stubborn. He also began having nightmares about God punishing him for his sins, and met regularly with Archbishop Cranmer for religious counsel. Perhaps prophetically, it was to be in a religious debate that Henry would secure his image with the public, and end widespread dissention with his policies.

10.1 The Kritchen Debate

In 1546 there was one remaining publicly "willful papist" that the regime had yet to eliminate. Pamphlets were being printed by a commoner named Reginald Kritchen—doubtless with backing from secret wealthy interests—criticizing the reformers for "intransigence against God's rightful place" and calling for willful refusal to acknowledge the King as head of the church. He called the Queen a whore, accused her of sleeping with Archbishop Cranmer to solicit his "services" in the church, and labeled Henry a demon whose sole motive was to control the people's minds with his dangerous and false prophetic language. These pamphlets said that the reformers had committed such grave actions that they should be labeled both heretics and traitors, and called for their execution. Further, he encouraged loyal Catholics to stay true to the Vatican. This commoner was taking unusual license in his statements, indeed, and would prove to be an important factor in the history of Henry VIII's reign.

Kritchen was born in Shrewsburyshire in about 1487, the fourth of seven children of John and Margaret Kritchen, who had married around the late 1470's. His father was a butcher, his mother a house servant. Little is known about his six siblings; Reginald would be the brightest and most renowned of the family. His family had been in the area since the 12th century, and a small parcel of land had been in his family's ownership for at least six generations. Initially, this land had been used for sheep farming, but over the years it had grown to encompass over 57 acres, including one of the largest farms in the area. During the enclosure crisis, these lands were reduced to a mere 13 acres, dramatically affecting the family revenue.

Reginald's most important influence was his father. As a child he had embraced hunting alongside his father, who would then carve and sell the meats they had killed together. His mother was a strict disciplinarian and ran the household with an iron fist. Each child was responsible for their part of the running the house. Meals were regimented and religious holidays always observed. They encouraged religious teaching in the home, although Reginald was initially bored with church. As he grew older he began to cling to their Catholic faith because of its promise of redemption and paradise, in contrast to the family's meager accommodations on Earth. In adolescence it was rumored that he stopped courting a local village girl because she refused to admit she enjoyed church. As with most of the commons, religion was the only thing they had to turn to for hope and for explanations for life's many unfortunate ills, from sickness to class structure. The church offered the oppressed peoples of all of Europe one simple explanation and promise for all ills: *"It was God's will, and if you have faith you will find eternal reward in the Afterlife."* Reginald took his Priests at their word.

In his early twenties, he began to re-evaluate Priestly teachings and would often speak out during sermons he found inconsistent. His objections to authority chiefly rested on his growing realization that the church was run like any other business, with just as much scandal and corruption as court life. Nevertheless, as a commoner with no experience in politics or international affairs, Kritchen remained a devout Catholic and saw abuses in the Church as merely being examples of local clergy exploiting their positions as intermediaries between the common people and the—no doubt—far more holy and righteous Pope.

To Kritchen, the resolution of abuses lay in reforming the clergy's lifestyle and bringing them nearer the true Church. In essence, he felt that the papacy neither encouraged nor approved of the abuses of a parish Priest. In the eyes of Christ, such actions would be deemed a cardinal sin. How could the very instruments of God be disobeying their vows of poverty and chastity? Prior to its being shut down, Kritchen saw his local monastery's Abbot living like a noble. Even the monks and nuns wore beautiful cloth, had rings of gold, and several had even taken missionary trips to the Vatican in the early 1510s, all at the expense of the townspeople. That very money Kritchen believed should have been going for the better treatment of the poor.

One evening in 1521 he snuck into a monastery and stole the house's accounting records. Going through it line by line he discovered that, not only were they misusing their funds, they were paying for illegal and sinful products such as various exotic wines, written off as routine expenses, for use as sacramental wine, despite such wine never being used at Mass. The truth was that this wine had come from some of the most expensive vineyards in France, vineyards from which the King of France drank. His church was spending upwards of 3,000 pounds a year on importing this wine, and a mere 130 pounds a year on Actual sacramental wine. He also uncovered recurring payments to a local tailor maid with no note as to their cause.

He held onto the books and sought out the maid under the guise of soliciting her services. He flirted with her a bit during the visit and, while she did not directly give away that she was sleeping with the local Priest, she confirmed with a very affectionate tone that she was very fond of the Priest and enjoyed providing her services to him. This was merely circumstantial evidence at best, but enough to satisfy Reginald's suspicions. The following week he confronted the Priest, who denied everything. Sometime soon after, Reginald was suspected of setting the church on fire, nearly destroying it. With his minimal understanding of the greater institution of the Catholic Church, he would come to think that the problem of corruption resulted not from the common church being too near to Rome, but too far from it.

In 1528, Kritchen applied to serve as a clerk to the clergy at Westminster. He was rejected with no reason given. Most likely he was rejected because he lacked formal experience and had no recommendations. Regardless, he held onto that rejection as a personal affront. He was forced to continue working on his father's farm. As the reformation got underway, he came to resent Henry's leadership and his involvement in religious affairs as an example of further corrupting the church by injecting into it the well-known abuses of secular leaders.

When Anne became Queen, Kritchen was livid. He had been a loyal and loving supporter of Catholic Queen Katherine, viewing her as a true model of a Catholic royal. He viewed Anne as the devil's handmaid and spread around town malicious rumors that she had used witchcraft to make the King love her (how else could the "Defender of the Faith" be so persuaded to the abominable Act of divorce?). While it took seven years for Anne to finally become Queen, to the people it did not feel merely long enough. Most of them hated her from day one, for the very same reasons that Kritchen despised her.

In the 1530s, when the *Valor Ecclesiaste* report came out and cited the continued abuses of the Shrewsburyshire monastery and recommended its closure, Kritchen could not have been more pleased. Personally, he had enjoyed some graces, finally marrying and having two daughters, but his wife died during the second birth, leaving him even angrier and convinced that God had punished him for not doing enough to support the true faith. This decade had indeed been a very trying time for him, including the death of his father and an elder brother, leaving him with the responsibility of managing the family farm and butchery. He was now a single father of two, running a stressful business he had no interest in working. Despite the difficult times, he took his family into town every weekend to hear the latest religious news and read to his girls nightly a new passage from the Bible. He saw his new destiny as in raising his children in the true faith and voluntarily took a vow of chastity following his wife's death, in a desperate attempt to prove himself worthy of God's acceptance. He often flagellated himself in private.

As the 1540's came Reginald found himself more and more despondent with the state of religious affairs in his country. In 1545, his eldest daughter Ellen married a neighbor's son, Jeremiah Wallace. Jeremiah had arranged for a modest cottage for the two, with an acre of land to work half a mile away from their parents. Reginald now had his youngest, Alice, 15 years old, to care for. Alice was a precocious young woman who made her father very proud. He was negotiating a pre-contract for marriage between Alice and another neighbor's son, and was haggling over the price of her dowry. As he saw his role as a parent fading fast, he decided to get more involved in the religious affairs that he so passionately believed in.

By the summer of 1546, Kritchen, then alone in his house with no children to care for, pursued his path of examining religious affairs further and gathered inspiration through prayer. In the cold and bitter darkness he prayed for hours to understand his true purpose on this new journey. After coming to a resolution, he decided that the only way to spread God's true word was to be bold, direct and without fear. He saw how the righteous, such as Sir Thomas More, Bishop Fisher, Robert Aske, Queen Katherine, and the Lady Mary, had been condemned for their compassion and silent allegiance to the Roman church. He resolved not to make the same mistakes. He sat to write down his thoughts and began openly preaching to his town. Deciding that his hometown was too sparsely populated to build a base for action, he moved with all of his meager possessions to the outskirts of London, where he was certain to find a far larger audience for his message.

Kritchen would choose a safe spot in the morning, before the sun became unbearable, and began preaching about the corruption at court. He focused his "lay ministry" on London due to its sheer size and thus ability to spread his message to large masses. Kritchen witnessed up front the lack of morality, sanitation, and what he viewed as the devil's influences all around the great city. His passion for the papacy gradually led from speeches in the town square to the city. One night in 1546 a person suspected to be Kritchen gathered a pile of the new English Bibles and lit them ablaze. Because the fire was set near the outskirts of London, and no one claimed responsibility for the Act, Kritchen was never tried for the crime.

Early in the morning of November 6th, 1546, pamphlets by Kritchen, condemning the reforms and his King and Queen, were delivered to nearly every household in London; the printing was funded by an anonymous benefactor who some believe to have been Cardinal Pole. The news spread back to their majesties before supper. Anne presented a copy of the pamphlet to the King as to provoke him and called for the Archbishop to dine with them to share his thoughts on the matter. Cranmer was particularly insistent that those responsible were heretics and even traitors who sought nothing less than his majesty's disgrace, the replacement of Prince Henry, and a return to the Catholic faith. The King ordered that Kritchen be found and brought in for questioning. This would prove easier said than done.

By winter of 1547, Kritchen had been roaming London for some time, teaching that the religious and educational reforms were nothing more than a call to turn good Christian people into heretics. He urged the good people of England to purify themselves and not fall for the state's ploy, which would lead to the damnation of their souls. Initially his followers were few, and over the weeks to come, as the new religious courses had started, instructors noted a significant drop off in their numbers of students.

Henry was outraged to learn that this Kritchen's sedition had been finding a willing ear in so many of his subjects. He raged to Anne at the Acts of this commoner and said he would have the traitor pulled limb from limb for daring to confront the throne and spread his sedition to the masses. Anne comforted the King, assuring him that he was right in his indignation against the papist Kritchen. Anne then took a step Henry had not anticipated. Upon cooling the King's temper, Anne suggested that a far greater victory might be in Henry's grasp. This won the King's attention.

Anne, again showing both her skill at politics and her influence over the King, suggested that perhaps the King could turn the heretic's Acts to Henry's own advantage. She suggested that Henry could help put down not only Kritchen, but any potential followers, by confronting the commoner directly, and in so doing, also show that the reforms the crown had instituted were not being decreed and enforced solely through the power of the state to intimidate and suppress, but because they were right and true. His interest peaked, Henry asked his wife to go on.

She suggested that God might be presenting him an opportunity to appear both a man of reason and the best man in the Kingdom to head their faith. She asked whether the King, so learned in the faith—remember, he had initially been trained for the cloth and had once been called "Defender of the Faith" by a Pope—might benefit from publicly debating the seditious heretic, and showing the truth of his position before all the world. As Anne reasoned, even an impressive showing by Kritchen could be portrayed as the commoner's merely spouting forth words put forth by a foreign agent, such as the Vatican or Spain, while a victory would forever cement Henry's rightful status as head of the church. Henry was intrigued, and inwardly pleased to think that he was, indeed, more than up to defeating a challenge from a papist mouthpiece.

Henry sent agents to Kritchen's home and, when the critic expected arrest and martyrdom for the Roman Church, stunned the commoner by instead presenting an invitation to court. Henry had decided, upon Anne's advice, to address the matter directly by challenging Kritchen to an open debate at Westminster. She felt it would make Henry appear more civilized and show his people that all the executions had been at the hand of evil ministers before him, a play he fell for immediately. George prepared his speech for the debate; it would later be heralded as one of the best in his reign. Henry had come to see this as an opportunity to once more show that he was one with his people and to dispute papist claims head on. By disputing such statements outright and in person, he had become assured that his words would have even greater weight, and he could further consolidate his rule, this time without having to resort to force that might inspire further dissent in the future. The great question might at last be settled forever.

The debate was set for December of 1547, just before Christmastide. Kritchen spoke first, submitting his arguments alleging abuses by the crown in attempting to suppress those who remained loyal to the Roman church. He argued that the crown's claims of seeking to free the people from idolatry were Actually an attempt to deny the very foundations of Christianity. He presented a very persuasive argument that the King had well enough authority to break with the political and business ties to any foreign power, including the Vatican, but said that it was beyond an earthly monarch's authority to dictate the manner in which a subject showed spiritual allegiance to Christ. Attempting to minimize the charge that he was merely a zealot or foreign agent, Kritchen then applauded the crown for making such bold strides against corruption and abuses in the church. He also thanked Henry for weeding out those in the clergy who abused their offices. His praise, however, ended there. Kritchen went on to inflame the audience with the polarizing rhetoric he had promoted in his pamphlets.

The King's response, carefully planned with Cranmer and Anne, was intelligent, poignant, and precise; his words struck Kritchen's arguments like daggers. The King emphasized the virtue of promoting public education—particularly by allowing them to learn the Holy Bible in their native English—as being the truest means of bringing about reform. He stressed the importance of male education specifically, but said also that women should be able to know and understand the gospels, so they would be assured of their salvation even if they found themselves spinsters or widows. The King asserted that his educational reforms were meant to empower his people and set a standard for all of Europe that would forever lift them from the days of darkness that followed the collapse of Rome.

The King saw himself as God's messenger to bring about the Lord's truth. He railed against his European brethren for not invoking their divine duty to better their people and damned their realms for their insolence at the clear will of God that Christ's message be spread. While powerfully moving, revisionist historians have questioned whether Anne's guiding influence was present in the crafting of the speech. The attendees that day received free English Bibles and wine, along with being given the rare privilege to ask questions of and receive blessings from the King.

The debate was exceptional public relations, and won mass approval for the King. Kritchen, humiliated and at a loss, would return to his home, by leave of the King. He would have a single return to the public eye yet before him.

10.2 Educating the Commons

Tudor England had one main industry, agriculture from farming or from fishing in coastal waters. The majority of the working class wound up serving in some agricultural capacity, with the rest in subsidiary industries such as creating textiles from farmed wool and cotton, working as servants to landowning nobles, mining and blacksmithing, or service in government. There were few comforts and no standards for setting a worker's hours. Some commoners worked from dusk to dawn in back-breaking labor. Medicine was still very much in its infancy and Henry and Anne's efforts to spark a medical Renaissance would only pay England large dividends much later. Coupled with disease, unsafe food and water, and the difficulty of the working conditions, the average life expectancy for those who survived childhood to become adults was only the mid-fifties.

Education was a privilege for those wealthy enough to afford it. Access to learning was believed to be divinely determined by order by birth and noble status, and not meant for the general population. Were one unfortunate enough to be born into poverty, it was unlikely that such a person would even achieve enough literacy to read and write one's own name. With literacy rates so low, an entire profession began for clerks who made their living off of being paid to read and write letters to and from the government and family members, along with legal documents. Most times the only way to rise from the lower social classes to achieve higher standing came through having won the generosity of a benefactor who saw potential in a person's mind or abilities and provided for their further education.

The feudal system was an accepted part of life, but as Henry VIII ruled with Anne's advice, the times became increasingly ripe for change. Many subjects recalled the recent and bloody War of the Roses and saw the death and destruction that accompanied that contest for power. Those memories reinforced the people's obedience to an ideology that kept rebelliousness in check. These fears were exploited heavily by the sitting regime to maintain its position in the system. The Pope also exploited these fears to preserve the Church's authority by promising an eternity of bliss in exchange for supplication to the clergy, and by threatening the loss of such paradise by means of expulsion from the Church.

Anne felt that education could be used to give the people the analytical tools needed for them to recognize corruption and injustice, and see the correctness of her religious reforms. Maintaining a general level of ignorance had been the preferred means for the ruling class to keep the commons in line, with the people kept aware only of technical matters that were necessary for them to fulfill their assigned roles in the social order. As to religious education, the people had long been encouraged to remain pious and dutiful subjects based on religious obligation. However, Anne proposed that this type of oppression could only last but so long, and that a monarch who called for broad public education would win the loyalty of the people for all his reign.

The first detailed plans for educational houses were drawn up by Hugh Latimer, a reformer and devoted scholar and theologian who was well trusted by the Queen. The plans called for groups of male children aged 6 to 11 to be paired together in groups of 12 to learn to read the Bible in English, and be taught the rightness of the King's religious reforms, with similar lesson plans to be set for groups of children aged from 12 to 17, and for subjects aged over 18. Latimer advised the Queen that this strategy of separation by age group had produced excellent results in trials, such as with the Children of St. Mary's. The teenage curriculum would also contain English history, reformation principles, and training in a skill such as farming, blacksmithing, or one of the clerical trades.

His original plan called for only males to be allowed into the classes. Young girls would learn how to read and write limited English, barely more than enough to sign their names and understand marital contract clauses. They would also be required to study the English Bible. In wealthy homes girls would be taught by a Governess and would only be sent to formal instruction at the age of 12. In poor communities, lessons would be taught at their local monastery at the most appropriate time for the town and the children. The majority of commoner children would have to walk several miles to town just to attend. Teenage girls were originally intended only to learn basic English and home management skills, such as child rearing and sewing, but the Queen insisted that children of promise be offered the opportunity to further their education, at the crown's expense, in either a monastery or the Queen's nursing college.

Anne further insisted that girls' classes also include learning to read and write to the same standards in English and Latin as the males. She successfully argued that a woman could not be prepared for this world if lacking in understanding of the very languages used in life and so much religious discussion. Cranmer reluctantly took Anne's side and Latimer agreed to attempt to work the Queen's wishes into the overall plan.

In an increasingly rare reversal by the King, Queen Anne's amendments to the plan would fail. Girls would be taught to lesser standards, "based on their diminished need for such learning," but the Queen understood to personally finance further education for girls in London and required monthly briefings on their progress. She also insisted upon the right to visit the children and attend their lessons.

The crown also agreed to finance the supplies needed for the lessons for a single year, subject to reassessment based on the results of the initiative. The royal exchequer had no concrete way of measuring the cost, and benefit, of a social program of this size. Their only experience to date had been in managing the cost of various court expenses and the cost of the armed services, which included salaries and equipment, and salaries for various government agents. The training of instructors for the education program was to be done by Latimer, Tyndale, and other professional educators they recommended, to ensure that the courses were adequately taught. For these courses to win support they would begin at court, as trial sessions, and gradually spread to cover the whole of the realm. Latimer proposed to begin himself tutoring the first group of 12 boys, in the presence of the royal court.

Adult classes would be taught in church, with a mandatory attendance for one hour per week following Sunday mass. Enforcing this mandate would prove difficult. Many subjects of the crown would obey partially out of fear of reprisal; many more would feign excuses or simply leave after the Priest's sermon. Churches of that time only kept records for tax purposes and evaluating land. Adding education to Sunday mass would be the easiest way to spread the program to a mass group of people without causing disruption to labor productivity. Holding the programs apart from church services would risk losing valuable work in the fields and other industries.

For adult males, they would be provided with a more in-depth understanding of the abuses of the Catholic Church, the foundations of the Reformation and instruction as to how the reforms would affect their daily lives. They would also be taught to read and write limited English. Latimer designed the curriculum under the theory that by the time a person reached adulthood the majority of their skill level had already been set, and adults were not as capable of learning new ideas as were children. It was also thought at the time that women were intellectually inferior to men and thus that curricula designed for females should be less demanding; even with Anne's influence and example, Henry would decree that learning would remain a privilege reserved for men.

The first series of trial classes were set to begin in London in February 1547. Sufficient time had to be allowed to coordinate logistics, including selecting and training tutors, and procuring supplies for each province in the country. These trial classes would test how receptive the people were to the content and allow for improvement before a final version of the courses could be designed and taught. Royal proclamations were ordered and posted all about the city of London, advising everyone of the purpose of the new requirement and urging all who were interested to tell the Mayor's office of their interest, so as to provide the crown some indication of how many instructors and supplies would be necessary. An overwhelming number of respondents flooded the Mayor's office, so many that armed guards had to be paid to wait by the door at all hours and additional clerks needed to be hired by Cranmer.

Despite the obvious interest of the people, it remained difficult to gauge King Henry's commitment to the program. In certain areas, especially on male lessons, he was encouraged and even eager for greater involvement in designing the curriculum. He even volunteered to write an accounting of his own reign for teaching to the people, to inform them of (a pro-Henry) description of current English history. When it came to educating women, the King was less than pleased. He argued that, while women should know homemaking and childrearing skills, they had little need for reading and writing of English, much less Latin. He argued that they were vulnerable, in need of protection from unsavory ideas, and ordered that literacy education be stricken from the girls' program, with the exception that females be taught enough to sign their name.

Anne was not present at the meeting establishing this change in the program, and accounts from her ladies-in-waiting indicate that the couple had a rather intense fight when word got back to her. Indeed, the wood paneling in the King's Privy Chamber would be chipped from the Queen having thrown her dinner plate at the wall. Henry reportedly grabbed the furious Queen and shook her so hard that she lost an earring. He bellowed that he had let her get away with far too much already and that she was the proof of the wisdom of keeping women uneducated and un-opinionated, before storming from the room. The couple did not speak for three days. By the fourth day, Henry was seen going into the Queen's chambers and, after a good deal of shouting, followed by hours that could not be heard by staff outside the room, all was well again. The King's order remained that reading and writing lessons be reincorporated into the female lesson plan, with an emphasis on learning enough to understand the Bible and 10 Articles. Tyndale, Cranmer and Latimer set about their preparations.

Were these courses to be successful, they would establish the first mandatory and formal public education system in all of Europe. The idea was both controversial and revolutionary. This program would create a lasting change in English society. The King understood that educating the commons was a matter none of the other European powers had dared to tackle. Friends of the realm viewed it as a clever way to educate the public at large and spread information legitimizing the King and Queen, while enhancing all of society in the process. Critics viewed it as nothing more than indoctrination of reformist principles.

When word spread of the new program, the public expressed both outrage (from the nobles) and delight (by the commons). The people for the first time would be allowed to truly understand the world in which they lived. Even being able to write one's own name had long been considered a privilege set aside for the rich. Many commoners felt that they would never acquire enough wealth to be educated and would die ignorant; and the nobility wished to keep them that way. Instead, the crown itself had decreed that a basic education would be provided to every several English man and woman. Anne had managed to alter the course of English society.

10.3 A Royal Family

To prepare for his own mortality, Henry ordered that his son's household be upgraded, and gave him lands previously owned by Lord Rochford, Lord Audley, and Sir Southwell. He also drafted in his own hand the Second Act of Succession of 1547, declaring that Prince Henry be heir to the throne of England and English lands in Ireland, and declaring that the future Prince's children be immediate heirs to the throne, followed by the Princess Elizabeth's issue; Elizabeth would herself be monarch if Prince Henry or his heirs had died.

Although he had less time to frolic and hunt, Henry came to enjoy the responsibilities of running the entire government, which came to him upon having dissolved the position of Chancellor. While his duties became far more demanding and afforded him precious little personal time, he relished the exercise of power. He kept on a clerk to handle most of the writing, but the main decisions in running the kingdom, down to the smallest matters, were solely up to him. He consulted the Privy Council when he felt he needed to, but as he aged he became more confident in his choices. The responsibility also kept his mind fresh as he aged, although he relied more and more heavily on Anne as his principal advisor.

He had given a great deal of thought to the legacy he would leave behind and spent the free time he did have with his son, hunting, teaching him statecraft, instructing him how to behave at court, and delighting the young man with tales of his own exploits in romance and how to pursue a lady. His son genuinely loved his father and Henry enjoyed being once more the center of attention. Father sparred with son while teaching him combat and Henry lavished the boy with the finest robes that could be found in all of Europe. Prince Henry was a constant delight at court, with the boldness of his father and charm of his mother. The King also spent more time with Elizabeth as well, visiting her household, showing her how to hunt, and often speaking with her in Latin and French. She far exceeded his expectations, not only for a daughter, but as a Princess. He had every confidence she would make an exceptional match to a Prince of Europe. In fact, Henry and Anne would often discuss potential matches for both of their children, without coming to any solid conclusions, at least for the time being.

While Henry tended to the country's affairs, Anne maintained a high profile at court. She ran up high expenses from French and Italian tailors for the finest quality fabrics, jewels of magnificent weights and dimensions from the Indies, and all of the accessories she could get her hands on. She would often take Elizabeth with her on shopping excursions and, now that the Princess was heading into puberty, Anne took enormous pride in developing her as a young lady.

The two were very close; Elizabeth preferred to stay with her mother instead of at her own household most of the time. Besides shopping, the mother-daughter pair also enjoyed long walks in the gardens, dancing, and both shared a fondness for debating religious philosophy. Having Elizabeth in residence brought Anne an enormous amount of joy and kept her calmer. It also helped her to avoid the pitfalls of loneliness that might have resulted from not seeing Henry as much as she had been used to. Without a state minister, his new schedule consisted of rising by five A.M. and retiring to bed shortly before 11 P.M. He would often try to share supper with Anne and Elizabeth when he was able, but most of the time he would miss it.

Now that the children were getting older and excelling in their studies, Anne brought the Prince to court to stay with the family as a whole. For Queen Anne, Princess Elizabeth, and Prince Henry, 1546 was a period of happiness and comfort. They wanted for nothing, the country was at peace and they were all together. As a mother, Anne was loving and protective. She did not intend, even as a Queen, to be a standoffish mother who sent her children to be raised permanently by a Governess. Even when the children were younger she spent considerable time at their residences or taking them on trips. Henry both admired and grew frustrated at her parenting style. He had expected Anne to be like his own mother. As Queen, certain duties were unbecoming of one's role, and emotional bonding was not seen as a requirement for royalty. Anne did not grow up as a royal, under such stringent conditions. She had also endured many harsh lessons over the years over having to learn so much on her own, and so she would forge a new model for of royal parenting.

At Anne's insistence that they needed to spend some time together away from the formality of court, in summer of 1546, the entire family would go on summer progress to Dudley Castle in the north. The Dudley property had been taken over by Lord Dudley from the Buckingham family in 1537 and had been in continuous renovation since then. The King left Thomas Howard, the 2nd Earl of Surrey in charge as regent in their absence, with extremely limited powers. Surrey was Lord of the Treasury and a trusted cousin of the Boleyn family. To some, the Earl was a highly ambitious man who used lethal methods to retain his standing. To the King and Queen he was nothing more than a trusted friend and loyal adviser.

As the progress moved through Birmingham en route to Dudley, the Queen greeted the people of the town and gave out alms on Sunday. She performed beautifully, was dressed sumptuously, and clearly wanted it known by all that although she was aging, she was still very much their Queen. Anne had chosen to dress in sumptuous blue velvet with a white damask underlay, threaded on the edges with cloth of gold, and wearing a gold string necklace of pearl and sapphire. The King matched her in his royal sapphire robes and accoutrements. Her almoner, John Skip, preached a sermon to the congregation that day concerning obedience to God and spreading the Lord's message of good cheer. The positive yet powerful message worked well and afterwards a great banquet was held with dancing by the town folk and a presentation of gifts to their majesties from the people.

Townspeople from Birmingham and surrounding areas came out to showcase their singing, dancing, juggling and other talents for the couple. In return, Prince Henry and Princess Elizabeth performed a brief play for the town and gave out charity to the locals. Their final evening in town, a great bonfire was held and the royal family got to know their subjects even better. The King was incredibly pleased with how the progress turned out. Being with his family lifted Henry's spirits immensely and, at least for a time, allowed him to forget about the stresses of his office.

Chapter 11

The Last Years of Henry VIII

Most historians agree that the Church of England was initially quite unstable, but Henry would end his reign as a confident monarch firmly in control of both his church and his state. Henry's early political actions against alleged enemies of the state and forceful suppression of early rebellions like the Pilgrimage of Grace had earned him a reputation for brutality, at least until his debate with Kritchen, but the enactment of the Ten Articles, the publication of the English Bible, and Anne's education program spread the reforms in an increasingly positive way.

In truth, the Ten Articles were not radically different from established Catholic doctrine, and certainly did not go as far as many Lutheran reformers hoped. Nevertheless, because the King had become head of the church, Catholics became the equivalent of political enemies. Reformationists in England argued that any opposition to the changing religious doctrine should be counted as treason, and under the Act of Supremacy of 1534, they would be. The crown needed no solid evidence to accuse a person of heresy and treason and the country's subjects lived in constant fear that any poorly worded statement could be misconstrued as denying the oath. Any papist who wished to deny the reforms had no freedom to do so and speaking such thoughts aloud was sure to result in imprisonment, trial, and execution. Freedom of speech in 16th century England was permitted only for those privileged enough to be close to the crown, or in limited fashion, to the court jester.

The English legal system of the time was heavily weighted against a defendant. The crown did not permit defendants to be represented by their own counsel; only the crown was allowed a lawyer. Additionally, any speech the accused would make—including confessions made under torture—could be used by the prosecution, or be stricken from trial transcripts entirely if reflecting negatively upon the state. The only religious and political enemies left to dare challenge Henry's rule publicly were Cardinal Pole, who had fled abroad and was never captured, and passionate Activists such as Reginald Kritchen, who had been humiliated by the King in open debate.

11.1 Counter Reformation

Elsewhere in Europe, the flames of reform had been ongoing. The Vatican had begun a "Counter-Reformation" in 1545. At the Council of Trent, beginning that December, the Catholic Church called a Council of Bishops together to more clearly define church doctrine, lay out specific Protestant heresies, and reform the church to bring back followers. This council would meet under several Popes, last over 18 years, and make some highly controversial decisions. Despite the best of intentions, the church failed to prevent the advance of Protestantism, especially in England. The Counter-Reformation came and went without impact on daily life. Only the theological community was interested in its debates, but Henry still headed the English church and no actions would be taken to undo reforms unless at his command; in response to the Council of Trent, he would do nothing.

Initiatives like the Council of Trent took place because of growing schism in Europe, including open war between Catholic and Protestant. In Germany, a group called the Schmalkladic League formed in the 1530s to further the Protestant reformation. Charles V, as Holy Roman Emperor, nominally ruled the city of Schmalkalden where the league began, but the league repudiated the Catholic Emperor. When the league formed, it had a powerful military, with over 10,000 soldiers. This was enough to catch Charles' attention.

Charles turned his focus from constantly preparing for an invasion of England to instead fighting the spread of Lutheranism in the Holy Roman Empire. Known as the Schmalkaldic War, Charles allied with Papal forces to battle the league. At the Battle of Muhlberg in Saxony, the Spanish and

Italian forces succeeded in crushing the Lutheran troops. Spanish forces captured the league's high-ranking members and forced the remainder to convert back to and abide Catholic tenets of faith. Only two cities were able to hold off the Spanish forces, but with the writing on the wall, those leaders fled to other parts of Europe, mainly to England.

England welcomed the fleeing reformers, including the highly influential Martin Bucer. Like many reformers, he was influenced by Lutheran ideals and became a staunch advocate for the move towards Protestantism. In a sign of commitment to his reformed beliefs, he had his monastic vows dissolved, cutting his personal ties to the Catholic Church community. He was one of the leaders of the Wittenberg talks that brought together political and religious community leaders and heads of state for open dialogue on reformist principles. In all of Europe at that time, the northern German states were by far the most open and accepting of Luther's ideals. Bucer united these various German factions of reformists with like-minded reformists in Switzerland, and the Low Countries, proving himself a skilled Activist, diplomat, and scholar.

Archbishop Cranmer warmly welcomed Bucer upon his arrival in England; Cranmer was an admirer of the German's work and had sponsored his travel to England. Cranmer enthusiastically sought Bucer's ideas on how to continue reforms in England. Cranmer and Bucer struck up a great friendship and the Archbishop ensured that his guest was introduced to the best scholarly and theological social circles in London. Shortly after he had arrived, he received the honor of a professorship in Divinity at the University of Cambridge and he dined with the King and Queen, who invited Bucer to join their educational council and help implement changes to their program.

Anne was asked to help with the preparations for the education program by rebuilding King's Trinity College at Cambridge. The Queen was successful and the college retained its charter in 1546. The one stipulation of receiving its charter was that the school had to volunteer professors to teach the King's courses over the period of one year. The college still operates today and houses both undergraduate and graduate students learning a wide variety of subjects.

Despite mixed emotions about having to leave his homeland Bucer was optimistic at all the progress he saw in England and had hopes for England's continued reformation. Bucer had every intent of getting the English reformation where it needed to be. Anne had given Lutherans fleeing Europe refuge and permission to stay at Westminster Abbey as long as they needed to. They would be fed, housed, clothed and be provided all the materials they needed. Their repayment for the Queen's generosity would be to tutor English subjects on the reform plan alongside Tyndale and the others. Henry and Anne would publicly welcome the religious refugees, allowing them sanctuary in England as long as they needed it. This provision of sanctuary to "German heretics" had been one of the factors influencing Reginald Kritchen to condemn the crown, in his early days of protest before his defeat by the King.

11.2 The Last Papist

While Henry and Anne pressed on with their reforms, a different sort of reform program would lead to a return by the King's most vocal opponent. With approximately 100,000 inhabitants, London was the Kingdom's largest city, and had a booming economy. Unfortunately, most of that economy stemmed from illicit operations. Criminals specializing in providing access to vice earned a healthy profit from their trades and used those funds to bribe court officials to keep silent as to their activities.

With the King on progress, the Mayor of London appealed to the Earl of Surrey to put an end to these vile practices. He requested additional guards and five hundred pounds to pay informants to find the sources of these operations and shut them down. In return for the crown's help he promised 10% interest on the 500 pound loan, to be repaid over a period of two years. This was quite a generous sum, considering that average interest rates at that time were far lower, hovering around 4%. Granted, the massive interest would come from intercepting the monies being transferred by the criminals, but the Mayor needed to ensure the crown's assistance in bringing these people to justice. He also requested that the crown allow pamphlets be put up around the city promising rewards in exchange for information leading to the capture of these criminals. The Earl did not feel comfortable going beyond the bounds of his authority in accepting the loan and repayment terms; he would need to consult Henry directly on the reward campaign. Fortunately it was near September and the King was due to be back by the 18th. The Mayor would not wait for an answer; he began hunting down criminal bosses on his own.

As word of the crackdown on vice crimes spread, the Lord Mayor would come to have an unwelcome sign of support. Kritchen, after a period in seclusion following his verbal drubbing by the King, had returned to his usual activities. He visited the Mayor personally to commend him on the exceptional job he was doing in ridding the city of such vile persons, and offered his services. The Mayor felt that the anxious volunteer was not mentally sound and denied his request. Rejected once again by the state, Kritchen turned to the means of forcing change that he knew worked best.

As was later determined, around midnight one evening in May 1548, Kritchen waited until the last clerk had left the book repository of a local printing shop. The clerk had, as usual, closed up the shop and extinguished the fire lit lamp before heading home for the night. Kritchen manipulating the lock, broke in, and set fire to the entire depository. The blaze destroyed all copies of Latimer's lessons, including the Ten Articles and copies of English Bibles for the children being taught under the new program. The fire engulfed the entire building, destroying it in minutes. No witnesses had seen anyone fleeing the building, and the fire was ruled an accident.

Kritchen came home in the dead of night, waking up his daughter Alice by loudly scrubbing his clothes, which were stained with lamp oil and soot. He had accidentally poured the fuel on his clothes; Alice offered to help only to be yelled at to go back to bed. The following day Kritchen went back into town to see the damage for himself and to purchase new sets of clothes. The problem with arson is that the person who sets the fire often has remnants of the fire particles backfiring on their clothing, along with any remnants of accelerant. If not treated with the right chemicals it smells just as strong as the remains of a burning building cooling. The sales woman assisting him noticed what appeared to be either ashes or soot on his clothing, his anxiety and insistence to get the new clothes quickly and alerted the magistrate. Unfortunately he managed to escape before he could be caught, new clothes and all.

He turned up later on the other side of the Thames preaching about God's judgment in burning a repository filled with heretical documents. He claimed that the evil works within were what brought about its destruction and he blessed God for the miracle that no one was harmed. He praised the fire, damned the King and Queen publicly, and called for the people once more to raise arms against the crown's heresy. During his brazen rhetoric, he called for the King and Queen's death, treason by itself.

His arguments were very persuasive and after several speeches, he now had a loyal following around 40-50 people.

Kritchen openly preached class warfare and that the Catholic commons should overthrow the heretic Protestant ruling class. At one point, he would unintentionally find one of those very nobles hearing every word. The Earl of Cumberland happened to be leaving the market when he stumbled upon the crowd and heard Kritchen's preaching. He listened to the whole speech and saw that the layman could work the crowd like a fiddle. When his preaching started, there was only some mumbling and a few people present. By the end of his nearly twenty minute rant he had a crowd of over twenty who were angry and shouting *"down with the crown! Down with the crown!"*

As Kritchen stepped down from the box he was using as a makeshift podium, Cumberland slipped out of view and headed for court. When denied access to the Queen, he went back home, writing her an urgent dispatch describing to her Kritchen's latest activities. The court was back in residence at Hampton Palace and it would not take long for his dispatch to reach her. Less than two weeks later Cumberland was called to appear before Anne to brief her on his letter. Anne paced back and forth nervously. She asked if Cumberland thought Kritchen could turn violent and then went on as the Earl sat through a barrage of questions. At the meeting's end, she tasked him with reporting on Kritchen's speeches, his daily routine, pamphlets he had written, and any additional details of note. He was to send her a bi-weekly report of his actions and would receive further instructions in the future.

While Kritchen was preaching one day, the Earl paid a visit to Alice, claiming to be a believer of her father's teachings and asking to know more about the man himself. Alice recited her family's history in detail, including the events that led her father to take up public speaking. Clifford thanked her for her help, provided her twenty ducats, and left to report what he'd learned to the Queen. By the time he arrived at court, Anne told him that Kritchen would at long last be arrested and that the Earl's services as spy were no longer needed. She did tell him that the final service she would require of him would be to testify for the crown and provide evidence of Kritchen's crimes. Since the Earl had witnessed treasonous speech himself, he made the perfect witness to bring about Kritchen's destruction.

Kritchen would be arrested by royal guards while in the midst of a particularly seditious call for the King to be overthrown and the country returned to Catholicism. The same day of his arrest, the magistrate had him moved, per Henry's express command, to the Tower, where the King personally interrogated him. Henry questioned him relentlessly for hours about his motives, his statements, the number of his regular followers, his connections at court and abroad, and finally about his death threats towards himself and the Queen.

Kritchen proudly admitted setting the book depository ablaze and insisted that he meant every vile word of his speeches, but that he had not yet come around to planning the details of the King and Queen's execution. He went on to berate the King, as one would a child, about the ills he had inflicted upon his own people. This only further enraged an already angry King. Henry stormed out of the room repeating *"kill him!"* several times. Before he left the Tower to draw up the execution papers, he ordered that Kritchen's daughter be brought to the Tower as well, so that she could be questioned and watch her father die. Later that evening Henry drew up the execution warrant; Kritchen would die at the stake.

When Alice arrived at the Tower it was under cover of darkness. Having been kept unaware as to where she was being sent and where her father was, she became hysterical upon recognizing the imposing edifice she was being brought into. Crying uncontrollably, she fainted several times before reaching her cell. Constable Kingston finally told her why she was being held, which news was met with only more sobbing. Feeling sorry for the poor child, the Constable and his wife lodged the girl in one of the more spacious cells, and she was even permitted to dine with them that evening. However, Henry expressly forbade her from seeing or saying goodbye to her father, and commanded that she be made to watch his burning from her cell. Alice had not slept all night, and she did not touch a bite of her food.

Since Henry had continued consolidating power unto himself, he no longer needed Parliament's approval to execute suspected traitors, and since Kritchen's Acts had been so public and blatant, the King decided to forgo the customary show trial. Instead, the King ordered Kritchen taken to the stake by 6 A.M. the following day, as his daughter Alice watched the King's henchmen stock the area with kindling, larger blocks of wood, and twine. Kritchen's final words were to thank his majesty for helping him achieve his objective of being martyred for Christ and the church, proclaimed his love for his daughters and his persistent faith in the one true church. He was then tied to the stake and set alight. The burning lasted 13 excruciating minutes before the condemned grew silent and still.

When Henry was told of Kritchen's last words he was outraged. Implying that the King had been manipulated into doing a traitor and heretic's bidding, and the several references to the "true church" demanded that Henry make further example of the rabble rouser. Even though both Kritchen's daughters had sworn to both the Oath of Supremacy and Succession, Henry well knew there were lying traitors about his kingdom. Now he was faced with the likelihood that the daughters believed as had their father. He sought Anne's advice as to their fate.

Her advice was simple and direct: "*they should join their father.*" She then went about her business, as if she had merely selected a type of fabric for a dress. Alice was burned less than 3 hours later, on the same stake as her father, and Ellen was sent for from her estate and burned about a week later. These would be the second and third times in Henry's reign that a woman's execution would be sanctioned by the state. Now truly no subject was safe. The entire Kritchen family had been destroyed. In Reginald's will he bequeathed all his religious papers, including drafts of his speeches, papal relics, and Bibles, to Cardinal Reignold Pole for *"staying true to the righteous faith."* Six months later, out of enormous guilt for his unintended role in the execution of the daughters, the Earl of Cumberland committed suicide, leaving a note stating that he had sold his soul to condemn that of another, and he would burn for it.

11.3 An English Renaissance

Nearing 50, Anne realized that for all her efforts and all Henry's success in solidifying his power, the English court had dramatically lost its appeal; she would seek to bring glamour and support for the arts to the English court in Henry's last years. The ever-evolving Italian courts were patrons to the best painters, sculptors, musicians, and literary geniuses of the period. The Queen wanted a court reminiscent of France in her younger years and that would require significant sums of money. Exclusive artists, musicians and literary talents of the day from all over Europe, and some from the Indies and even Asia, were brought in to entertain their majesties.

Anne also ordered three new tapestries to be completed by 1555, a relatively fast order considering that these beautiful weavings could take nearly a decade each to create. During this period, tapestries were among the most impressive representations of a court's wealth. Kings fought over them because their value was enormous. The more tapestries a King had, the more powerful they were viewed in the eyes of not only their court but the rest of Europe. Tapestries still existing at Hampton Court belonging to Henry VIII are valued at over 40 million per weaving in today's current prices. She also arranged for Hans Holbein the Younger to paint her and her children together in the Hampton Court Gardens, a painting that unfortunately has been lost to us.

Her desire to improve the image of the English court extended as well to food. She imported exotic wines from Italy, France, and exclusive vineyards in Austria. She became more involved in the cuisine served at court functions and reduced the number of meals from over 30 per event down to a mere 5. She reasoned that the reduced portions would allow the kitchen staff to be less stressed and to be able to feed the entire court for a lot longer period. She also worked with the head cook to modify her favorite sweetbreads recipe and demanded it be served to her alongside her other meals. She also ordered, after advice from her medical consultants from abroad, that the kitchens, basements (in which food was stored), and chimneys be cleaned thoroughly at least once a month, with the expenses taken from the King's household fund. This measure led to a significant decline in the amount of food-borne illness at court.

Also improving England's reputation in the arts was the work of literary artists such as the reformer John Bale, Bishop of Ossory. Bale wrote tragedy and morality plays with the central theme of religious obedience to God. All of his works were angled to be compatible with reformist views, often belittling the Catholic community and papal doctrine. His works included highly popular books and plays such as "*The Three Laws of Nature, Moses and Christ, corrupted by the Sodomytes, Pharisees and Papystes most Wicked*" and *Kynge John*, which came out in 1548 as the first attempt to transform literary plays into historical dramatic pieces. His plays were a valuable public relations tool for the reformist cause and Bale took enormous pride in his works. *Kynge John* was a play where the protagonist faces a struggle in breaking free of Rome to tell God's rightful truth. Bale even recognizes King Henry VIII in one of his verses, proclaiming that the good King Henry saved the English people and brought them into a new land, comparing it to a land of milk and honey. The King praised his work and ordered a fully bound illuminated copy for his library and for the play to be performed for his birthday.

Anne's improvements to court extended to physical renovations as well. She called in the finest architects from Denmark to completely redesign the court space, expanding how many members it could hold, creating a formal stage for entertainment, and increasing the lighting by designing more easily replaced candles. She also had the royal tailor, with Henry's blessing, re-upholster a new royal throne. The cushions on the seat of state had not been replaced since Henry VII's reign and were beginning to wear. Henry designed the replacements for his and Anne's chairs, down to detailing the appearance of the "HR" logo with a Tudor rose located squarely in the middle of the pattern, sewn into velvet fabric with diamonds sewn around the edges of the pillows. The cushions were held in place against the back of the chair by a string of pearls. The architect recommended moving the position of the state chairs to allow the greatest amount of light to fall upon the fabric and the jewels that now ordained it.

The Throne Room was completely outfitted by early 1547 at an enormous cost, equivalent to some $6 million in 2011 US dollars. Heedless of cost, it was vital for both Henry and Anne to showcase their God given rights as monarchs. The only way to do this was by continuously enhancing their estates to show just how glorious their status was. Henry wanted his court to outshine the courts of France and Italy. Both countries had been well known for their lavish furnishings, marble floorings, large number of tapestries, and extensive use of rare jewels. It was all very impressive and Henry and Anne sought to not only recreate that opulence in the English court, but to surpass their counterparts. Anne worked closely with Thomas Howard, the Lord Treasurer, on how to execute obtaining these materials. The renovations were anticipated to be shown either late 1547 or early 1548 for New Year's celebrations.

11.4 The Beginning of the End

The couple went on their final royal progress in the summer of 1549, visiting Cardiff in Wales. Henry's increasingly failing health made the trip slower than expected and it took them and the entire court nearly three months to make the journey, stopping at countless towns along the way to provide the people a glimpse of their majesties. Along the way the couple also tarried to visit with various nobles and even attend public plays put on in their honor by the people. In one of her final letters, Anne wrote to Elizabeth in French about the progress and her father's health, assuring her not to worry and that all was well. This letter in particular is insightful as to Anne's state of mind about her daughter; possibly seeing her as stronger than her brother and more fit for rule. Interestingly enough, the letter also contained a prophetic warning about the need to guard against ill advisers; she knew all too well how she had been handled in the past. The Queen also wrote to Prince Henry, with her letter to the Prince being far more personal, perhaps suggesting a desire to forge a deeper bond with him:

"My dearest child, you are but young man now, yet one day you shall grow to manhood and be prepared to rule over the Kingdom that will be yours. Be strong and be bold, my heart, you are your father's son. You will become a great King and you must learn great piety, dignity, and faith in God's plan that you be placed upon the throne of England. You make both your father and your mother proud every day. Be well my son as you must, your loving mother, Queen Anne."

After a long, hot and uneventful summer progress, the couple headed back to Hampton Court, reaching it about the end of October. Henry decided to recall Parliament and call a session of the Privy Council in November to discuss further reforms needed to in kingdom. Winter would bring with it a series of Parliamentary laws recognizing several new religious statutes, humanitarian Acts, and statues regarding sanitation and medicinal grants.

The educational reforms were also progressing apace, with the trial classes held in London proving to be a resounding success. Initially, much grumbling and frustration was because the teaching materials—delayed by Kritchen's fire—were ready late. The children also resented having to attend, with some families altogether fleeing London so that their children would not have to be a part of these lessons. However, for those who stayed, the children (both boys and girls) were able to reach basic literacy, starting with their own names, in less than six weeks; an astonishing feat considering that many adults at the time were unable to do the same.

Latimer was impressed with the progress of the courses and sent for their majesties to attend a session of the child and teenage lessons to see for themselves. In anticipation of their visit, Latimer taught the children to sign a hymn praising their majesties and thanking them for being able to attend. The hymn was very clever in its wording, it rhymed and the children performed a small dance at the end.

From what little we know the Queen began experiencing severe cramps in autumn 1549, followed by dizzy spells and sometimes fainting. Her physician's exams determined little. She began to bleed, although slightly past her time of menopause, which her doctors thought strange. With no remedy apparent, she turned to the midwife who had so delicately helped her carry her pregnancies to term. The midwife told the Queen that she was experiencing a shutting down of her feminine organs, and it was best to take meadow seed and pray for absolution against the wickedness that was plaguing her.

Soon after, Anne sought out Cranmer to toll the bell of his church 20 times in prayer and to hold a special vigil for her, but she remained unwell. Along with her cramps, bleeding, and dizziness, Anne came to suffer from frequent migraines and arthritis that made it difficult to read, sew, and plant in her garden; all her favorite activities. Henry checked on her and monitored her progress closely with her physicians, comforting her as much as he could. For the first two days after her examination by the doctors he stayed by her bedside refusing to leave. On the third day he came down ill himself so the doctors removed him to his own chamber. Thankfully, the Queen's symptoms subsided and she recovered over the next weeks, although she would from time to time continue to suffer painful migraines. Over the next year, it was the King whose health would be the grave concern.

During Christmastide celebrations in 1549, Henry publicly surprised Anne by toasting to his Queen's grace and skill in renovating their court, boasting that, thanks to the Queen, they enjoyed the most splendid court in Europe, and affirming yet again her hold upon the crown. He then went even further and dropped to his knee to give a glowing statement of praise for how much she had meant to him over all of these years together, and to thank her for her gifts of their children. The Queen cried and made a speech of gratitude in return, thanking the King for his immense kindness and showing genuine affection towards him. The joy would not last long.

The King's councilors were secretly preparing for the possible succession. While the Act of Succession in 1547 still stood, revisions were made providing financially for the Queen and her heirs. Henry was by no means a frugal monarch and by this time his crown was in debt by over an estimated 213,788 pounds annually. The growing cost of the court, primarily at Anne's insistence, was taking its toll on the country's economy. With money again becoming an issue, even before the worsening of Henry's health, it became necessary to renew discussions of marrying off the heirs.

11.5 A Royal Wedding

Henry focused his remaining days on executing the marriages negotiated over the preceding few years. For Prince Henry, the only ladies of suitable standing ladies were Joan, Princess of Portugal and Margaret, Duchess of Berry in France. While both ladies made fine candidates, Anne—as could be expected—favored the French candidate. Margaret was 24 in 1547, a highly refined and sophisticated daughter of King Francis I, and the sister of the current King Henry II of France. The dowry paid to England for this marriage would be sizable, but the King would gladly negotiate the handing back of control over Calais to the English in place of a cash dowry.

The pre-contract was drawn up April 1547 for the marriage of Prince Henry to Duchess Margaret in 1550 when the Prince was to turn 13. Margaret was 13 years older than her betrothed, but that mattered little, she had no formal proposals of marriage up until that point, and her brother feared that none may come. When the offer was on the table, the French King immediately embraced it. The English were willing to take Margaret immediately to introduce her to the Prince and life here in England. King Henry II gladly took Henry's offer, but he rejected the Calais proposal, instead promising a dowry of 2 million pounds and sending Margaret on her way to Dover in May 1547 to meet her future husband.

The King and Queen celebrated handsomely over this joyous news, inviting the French Ambassador to visit the English court as guest of honor. By the time Margaret and her marriage contract arrived, the renovations at Hampton Court had been completed. The French delegation were greeted to stunning surroundings, and the Queen herself gave Margaret a two carat ruby and diamond necklace with matching earrings from the West Indies, and cloth of gold for preparation of her upcoming wedding gown. Anne also offered to have her own tailor fashion the cloth into any piece she would like for her wedding.

With his masculine features and height of 5'11", at only 13, Prince Henry was a force to be reckoned with. He truly was his father's son, with bright blue eyes, dark hair, and a fair complexion. His father's health now in question, the Prince needed to be continually groomed for his time to take the reins of power should the need arise. Henry had been a loving, even doting father to his first born. He showered him with gifts, personally taught him the Greek classics and how to hunt. He had also made the Prince a member of the Privy Chamber and given him several estates, so that he could begin to practice developing the habits of command.

A magnificent joust was held for Prince Henry to celebrate his betrothal. It would be a chance to show the court and foreign dignitaries all that he had learned under his father's strict but guiding hand. The Prince was measured for armor, and fitted with appropriate weaponry. Artisans were even brought in to sculpt the Prince in all his regal glory; the resulting statue was made of marble and served as another example of his father's brilliant public relations stunts. He wanted everyone to know that Prince Henry was to have a glorious reign ahead of him and that the succession would at last be confirmed. The sculpture took months to complete. Anne also commissioned yet another portrait of the entire family by Hans Holbein; it was to be displayed at Hampton Court with copies to be reproduced for the elite to hang in their homes. This great work was, unfortunately, lost in the Great Fire of London in 1666, while on display in St. Paul's cathedral.

To increase his accounts, in the face of this continued profligacy, Henry increased the tax on ale, wheat, and licensing fees for midwifery and to operate as a surgeon. This may have made up only a small portion of the revenue and require additional revenues be found. The nobles had been hoarding their properties and cash for years, so Thomas Howard suggested that Henry increase land taxes by 2%. Henry agreed and instructed Howard to draw up the proposal for his signature and post the proclamation immediately. He then summoned Parliament to tell them of the measure, which was met with jeers and boos. The King's programs were proving popular, however, leaving Parliament without much ability to deny the King anything he might wish.

Prince Henry was about to turn 14 in June and the Queen had been busy preparing for his reception at Hampton Court. During the three years of their betrothal, Henry and Margaret enjoyed themselves immensely. Ladies of the court had attempted to turn his head, but he stayed true.

Margaret had turned out to be stunningly beautiful and Prince Henry took an immediate liking to her. Not only gorgeous, but also highly intelligent, she challenged the Prince's intellect and he respected her for her wit.

One would think the significant age difference between the two would have caused an issue, especially for such a refined lady, but instead he made her laugh and she found him moldable to her whim. As a result, age did not often arise as a concern and for the most part the two became great friends. The two seemed to enjoy a genuine courtship, spending long walks together, playing chess, reading with one another, and discussing the classics. As far as anyone could tell, they both genuinely fell in love, a rare feat for any politically arranged match. Both Henry and Anne happy at the success of their son's union.

The pair was warm with one another and it was Anne's hope that Margaret would provide her with several grandchildren. Anne was nervous about Margaret's true religious leanings but found her a great comfort and a dear friend. She treated her already as a daughter and often Margaret, the Queen, and the Princess Elizabeth would dine together.

Henry thanked his parents for finding such an agreeable match and requested if possible that the wedding be moved up sooner, to 1550. This was quite an unusual request, but it could be done. Since France had paid Margaret's dowry in full upon her arrival there was no reason to hold off, beyond allowing more time to gather guests and supplies for the wedding day. For all intents and purposes, the future heir was truly happy and had every reason to be. Theirs would prove a lifelong marriage of contentment and happiness. With Prince Henry betrothed, now it was Elizabeth's turn. She was 24 in 1547 and it was appropriate for her to find a husband.

The marriage took place February 2nd, 1550 at Westminster Abbey. Archbishop Cranmer presided over the union, Tyndale assisted Henry in writing his vows, and Anne helped her new daughter-in-law design her wedding dress using the Queen's personal tailor. She would wear gold silk with a three-foot lace train, pearls and diamonds about the square neckline, and her Valois family crests as a broach. Her earrings were pearl and diamond drops of three layers. Elizabeth was Margaret's maid-of-honor and the Queen let the bride borrow her own 3.5-carat diamond necklace, an anniversary gift from the King. Per tradition, King Henry II of France happily walked his sister down the aisle. After the exchanging of vows and rings, Cranmer pronounced them man and wife.

King Henry VIII then publicly announced their new titles to the waiting crowd of nearly 300 guests, introducing them formally as His Royal Highness Prince Henry, Duke of Richmond, Prince of England, Ireland and Wales and Her Royal Highness Princess Margaret Valois of Berry. The King kissed them both on the cheek and declared them married to much joy. Both Anne and Henry wept during the ceremony. A grand reception was held in the new couple's honor at the Grand Hall in Greenwich Palace. The palace was granted to Prince Henry as his wedding gift, along with an increase in his income. Anne had her jeweler tailor-make a crown for Princess Margaret to wear at formal events made of brilliant sapphires, emeralds and diamonds; apparently Margaret's favorite combination of gems.

News of the marriage was welcomed in Europe, except in the Vatican. The Pope vehemently opposed the match, claiming that the King of France was foolish to let his sister marry an illegitimate heir to the English throne. Thankfully, King Henry II paid no attention to this insult and for at least a period of several years kept a close relationship with England. Henry II and the future Henry IX shared many interests and got on together well. Within the first year of their marriage, Margaret was pregnant with the first of their five children. This child, born in December 1550, would be named Princess Anne of England.

11.6 The Death of Henry VIII

1551 marked the beginning of the end for Henry VIII. His health had been fading rapidly in the last few months and the harsh cold of winter did little to better his constitution. The King had come down with consumption, or tuberculosis. Because tuberculosis is an airborne pathogen, the disease is spread as people talk, laugh, and cough. It is difficult to pin down a precise day when Henry contracted the disease, but he began showing the early stages of it in late 1550. He displayed flu like symptoms in October of that year, with heavy coughing and fever, chills, fatigue, and lack of appetite. He dismissed his physicians from treating him, feeling that their remedies often made him tired. He was still eager to impress upon his young son and the rest of the court that he was just as capable as ever. This led him to over exert himself, staying hours in Privy Council meetings arranged merely for show, even when there were no substantive issues at hand.

Other times he was seen in the royal chapel praying more heavily than ever before, possibly a sign of his growing realization that his body was failing him. Once so Active, now his frail immune system was keeping him in his chambers. He complained often of humidity in the middle of cold winters, and of a chronic slight cough that seemed to get deeper as the months grew by. His doctors were concerned that Henry would not survive his battle with this affliction. The King was also prone to night horrors and would on occasion cough up blood.

Whether wet or dry, as 1551 wore on Henry coughed more and more constantly, and his chest bothered him at all hours of the day. As a result he slept little and was often irritable. Despite his size, he was now starting to lose weight at a rapid pace. Royal household records show that tailors were redesigning clothes for him every few months, each time a smaller size than before. He woke up in sweats with fevers. Each time the groom wanted to call for a doctor he forbade it. Never one to want to face his own mortality he demanded instead that his groom remove himself so he could rest. When Henry did manage to sleep, he would wake at strange intervals experiencing a high fever his doctors were unable to break.

Physicians bled him often, sometimes twice a week to relieve the chills but to no avail. His doctors did not have the resources or technology available to recognize that it was a deadly bacterium killing the King. If it was not treated, it would prove fatal. Even with modern medicines, tuberculosis is a deadly illness that requires that patients in later stages to be isolated to prevent infecting others. It would be another four centuries before a cure for this would be developed. A weakened immune system would allow the bacteria to flourish virtually unstoppable. In the 21st Century, multiple therapies are used for the successful treatment of the condition; including heavy doses of strong antibiotics which would not have been available during Henry's time. X-ray exams are also used to verify the progression of the disease and to assist doctors in advising correct treatment therapies.

All that Henry's physicians would have known is the color of his vomit, which would have been dark. They would have analyzed the waste and compared it with the four bodily humors to determine the appropriate cause for the illness in question. The only remedy they had was to quarantine him, alter his diet, ensure he got plenty of fresh air, bleed him, monitor his vital signs, and make him comfortable as the disease ravaged his body. His doctors were in a precarious position. Since it was treason to speak of the King's death, they could not truly advise their highest patient of the full extent of his illness. Henry was never told the official condition that made him sick.

With Henry sick, Anne became increasingly occupied with the hygiene habits at court. She demanded that upon entry to court each person be checked by a physician. She also limited the size of the court in the summer in a vain attempt to prevent infection by plague, lice, and possibly to ward off another round of the sweat, should it appear. The King gave strict instructions that no one, not even the Queen, was to know his weak condition. He mustered up the strength to show himself to the court, hold Privy Council meetings and meet with Anne, all while maintaining appearances that he had only a mild cold. It did little good, she knew all too well he was sick and she received regular reports in secret from his doctors about his condition. She played Henry's game and disavowed knowledge of his illness.

For weeks this charade went on until, finally, in May 1550 Anne wrote the Ottoman Ambassador to seek his guidance on any new remedy for the King's condition. The Ottoman Empire had been known for unique herbal concoctions that treated a variety of ailments, and while it was a far hope, she still had to try. Henry was very selective about whom he let treat him; he had the same physician for nearly thirty years and nearly always refused Anne's requests that he seek out new opinions and treatments.

When Henry found out about Anne's maneuvering behind his back he was outraged; her diplomatic activities had more than once brought ill intended consequences, but this was a new blow. She had Acted out of great concern for her husband, but Henry wanted to maintain the illusion that he was the great physical force he once was in his youth. A great row erupted between the couple lasting for hours; the grooms knew better than to interrupt these violent tirades. The arguments were usually intense but brief, with the couple perfect friends thereafter. His ego had been bruised but Anne knew well how to manipulate these arguments to her benefit and persuaded him to her cause. In the end he finally relented to trying new treatments.

The Ottoman Ambassador received the Queen's letter warmly. He responded that he had dispatched the famous surgeon Ambroise Paré to come examine Henry as discreetly as possible. Pare had gained an international reputation in healing important 16th century clients such as Dukes, Earls, and several Kings of Europe. He had learned his great craft treating war wounds and had blazed the trail for surgery in modern medicine, being credited with introducing the suture technique for closing wounds. While his craft was impressive, he typically did not deal with infections, unless there was a need for operation. His reputation greatly preceded him; he was a man of few words and great talent. As recently as 1549 he had been employed in the service of King Henry II of France. Paré was released for his special errand to examine Henry VIII in January of 1551.

When Paré arrived he found Henry in a terminal state. He could do little for him beyond provide him means of finding comfort. His new methods would do little beyond buy him additional time; he could promise nothing. He left the Queen and aging Dr. Butts with additional herbal supplements unique to the East and left copious amounts of Opium—used for centuries by the Chinese—for Henry's pain. He warned Dr. Butts not to let the King have all the drug he would want, as it would become addictive. He wished the Queen well and headed back home with a handsome payment and absolute certainty that King Henry VIII would be dead within the year.

Henry did the best he could to take short walks in the garden with Anne, write Elizabeth, and on occasion attend to matters of state. Over the summer of 1550 he appointed what he called a "temporary state minister" and had the Privy Council insert a clause that Prince Henry would take over his role as soon as he returned from tending to his estates with his new bride. Soon Henry's condition became too severe to keep up pretenses. In March 1551 he finally took to his chamber. He never made another public appearance and was not to be disturbed.

The management of the kingdom was left up to the Privy Council and the Queen as regent. Life at court thereafter began to slow down; no new tournaments or jousts were prepared for any reason. Gossip was rife in London that Henry had already died and that Anne was holding the notice from going public so that her evil council could proclaim her monarch in full, instead of their son. Privy councilors met with the Queen to discuss arrangements for implementing the Act of Succession of 1547. The Queen refused to hear it and sent them from her presence.

By April, the King's condition had rapidly deteriorated; he started coughing up blood in large amounts and the coughing rarely ceased. He was barely conscious and spoke in delusional sentences. His doctors had given up all hope of him being able to beat the disease; he was simply too far gone and used up great reserves of his energy in the weeks before, while attempting to prove he was someone he no longer was. The physicians had called for Anne to attend her husband on April 29th and she resolved to stay with her husband for as long as possible, for he was about to greet God. Cranmer, Prince Henry, and Princess Elizabeth also were summoned by the Queen. All of Henry's family was at his side in his final days. Anne sat with him the entire time, praying over him as he lay slowly dying. She was present when he lapsed into a coma the following day. His last words were unrecorded.

At 4:38 on the morning of May 1st, 1551, King Henry VIII died from consumption at Whitehall Palace. He was survived by his wife and his children, Prince Henry and the Princess Elizabeth. Anne stayed by his bedside for nearly two hours after his death, wailing loudly. Only the Archbishop was allowed to stay with her; she clutched him by the arm as they prayed together for Henry's soul. The bells at Westminster Abbey tolled, and word was quickly spread that Prince Henry would be crowned the new King.

Chapter 12

King Henry IX

Henry VIII was buried at St. George's Chapel in Windsor Castle. His body was encased in lead and taken in a solemn procession from Whitehall to St. George's. Henry's coffin had a wax effigy of his likeness and was carried through the streets with blue and gold velvet over his casket, while the people mourned his death. They had come out in record numbers to watch as the King's body moved through the streets, the Queen and Princess Elizabeth trailing behind it in mourning. Due to restrictions to preserve his health, the new King, Henry IX, was not allowed to attend his father's funeral, but he grieved for weeks in private. The subjects removed their caps and many sank to their knees as the coffin passed. Anne would now be referred to as the Queen Mother, per custom, and Elizabeth would remain Princess. Margaret was now the official Queen Consort.

King Henry IX's coronation took place noon of May 6th, 1551, at Westminster Abbey. With the change in regime the new King changed ministers. As the family had grown quite close to William Buxton, he was created "Master of the Rolls" and made a member of the Privy Chamber. The King also paid for his formal legal education and trusted him as his closest friend and confidant. Now fully vested in his title, the new King set about understanding all elements of his kingdom. His reign would be hailed as a true period of learning and prosperity. He immediately reinstated the Privy Council and hand selected those members of the peerage he felt were worthy of the honor, along with two of his former tutors of military studies and history.

The King's death had been difficult on Anne. The next six years she continued to suffer from occasional bouts of intense abdominal pain and bleeding. She confined herself to her chamber at Whitehall taking only two maids with her, Lady Marla Benidici and Lady Audrey de Vere. These women were her companions and saw her through the darkest days. Her King, husband, friend, lover, companion, and father to her children, was now dead. The last thirty years seemed to go by like a blur. By him she gave birth to two children, miscarried several others, and secured the Tudor line. Menopause had come and gone and she was now in the third and final stage of her life.

Her children continued to visit her when permitted, Elizabeth reading to her almost daily in Latin. These visits brought the only comfort she entertained. She enjoyed the visits with her daughter very much and they often talked about marriage proposals for the Princess. Her son visited as often as he could, but with a country to run, it was difficult for him to find the time. There were also rumors that the King found it difficult to see his mother because it raised in him painful memories of the loss of his father.

When her son took the throne, Anne nearly removed herself completely from many of the political activities she had once engaged in with such passion. Partly due to her failing health and partly because of Henry's death, she no longer held the interest she once did to cling to power. She had seen her son become the next ruler and that now in her condition had to be enough. She continued to sew for hours despite her arthritis, and invested in charitable causes including sponsoring several orphanages and artists. She took up painting, continued playing cards, and spent hours in prayer. She also monitored how the education classes she had helped design were progressing, and received regular reports on their progress from Archbishop Cranmer. She and Elizabeth continued their very close bond and she came to rely on her daughter most heavily.

Anne began staying in her chambers more after Henry's death. In 1552 she had suffered massive vaginal bleeding; physicians attended her for any sign of serious damage. Her body carried signs of severe hemorrhaging. The physicians thought her uterine line might have ruptured. With the bleeding came heavy cramps and her screams could often be heard ringing down the hall. The pains peaked in the evening and she had difficulty sitting for long periods of time, even in bed. Her breathing was slow and difficult. Fatigue and frequent urination had been taking place for the last several weeks. Doctors were puzzled at her condition and had only the most elementary understanding of cancer and how it might develop. They attributed most mysterious illnesses to being curses from God for one's sins. Anne certainly had a long list of those to atone for.

Her illness, in modern terms, was likely ovarian cancer, known as "the silent killer" for so many women whose symptoms commonly masquerade as other problems. She had all but stopped eating and lost nearly fifteen pounds within a month. Doctors ordered her to rest in her chamber, eat soft foods, not too many heavy meats, not a lot of salt, and to avoid walking for lengthy periods. Stubborn and willful to the last, it was nearly impossible for her to abide by these restrictions. After a long and exhausting life, Anne was at her end.

Anne Boleyn, the Queen Mother, instigator of the Reformation in England, and co-founder of the first public education program in England, died shortly after 2 P.M, on August 7th, 1553. Cranmer and Elizabeth were by her side and she was attended by her ladies, these servants recording her last will and testament. Her funeral was held 3 days later; she was buried beside Henry VIII in their tomb at Windsor. Despite her unpopular reputation, thousands turned out for her burial. Contemporary accounts remark that Anne had twice as many mourners at her procession than had been at Henry VIII's. Perhaps the onlookers were more curious than grieving, but whatever their motivation, she was finally receiving the recognition due a Queen. Her tomb was made of marble with gold casing and her motto etched on the side: *'The Most Happy.'* She remains at rest there today.

Henry IX and Princess Elizabeth gave a touching eulogy to the crowd of mourners that day. Among the many accomplishments they listed for their mother was being a key player in the Reformation, securing the Tudor dynasty, instilling the English language in Bibles, and freeing England from domination from abroad. This latter claim was never fully explained, but no one dared to question the statement. On the day of her death, a dozen red roses appear at the foot of her tomb; the figure who delivered them has never been identified. Given her lifelong dedication to theological, medical and educational reform her burial crest bares only the special scalpel she had been given by Dr. Butts for instituting medical licensing. At the time mourners passed her gravesite but today, she is a popular tourist attraction and every year receives a dozen roses anonymously on the date of her death. While at the time her legacy may not have been appreciated, in the nearly 500 years since then it has been exploited and certainly not forgotten. Her legacy reminds us of how a strong will of mind can truly change the world.

What Henry and Anne started changed the entire British landscape. Henry IX would rule England for fifty-seven remarkable years that would come to be called England's "Golden Age," with the country seeing unparallel improvements in education, economic reform, and territorial acquisition. Princess Elizabeth and her brother remained close and she would help her brother to build heavily on the education programs and patronage for the arts and sciences that his mother had instituted. He would come to be known as "*Henry the Enlightened.*" He also took up his father's cause of reclaiming French territories and made England a competitive player on the field of global exploration. He and Margaret would produce five living heirs who would go onto to spread their lineage around the world, partly responsible for expanding the British Empire. Their children were Princess Anne of England, Prince Charles of England, Anthony Duke of York, Michael Earl of Ormonde, and Isabelle Duchess of Burgandy; all would all go on to forge successful European alliances.

Elizabeth took up her mother's passion for reform and thrived on debates of theology with members of the court. The Princess had truly blossomed into a ravishing young lady filled with intellect, passion, and maturity rare for a woman of her age. She also continued to keep in touch with the St. Mary's Orphanage. When Ms. Astley could no longer run the establishment she left her daughter in charge so a second generation could continue the work.

Due to Anne's enormous generosity during her lifetime, the orphanage was able to take in twice as many children and adequately house them. It was hailed as the best model orphanage in the country. As a condition of entry all orphans had to enroll in the education program; all would learn how to read and write. It truly was a remarkable turn of course. Several of the children that Elizabeth played with as a child had gone on to accomplish great things. A few served in the English army, one woman went on to design fashions for the English court, and others became teachers.

The Grand Duke of Tuscany, Francesco de'Medici I, in 1553 offered Henry a pre-contract of marriage for the hand of the Princess Elizabeth;

she immediately agreed. She had met him at a state dinner back in 1548 and remarked that he was quite handsome. The Duke would be turning 17 in August, leaving only a three year age difference between the pair, with Elizabeth the elder. After persuading her brother to agree, Henry called for the Tuscan Ambassador and sent word back of his consent. The Princess was eager for a successful marriage alliance. She was deemed one of the finest prizes in the European marriage market, but her staunch Protestant views were a concern. In light of such conditions, Henry offered twice the originally agreed to dowry and in December 1554 Elizabeth and Francesco married.

Arrangements were made that Francesco would marry her in England, surrounded by her family and friends to solidify the official alliance. Elizabeth chose to marry at Hampton Court, it was her favorite of all the palaces, and the gardens were the most beautiful. She personally designed a dress with a six foot train of lace. The bodice had diamonds and pearls sewn into the fabric. She wore a seven carat diamond necklace given to her by Anne, with modest pearl earrings. Her tiara was made of sparkling pear and Princess cut diamonds, holding her veil in place. There were over 2,000 attendants present to witness the nuptials, with Henry IX giving away the bride. The aging Archbishop Cranmer presided over the ceremony. After a lavish feast later that evening Elizabeth boarded the ship waiting to take her and her retinue of over three hundred persons to her new home. For her wedding gift, Henry had Anne's Book of Hours reset with new binding, leaving the original pages intact, with a handwritten letter wishing her well on her new journey in life. He bade her farewell, calling her *"my own special angel."*

Elizabeth settled into her new home with remarkable ease. The fresh country air and the beautiful countryside fit her disposition perfectly. She became the first lady of the Tuscan court and, like her mother, became famous for trend setting. Elizabeth loved the vineyards and used her own inheritance to buy a vineyard of 132 acres that remained in her family lineage until 1784. She bore the Duke three sons, Giovanni, Maxwell, and Marcus, all of whom entered either the military or government service. She kept in close touch with her brother and family, returning to England every other summer. Thanks to Anne, the Tudor dynasty would survive another two centuries.

Epilogue

Anne Boleyn was a captivating, powerful, and one of the most polarizing women in English history. Her story is known very well to us today but as having played out very differently from how it transpired in this book. Most who know Anne's story either love her or hate her and both sides have excellent reasons for their cause.

Her real death, on May 19th, 1536, resulted from false charges crafted by Thomas Cromwell that led to Anne's conviction for treason. An increasingly erratic Henry, suffering from wounds that in this book were instead sustained by his friend Charles Brandon, had been persuaded that Anne had been disloyal, and had committed incest with her brother George. Having miscarried a potential male heir to the throne—partly due to shock at Henry's having sustained such serious injuries—Anne was in little position to defend herself against Cromwell's charges. His plot was hatched and carried out in under a month and remains one of the swiftest eliminations of a political opponent in British history.

Ironically, had history gone a different way, perhaps she would not have had the lasting cultural impact that led to her story being sensationalized into television, stage plays, films, and other cultural media over for nearly five hundred years. In preparing the research for this book I got to know an incredibly complex woman, far ahead of her time, whose life ended far too quickly. It was an incredible journey for me, as an author, to connect with Anne Boleyn, and imagine what she might have accomplished had she remained Queen.

As my version of events leaves off, the son she never actually bore succeeded his father to be crowned King Henry IX, instead of her daughter becoming Elizabeth I. How England might have developed differently were these changes to have occurred is a subject of continuing interest to myself, I hope to you, and will be explored in my next book.

In any such story, with such complicated, influential figures, the options are simply limitless.

References

Real people and events—especially in the Prologue and early sections of this book—have been used, and then modified as little as possible, in constructing this alternative history. For those interested in the full, real history of the period, below are the sources I consulted heavily. The work of these historians made this book possible.

https://www.cia.gov/library/publications/the-world-factbook/geos/uk.html

Huddleston, G. (1910). St. John Fisher. In The Catholic Encyclopedia. New York: Robert Appleton Company. Retrieved May 19, 2011 from New Advent: http://www.newadvent.org/cathen/08462b.htm

Tyndale, William (1528) *The Obedience of the Christian Man*. Reprinted by Penguin Books, 2000 Edition. London: England.

Turner, Sharon (1828) *The History of England from the Earliest Period to the Death of Elizabeth*. Longman, Rees, Orme, Brown and Green

Cressy, David (1997) *Birth, Marriage and Death: Ritual, Religion, and the Life-Cycle in Tudor and Stuart England.* Oxford University Press, New York.

Denny, Joanna (2005) *Katherine Howard: A Tudor Conspiracy.* Piatkus Books, London.

Hutchinson, Robert (2007) *Thomas Cromwell: The Rise and Fall of Henry VIII's Most Notorious Minister.* St. Martins Press, New York.

Ives, Eric (2005) *The Life and Death of Anne Boleyn.* Blackwell Publishing United Kingdom.

Lipscomb, Suzannah. (2009) *The Year that Changed Henry VIII: 1536.* Lion Hudson Plc, Oxford England.

Norton, Elizabeth. (2009). *Jane Seymour Henry VIII's True Love.* Amberley Publishing, Gloucestershire, United Kingdom.

Marius, Richard (1999) *Thomas More A Biography*. Harvard University Press, United States.

Weir, Allison (2001) *Henry VIII.* Ballatine Books, New York.

Weir, Allison. (1998) *The Life of Elizabeth I.* Random House Ballatine Publishing, New York.

Weir, Allison (2009) *The Lady in the Tower: The Fall of Anne Boleyn.* Random House Publishing, New York.

Wilson, Derek (2009) *A Brief History of Henry VIII.* Constable and Robbin Ltd, United Kingdom.

About the Author

Raven A. Nuckols is a first time author living in the Washington, DC metro area. She holds a Bachelors of Science Degree in Economics from Strayer University and actively engages in philanthropy and humanitarian causes. She lives with her boyfriend and two cats in the Washington, DC metropolitan ea. An avid fan of the Tudor period, she became particularly attached to Anne's story several years ago. The Queen's tragic story led her to question how different English history may have been if such a politically ambitious wife had stayed at Henry VIII's side. This book was an enormous honor to have written and she is eager to engage with the Tudor community.

Made in the USA
Middletown, DE
14 November 2021